turn the page for more rave reviews . . .

Death of a Colonial

"The author renders [the London streets] with the marveling eye of a time traveler . . . a rich rewarding trip for everyone."
—*The New York Times*

"Charles Dickens and Arthur Conan Doyle must be beaming down from literary heaven at Bruce Alexander's splendid series. Alexander's eye for period detail is sharp and subtle; he brings historic England back to life in layers. Isn't it time that some sharp producer began to turn these fascinating Fielding books into an A&E mini-series?"
—*Chicago Tribune*

"Alexander's Sir John Fielding novels aren't as well known as Anne Perry's historical mysteries, but they should be . . . cleverly plotted, rich in historical ambience, and written with flair and a keen eye for detail. A mesmerizing tale certain to delight all historical-mystery lovers."
—*Booklist*

Jack, Knave and Fool

"If there's truth to the raucous scenes of urban life in Bruce Alexander's atmospheric period mysteries, then London in the eighteenth century was a carnival of thieves, cutthroats and re-fined folk who ate with their hands."
—*The New York Times*

"As Jeremy bustles about the city collecting clues and allowing fugitives to escape, he serves as the reader's eyes as well as Sir John's, capturing the flavor of life in old London."
—*The Christian Science Monitor*

"A fascinating tale. Alexander does a great job of acquainting the reader with the dirty, grubby back streets of London and the high-ceilinged snobbery of the upper classes."
—*Sarasota Herald-Tribune*

"An enjoyable adventure for the reader."
—*The Providence Journal-Bulletin*

Person or Persons Unknown
One of *Publishers Weekly*'s Best Books of the Year

"Evocative."   —*Chicago Tribune*

"Alexander provides rich period detail and a wonderful supporting cast . . . making this story intriguing from first page to last."
                                    —*Publishers Weekly* (starred review)

"The Dickensian detail and characters bring life to the sordid streets and alleys around London's Covent Garden . . . Highly recommended, especially for lovers of historical mysteries who like to see another time and place blaze into life as they read."
                                    —*The Washington Post Book World*

Watery Grave

"Wonderful. . . . The high-minded and always astute Sir John is as companionable as ever in *Watery Grave,* and young Jeremy, wide-eyed but maturing fast, makes for a winning narrator. . . . Packed with history and lore."   —*The Washington Post*

"Enthralling. . . . It's a joy to watch the great magistrate apply his formidable intellect to this sordid business."
                                    —*The New York Times Book Review*

Murder in Grub Street
A *New York Times* Notable Book of the Year

"A fine tale. . . . Historical fiction done this entertainingly is as close to time travel as we're likely to get."   —*Newsday*

"First-rate, original, and persuasive."   —*The Boston Globe*

"Alexander has a fine feel for this earthy period, with its interplay of serene reason and irrational cruelty and violence. A bewildering time, to be sure, but Sir John's judicious insight and Jeremy's naïve fascination supply a novel perspective on it."
                                    —*The New York Times Book Review*

"Noteworthy. . . . A stunning double climax."
                                    —*Publishers Weekly*

SMUGGLER'S MOON

Bruce Alexander

BERKLEY PRIME CRIME, NEW YORK

SMUGGLER'S MOON

A Berkley Prime Crime Book / published by arrangement with the author

PRINTING HISTORY
G. P. Putnam's Sons hardcover edition / October 2001
Berkley Prime Crime mass-market edition / October 2002

Visit our website at
www.penguinputnam.com

ISBN: 0-425-18690-3

Berkley Prime Crime Books are published
by The Berkley Publishing Group,
a division of Penguin Putnam Inc.,
375 Hudson Street, New York, New York 10014.
The name BERKLEY PRIME CRIME and
the BERKLEY PRIME CRIME design
are trademarks belonging to Penguin Putnam Inc.

PRINTED IN THE UNITED STATES OF AMERICA

10 9 8 7 6 5 4 3 2

For the Members of the Suicide Club

ONE

*In which Sir John
receives a special
assignment*

I t had been agreed that there was no need for Sir John Fielding to accompany Lady Fielding to the Post Coach House for her noon departure north to York. After all, he had his Bow Street court to convene at that same midday hour; and later in the day, he had an appointment to keep at the residence of the Lord Chief Justice. "Something," the magistrate had muttered to me, "that will mean trouble for us, you may be sure of it."

And so it was that Clarissa and I stood at the open door of the hackney coach as Sir John and his wife whispered their farewells and kissed in proper loving fashion. He then did accompany her to the hackney where we waited in attendance.

"I shall return, Jack," said she, "just as soon as Mama shows signs of a good recovery—or, on the other hand . . ."

"She will pull through, Kate, I've no doubt of it. Your

mother is of hardy northern stock. No doubt she has a good ten years left in her."

"I do hope you're right," said she with a sigh. "We shall see."

With that, they kissed again. I pushed her portmanteau up to the driver. Sir John retreated unaided to the entrance of Number 4 Bow Street, as I gave Lady Fielding a hand up into the coach and followed her inside. Then were we underway. For the most part I remained silent as my mistress gave most of her attention to Clarissa, imparting to her directions, reminders, and all manner of encouragement for the days ahead. I came in for instruction only in the most general sort of way as we bounced along through the London streets.

She leveled a forefinger at me and said with great seriousness, "Now, Jeremy, I shall ask you to offer Clarissa all the help that you can. I'll not have reports of you two wrangling and fighting, shall I?"

"No, ma'am, certainly not."

"I should hope not," said she. "Now, this will be a difficult time for all of us. Only if we remember to cooperate in all matters can we manage to pull through it. You do see that, don't you?"

"Yes, ma'am, I certainly do."

Once arrived at the Post Coach House, I hied off to purchase her ticket. When I returned with it in hand, the coach to York had pulled up to its station, and Lady Fielding's baggage was secured atop it. I handed the ticket to her as she looked about her anxiously.

"I had best claim my seat," said she, "else I shall find myself riding in the backward way. I must face front, or I shall grow sick, I know." As she looked upon us, I saw tears glistening in her eyes. She dabbed at them with her kerchief. "Do be good, children," said she. "And take good care of Jack, won't you? See that he gets enough sleep—and you'll help him dress, Jeremy? I can count on you?"

"Of course you can."

"Then God bless you, both of you. Goodbye. I hate long farewells."

With that, she turned and handed the ticket to the coachman, and he assisted her into its dark interior. Then did I step forward, and out of sight of Lady Fielding, I placed a shilling in his hand, as Sir John had instructed me.

"Your passenger is the dame of Sir John Fielding, magistrate of the Bow Street Court," said I. "He would greatly appreciate any courtesies or considerations that you may show her." Then, most direct: "What is your name, sir?"

Taken somewhat aback, the fellow could but blink in reply. But after a moment, he nodded and spoke his name. "I am Henry Curtin," said he.

"Very good, sir. I shall pass that on to Sir John. He does not forget those who offer him or his lady assistance."

"You may be sure she will receive the best of care."

"I'm sure she will, but . . ."

"Yes? But what?"

"But do not presume upon his generosity in matters before his court."

"Oh, I would not think of it. And thank you, young sir."

He tipped his hat to me, and I bowed in return. Taking Clarissa's arm, I swept her from the coach yard. She, who had looked upon all that had passed with great interest, offered me a sly grin and a wink.

"So that is the way the world works, eh?" said she to me.

"Sir John thought it best," said I.

"But did you not give that man license to commit murder—and a shilling to boot?"

"By no means!" said I, most indignant. "Did you not hear me say that he was not to presume upon Sir John's generosity?"

"Oh, I heard, but I wonder, did he understand the limits put upon him?"

"He had better, else he will be sorely disappointed."

"Well then, what sort of preferment has he been offered?"

"Oh, how should I know? Chiefly misdemeanors, matters of sentencing, that sort of thing. Let us say, he comes before Sir John for public drunkenness, a common enough charge in Bow Street. He might then be sentenced leniently, perhaps have it suspended altogether."

"What sort of justice is that?" She wailed it out so loud that all around us turned to stare.

I grasped her tighter at the elbow and moved her quickly through the crowd. And as we went, I whispered sharply to her.

"See here," said I, "you know and I know that Sir John is the most just of magistrates. He would handle it as it should be handled. Now, let us speak of it no more."

"*That*—" She seemed about to offer an objection, yet she held it back: "That suits me well, for Lady Kate has filled my head so full of instructions that I can scarce contain them all. If you will excuse my silence, I shall now attempt to review them all."

Then did she go silent for a short space of time.

"Jeremy?"

"Yes? What is it?"

"You may release my arm now."

"What? Oh yes, of course." I did as she bade me.

"And if we might slow our pace a little?"

That we did, settling into a comfortable walk which would no doubt get us back to Bow Street in plenty of time to continue the day.

Truth be told, reader, Clarissa had caught me out. Sir John had told me to give to the coachman a shilling and ask him to look after Lady Fielding. Nothing more. It pained me at that moment to admit, if only to myself, that the rest—asking the coachman's name, the vague statement that Sir John did not forget favors done him—all of that had been my invention. Even at the moment all was said, I thought I had perhaps gone a bit too far—hence my warning that the coachman was not to presume upon Sir John's generosity. Why had I done so? Even now, near thirty years after the fact, I can but guess the reason: I was at that time (my age was seventeen in that year of 1772) impatient for my life to begin; and, wishing to get on with it, I was inclined upon occasion to give the impression that I was both better situated and more powerful than I was. In this case, I realized that I had overstepped myself, and yet I had not a notion of how things might be put right. Thus was I quite resentful of Clarissa for calling all this to my attention. Though we were often at odds, and I was in this instance quite annoyed at her, I was nevertheless forced to concede that, with the added duties that had fallen upon her with Lady Fielding's departure, she was right to withdraw from our contentious conversation and concentrate upon all that must be done upon her return.

Lady Fielding had been absent from our home atop the court on only one previous occasion, and that was for a brief visit with her son, Tom Durham, then recently promoted from midshipman to lieutenant. She met him in Portsmouth, where he had been transferred to the *Endurance*, a ship of the line, ere it was ordered out to the Caribbean. She had been gone but five days, and at that time Annie was our cook and well able to keep things running smoothly. Now Annie was gone, an apprentice in the acting company of Mr. David Garrick at the Drury Lane Theatre. Lady Fielding had since then been filling in as cook as best she could as we searched to find another like Annie (vain hope!). Now, with Lady Fielding gone, it was up to Clarissa to fill in—and she with little training in the culinary arts. Nor was she to neglect her regular duties at the Magdalene Home for Penitent Prostitutes.

Clarissa, then just fifteen, had taken a path into the Fielding household in a manner similar to my own. She was the daughter of a felon—or one who would surely have hanged as one—educated beyond her station and bright beyond her years. Yet Lady Fielding took pity upon her and saved her from the Lichfield poor house, or service in some aristocrat's downstairs crew, by persuading Sir John to take her on that she might have a secretary to aid her in her work at the Magdalene Home.

As for myself, I, an orphan, did come before Sir John falsely accused of theft. That most just of magistrates saw through the perjured testimony that had brought me to him. He made me, after his fashion, a ward of the court and eventually took me into his household. Thereafter, I helped with the housework and soon found myself able to give him aid in his work as magistrate. And how, you may ask, could a mere lad of thirteen (which was then my age) be of help to one noted as a lawyer and as an enforcer of the laws? Why, by performing all those duties for him which he might have been capable of had he the faculty of sight. For yes, strange though it may seem, and amazing though it would have been to see, he had so distinguished himself as a magistrate that he had been knighted—even though he had been blinded many years before.

All the while, as we wended our way through the tight streets, Clarissa kept her mind upon the awful tests that lay ahead. That is to say, I was reasonably certain that it was thereupon she had concentrated her thoughts, for as I glanced over at her once or twice, she seemed to be repeating Lady Fielding's instructions to her word for word, over and over again, almost as a litany, a prayer. But then, of a sudden, she did turn to me, stopped in the busy walkway, and confronted me.

"Jeremy," said she, "you will do the buying for me, will you not?"

"Why, certainly," said I, "if that is what you require. I did the buying for Lady Fielding, for Annie, and for Mrs. Gredge before them all. But perhaps you ought to accompany me—if not this day, then another—that you might see how the buying is done. I would introduce you to Mr. Tolliver, the butcher, and to some others. They can be very helpful."

"Well . . . ," said she, in a manner a bit less certain than her usual, "as you say, if not this day then another. I believe another would be better."

Thus we came to Bow Street and sought entrance not into the courtroom, for Sir John's voice could already be heard through the stout oaken door, loud and commanding.

"Come along upstairs," said she to me. "I'll prepare a list for you."

Returning from Covent Garden well over an hour later, I was fair loaded with all manner of comestible cargo—packages of carrots and turnips, a sack of potatoes, a loaf of bread, and last (though not in the order of importance), some good pieces of stew meat bought from Mr. Tolliver, our butcher. That last came with detailed instructions for preparation, which I was to pass on to Clarissa. And that I would have done had I not been hailed by Mr. Marsden, the clerk of the Bow Street Court, the moment I struggled through the door.

"Here, you, Jeremy! The magistrate wishes to see you most immediate."

It had been my experience that when Mr. Marsden referred to Sir John by his position, it bode ill for me—and so it proved that day, as well. The moment I looked into the modest room at the end of the hall, which he referred to somewhat grandiosely as his "chambers," I was greeted by a blast that near singed the hair upon my head.

"Who is there? Is that you, Jeremy?"

"Yes, Sir John, I—"

"Where have you *been*, boy?"

It had also been my experience that when I was addressed as "lad," then all was well, but should I be called "boy," I was then to expect the worst.

"Why, only to the Garden, Sir John. I—"

"It is not a fit place to spend your time," said he, interrupting again. "There are too many of the young criminal element thereabouts. Your friend Bunkins, now that he is reformed, no longer lays about on the steps of St. Paul's, Covent Garden, as he once did. Why, praytell, should you go there, then?"

"To do the buying for supper—at Clarissa's request."

"What? Oh, I . . . I . . ." Taken off guard, he stammered for a moment as he sought to adjust himself. "But did I not tell you that we were to meet with the Lord Chief Justice this very afternoon?"

"Yes sir, you said that it was bound to mean trouble. But you did not say at what hour on the clock we were to depart."

"Well, never mind that. Did I not say the meeting was to take place in the afternoon?"

"Yes sir, but—"

"But me no but's. Is it not now the afternoon?"

I sighed. "Yes, Sir John."

"Then let us be off." He jumped up from the chair where he sat and, feeling about the top of the desk for his hat, he found it and planted it firmly upon his head.

"I must bring what I have bought to Clarissa," said I, shifting the packages noisily in my arms.

"Well, yes, I suppose you must. I shall meet you at the door to the street."

"Done," said I and hastened back down the hall and up the stairs. Yet I found when I reached the top that I could not quite manage the door latch, so full were my hands. I kicked at the door, but it did not budge until, after a brief pause, Clarissa threw it open.

"Ah, Jeremy, just in time. I'll need you to peel the potatoes."

"Sorry," said I, pushing past her, "but I must accompany Sir John to his meeting with Lord Mansfield."

I deposited the load in my arms upon the kitchen table, then made for the door.

"Must I do it all myself?" Clarissa wailed.

"Why not? Annie managed it so."

"Well I know that I'm *not* Annie. You *needn't* remind me of my limitations."

That I caught just as I started down the stairs.

"Don't worry," I called back to her. "You've hours before dinnertime."

By the time I reached the foot of the stairs and spied Sir John waiting by the door, it had occurred to me that I had not passed on to Clarissa the instructions given me by Mr. Tolliver on cooking the stew meat. There simply had not been time for that. Ah well, I assured myself, Lady Fielding had no doubt covered all that earlier. Besides, women knew all about such matters as cooking, didn't they? It was second nature to them, was it not?

"You had best fetch us a hackney," said he to me. "I have the feeling that we are awaited."

Sir John Fielding had often said to others within my hearing, "If a man lacks one of his senses, then he must compensate by strengthening the other four." Since he had lost his sight more than three decades before whilst in the Royal Navy, he had so strengthened his smell, touch, taste, and hearing that through them he could perform prodigies of "seeing" with his blind eyes that astounded all but those who worked by his side each day. And if this were not sufficient, he seemed, during this same period of time, to have developed still another sense nearly as reliable, and even more impressive, than the other four. He would identify a visitor by his knock upon the door, a criminal by the tone of his voice, and who, among a silent dozen, had been discussing him only moments before he entered the room. Therefore, reader, I was inclined to take him quite seriously when he said that he had the feeling that we were awaited. And furthermore, I took it that his tetchiness regarding our departure had to do with his feeling that the meeting ahead was of greater importance than he had previously supposed. And so it proved to be.

As we bumped toward the residence of the Lord Chief Justice in Bloomsbury Square, it occurred to me that this might be the moment to raise this embarrassing matter of the implied promise of consideration made to Mr. Henry Curtin. Yet soon as it had entered my mind, I dismissed it: no, this was emphatically *not* the right moment. I recognized that, after all, I should have to confess to him what had been done and said, embarrassing though it be, but with him now in this odd state of upset, the matter could and should wait.

The hackney driver reined in the horses before the residence of William Murray, Earl of Mansfield, the Lord Chief Justice. It was an imposing structure by any standard, the largest of any of the grand houses in the square. As I paid the driver, Sir John sought to find his bearings that he might reach the front door without assistance. Alas, he could not. He wandered, looking somewhat befuddled, awaiting my assistance.

By the time I caught him up, the door to the residence had opened, and there stood two men, obviously saying their goodbyes. One of them I recognized immediately as Lord Mansfield; the second I had never seen before. Both seemed to catch sight of Sir John at the same time; it was Lord Mansfield, however, who waved to him.

"Sir John!" he called out. "How fortunate you've come!"

They were together in a moment's time; Lord Mansfield introduced him to George Eccles, who had just been taking his leave. Mr. Eccles, it seemed, was Chief Customs Officer for eastern Kent. He explained that he would be unable to stay longer, much as he would like to, for he had, at the last moment, been given an appointment with the Chancellor of the Exchequer.

"And it's either take it when it is offered or wait a week or a month for another bit of time to come open."

"Never having had dealings direct with the Chancellor of the Exchequer," said Sir John, "I must take your word for it, but from what I have heard, Mr. Eccles, I can well imagine your difficulty."

"Though I should like to stay on and explain the situation to you, I cannot. Yet in any practical way, it is of no matter, for Lord Mansfield here has all the details—at least all those which do pertain to the judiciary's part of the problem."

"Oh?" said Sir John. "And what is the problem?"

"I shall explain it all," said the Lord Chief Justice.

"Very well, Lord Mansfield, I shall look forward to a more complete explanation from you."

Taking that as the proper moment to depart, Mr. Eccles inclined his head sharply in a precise little bow, seemed to wait for Sir John's answering bob of the head, and then scampered off to claim the hackney in which we had arrived from Bow Street. Somewhere between the door of Lord Mansfield's residence and the door to the coach, he called out a goodbye. I did not like the fellow.

"Was I tardy?" Sir John asked Lord Mansfield.

"By no means," said the Chief Justice. "I was given to understand that he wished to come and discuss a matter at length. As it happened, I had the day without cases, and so I was willing to devote the entire afternoon to it. That was how I framed my invitation to you, was it not?"

"Yes, but for some reason, about half an hour past I suddenly felt a great sense of urgency in getting over here."

"Hmmm," said Lord Mansfield, looking at him a bit queerly, "that would probably have been about the time that he arrived. He came in, blurted out an accusation, and explained that he must get on to an appointment with the Chancellor of the Exchequer. He certainly lets one know where he stands in relative importance to members of the government, does he not?"

"Yes, I see what you mean."

This brief conversation took place at the open door to the residence. It concluded there when the host offered an invitation to "come along to my study, and we shall talk this matter through."

We entered, and the butler—my old adversary—closed the door after us and then brought us to the study. The Lord Chief Justice seemed quite content to allow him to lead the way, which struck me as odd. Was he unsure of its location? The butler stood aside at the open double door of the study. He frowned at me as I passed him by. It was a look which to me did say, "They seem to want you inside, and so there is naught I can do to keep you out, and yet if it were left up to me . . ." He closed the doors after us; that is, he must have, for next I looked at them they were shut—though I had heard not a sound. Ah, butlers! How do they manage?

"Sit down, Sir John," said Lord Mansfield. "I daresay we shall have more to talk about now that Eccles is gone than if he were here."

I guided Sir John to a chair, and once he was settled, I looked round for one for myself.

"Your young fellow can take notes if you like," said the Chief Justice. "I'll provide paper and pen."

"Should it be necessary?"

"There are a few names to remember."

"Oh, I'm good at names," said Sir John. "Numbers are sometimes a bit of a problem. But let us begin. I assume the problem to which he referred is smuggling."

The Lord Chief Justice looked up, an expression of surprise upon his face. "How did you guess that?"

"Ah well, simple enough. Our friend Eccles is Chief Customs Officer for east Kent. Customs means import duties, which smugglers evade. And of course east Kent has the most active smuggling trade of any part of England, for it lies just opposite France."

"Well . . . quite right."

"And he is now on his way to see the Chancellor of the Exchequer, no doubt, to ask for more money to combat the trade," said Sir John. "But indeed the truth is, it is the Chancellor of the Exchequer who caused the problem to begin with—his exorbitant import duties, taxes and so on. Tea and wine are taxed at over double their value, are they not?"

"Yes . . . I suppose they are. But see here, Sir John, we've been at war for a good part of the time for as long as I can remember. We've gone in debt. Money must be raised in some way to retire that debt."

"And each time they raise the import duties, smuggling increases."

"That is true," said Lord Mansfield, "but smuggling must be stamped out. It is a simple matter of enforcing the law, is it not?"

"Smuggling will never be stamped out, so long as import duties continue so high."

The Lord Chief Justice sighed and said nothing for a goodly space of time. He simply studied Sir John, perhaps trying to suppose some means to dissuade him from his contrary position. Apparently there was none.

But then the magistrate did clear his throat and speak up once more: "I have an addendum to that which I have just said—an alternative."

"Oh? And what is that?"

"Either import duties be lowered, *or* . . ."

"Yes?"

"Those of the aristocracy and the nobility refuse to buy what they know to be contraband goods."

"How would they recognize contraband from what has entered legally? Both may carry the proper stamp, or something forged to look quite like it."

"True enough, but smuggled goods are luxury goods—perfume, tobacco, wine, all of that. Persuade those who can afford them to forgo such pleasures, and you will have solved the problem."

Lord Mansfield regarded him with dismay. "I thought for a moment that you were being serious. I shall know better next time."

"I *was* being serious—or at least I was trying to make a serious point. And that, Lord Mansfield, is that there is no practical likelihood of reducing smuggling in east Kent, or in any other part of England—not now, in any case."

"Mr. George Eccles says otherwise."

"He would, wouldn't he?" said Sir John. "I did not like the man, you know, rather a self-important sort."

"That may be, and for that matter I did not like him, either. Nevertheless, I fear we must take what he says seriously."

"And what has he to say?" Sir John put it to him as a sort of challenge. "There was something about an accusation, was there not?"

"Indeed there was—and a very serious one it is. According to Eccles, nothing of substance can be done to diminish smuggling in his section of Kent unless we get rid of the local magistrate, a young man named Albert Sarton."

"He says that, does he?"

"Oh, he says far worse. According to Mr. Eccles—and I quote him—'The man is either corrupt, or the most incompetent ever in the history of the magistracy.'"

"That indeed is a powerful indictment," said Sir John. "Yet I have known colleagues who impressed me as *both* corrupt and incompetent." A sly smile spread across his face. "Please don't press me for names, Lord Mansfield."

"The odd thing is," said the judge, "I've met the fellow, and he didn't seem at all as Eccles described him."

"You've met this Albert Sarton?"

"Yes, I have, and I remember him well. As it comes to

me, I had been invited up to Oxford to address the law faculty and students. The invitation came from an old friend of mine, a former classmate he was and now a professor there. At the party given me afterward, he brought forward a good-looking young fellow not much older than your lad here"—nodding toward me. "He gave his name as Albert Sarton and said that he was quite the most promising student lawyer they had had at Oxford in his memory. He urged me to keep young Sarton in mind for the judiciary—after a proper amount of seasoning, understand. Well, then he left me with this young fellow, and I had a chance to talk with him myself, and I must say, I was very favorably impressed by him. Not only did he show great intelligence, he also showed something far rarer among those young university fellows—good sense.

"All this was a few years past," he continued. "But when, just last year, the post in Deal came open, I remembered meeting this young Sarton, and I inquired after him. I found he had just passed the bar and was looking for a post. Work as a magistrate has always seemed to me good preparation for a career in the judiciary—as I've said to you, Sir John, each time I've offered a judgeship to you."

Sir John waved a hand in a dismissive manner. "Well, we needn't go into that again," said he.

"As you wish. But to continue, I happened to have another old friend in Deal, a squire who lives in a manor house up above the town—a Sir Simon Grenville. Do you perchance know him, too? I was specially close to his father at Oxford."

"I fear not, Lord Mansfield. I leave London only on those errands on which you have sent me. I know no one in Deal."

"Ah, well." The chief justice shrugged indifferently. "In any case, he is quite influential in those parts, and when he heard that young Sarton came so highly recommended, he promised to do all that he could to see that the post was offered to him. That, essentially, was all that was necessary, though Sir Simon did say that there was some slight opposition to Albert Sarton because he was not from east Kent."

"They don't like outsiders, I take it."

"Don't seem to—no, they don't. In any case, Sarton got the job, partly through my sponsorship, and I'd heard nothing ill of him until this man George Eccles came forth with these complaints. They all have to do with the smuggling trade thereabouts. Deal seems to be the center of it, at least currently. Eccles says he is letting known smugglers go free, and so on. Says he even consorts with them. Frankly, I find it difficult to credit his complaints. First of all, they were not at all specific. Secondly, I know Sarton is not stupid—and therefore not likely to be incompetent; and as for him being corrupt, well, having met him and talked with him at some length, I can only say, I doubt it."

"Did you express these doubts to Mr. Eccles?" asked Sir John.

"No, I did not. His appointment with the Chancellor of the Exchequer intervened. As soon as ever he had unburdened himself against Albert Sarton, he leapt to his feet and announced that he must be off to meet with no less than the Chancellor of the Exchequer himself. I had the awful feeling when he told me that he meant it to impress me."

"Surely not," said Sir John, suppressing a snicker.

"Well, one does get these suspicions from time to time."

"Hmmm, tell me then, what do you wish me to do about all this?"

"Oh, I think you know. I'd like you to go down there to Deal and meet this Albert Sarton, look at his court records, interview him, ask round town about him, and form your own judgment of him. If it goes against him, then I shall pull him from his post immediately. Even if you have naught but misgivings, I shall remove him. I cannot have the power of one magistrate challenged, for it calls to question the authority of all the rest."

Sir John sighed and said nothing for a long moment. At last did he speak up, saying, "You give me greater right to judge him in this matter than I desire. How long would you say I should devote to this matter?"

"Oh, a few days, a week at the most."

"Well, I doubt I can make an investigation of such importance in such a short time. The future of this Sarton fellow depends upon it, after all."

"Then take as long as you must."

"I have another objection—a personal one."

"All right, let me hear it."

"You could not have asked me to go at a worse time. My wife has gone up north to care for her ill mother, who seems near death. Departing thus, she has left me in charge of the two children—the lad here, who offers no problem, and a girl of fifteen, who does. I cannot leave her here, yet even less easily can I bring her with us to Kent."

Lord Mansfield considered the matter. "I would call that a problem," said he, "albeit not an insoluble one. Let me tell you what accommodation I can make. I shall find you a place at the residence of Sir Simon Grenville. If I write him within the next hour, I can catch the last post coach, so that he will have a day's notice before your arrival. The fellow is ever after me to come down for a visit. He'll be happy to welcome you."

Sir John appeared a bit troubled by the suggestion. "I should say, sir, that it does not necessarily follow that he would accept me as a reasonable substitute for your distinguished self."

"He will if I tell him to," said the Lord Chief Justice in a manner which made it clear he would brook no argument from Sir Simon, Sir John, nor indeed from any other.

"Perhaps."

"It would be far better," said Lord Mansfield, "to have the girl you mentioned in the manor house than in such quarters as the town of Deal might provide."

"I'll grant you that."

"And I daresay Sir Simon will be your best contact there in Deal. He knows Sarton, of course, having connived with me to put him in his position. And he must know Eccles, as well. In fact, he should be able to introduce you to any number who can be helpful there in Deal. It is, after all, no city." Lord Mansfield stopped abruptly at that point, thrust forward, chin first, and growled, "Well, what do you say?"

"What indeed? You seem to have thought of everything."

"No, not quite. I'll tell you what I'll do. I'll provide transportation, as well. I'll not need my coach for the next few days and Lady Mansfield is up at our place in Hampstead. I can get by in hackneys. My coach and coachmen are yours for the remainder of the week."

"I am quite overwhelmed. But tell me, who will take my cases?"

The Lord Chief Justice fluttered his fingers, as if to say that this was a matter of negligible importance. "Oh, Saunders Welch, I suppose. I shall speak to him myself about it. He'll not dare to show reluctance."

Thus was it settled. The two talked on a few minutes more and between them arranged the details of our departure. I, for one, looked forward to the journey. With Sir John I had visited Portsmouth, Bath, and Oxford, each so different from the other two. Quite naturally I wondered, too, in what way Deal would differ, little knowing the brutal and bloody history that I would write from the events we endured there.

Lord Mansfield bade a swift farewell, declaring that he must write that letter to Sir Simon Grenville if he were to be given a proper day's notice. He rang for the butler, who appeared instantly (he must have been eavesdropping at the door) and showed us out to the street.

Once away, Sir John turned in my direction and asked, "Is there a hackney about? Can you find one for us?"

This surprised me. While there had been reason enough to take a coach to Bloomsbury Square—at least it was so in Sir John's estimation—there seemed little need now to hurry back to Bow Street. Why did we not walk? It was not Sir John's custom to be so free with his cash.

I was thus doubly surprised when, after bringing a hackney to him from Hart Street, he called up to the driver the address of a dock in Wapping. I had not the slightest notion of where he might be taking us—nor did I discover until after we had arrived, so tight-lipped was he. During the entire journey he spoke not a word but fell into that state in which it was impossible to discern whether he thought deeply or slept. The black silk band that hid his eyes concealed all from me. Nevertheless, when at last we came to a full halt upon the wooden timbers of the dock, he responded quickly enough, moving so swiftly for the coach door that I had bare time enough to get it open before he launched his leap to the dock.

It was not until I, too, had alighted and heard a most familiar voice that I called to mind what Sir John had told me days before: his friend (and mine) Black Jack Bilbo had bought a ship. He was ever so pleased with it, I was assured. Yet because he had bought it from the Royal Navy as a ship decommissioned and brought out of service, there were certain alterations to be tended to. It was a sloop and no great man-of-war, but there were cannon on board, thirteen in all, and these would have to be melted down. And since it had had twenty years hard service, there were ordinary repairs to be made upon it. And that, reader, is why the *Indian Princess*, as Mr. Bilbo had re-christened her, was in dry-dock there in Wapping.

Now, one question should perhaps be settled before we go further: Why would the owner and operator of London's most popular gaming club wish to own such a ship? That you might well wonder, reader, and the answer lies in Mr. Bilbo's dark past. For years there had been rumors that he had been a pirate in the Caribbean and the waters off the North American colonies before coming to London to launch his gambling enterprise. In fact, it was claimed he had used the proceeds of his free-booting to build and bank his club. Because of these rumors, Sir John often remarked that Mr. Bilbo was a dangerous man for him to know. "I should not like the fellow," said he, "but I do, and there's an end to it." And since they were friends, as indeed they were, Sir John had learned from him the kernel of truth at the center of those rumors burgeoning about his past. The truth was, Mr. Bilbo had been not a pirate but rather a privateer, "too fine a distinction for the London rumormongers." Quite legally (that is, with a letter of marque), he had plundered French shipping during the Seven Years' War, taken merchant ships and their cargoes, and sold them, thus amassing his fortune. Those who were in a position to know had told Sir John that there was not a finer captain in a fight than Black Jack Bilbo and that all that he had taken, he had taken fair. The ship he commanded then was a sloop, like unto the one now in dry-dock here in Wapping. With it, under-manned and under-gunned, he took on French vessels of more than twice the tonnage. And so to repeat the question, what did he want with such a ship? It should be obvious: he wanted, in some sense, to recapture his youth; to relive those days of danger—without the danger—or so I now suppose.

In any case, when from the deck swarming with workmen Mr. Bilbo espied us standing at the edge of the dock as the hackney pulled away, he gave a mighty wave and shouted out, "Ahoy, you two! Come aboard. Your presence is most welcome!"

"Is she in or out of water?" Sir John responded.

"Out for caulking. But she's steady, and the gangplank's well set."

"Come along, Jeremy," said he to me. "Take me there and lead me across."

And thus we went. Though the gangplank seemed a bit narrow to me, Sir John seemed not to mind in the least; he went behind me with both hands upon my shoulders. In fact, he urged me to pick up the pace when we were but halfway across, yet in the absence of ropes or banisters, I refused—let him think what he would of me!—for it seemed a mighty chasm below.

"Welcome aboard, both of you," boomed Mr. Bilbo. He grabbed my right hand with his left, and with his own right hand he pummeled Sir John's shoulder and back. It occurred to me that I had never seen him before as truly happy as he seemed at that moment. "Glad I am to have you." He hesitated, but then came out with it: "But I was expecting you a bit toward the end of the week."

"Well, John Bilbo," said Sir John, "'Twas either come now or miss the chance altogether, I fear. The Lord Chief Justice has another errand for us."

"Where to this time?"

"Oh, not far—east Kent. Deal."

"No, not far at all. But you're here now, and that's the important thing, so let me show you about the *Indian Princess*. I can describe to you what's being done to her, though with your nose you can probably tell what's going on right now."

"Well, I smell pitch and varnish, right enough."

Indeed there was a strong odor of both, as indeed there should have been, for there were workmen about applying both where needed—the pitch between the deck timbers and the ship's varnish upon all wooden surfaces, save the deck timbers upon which it had already been laid down in multiple coats.

"When was she built, Mr. Bilbo?"

"In 1750, sir. A lot like her was built and launched to combat the smuggling trade." He gave a cynical little chuckle. "Whole lot of good they did, howsomever."

"You mean, of course, that they did no good at all."

"Well, perhaps a little but only a little."

"Exactly my belief. I take it she's seaworthy."

"Oh, and then some. Indeed she's in good shape, considering she's never before been brought in for an overhaul."

"Then why are they selling her off in such a way?"

"Why, they're still trying to pay for the war with the French. They'll be selling off the whole navy, ship by ship, before you know."

"And all the while, the smuggling trade prospers."

"Aye," said Mr. Bilbo, "but I've naught to complain. I'll have a ship beneath my feet again, and I've wanted that since first I came to London."

"Oh, I've no doubt of it. I felt the same for years."

Though they spoke of it seldom, this love of the sea and ships was what held these two men, in most ways so different, so close together. It may not have been widely known, but Sir John Fielding lost his sight as a midshipman at the siege of Cartagena during the War of the Austrian Succession. He had, up to that dreadful event, expected to make the Navy his life, and while afterward that proved impossible, he never gave up his love for the sea. In Black Jack Bilbo he found one who, like himself, felt in exile so long as his feet touched solid ground.

"Why not take my arm, Sir John, and I'll walk you about the deck and call out to you the points of interest."

He did as Mr. Bilbo suggested, and the two started off together; I trailed close behind.

"What points of interest had you in mind?"

"Well, not all that pitch you smell is going on the hull. Decks in these sloops can be pretty leaky, so they can. A bad rain or a rough sea can damn near drown the men sleeping below. I care more for my men than the Royal Navy ever did, so I've tightened up the leaks between the timbers with pitch and plugged the holes with wood."

"Hmm . . . well . . . yes. But tell me, Mr. Bilbo, how is she rigged?"

"Ketch-rigged, she is—main mast and mizzen—which is a considerable improvement over my first down there in the Caribbean, a Barbados sloop. Single-masted, she was. I got one like the *Princess* here as soon as ever the fortunes of war permitted."

Thus they toured the ship. At some point, perhaps as I lagged behind and viewed them from a distance, it occurred to me that they made quite a strange pair, so unlike were they. The bearded Black Jack Bilbo, near as wide as he was tall, rolled about on thick, powerful legs, walking a seaman's walk even there on a steady deck. Sir John, much the taller of the two, walked with the ease and steady gait of a city man; but for the silk band that covered his eyes, he might not have appeared to be blind at all.

Mr. Bilbo did most of the talking. His comments and description of the improvements and repairs upon the ship were well mixed with tales and reminiscences of the sort that only seamen seem to tell to others like themselves. Sir John responded in kind. Though I understood little of it, it pleased me greatly to hear them talk so.

My only disappointment in our visit was that my friend Jimmie Bunkins was not also on hand. We two had been chums since my first days in London. Mr. Bilbo had taken him in hand in much the same way that Sir John had shaped my own life, overseeing his reform and education as a proper father ought to do. Yet there was still in Bunkins something wild. Though he no longer stole as he had during his days as "a proper village hustler" in and about Covent Garden, he was quick and sharp with his tongue and accepted no nonsense from any quarter. Whatever he had to say made great good sense. In short, he was my best friend.

I wondered that Bunkins was not there with Mr. Bilbo on the deck of the *Indian Princess*. He had talked of it to me as much and as excitedly as Mr. Bilbo had discussed it with Sir John—nay, more so, I believe. But as I wondered, Jimmie

Bunkins made his appearance, and rather a dramatic one it was. He came along seated upon the wagon box of Mr. Bilbo's coach-and-four. And 'twas he who drove the team of matched blacks. The regular driver and the coachman sat at either side of him, shouting encouragement as he brought the team and coach to approximately the same place our hackney had stopped and halted them there. It was all done so swiftly and with such dispatch that I, for one, was quite dazzled by Bunkins's accomplishment. Mr. Bilbo, on the other hand, was less than pleased.

"Next time you come, you'll be drivin' them off the dock and into the Thames," he shouted out to him.

"Aw, Captain," the driver called back, "he's comin' along fine, he is. Got good hands."

"He took us clear through town," the coachman added.

For his part, Bunkins simply chuckled modestly. He had done well, and he knew it. But then did he catch sight of me, and he gave a great wave.

"Jeremy, chum," he called, "an't I quite the driver?"

"You are, and that's naught but the truth!"

"Don't encourage him, lad," said Mr. Bilbo to me. "His opinion of himself and his abilities is far too high already."

The appearance of the coach-and-four signaled to Black Jack Bilbo that his day at the dry-dock had ended and that his day at the gaming club would soon begin. (I had heard it said once that Mr. Bilbo slept less than was natural for a man, and I believe this was so.) He assumed rightly that we would travel back from Wapping with him to Number 4 Bow Street. He gathered up the pieces of clothing he had shed against the heat of the day and talked with the foreman about the work remaining to be done. As he did, Bunkins climbed down from his perch high above the horses and jog-trotted across the gangplank to me.

"Hey, chum," said he, "an't this the rummest, grandest thing that ever you saw? A sloop! And the cove says it's just like the one he plagued the French with."

(If one or two words I have quoted above are not immediately comprehensible, reader, it is because Bunkins
spoke still the patois of the streets surrounding Covent
Garden, known as "flash talk." A quick, second glance
should suffice to reveal their meaning.)

I quite agreed with him, noting only that the cannon
seemed to be missing.

"Aye, so they are," said he. "And I think it sad, don't
you? There's nothing like cannon to dress a sloop proper."

We laughed at that, and then did we begin the sort of
banter with which we customarily passed our time together. Not worth repeating, perhaps, but one curious fact,
communicated in a whisper, did emerge from our jocular
exchanges: Bunkins confided that Mr. Bilbo was told by
the Navy office that as a condition of the sale he must remove the thirteen cannon and have them melted down.
Though he arranged proof that he had done so through an
obliging metal merchant, he had, in fact, secretly stored
them against an uncertain future. "You never know, Jimmie
boy, what fate has in store," he had said to Bunkins.

"You must never tell no one of this, Jeremy," said Bunkins to me, "not even your own cove. Otherwise, I'll never
trust you with another secret."

It was not long until we four were settled in the coach
and bouncing along in the proper direction. Sir John and
Black Jack Bilbo sat close and talked in low tones. For our
part, Bunkins and I sat silent, straining forward to listen to
them. What we heard was a report and discussion on the
earlier meeting with Lord Mansfield which I had, of
course, attended with Sir John. Nevertheless, Sir John's
summary and Mr. Bilbo's comments were both of interest
to me: the former because he managed to present all the
facts in the most neutral and least prejudicial manner possible—one would gather from what Sir John said that he
simply had as yet no opinion in the matter; and the latter for

the very opposite reason—Mr. Bilbo did immediately choose a villain.

"You'll want to watch out for this man Eccles," said he to Sir John.

"And why do you advise me so?"

"Because, if you ask me, it's the customs service that's corrupt, always has been, always will be so."

"Oh? And what is it prompts you to say that?"

"Personal experience," declared Mr. Bilbo. "It didn't matter which port I'd bring in a ship and cargo, first person to meet me at the dock was always the customs man. He'd have his hand out, expecting me to pay duty on the cargo, just like I was the regular shipper. And when I'd refuse, they'd seize the cargo of the ship in tow, saying they'd hold on to it until the prize was bought and the buyer had paid the duty. Now, some of these cargoes was perishables— fruit and such like—and what the customs man really wanted was to get it in the customs warehouse so he could sell it out the back door. They was always selling out the back door. 'Twouldn't matter where: Kingston, Charleston, Savannah—wherever—even Boston."

"Good God," said Sir John, "what an indictment! All customs men everywhere. Is that what you mean?"

"Oh, I suppose not. Just watch out for that Eccles— that's all I have to say."

They talked on, but by now we were well into the city. The Tower of London loomed just ahead, and the street noise had mounted to a pitch comparable to what we knew in Covent Garden. Horses whinnied and clopped, hawkers yelled out in praise of their wares, workmen hammered and shouted. It was quite impossible to hear more, and so Bunk- ins and I sat back during the rest of the journey and relaxed, so far as it is possible for boys of that age to do so.

In his farewell at Number 4 Bow Street, Black Jack Bilbo did lament that Sir John would not be along when he took the *Indian Princess* out on her test voyage. "I was countin' on havin' you aboard," said he.

"Not more than I," said Sir John.

"But may I give you a bit of advice, sir?"

"Of course you may, Mr. Bilbo."

"With all due respect to Jeremy here, who has proved his worth again and again, I do believe you would be well served to take with you one of your Bow Street constables, if you get my meaning."

"No, not quite. To what end?"

"As protection. They take their smuggling seriously down there in Deal. I believe you may need a bodyguard."

"You do? Truly? Hmmm. Well, I shall give the matter serious consideration."

Mr. Bilbo did not belabor the point but wished us both Godspeed and a safe return. Bunkins waved and called out his goodbye as the coach and its impressive team of four pulled away.

"If I may say so, Sir John, I believe that Mr. Bilbo is right," said I, rather boldly. "I believe one of the Bow Street Runners should accompany us, and I believe I know which it should be."

He chuckled at my certainty. "You do, do you? And just who is it you have in mind?"

"Constable Perkins, and no other," said I, "for he is as able as any man among your force, and he knows the territory to which we travel. He grew up on a farm in Kent, and I do believe he mentioned to me once that the nearest town of any size was Deal."

I had given him pause. Right there in the walkway before the Bow Street Court he took a stand, ruminating for near a minute as the passersby passed him by.

At last said he, "I daresay, Jeremy, you are indeed right! I shall need a constable in Deal, and Constable Perkins is the constable I shall need. I leave it to you to inform him when he reports for duty this evening."

• • •

Alas, the dinner prepared by Clarissa was no great success. Even in describing it as "no great success," I praise it beyond its due. And for its failure, I fear I was partly to blame. I now know enough of cookery to realize that the instructions given me by Mr. Tolliver to be passed on to Clarissa were quite essential, and I have been thoroughly disabused of the notion I once had that members of the female sex come quite naturally to a knowledge of the kitchen arts. No, they have to be taught, just as I have had to be taught the law. And the particular lesson she was intended to get in the proper use of meat in the preparation of stew was not taught her because I was in such a great rush to be off with Sir John to visit the Lord Chief Justice.

After all, Mr. Tolliver's advice was simple enough: "Just have her cut the fat off the meat, all but half an inch or so. That should be more than plenty. Simmer that in the stewpot for the last half of the afternoon with potatoes and carrots and an onion, and you'll have a good stew for yourself."

That was what he said to me, and that was what I should have said to her—but did not. As a result, Clarissa did her best, but with no previous experience, that best simply was not good enough. She tossed in the meat as it had come to her from Mr. Tolliver, thick with fat with gobbets of flesh scattered through. And, knowing no better, she cooked it in the stewpot with the vegetables for the whole of the afternoon. The result was a viscous gray mess, bubbling greasy bubbles in our plates even after she had ladled the concoction out to us. It did not taste so bad as it looked. Yet what were we to do with these large pieces of light-colored, inert stuff which looked more or less like meat yet squirted pure grease when we bit down upon them? And the vegetables, dear God, the vegetables—they had cooked down so that they had lost their distinct identity: no longer were they potatoes, carrots, and onion, but rather mere lumps in the slime.

"Quite tasty," said Sir John. "I do believe, however, that I should have a happier time of it with a spoon. Will you fetch me one, Jeremy?"

I did as he requested and watched him empty his plate with great relish. He asked for more. It was provided him. He attacked it with the same enthusiasm. Inspired by his example, I dug in once more, trying to eat without looking at what I ate. That worked well enough for half a plate or so, but then a fit of belching overtook me, and I was forced to end my dinner there.

For her part, Clarissa took a bite, or possibly two, then began pushing her food about upon her plate, as if looking for uncontaminated bits. Finding none, she looked across the table at me quite miserably, shook her head, and quietly laid down her knife and fork. Through it all, Sir John continued to eat until he, too, began to belch with such alarming frequency that he was forced to end his meal rather abruptly.

As I did the washing up afterward, I confessed to our dejected cook that I had failed to tell her of Mr. Tolliver's instructions and must therefore shoulder some of the blame she claimed for herself.

"Ah no," said she, "I should certainly have known better. How many times have I sat here in the kitchen with Annie, watching her trim the fat from the stew meat? You'd think I might have picked up a thing or two just being round her."

"Ah, but Annie was one of a kind."

"Indeed she was. Why couldn't I have realized that while she was here and learned something from her?"

"But, well, you should be happy at least that you're going down to Deal with us. They say that the sea air is quite beneficial. Think of it as a holiday."

"Oh, I will. I do. But when we return, I shall have another test in the kitchen, then another, and another."

"Well, if it is any consolation to you, your stew was no worse and probably better than most Mrs. Gredge cooked up."

"Gredge? She was the old woman Annie replaced, wasn't she?"

"She was," said I, "and not a moment too soon."

Sir John had asked me to visit him in his study when I had finished washing up that he might dictate to me a letter to Lady Fielding explaining why it was he must leave London for Deal for a week, give or take a bit, and further, why he must take Clarissa with him. He promised that she would be well taken care of, and would, in fact, be staying at the home of a local squire, Sir Simon Grenville. In closing, he voiced his concern for Lady Fielding's mother. Yet he declared that he was certain her mother would pull through her illness, as he had predicted, and that she, Kate, would soon be back in London. "Until the happy day when we are reunited, I shall be but half a man, wandering about this lonely city, thinking only of you." And then did he stipulate that the letter be signed, "Your loving husband." Unused to putting his name as "Jack" upon correspondence, he asked my help in forming the letters. We practiced together two or three times, then did we sign him informally at the bottom of the text. I addressed the letter as he dictated and prepared it for mailing. But my mind being yet troubled by the matter of Henry Curtin, I remained on in that little room and attempted to think just how I might begin.

"Was there something more?" he asked.

"Yes, there is a matter I should like to discuss," said I. "Or perhaps better put, a matter I should like to confess."

"Well then, let me hear it."

I told him the whole tale. I told of how I had given the shilling to the coachman and asked that he see that Lady Fielding was well taken care of—all as Sir John had told me to do. But then, I went on to tell him how and how much I had enlarged upon his instructions. Insofar as I was able, I quoted myself exactly, though it proved embarrassing. I even told him how, when I feared perhaps I had overstepped myself, I told Mr. Curtin not to presume upon Sir John's generosity; and thinking I had told him all, I ended it there. But then I did add that Clarissa had said I had done wrong, and as I thought about it through the day, I saw that she was right.

"Indeed she was," said Sir John. "But you realize it, too, and we may be grateful for that."

Was I to be let off so easily?

"You see what you have done, don't you?"

"I . . . believe I do."

"Perhaps not. Let me lay it before you. What you have done is to blacken my name. You have suggested to this Henry Curtin that I would sell myself so cheap as to give leniency to him in court simply for doing what he is paid to do—look after one of his passengers. Who knows? Perhaps he will spread the word. I may wind up with a reputation so sullied that it may never be clean again."

I hung my head, unable to look him square in the face.

He continued: "But that is not likely."

"Sir?"

"No, the chances are good that we shall not hear of Mr. Henry Curtin ever again. I hope that is so. I expect it will be so. Let us leave it at that, shall we?"

There was but one more matter, quite unrelated: "I wonder, Jeremy, if you could go to the apothecary shop early tomorrow and get from him some preparation to bind my bowels. I've been troubled ever since dinner."

TWO

In which Sir John
arrives and is given
a warm welcome

I t took over a day of hard driving to bring us to Deal.
Lord Mansfield's coach-and-four awaited us, as previously arranged, at the end of Sir John's court session. Constable Perkins and I handed up our bags and portmanteaus to the coachman, who stowed them, secured, atop the vehicle, just as might be done upon any stagecoach. That gave us far more room inside in which to bounce about. Though I'm sure that the driver provided exemplary service going about London, he apparently could not resist running the horses once we were out on the open road. As a result, after hours of having our backsides brutalized, we were happy to put up at an inn somewhere beyond Chatham which had been recommended by Lord Mansfield.

Next day, however, was a bit different. It may have been that we had grown used to being battered about, or perhaps our backsides had hardened, or again (though less likely), perhaps the driver had taken pity upon us and slowed the pace appreciably—whatever the reason, we traveled so much more comfortably that we actually found it possible to talk amongst ourselves. It must have begun as we slowed to drive through Canterbury. Clarissa remarked that it was the first walled city she had seen. Always trying to best her, I countered that London itself was a walled city—or had been such. When Clarissa leapt in to challenge my assertion, Sir John settled it by declaring that it was indeed so, but that so many centuries had passed that so far as he knew nearly all trace of it had disappeared.

Then, perhaps to keep us two from wrangling further, Sir John called upon the fourth passenger, rousing him from a bouncing doze.

"Mr. Perkins," said he, "what can you tell us of this territory to which we're headed? So far as I am concerned, east Kent is naught but *terra incognita.*"

"*Terra* which?"

"Oh, 'tis a phrase meaning 'unknown land.' Do please forgive me for resorting to Latin, won't you?"

"Certainly I shall, sir." Then, having come full awake at last, he glanced round at the rest of us, and said, "So you'd like to hear a bit about east Kent, would you? First of all, you know what they call it, don't you?"

"I believe I have heard," said Sir John. " 'The garden of England,' isn't that right?"

"It is indeed. That's for all the farming that's done here. Most of what's sold in Covent Garden, all them fruits and vegetables, they come from right here in Kent. The hops they make the ale from—that's grown here, too."

I could well believe it, reader, for if you have ever visited that corner of the realm, it must surely have struck you what a verdant and fruitful spot it is. If all the world were as this, then hunger would be quite unknown.

"Now, that's both good and bad," continued Constable Perkins, "my point being that a man an't got much choice here in Kent for honest employment. There used to be iron smelting done here, but that's gone up north, and the wool weaving that was done here, that's moved up north, too, to those big mills where it's all done by power loom. So the result is you got to work doing old-fashioned farm labor for seven or eight shillings a week, and at best that's just seasonal work. That's *honest* employment I'm talking about."

"And for those who would sully their hands with *dishonest* employment—what choice have they?"

"Just one other, and that be the owling trade."

"The owling trade?" repeated Sir John. "What, praytell, is the owling trade?"

"That is what others might call the smuggling trade. Out here it's the owling trade."

"Whatever for?"

"Oh, in truth, Sir John, your guess would be as good as my own. All I can say is that owls fly by night, and that's when the smugglers conduct their business, as well. And let me tell you, sir, it can be a very profitable business, too. Instead of the seven or so shillings a farm worker might make in a week, he'll get ten shillings in a single night."

"Would that be ten shillings every night?"

"No sir, that an't the way it works. It an't every night that you go out, but when there's a boat coming in from France, the word goes round that men are needed down on the beach, and half the town turns out to unload what's been brought across."

"So it's that way, is it?" said Sir John. "And how often might this great crowd be needed on the beach?"

"Oh, no less than once a week, nor more than three times."

"Then an average of two?"

"I suppose so, yes sir."

A teasing smile twitched at the corners of Sir John's mouth. "It strikes me that you know a good deal about this . . . owling trade, as you call it."

"You could say that, sir." And there was a similar air of playfulness in Mr. Perkins's response.

"Could it be you have had some direct personal experience of all this?"

"Oh, it could be indeed," said the constable. "Yet I always figured you knew all that and took me in the Bow Street Runners anyways."

"Well, I'd heard a few rumors, but I put no great stock in them. It was your army record interested me far more."

"Glad to hear it, sir."

"Tell me, Perkins, could your direct personal experience of the owling trade have had some relation to your later experience in the grenadiers?"

"It could. It did."

I had been watching the two men carefully, greatly enjoying the game they played between them. Clarissa, equally fascinated, seemed nevertheless to be somewhat confused by what passed between them. Were they teasing, or were they in earnest?

"There is a tale to tell there, Sir John," said Mr. Perkins.

"Then tell it by all means," said the magistrate. "And you may rest assured that naught in the telling will be held against you."

"Ah well, in that case, I'll not hold back further." And with a wink at me and a nod to Clarissa, he began his story. "I was a lad about the age of Jeremy here, doing farm labor for a family by the name of Griggs. It wasn't quite year-round labor, for I was not paid in the winter when there was naught for me to do. Still, the Griggses were decent people, and they'd given me a place to sleep behind the kitchen and kept me fed through the winter, so it was *almost* year-round. I was orphaned by then, and this was the best I could do for myself at that time in my life. I was reconciled to it.

"There was a Griggs daughter about my own age I used to dote upon, and I had saved up a bit to buy her a Christmas gift. So one Saturday in December I walked into Deal bright and early and found a locket and chain of silver which I thought just right for her. The problem was, y'see, I didn't have the price of it, though I'd been laying a bit aside each month for just this purpose. It was just that I'd not laid enough aside—and so back into the store window it went.

"I was fair crushed, so I was, and so I took myself over to an inn in High Street right there in the middle of town to have an ale so as to console myself. Whilst I was there, I fell to talking with a young fellow a bit older than I was. I told him what brought me into Deal and how disappointed I was to be caught short.

"'Well,' says he, 'I know how you can earn enough in a night to buy any locket and chain in Deal.'

"'How's that?' says I. 'Is it legal? Is it respectable?'

"'Well, it may not be legal,' says he, 'but in this town it's work that's damn near respectable. There's a lugger coming in tonight just filled with Christmas dainties for the lords and ladies of London.'

"I'd no idea what he meant. Finally, with him dropping hints and me trying hard to understand, it come to me that it all had to do with smuggling, that a ship was coming in from France loaded with items of the sort that would be very popular with those in London who had money enough to pay for them. Men would be needed to unload the cargo from the longboats and pack them onto horses and into wagons. It was the offer of a job.

"My newfound employer, whose name was Dick Dickens, told me to be there at the inn at closing time and we'd be right on the hour and the minute to meet the lugger. Well, I was there right enough and went down with Dickens and a whole gang of men to the beach. It was all work once we got there. Once the boats started to ply back and forth from the ship to the shore, it was just a matter of getting them unloaded and the goods transferred to the wagons. We worked fast, for Dick Dickens or one or two others who were in charge were always about telling us to pick up the pace, that it would soon be morning. As it proved out, we was well paid, as promised, but that didn't mean we didn't work for it. Strangest thing was, it didn't *seem* like we was breaking the law at all—just working hard.

"By dawn the last wagon was gone, and the ship out there off the beach had weighed anchor and was sailing away on the tide. That was when we was paid off. I could scarce believe it when Dick Dickens counted out ten shillings into my hand. He told me I'd earned it, and that I was a good worker, and he wanted to know would I be able to work next time a lugger came across. I told him I would, and we worked out a way he could let me know when I'd be needed. So from then on I was working down on the beach one or two nights a week.

"So for certain sure this wasn't the sort of winter I'd expected. The way it had been I was happy just having a place to sleep and something to eat each day, but now of a sudden, I was making more money than ever I had in my life. Well, of course I went a bit daft. Instead of the silver locket and chain, I gave the Griggs girl one of gold for Christmas. Naturally, her ma and pa must have wondered where I got the money to pay for it, but they said nothing. And I bought myself a new suit of clothes, though where I supposed I would wear those new duds, I have no idea.

"And through all this, the work on the beach continued. The luggers made the run from France whenever the weather permitted. As it improved, the ships would be coming over often—or so I supposed. I saw, looking ahead to the coming of spring, that I would soon have to make a decision. Was I to continue in the owling trade, or was I to return to my life as a farmhand? How could I, after all, leave the Griggses after they had kept me all winter long? Well, I was saved from that choice by what seemed to me at the time a dreadful circumstance, but was surely a blessing in disguise. I was caught in a raid on the beach carried out by the excisemen together with the Deal constables. Just why I, or Dick Dickens, or any of them, thought this sort of thing on the beach could go on without getting the notice of the excisemen and the magistrate I'll never know. Or maybe Dickens and those shadowy men behind him thought their bribes had purchased a free hand to operate indefinitely. Or maybe, as Dickens told me on a jail visit, it was all just a misunderstanding. Anyway, this raid looked specially bad, for an exciseman was shot and killed by one of the wagon drivers, an evil old ne'er-do-well named Rufus Tucker. When I heard the sound of that shot, I took off running—and went right into the arms of a constable. Others were better than I was at getting away. In fact, most were, but because a man had been killed, there could be no question of getting off with a fine and jail time. The five of us who went before the magistrate—Rufus Tucker was one—could all have been sent on to Old Bailey, judged guilty, and hanged on the next hanging day. But as it happened, only one was executed, and that was Tucker. The remaining four, not one of us over twenty-five, were given the opportunity to enlist in the Army, and given the chance, we took the King's shilling. The year was 1758, you see, and replacements were needed for those lost in the American colonies in the war against the French. Well, you see the result: Here I am, a veteran of campaigns in the Ohio Valley and Canada, alive and healthy, though missing an arm. Yet that—as you, Sir John, and you, Jeremy, well know—was lost later in the Grub Street campaign."

Sir John, who had been squirming a bit during the last sentence or two of Mr. Perkins's tale, banged upon the ceiling of the coach with his stick, signaling thus to the driver for a stop.

"A good story, well told," said Sir John to the constable. "But I fear I must interrupt now and make for the bushes. Pray God this will be the last such stop on this journey."

The coach came at last to a complete halt. He jumped

down to the road below, and I followed with the latest issue of the *Gentleman's Magazine* in hand.

"Do you see a likely place, Jeremy?"

"Over this way, sir," said I, taking him by the arm. (Only in emergencies did he permit this.) I led him off the road to a copse of trees with sufficient undergrowth to provide a blind.

"Paper?"

I put the magazine in his hand.

"You may leave me now, Jeremy. I shall call you when I need you."

And so leave him I did. There was no arguing with him at such times as these. Insofar as he was able, he maintained his privacy in spite of his blindness.

Returning to the coach, I found Clarissa and Mr. Perkins had taken this opportunity to loosen the knots in their limbs. As I approached, I saw that their attention was wholly taken by something down the road and just out of my sight. The driver and coachman seemed also to be staring off into the near distance. Once I reached them, I saw that the object of their interest was a kind of large cage suspended over the road from the strongest limb of a stout old oak tree. Inside that cage was a skeleton which, as if in some grotesque All-Hallow's-Eve masquerade, was dressed in a tattered, dusty, and faded suit of clothes. I had heard of such before, though never before had I seen one.

"They call it a gibbet," said Mr. Perkins, thus informing Clarissa. "'Twas thought a terrible disgrace amongst condemned men to know their bodies would be put on display in such a way."

"As indeed it should have been," said the coachman. "Dead or no, who would want the corbies peckin' out his eyes or pullin' off his nose?"

"Gibbets used to be common as flies on a carcass," said the driver. "Seemed there was one decorating every crossroad from one end of England to another. Don't see them so much anymore."

Clarissa, quite unruffled by the gruesome sight, stared thoughtfully at the gibbet and its contents. "Who do you suppose it was?" She asked it most indifferently, as if she were merely wondering aloud.

Yet Mr. Perkins took her idle query most seriously. "Why, I don't know," said he, pondering, rubbing his chin. But then did his eyes come alight of a sudden. "Or perhaps I do," said he to her. Then did he call up to the driver of the coach: "How far are we from Deal?"

"Not far at all," said the driver. "I should not doubt we will see it take shape when the road next climbs a hill."

"In that case, I would give a good wager that yonder hangs all that is left of Rufus Tucker."

"The one you were talking about? The one who killed the exciseman?" I had not seen Clarissa so animated since her first meeting with Samuel Johnson.

"The very same, miss, for I know very well that there was no such body on display before I left here. And I now remember running into a lad from Deal whilst I was in Aldershot waiting transfer to another regiment. He told me old Rufus's body had been shipped back to Deal for display purposes. The idea was that he was to hang there to warn all against shooting excisemen."

"Imagine!" sighed Clarissa. "That could be Rufus Tucker."

"JEREMY!"

That was Sir John's bellow from across the road. Quite unmistakable it was, though not near so fierce as I may make it seem, writ so in capital letters. It was loud enough, nevertheless, to suggest to me that he might be in distress. Adding to that, he was not where I had left him. I looked uneasily about but he was nowhere to be seen.

"Jeremy!"

Another bellow, somewhat more impatient, rose from a

spot a bit behind me. I hastened to the place and found Sir John lying disheveled and somewhat disappointed with himself at the dusty bottom of the deep ditch which ran along that side of the road.

"Is that you, Jeremy?"

"It is, Sir John. Are you hurt?"

"No, no, though my pride is a bit bruised. I fear I must ask you for a hand up."

That I gladly offered him. I tugged hard, and up he came. Yet though on his feet, he still required help in scrambling up the crumbling wall of the ditch to the road. I pushed— though that did no good at all. But then, as I bent low from the road level to grasp one of Sir John's hands, I found a helper beside me—none other than Mr. Perkins. The constable gave his only hand to the magistrate, and we two hauled him up.

"Who is that helping poor Jeremy? Is it you, Constable Perkins?"

"It is, Sir John."

"Ah well, I should have called earlier for Jeremy to lead me back but I heard your voices, and I thought I could simply walk to the sound of them. But I misstepped, lost my balance, and fell to the bottom of that . . . what would you call it? A ditch?"

"It was a ditch, yes sir."

"Sometimes I fear that I attempt too much. Perhaps I should accept the limitations my blindness has put upon me."

"Ah, do not say that, sir. If you was to give in to your fate, there's a certain one-armed constable might be forced to give in to his."

Sir John chuckled. "Well, I would not wish to encourage that—no, certainly not."

Sir John had accepted my help in seeing him back to the coach. Yet without notice, he stopped of a sudden and said to me, "Jeremy, I have something to discuss with Mr.

Perkins. Would you then go to the coach and tell all that we shall be with them in just a few moments' time?"

Having no choice in the matter, I agreed, though I saw little need for such secrecy. Ultimately, their conversation lasted many more moments than a few and became at one point quite heated before it was done. When at last they returned to the coach, Sir John called up to the driver and asked that he stop when the town of Deal came into view. Only then did he ascend to the coach's interior, bang upon the ceiling, and set us into motion once again.

"Jeremy," said he, "you serve as treasurer on this expedition. Give Mr. Perkins a few pounds. How much would you be needing, constable?"

"Oh, a pound or two. Two pounds should be more than enough."

"Then give him three."

I counted out the amount and handed it over.

"Mr. Perkins will be going out alone to do some listening for us. It will be to you that he reports if indeed he has anything to report. Where might you two best meet?"

"There is an inn on High Street, name of the Good King George," said Mr. Perkins. "Suppose we get together there about noon each day and have us an ale, and I'll tell you what I know. How does that strike you?"

"Why, I'm thirsty already."

"Enough of that, you two. We'll—"

Sir John, interrupted by the sudden halt of the coach, gave a firm nod. "God bless you, sir," said he to the constable. "And remember well what I told you."

"Goodbye, all." And so saying, Mr. Perkins threw open the door and jumped from the coach. I pulled the door shut behind him, took his wave through the window and returned it.

The magistrate said nothing during the rest of the trip. That left it to me to puzzle out what he had discussed with Mr. Perkins there in the road. It seemed likely that Sir John had asked him to serve as his spy. After all, Mr. Perkins was, if not well known in Deal, at least remembered. He had known his way round the owling trade and been forcibly enlisted into the Army. The last any of the townsmen had seen of him, he was no doubt being led away in chains by the recruiting sergeant and his party. Those who did recall him would quite naturally assume that he had lost his arm in military service. They would be willing to answer any of the questions he might put to them. He would be perfect in such a role.

Yet having formed that notion, I dismissed it immediately. There was something in it which rang false for both men, yet I could not determine what it was for either. Ah well, perhaps Perkins would be more forthcoming than Sir John when I met him next midday.

But for now, here was Deal before me. As I stared out the window at the shops along Broad Street and at those we passed by, I realized how much more prosperous-looking was the picture before me than would have been a tableau from any comparable section of London. The people were better dressed; they walked with a more confident step. The shop windows were filled with goods of a quality that only the grandest shops in lower St. James Street might carry. The smuggling trade may have been illegal, but it had certainly brought good times to Deal.

Looking away from the coach window for a moment, I happened to catch Clarissa's eye. She was obviously most impressed by what she saw all round us. Her eyes were wide with excitement.

"Why, Deal is near as grand as Bath!" said she. "Had you ever imagined it so?"

I admitted I had not. But then, as we came to the bottom of Broad Street, the driver turned the team right. And there, through the window, off to our left, was a great body of water.

"Oh, there it is," said Clarissa, "—the sea, the ocean, the English Channel."

"And there beyond it," said I, "is France. Can you see it?"

She studied the horizon carefully. "I . . . I don't know. I think I can. How far is it?"

Before I could respond, Sir John spoke up: "Thirty-five miles, give or take a mile or two."

"So close?" Clarissa exclaimed. "Why, we're nearer to France than we are to London."

"Indeed we are," said he.

The driver reined the horses to a halt. I heard him call out, asking another for directions to the residence of Sir Simon Grenville. The response I heard not quite so clearly, but in a moment more we were off. We drove up a street, and in less than a mile the street became a road, and so on until we were back into the country. Ever upward we went by easy degrees, so that when at last we turned off the road and into a driveway, we must have been a few hundred feet above the town and the sea. We were so long on the way that I began to suppose that we had taken some secondary road that led still farther upward. But not so, for the team of four slowed at the driver's direction. I heard the brake applied. We came to a halt just at the door of a manor house, which had been added onto so often and grandly that it had reached the proportions of a small castle.

And yet it had no grand entrance, no portico with which to impress the visiting aristocracy and nobility; perhaps hereabouts Sir Simon was the only one of his class in residence; perhaps then Deal was his fiefdom.

As these thoughts did thus flash through my brain, a man emerged to meet us and, leaving the door symbolically open behind him, to bid us welcome. Among the landed in the country, a great host of house servants seems to be considered something of an embarrassment. They keep, rather, a number of retainers who are capable of duplicating the work of the rest. The man who came out to greet us was one of these and should not be thought of as a butler. No, indeed, he was no butler, for he lacked the degree of coldness any proper London butler would surely have had. He was simply a Kent fellow of middle years, big and strong—a proper countryman—and he had come out to assure us that we were expected but most of all that we were welcome.

He managed to convey that just by stepping out upon the little porch that was raised a step or two above the ground. He chuckled to himself as he bowed and approached the door of the coach and threw it open.

"Here, miss, give me your hand, and I'll help you down."

Clarissa took advantage of the offer and stepped down very lightly indeed. Sir John was next: he did not attempt to jump, as was his wont, but accepted the proffered hand with good grace and hopped down quite nimbly. Only I, who was last of all, displayed a certain clumsiness in exiting the coach; my heel caught in the step, and had the jolly retainer not been there to catch me, I should have tumbled face-first into the dust of the driveway.

"Hi, watch it there, my lad. I'd not want to present you to the master with a broken head. Steady as she goes, eh?"

He pulled himself to his full height, put a hand atop his protruding belly, as if to hide it from sight, then spoke forth in the manner of one who had memorized a piece in order to have it down precisely.

"My master, Simon Grenville, Baronet, was unavoidably called away this day. He deeply regrets not being present to welcome you himself, but he assures you that his household staff will do all that they can to make you comfortable in your rooms until dinner, at which time he will join you."

"And the horses? Our driver and coachman?" asked Sir John.

"If they will but drive round the house to the stable, sir, the staff there will do all that needs be done for the horses. The driver and coachman will be taken care of by us in the house, you may be sure."

"And one last question: How may we call you?"

"Will Fowler, sir, and my family has been in service to the Grenvilles for three generations. Now, if you will step this way, please?"

And so it was settled. We were assured that there would be time for a nap before dinner, and that we would be knocked up in time to dress.

"I am grateful for that," said Sir John to me once we were alone in the room we shared. "I had briefly entertained the notion of visiting the magistrate. Yet when a man is as bone-weary as I from travel, all he can do is seek rest."

After we woke and dressed, we were ushered in to the large formal dining room where we found a tall and rather handsome man awaiting us, obviously our host, Sir Simon Grenville. I saw no sign of a hostess—a Lady Grenville— and I wondered at that, but Sir Simon made no immediate explanation, and I thought perhaps there was no Lady Grenville. We took our places, with Sir John at his right, of course, and the longest meal of my life began. There was course after course. Plates of various foods appeared and vanished before me, apparently of their own power—I always seemed to be looking the other way when the server whisked one plate away and put another in its place. And with each course there was a new bottle of wine of a different color and a different flavor put before us. That all this was done according to some intricate plan, and not simply as a demonstration of great abundance, I learned as Sir Simon himself explained his situation to us.

"You will note," said he, "that I am alone here. Lady Grenville is on the other side," he made a vague gesture toward the Channel, "visiting her family. She is, as you may gather, French. And being French, she brought with her into our happy marriage, a French cook; indeed the finest French cook who ever came to these shores, or so he keeps declaring. His name is Jacques, you see, and Jacques feels unused and unappreciated because we do not often have occasions here in our sleepy little corner of England to make full use of his talents. Especially does he enjoy showing them off to my wife, for she is French, and only the French can fully appreciate their cuisine. Yet she has been away a considerable length of time due to an illness in the family. This is, in fact, the first occasion on which he has prepared a full-course dinner in the grand style in her absence. Ordinarily, that might seem reason to caution you as to its quality. Nevertheless, first of all, Jacques has not been put to the test for far too long, and he has been eager to prove himself. And secondly, say I in prideful mock-humility, I believe his work speaks for itself."

"Indeed it does," said Sir John, "oh, indeed so."

Had there been any need to do so, I might have raised my voice to second Sir John, for while I commented a moment ago upon the great abundance of the food, it should be said that it tasted remarkably well. It was perhaps a bit too delicately spiced for one, like me, who sought grosser gustatory satisfactions. Which is to say, I knew that the turbot, the quail, and the lamb that were put before me in their diverse sauces were in every way exceptional, yet I still preferred Annie's well-garlicked beef stew.

"Remarkable coincidence," said Sir John.

"Oh? What is that, sir?" queried our host.

"That your wife should be away visiting an ill member of her family. So also is my own dear wife. Which of her relations is sick?"

"Pardon?"

"Which family member? Brother? Sister . . . ?"

"Oh, well, her mother."

"You see? Remarkable coincidence. It is her mother

also, whose illness has occasioned my wife's visit. Remarkable."

Sir Simon, for some reason, seemed disturbed by this exchange. He signaled the wine server to refill the glasses. Glancing uneasily at Clarissa, who sat next me, I wondered how much more she should or could drink of the wine. It was not that I feared that she would become boisterous or rude, yet she might become talkative. And the conversationalists at this table were to be Sir Simon and Sir John— and no others. Surely she realized that. Clarissa took a sip from the newly refilled glass, then turned to me with a lazy smile upon her face. Her eyes, I noted, were a bit opaque.

"I do regret Marie-Hélène's absence now, at the time of your visit," said Sir Simon, resuming their talk. "Lady Grenville, that is. She would be the ideal guide through this old house. She knows its history better than I."

"How old is it?" Sir John asked, showing little more than polite interest.

"Oh . . . let me see. The core of the house is quite old— fourteen-something. Marie-Hélène would have it exact."

"That is indeed old."

"There have been three major additions since then. It is one of those old houses which simply grew of its own volition. Why, it even has a ghost or two."

This was simply too much for Clarissa. Her eyes brightened. "A *ghost!*" She fair shouted it out. "Oooh! Tell us about it." And then: "*Ow*—Jeremy!"

That last was her response to the kick I gave her in the ankle. As I administered it, I leaned close and whispered, "Do you wish to have us eating with the servants?"

Lips pursed, she nodded primly, indicating that she understood and would cooperate.

Sir Simon Grenville, on the other hand, seemed to take no notice of the breach of etiquette. He smiled blandly at Clarissa and shrugged rather grandly. "The truth is, alas, I know not much to tell. It, or perhaps he, is said to be the ghost of the first Grenville Baronet, who would have been—let me see now—my great-grandfather, no less."

"And how does this restless spirit make himself known?" asked Sir John.

"Oh, by rambling about the house, making a good deal of noise and generally creating havoc."

"Havoc, is it? And how does he do that?"

"Why, by allowing himself to be seen from time to time. He looks rather different from me. His is a face that seems to run in the family. My father was quite like him. We've a portrait of him in the library. He appears in these visible visitations in dress of the last century, and there does seem to be something—though I risk his wrath to say it—rather evil about him, his expression, the look in his eyes, the rather frightening smile he offers the viewer."

"I can only gather," said Sir John, "that you yourself have seen this apparition on at least one occasion."

"Yes," said he, "I have, and on more than one occasion." Sir Simon had grown most serious of a sudden. Any hint of jocularity had vanished from his manner. "And each time I have counted myself lucky to survive unscathed."

"Why so? Is this spirit so dangerous?"

"Dangerous enough. His appearance, which is to say, his visible manifestation, usually means that someone in or around this house . . . will die, and die most horribly, within the next week or so."

There was a sudden and quite audible intake of breath next me. It was Clarissa, of course, so overcome by Sir Simon's lurid tale that she could but gasp for air; indeed she was truly afrighted.

Yet Sir John, having listened, primed his host with questions and comments through the recital, and in short, done all that a good guest might be expected to do, had finally had quite enough of ghosts, spirits, and apparitions.

"If you will forgive me, Sir Simon," said he, "I find all such tales naught but poppycock. Naturally, they frighten children like Clarissa, who deep down rather likes to be frightened. But frankly, it would take a great deal to convince me of their validity."

"What, specifically, would it take?"

"Well, since I am incapable of accepting the proof offered me by my eyes, I would have to be convinced by one or more of the other four senses."

"Did I mention the smell which comes with his appearance?"

"No sir, you did not."

"When he appears, and sometimes only when he is about and wishes to make his presence known, there is a rather overpowering smell of brimstone about."

"Brimstone?" Sir John puzzled that about in his head for a moment or two. "You mean sulphur?"

"That is what some call it today, yes."

"It is sulphur, is it not, which gives off the foul odor of rotting eggs? It can be quite overwhelming."

"Yes, that's it!" said Sir Simon in sudden excitement. "Rotting eggs—a terrible smell! That's it exactly!"

Sir John began laughing quite abruptly. He threw back his head and let it peal forth from him in great waves of merriment. I had not the slightest notion what had, of a sudden, struck him as so terribly funny.

Nor was I the only one. Sir Simon Grenville recoiled slightly from his guest as he looked upon him in utter bafflement. Then did the baffled expression turn to one of slight though open annoyance. At last, when Sir John's laughter had subsided, he risked a query.

"What, praytell, did strike you as so amusing, sir?"

"'Twas but a passing thought which tickled my fancy." And having gone only so far, he began snickering again. "It came to me that yours may be the only house in the realm that is haunted by a farting ghost." Then, having said it, he was once again beset by a laughing fit of a length and intensity quite like the last.

Thereafter the table remained rather quiet for quite some time.

For one unused to drinking wine of any kind, Clarissa did rather well drinking wines of every kind. In her own way, she kept up until the dessert course. It was not the piece of *gateau*, dripping with sweet sauce, that did her in. No, it was the accompanying sweet white wine from far-away Hungary which did finally seal her fate. She sipped it once in a manner most ladylike, then took nearly half a glass in a gulp. She replaced the glass upon the table, rested her chin upon her chest, and began snoring quite loudly.

It continued thus for less than a minute. Sir John did then become uncomfortably aware of the persistent drone.

"My ears tell me," said he, "that Clarissa has been summoned off to sleep. The poor child must be terribly weary. Perhaps we had best cut the evening a bit short and take her up to bed."

"Oh, do stay a bit longer, Sir John," urged the host. "We've matters to discuss, those which brought you here, matters that we have not even touched upon."

Sir John sighed. "Indeed, sir, you're right." He hesitated but a moment, then turned to me. "Jeremy, will you take Clarissa upstairs to her room?"

"Certainly I will, Sir John."

"Can you find her room? As I recall, it is directly across from ours."

I assured him I had the location of both firmly in mind and would bring her safely to her own.

"I could wake one of the staff," Sir Simon offered. (One by one they had disappeared.)

"No, Jeremy is quite capable."

By the time the discussion of my ability to deal with the situation had gone thus far, I had already persuaded Clarissa out of her chair, taken her firmly by the arm, and was marching her out of the grand dining room.

"I'll be back shortly," I called out quietly to them.

Yet I must have called loudly enough to bring her further awake, for she pulled herself up a bit and began to walk a bit more firmly.

"Where are we going?" she asked.

"Why, upstairs to your room, to put you to bed."

"Mmmm. That should be interesting." She had been making far too many such remarks of late to suit me—not quite lewd but of a sort which might be understood in a number of different ways. It had been so with her ever since that evening when we two had been trapped briefly in the darkened cellar of Number 4 Bow Street. I made no response to her sally but started her up the great stairway.

"Did I disgrace myself?"

"No," said I, "nothing of the kind."

"That's gratifying."

We continued to climb the stairs until, quite near the top, she spoke up again.

"What if the ghost should suddenly appear at my door?"

"Ghost indeed," said I with a sniff. "If he should be so unwise as to hang about your door, I should simply tell him to be gone. I should say to him, 'Here you, get back to your grave, if you know what's good for you. And none of your smelly farts.'"

At that she giggled, and she continued giggling all the way to her room. I opened the door and glanced inside: a candle was burning on the bedside table, and her bed had been turned back.

"Would you truly address the ghost so rudely?"

"I would! You must be firm with his kind."

"Then you are my hero and my champion, and I shall reward you by permitting you to kiss me good night."

"Ah well," said I, not wishing to kiss her but also not wishing to offend her, "perhaps another time."

"No," said she insistently, "*now*. I'm prepared to wait right here until you do—all night, if need be."

Well, why not? It would be the quickest way to be gone, would it not? I leaned toward her and chose a spot high on her left cheek just below her eye.

She stiffened and shrank back a few inches. "On the lips," said she in a manner which made it clear that she would brook no argument.

Steeling myself for a proper meeting of the mouths, I saw no way now to withdraw. Well then, thought I, in for a penny, in for a pound. I would do it all quickly and be gone.

But she would have none of that. Our lips had barely grazed when I felt her arms encircle me. Her lips pressed against mine. Her arms near squeezed the life from me. I felt utterly trapped. Yet it was for but a moment—for it was but the duration of a moment that she held me so. She stepped back, and I saw her cheeks redden with embarrassment: her boldness had exceeded even her own expectations, perhaps her own intentions, as well.

She leapt over the threshold and into her room. As she shut the door behind her, I heard her call a good night to me.

Well, thought I, hurrying away, the girl is obviously quite mad. Or perhaps it was the wine that she drank which has made her behave in this unaccountably wanton manner. She was truly making it difficult. Perhaps if I were to talk to her, reason with her, I might make her understand just how terribly awkward this will be for both of us.

I started down the stairs at a jog trot, but then did my pace slow somewhat, for as I descended, I heard a voice from the dining room—it was none other than Sir John's. Quite unmistakable, for when he spoke in argument, his voice fair thundered.

"Again, if you will forgive me, Sir Simon, what I cannot, for the life of me, comprehend is how you could so swiftly and so completely alter your opinion of Albert Sarton in so short a time. You supported him. Without you, he would not have had a chance of becoming magistrate of Deal."

THREE

*In which Sir John
meets Albert Sarton,
Magistrate of Deal*

We were late leaving for town the next morning. By
the time Sir John was up and had breakfasted, Sir
Simon Grenville was long gone on his daily round of in-
spection. His vast holdings, which numbered near a thousand acres of rich Kent farmlands, had just been planted
and so required his close attention—or so he told me that I
might explain his absence to Sir John. Before leaving, he
appointed Will Fowler, who had given us the speech of
welcome at our arrival, to be our guide round the manor
house. He took Clarissa on a proper tour of the place. I
asked only that I be shown the library that I might choose a
book to read whilst I waited for Sir John to rouse.

And so there I was, sitting outside the door to our room,
reading *A Sentimental Journey Through France and Italy,*
by the Reverend Mr. Sterne, listening for the familiar
sounds of snuffling and coughing which prefaced his ris-

ing. I liked the book not so well as *Tristram Shandy*, yet liked it well enough to wish to read it through. Therefore I was, I confess, a bit disappointed when at last the morning overture did begin. Yet dutifully, I set the book aside and entered the room.

"Jeremy? Is it you?"

"It is, Sir John."

"Is it late?"

"It's getting on."

In answer to that, he simply grunted, made use of the chamber pot which I fetched to him, and expressed his desire to be shaved. It took a few minutes for me to make preparations, during which he began a recapitulation of his discussion the night before of Mr. Albert Sarton's record as magistrate. Though it angered him to do so, he dwelt upon the details of the baronet's argument—or rather, the lack of them.

"I asked him to be specific," said Sir John, "and he could not be. Oh . . . well, he kept referring back to one case— only one, mind you—wherein Sir Simon had attempted to tip him on one gang of smugglers, yet he felt the magistrate had, ever afterward, turned a deaf ear to him and his tips. I must say, there seemed to be a good deal of personal pique involved in that. I should like to hear what Mr. Sarton has to say about it."

Sir John continued to grumble even as I proceeded to shave him.

"You heard him, Jeremy. Did I miss some several proofs of his? I ask you, was he specific?"

"No sir, he was not."

It is a risky matter to shave one who insists upon talking on, even as the sharp blade of the razor plays about his bobbing Adam's apple. I warned him twice against it.

"He did mention that Eccles fellow often, though, did he not?"

"Yes sir, he did."

"His contention seemed to be that if Eccles was against Mr. Sarton, then that was all the proof that was needed. He and Eccles may have formed a sort of alliance. I wonder who turned who against Sarton."

"Sir?"

"I mean to say, was it Sir Simon or Eccles who first became prejudiced against the magistrate? And who then won the other over?"

He went silent as he considered the questions he had raised. Carefully, watchfully, I resumed shaving him.

"And *why* sh— *ow!*"

I had cut him—or perhaps more accurately put, he had cut himself upon my innocent blade. Not, thank God, upon or near his throat. No, it was the tip of his chin that bled. Yet I was prepared. I reached into the kit and pulled forth the plaster preparation given me by our medico, Mr. Gabriel Donnelly. I dolloped a wad upon the cut and saw the bleeding stop.

"How is it?" he asked.

"All right now."

"Stopped bleeding, has it?"

"It has, yes."

"You should be more careful."

"*I* should be more careful? Why, I told you *twice* you were taking a chance continuing to talk whilst I was shaving you."

He said nothing for a long moment. "So you did," said he at last. "So you did."

When we two were deposited at Number 18 Middle Street, and I waved goodbye to Lord Mansfield's driver and coachman, I felt an odd, sinking feeling. It was as if Sir John and I had been cast away upon an isle from which there might be no return. They would go back with the coach to London. How much, of a sudden, did I envy them!

Yet why? Why this sense of desertion when, coming to Deal, I had been buoyed by a grand sense of adventure?

In any case, they were gone, and there would be no calling them back; even less was there a chance of stealing away with them. Ah well, with Sir John about to inspirit me, I had not yet failed to rise to the occasion, nor did I intend to ever in the future.

"Well, we are here, are we not?" said he. "Shall we go meet the magistrate?" He placed his hand upon my forearm, and thus together we made direct for Number 18.

Middle Street lay just above Beach Street, which fronted upon the sea, and just below High Street, where I was to meet Mr. Perkins in an hour's time. The better part of Deal was scattered along these three streets. Will Fowler had told us that at its farther end, near Alfred Square, Middle Street was not near respectable and downright dangerous. "You'd ought not venture there at night," said he. Yet Number 18 was, in his view, well within the safe zone, day or night. Middle Street was as tight and narrow as any of those in London. The houses which lined it on either side— all of them brick or stone, so far as I could tell—were crammed together, wall to wall, street after street. Number 18, in which Mr. Albert Sarton resided and presided over his magistrate's court, was a little larger (though not much) than the houses on either side of it. It was by no means imposing.

I grasped the hand-shaped brass knocker firmly and slammed it thrice against the plate. We waited. I could hear the voices of a man and a woman from some distant part of the house, though it was quite impossible to tell what was said between them. Just as I grabbed at the knocker again and made ready to try my luck a second time, I heard footsteps beyond the door; they seemed to be moving at a steady clip down a long hall.

And then a voice: "Coming! Coming! Who is it at the door?"

"It is Sir John Fielding, come from London," I cried loudly that I might be heard through the door.

A bolt was thrown, a lock turned, and the door at last came open. There stood a woman of about thirty years. She was pretty enough, but panted with exertion and perspired freely from her red hair to the nape of her freckled neck (and no doubt beyond). Clearly, she had been hard at work. Was she the maid? I thought not, but in London the lady of the house would never present herself in such a state of dishevelment.

"Good gracious, it's him, an't it?"

Since she was not looking in my direction but beyond, I could only assume that she spoke not of me but of Sir John.

"If it is me you speak of, young lady, then allow me to present myself a bit more formally. I am Sir John Fielding, magistrate of the Bow Street Court in London, and this is my young assistant, Jeremy Proctor. We are come to call upon Mr. Albert Sarton, magistrate of Deal. Is he in?"

"Oh, he's in, right enough, and he's expecting you . . . tomorrow."

"Well then," said Sir John, "perhaps we should leave and return on the day we are expected."

"Oh no, I'll not hear of it. Come in! Oh, do come in, please. We were just tidyin' up the place in expectation of your visit."

There was something quite disarming about the way she sought to make us welcome. She beckoned us inside, urging us through the door, grasping him by the arm in a way he usually fought against. She told him to mind the bump there at the threshold. Heading us forward, she left us in a small room to the left of the door with a promise to tell "Berty" of our arrival.

"He'll be with you before you know it."

I guided Sir John to a chair, which he eased into rather carefully. Very likely he was still fighting the effects of last night's wine and brandy.

We seemed to have been left in an office of some sort. The room was certainly no larger than the modest little chamber in our living quarters which Sir John called his "study." And it probably served Albert Sarton in the same way—providing him with a place to be alone and to think.

"Is she Irish?" Sir John asked. "She seems Irish."

"Well, she has red hair."

"That's a start."

He was silent for a bit. "Is she his wife?" he asked. "What do you think?"

"I believe so," said I, after giving the matter due consideration. "After all, she called him 'Berty.' If she were a housemaid, or any sort of servant, she would not have done that."

"True, yes, well, nobody told me that he was married."

I wondered how that might change things, yet I did not raise the question. Instead, I looked about me and studied the objects in the room and thus attempted to draw some picture of the man we had come to see. He was plainly a man of scholarly bent. A pile of books and papers upon the desk suggested to me that he was engaged in the writing of some weighty work—on the philosophy of jurisprudence, no doubt. I half-rose and strained to see the nature of the one book which lay open upon his desk: it was a Latin dictionary. Inwardly, I shuddered, for I had a great fear that my weakness in Latin might ultimately bar my entry into the legal profession. I brooded upon this, wondering where and how I might find a tutor in Latin and why, if I put my mind to it, I could not teach myself Latin—at least well enough to pass an examination of some sort.

So completely was I taken up with my own matters that I failed to hear the footsteps down the long hall until they were nearly upon us. In fact, it was not until Sir John rose from his chair to meet the magistrate that I became aware that the latter was anywhere nearby. I jumped to my feet and made ready to be presented to him.

Albert Sarton was short of stature and short of sight. I, who am even now no more than an ordinary average in height, was then near half a head taller than Mr. Sarton. As I ducked my head sharply in a quick little bow, I found myself face to face with him; he peered at me through spectacles near a quarter inch in thickness, smiled at me in friendly fashion, and shook the hand I offered him. Indeed I liked him quite well. But once the formalities had been observed, he turned his attention to Sir John.

"Please believe me, sir," said he to him, "when I say that I feel quite honored to meet you. You are known far and wide."

"Ah yes, the Blind Beak of Bow Street," said Sir John a bit dismissively, "—the penny papers and such."

"By no means! Why, I recall hearing you quoted favorably at Oxford. It had to do with the problem of making the law fit the crime—something about . . ." He hesitated as his memory worked upon it. ". . . about a villain who sold body parts taken from a murder victim . . ."

"Ah yes," said Sir John, "he was indicted on a charge of disturbing the dead."

"Grave robbing, in effect, before the grave was dug."

"Something like that," said Sir John modestly.

"Oh, but please sit down, both of you."

We resumed our places, and Mr. Sarton squeezed round us to situate himself behind the desk.

"Forgive me," he said, "for the mistake on the date of your arrival. I'd got a letter from the Lord Chief Justice telling me that you were on your way and that I was to cooperate with you in any and all ways which you might require. He did not name a date or a day, but said, rather, 'in two days' time.' You arrived only a day later."

"Ah well," said Sir John, "Lord Mansfield gave me the loan of his coach-and-four to make the trip down here. And his driver seems to go everywhere at full gallop."

"That then was no doubt the root of the misunderstanding."

"No doubt, but dear God, Mr. Sarton, did he truly say that you were to cooperate in any and all ways which I might require?"

"Those may not have been his exact words, but they are as I remember them."

"Then he has made it sound appallingly like a court-martial."

Mr. Sarton stared at him for a moment, saying nothing. Then: "Is that not the nature of your inquiry?"

Thus it came Sir John's turn to maintain a solemn quiet. "No sir," said he after near a minute of cold silence, "it is not. I have not the authority to act as a one-man tribunal in judgment upon you. I would not want such authority. I am here in answer to a complaint regarding the manner in which you have discharged your duties. I am here, to put it another way, to inquire into your methods and their effectiveness."

"Who made this complaint? Or have I not the right to know?"

"If you expect me to reject your question as impertinent, I must disappoint you. The identity of the accuser is indeed pertinent. A man has the right to face him who sullies his name, else we are all to be in mortal dread of every manner of rumor, false witness, and lie which is told of us. And so you may know that the complaint against you was made by George Eccles, Chief Customs Officer for east Kent."

"Eccles, is it! Indeed, I should have known. He has been against me from near the start. With what, specifically, has he charged me?"

"He has said that you are either corrupt in the discharge of your office, or the most incompetent ever in the history of the magistracy."

"But . . . the specifics, the incidents?"

"He gave none." Sir John paused. "Let me assure you,

Mr. Sarton, that Lord Mansfield, to whom the complaint was made, would not have taken Eccles's complaint seriously but for his position; nor would he have sent me down to look into these matters had he himself not taken a personal interest in you here in Deal."

"I . . . I know that he was quite instrumental in getting me this post," said he, faltering for the first time. "And for that I am still grateful, though a little less, perhaps, today than when I received the appointment."

"What have been your relations with this man Eccles?"

"Not good, I should say. As Chief Customs Officer for this part of Kent, he has at his disposal a considerable force of men—over sixty at Dover Castle, where he has his headquarters, and more scattered in various towns up and down the coast."

"How many in Deal?"

"Twenty, I believe. They are quartered at Deal Castle and report to the local customs officer, a man with whom I've cultivated good relations. My difficulties have been with his chief."

He hesitated, frowned, and traced a pattern upon the desktop with his finger as he sought words to continue.

"Like most country magistrates, I have but two constables at my command," said he, resuming. "You, I believe, have a greater force—the Bow Street Runners, they are called."

"I have been fortunate in that regard, yes, and that is because those in the government who apportion money wish to feel themselves safe in London," said Sir John, "And by the bye, though my constables be greater in number, they can never be sufficient to the task. London, it seems, will never be truly safe."

"Be that as it may, sir, would you care to hazard a guess as to how many here in my jurisdiction in Deal are involved in the smuggling trade?"

"I couldn't possibly put a number on it."

"No less," said Mr. Sarton, pausing for effect, "than two hundred."

It took Sir John a moment to respond. "So many? I had not thought it could be so many."

"I trust the figure," said the young magistrate, "for it was given me by the local customs officer, who grew up in Deal and has helped me on numerous occasions in ways his chief, Eccles, would never do."

"Yes, Eccles—let us get back to you and your difficulties with him."

"Yes, of course. Because these two constables are expected to keep order in the town and enforce the laws of the realm, et cetera, they are an insufficient number, pitifully insufficient, to do much to put down the smuggling trade here in this district. I saw that immediately I came here. And so I journeyed off to Dover to ask Mr. Eccles's aid in patrolling the beaches known to be used by the smugglers. He said no, it was out of the question, for there was work enough to be done in the Dover area. But surely, said I, he could spare us at least a part of the force of customs men quartered here in Deal. Again no, said Mr. Eccles, for they had their duties to perform and could not be spared from them. There was no arguing with the man—I tried, but to no avail. He simply would give me no help whatever. And now, I learn from you, Sir John, that he has had the cold gall to accuse me of incompetence or corruption in the discharge of my duties."

Mr. Sarton ended somewhat breathless. He could say little more in his own defense. And to me it seemed that little more need be said. Indeed I wondered if we might not return to London this very day. But Sir John seemed to have more in mind.

"Have you had no success in combating . . . what is it they call it here?"

"The owling trade. Yes, I have had—just once. It came through a tip given me by Sir Simon Grenville. He had

heard through his servants at the manor house of the sched-
uled arrival of a shipment from France of wines and brandy
on a certain night of the new moon. They made the crossing
in one of those galleys which are built on the quiet right in
Deal. I understand that they can make it here from Dunkirk,
with twenty men rowing, in five hours' time. They have a
shallow draft and can land upon Goodwin Sands or most of
the other beaches in the district. And with so many men
working, they can be unloaded in no time at all. So there
was no point trying to confront them on the beach. We
three—my two constables and me—would have been hope-
lessly out-manned and out-gunned."

He was warming to the subject, putting a good deal of
drama into the telling of his tale.

"That was wise of you," said Sir John. "What then did
you do?"

"Why, we waited till their two wagons were loaded and
had started up the hill, and the galley was departed from the
beach. We kept our silence and were well hidden, for we
sorely needed the advantage that surprise would give us.
We were but three in number, after all. We waited and
waited and waited until they were just upon us."

Reader, I had become acutely aware of the clock that
hung upon the wall behind Mr. Sarton. According to it, I
had barely five minutes in which to locate the Good King
George in High Street, where I was to meet Mr. Perkins and
hear his first report. How could I leave gracefully if Mr.
Sarton insisted upon spinning out his story to absurd
lengths? Would he never reach the conclusion?

But then, rather abruptly, he did end it: "And then we
jumped out at them and upon their wagons and persuaded
them to stop."

That, it seemed to me, was a weak ending to a strong
story. Why had he cut it short? Then did I note the quick
footsteps in the hall and saw how our host turned his attention past Sir John and me to the door that lay between us. I

turned my attention to it just in time to see the putative Mrs. Sarton appear. She carried a tray, and upon it were three cups and a steaming pot which I took to be filled with dark tea a-brewing. Best of all, I spied a plate of sweet cakes and all manner of dainties, near as tempting to the eye as they would be to the palate. Her husband rose, as did Sir John and I.

"You two have already met my wife, Margaret, I believe."

"We have," said Sir John, with a stiff little bow, "and a pleasure it was indeed."

"Ah, you're too kind, sir," said she to him. "I've just brought along some tea and cakes for all. I believe that talk goes better on a full stomach, don't you?"

"Absolutely certain of it," said Sir John.

She placed the tray upon her husband's desk and busied herself pouring tea.

I realized that I now had my opportunity to leave. "None for me, thank you."

"Oh? And what would you prefer, young sir?" asked Mr. Sarton. "Milk perhaps?"

"No, nothing at all. I've a matter to attend to on Sir John's behalf. It should not take more than an hour."

"Well then, be on your way. Quick to depart, quick to return."

"I'll show you out," said Mrs. Sarton. "But before I do, I would like to say to you, Sir John, and to you, young sir, that I have often heard that story told before by Albert—the one that he was telling just before I came in. But there is part of it that he always neglects to include at the end of it."

"And what is that, Mrs. Sarton?" asked Sir John, clearly curious at what she might reveal.

"What Berty, that is, Albert, never tells is that he was badly wounded in the arm by a pistol ball. It shattered the bone, and it looked for a time that he might lose the use of that left arm altogether. I've asked him again and again to promise that he will take part no more in such battles, but so far I've yet to squeeze such a promise out of him."

"Please, Molly," said he, "I can make no such promise. I'm sure Sir John understands that."

"Well, whether he does or don't, I intend to keep working until I get it from you, Berty." Then, turning her attention to me: "Come along, Mr. Proctor, if that's your name. Oh, and at least take with you a cake or two. I made them myself, and so I know they're good."

I took her at her word, grabbed a scone, and was then ushered out of the room and to the street door. I asked her the way to the George in High Street, and as she gave directions, which were quite simple enough, I noted that her eyes glistened as though she might weep. Nonetheless, she managed to get the locks off and push me out the door before tears fell.

The scone was quite the best I had ever eaten.

I found Mr. Perkins in the taproom of the inn, where ale and beer flowed freely. The bar was crowded with raw and boisterous men of every description who seemed to have little in common but their loud speech and their thirst for malt. They stood cheek-by-jowl, howling and shouting each at the other. I could scarce believe it was no more than midday and could not but wonder what the place might be like at midnight. No, he was not at the bar. I wandered round in search of him at one of the tables placed along the wall and found him at that which was farthest. All was as expected. What I had not foreseen, however, was that Mr. Perkins would be sitting in the company of another. I thought at first glance he might wish me to stay away; but no, he pointed me out to the man with whom he shared the table, and then waved me over.

I was not in a good position to see the face of the stranger until he turned to look at me. He was a man of about the same age as Mr. Perkins, tall and lean (somehow that was obvious, even though he maintained his sitting posture), with what appeared to be a saber scar across his left cheek. As I drew closer, I saw that he was smiling at me, though only with the right side of his mouth.

"Jeremy, meet an old friend of mine from bygone days, name of Dick Dickens."

Dickens reached across the table, offering his hand as I sat down. Mr. Perkins passed on to me a broad and most obvious wink. I gave a manly squeeze to the hand and a proper nod to the constable, signaling my understanding: I would follow his lead.

"What say you, Jeremy," said the constable, "have they kept you hopping to their tune?"

I shook my head in the negative. "Nah, 'tan't so," said I to him, effecting the manner of speech of a Covent Garden lay-about. "It's mostly just waitin' for when we're needed."

"It was Jeremy got me the ride down here," said he to Dickens.

"In a gentleman's coach? That an't half bad."

"No, it was *on* a gentleman's coach. You think you'd like to go bouncing about on your arse, just hangin' on for dear life atop a coach with four horses at full gallop—you think that, then you're welcome to my space back to London."

"No, but I thank you all the same," said Dickens with a chuckle.

At last did I remember whence I knew that name, Dickens. It was Dick Dickens who figured so prominent in Mr. Perkins's tale of his life in the owling trade. He had enlisted him all those years ago. By luck or by cleverness, Constable Perkins had made direct contact with the smugglers.

"Which gentleman is it has the coach?" asked Dickens.

The question seemed to be directed at me, yet I was unsure how I should answer. Thus was I relieved when Mr. Perkins came forth with the information—false information as it happened.

"It belongs to John Fielding, a knight by the pleasure of King George."

"Sir John Fielding, is it?" said Dickens. "An't he the blind magistrate there in Covent Garden?"

"That's the one."

"You work for him? Don't tell me you're a constable!"

"Do I look like a constable?" said Mr. Perkins. "You ever see one with just one arm?"

"No, I don't guess I ever did."

"I'm his dogsbody."

"What's that?"

"I do whatever I'm told to. Fetch what needs to be fetched, carry messages back and forth, just an errand boy, really."

"And what about you, lad? What do you do for the blind magistrate of Bow Street?"

"Just a footman," said I.

"Ah well," said Dickens. "We all got to start somewhere, don't we?" He then rose and said something that struck me as strange: "I must get back to the castle." He shook hands once again and bade us goodbye, leaving near a full half-pint of ale at his place at the table.

Once he was out of earshot, I turned to Constable Perkins and in a voice so quiet it may as well have been a whisper, I said to him, "That was the Dick Dickens you told us about, wasn't it? The one who got you into the smuggling trade?"

"That's who it was, Jeremy, and I was quite amazed when he walked into this place not long before you came along. I recognized him right away—he's not changed all that much—but he more than recognized me."

That seemed odd. "What do you mean?"

"Well, he came up to me right away, like he knew that I was here—and maybe he did."

Again, he had done naught but confuse me.

"What do you suppose he's up to now? Guess, Jeremy, just try."

"Why, I've no idea, really," said I. "Still in smuggling, I suppose."

"Oh no, not like that at all. But this is unfair. You'll never guess." He took a deep breath and uttered as softly as ever he could: "He's a customs man."

I heard what he said, though I did not quite trust my ears. "He's *what*?"

Perhaps I spoke too loudly—or perhaps it was Mr. Perkins's obvious wish not to be overheard which attracted attention—but glancing about, I noticed that a number of faces at the tables near ours had turned in our direction. Mr. Perkins noticed, as well. He jumped to his feet.

"Come along," said he. "Let's go to the bar. The crowd there is so loud, they'll pay no attention to us."

And thus it transpired that we concluded our conversation standing at the bar where he called for another ale, and I ordered coffee. We were two of that roaring crowd who roared along with the rest. Yet I daresay none of our near neighbors paid us the slightest heed. Mr. Perkins shouted his news to me loud as the town crier might have done in days gone by. None but me did hear him, though. Of that I'm sure.

As Mr. Perkins told it, he had been sitting at that most distant table, sipping an ale and awaiting my arrival when Dickens came into sight and walked straight over to him. Recognition was immediate. They greeted each the other like long-separated friends and immediately fell to talking about all that had happened during the years that had passed since last they met. Dickens's first concern was for Mr. Perkins's missing left forearm. He asked the usual questions: How had it been lost? Did it pain him? Was he able to do without it? Et cetera. These and other such questions Mr. Perkins answered quickly and directly, for he had prepared an elaborate story which concerned a wound given him in the battle for Fort Duquesne.

"I took a proper chop at the elbow from a tomahawk," he had told Dickens. "That, for your information, is a sort of Injun hatchet."

Dickens, properly impressed, had winced visibly. Yet he was in no wise helpful when Mr. Perkins hinted that he had returned to Deal hoping to find employment. Did he know of anything in that trade in which they had both once worked?

"Ah well," Dickens had responded. "Afraid I can't help you there. I've moved across to the other side of the street now."

When asked to explain that, he said that he was now with the Customs Service.

"I must have looked at him pretty queer," said Mr. Perkins to me, "for he laughed a bit and swore it was all true. Not only that, but then he tells me that he's the customs officer for Deal with an office in Deal Castle and twenty men to do his bidding. I wanted to hear more, of course, but it was just about then that you came by, Jeremy."

I thought about what had then been said by and to Dick Dickens, and I realized that there was something that had puzzled me.

"I've a question, Mr. Perkins."

"Ask it then, and I'll answer if I can."

"Why did you mention Sir John to him at all? You needn't have done. A complete fiction would have worked just as well."

"True enough, I suppose," said he. "But if you had seen the way that Dickens came up to me at that table, you'd understand. I happened to be looking in his direction when he come round the corner, and he wasn't looking left or right at all. He knew right where I'd be, and he knew exactly who I was. No, I figure that he'd been told about me—

somebody must've recognized me from the old days and told him where I'd be. As for why I then brought Sir John into it, it seemed to me that if I was being watched that close, they might just possibly see me around Deal sometime soon with Sir John—or at least with a blind man who answers his description. And if they did, I wanted to account for it in advance." He paused. "Why? Didn't you think much of the story I gave?"

"Well," said I, "I thought it a bit far-fetched. After all, a dogsbody? an errand boy? You seemed, rather, to be describing me."

"Aw, now you're not being fair to your own self."

Thus, in friendly raillery, we did continue our interview at the George to the very end, when, having finished my coffee, I prepared to take my leave.

"You can tell Sir John," said the constable, "that I'll continue to find out what I can about the trade hereabouts. Tonight I'll head over to Alfred Square. I understand it's sort of a gathering place, so I've heard."

"Well, watch out if you do," said I, "for *I've* heard that it's just the part of town to be avoided—a robbery a week and a murder a month."

"Sounds just like dear old Bedford Street in Covent Garden, so it does. I think I'll like it just fine."

On that I departed.

My interview with Mr. Perkins had not lasted near as long as I expected, and so I decided to take a bit of time and explore the town of Deal. I had seen some of it, of course, from the window of Lord Mansfield's coach. Yet the world seen from a coach window is simply a picture that moves. Where are the smells, the sounds, of the place?

Well, they were indeed present as I set off down High Street. I mixed with the crowd of buyers as they moved in and out of the rich shops along the way. There was a certain indefinable but real sense of prosperity and well-being among them. It was not so much what was said as how it was said. No doubt they gossiped of family, friends, and workplace, as they did in most other towns and cities. Nevertheless, they did so with smiles upon their faces and laughter in their voices; they did not go about muttering and cursing, as they seemed so often to do in London.

As for the smell of the place, there could be no doubt: it was the smell of the sea. I soon saw my way down to Beach Street, and I took it. Once there, I was immediately touched by the great flocks of gulls, flying over sea and shore and walking about upon the narrow strip of beach that ran along the cobblestone street. It seemed that whenever one of the great gray or white birds landed, another would take off. I wondered, were there not more gulls than people in Deal? Not far offshore, a number of boats bobbed in the tide—though not so many as I might have expected, for Deal was known then, as it is now, as a fishing port. Then, of a sudden, did it come to me that because it was not long past midday, the boats might indeed still be out upon the sea; perhaps they stayed out for days at a time. The smell of the sea and the fish was all about me, a strong odor even upon the walkway. I did realize at last that it came not just from the beach and beyond, but from ahead, as well, for there, at the next corner, were stalls which sold all manner of seafood to the citizenry, shellfish and finny fish, even eels and skates. I paused and surveyed the vast array of God's water creatures. What would they taste of? Why, of the sea, of course, but in truth, I had not tasted much seafood at that time in my life. I had no clear sense of it. Reluctantly, I continued on my way. I went on to the next street and the next. Then, when Beach Street ended, the shore, of course, did not. And so I crossed over and walked along the water line. What a grand thing it would be to live one's life by the sea and take such walks every day!

I had not gone far when I spied a vast structure back somewhat from the shore. Low and hulking it stood, with many cannon pointed out to the sea. I concluded immediately it was Deal Castle, where Dick Dickens lorded it over an idle force of twenty customs men. Did those who accepted him in the Customs Service not know his history? Did Mr. Albert Sarton not know it? He had spoken of him (without identifying him by name) quite respectfully. What if I were to return with the news that the local Customs Officer was once indeed actively involved in smuggling? Would he and Sir John suspect, as I did at that moment, that perhaps Dickens had only pretended to leave the owling trade? It could well be, thought I, that Dick—and perhaps his customs men, as well—were not near so idle as they seemed.

Thus my thoughts as I gazed upon Deal Castle. Had I known more at that moment, I might not have been near so certain. Yet if I had not been so certain, I should not have hastened, as I did, to Number 18 Middle Street in order to inform Sir John of what I had learned about the local customs officer. And had I not hastened, I might have missed him altogether.

Knowing no better way, I returned to the residence of Mr. Sarton just as I had come from it. No doubt there was a shorter route, but I did not know it, nor did I have time to ask it. I felt a strange urgency to Middle Street. Where before I had ambled, I now jog-trotted. Even there along High Street I moved at a fast pace through the crowd of local gentry, narrowly avoiding collisions, dashing at full speed past the Good King George, the inn where I had learned all from Mr. Perkins. And at last to Middle Street where, to my uneasy surprise, I spied a coach waiting at one of the houses halfway to the next street. I feared the worst when I saw that it waited before Number 18.

Upon the box, there in the driver's seat, sat Will Fowler, he of the welcoming speech who had acted as guide to Clarissa's tour of the manor house and its grounds. Fowler talked soothingly to the two horses, calming them with his voice, as only a good driver can do. But he gave me a wave of recognition ere I knocked upon the door. Because I read the look upon his face as one of concern, I asked if there were trouble back at the house.

"I fear so," said he, "trouble of the worst sort."

"And what is that?" I asked.

"Murder," said he, "of one of our own. I've come to report it and collect Mr. Sarton. That's as it should be done, with the magistrate, or so I was told."

"May Sir John and I return with you?"

"Already been asked, already been granted."

I nodded and went to the door, banging loudly upon it and waiting just as I had before. And just as before, I heard the steady tap-tap-tap of Mrs. Sarton's heels down the long hall. She called out to me, demanding to know who knocked. To her request I called out my name. Yet there was a lapse of some several moments before the bolt was pulled and the key turned in the lock. She had evidently forgotten who I was. We had never been properly introduced.

"Ah yes," said she, "I thought 'twas you, but we can't be too careful. Come in, come in."

I did as she bade, and noted that she did return bolt and lock to place the moment I was inside. I gave her my thanks and followed her pointed direction into that small room to the right of the door where we had sat earlier. Then did she depart. Sir John, and he alone, occupied the space at that moment. He stood, fidgeting with his walking stick, obviously eager to be off.

"Ah, Jeremy, you're here," said he. "I feared we should have to leave without you."

"Yes, Sir John, and I bear with me important news from Constable Perkins."

"Well, save it. I've important news, too. Let us wait till we are alone and may talk more freely."

"But," said I, "this is information that will be of great interest to Mr. Sarton, as well. I'm sure he would want to know."

"That may well be," said Sir John, "but if it came from Mr. Perkins, it must be saved. Remember, we are here as trespassers upon his private preserve. If he knew we had someone gathering information here behind his back, so to speak, he would be most displeased."

Reluctantly, I agreed to say nothing.

"Hush now, I hear him coming. Not a word."

"No sir, not a word."

FOUR

*In which Clarissa
proves herself a
reliable witness*

The conveyance in which we were taken to Sir Simon's manor house was of an unusual, probably local design, the like of which I had never seen in the streets of London. It was a bit like a hackney coach, though so much smaller and lighter that only two could fit comfortably in its interior. As a result, there was naught for me but to take a perch upon the box beside Will Fowler.

From my brief acquaintance with the man, I deemed him one of good disposition and a ready tongue. Yet the grave nature of his errand had saddened and silenced him so that in spite of my best efforts, I was able to get little from him. Nonetheless, the little I did get surprised me much. As I now recall, we were well out of town when I made what must have been my third or fourth attempt to draw him out. He had up to then left my questions hanging unanswered in the air, or at best responded with a gesture—a shrug or a shake of his shaggy head.

He had the horses moving along at a good pace so that it seemed we must be near the end of our journey. I expected the unmarked driveway into the great house to appear after the next turn of this winding road—or surely the next one after that. It was then, holding on to the seat grip for dear life, that I asked him (for the second time, I believe) who it was had been found dead.

Again he shrugged, but this time he added: "One of the new men Sir Simon took on. Don't know his name."

"It's certain he was murdered? Couldn't have been an accident?"

"What kind of an accident leaves you with your throat cut?"

"Well . . . yes," said I, in something less than a shout. "I suppose it was murder then."

"Course it was!" said he peevishly, punctuating his dec-laration with a rather fierce glance.

"Who found the body?" I was certain I hadn't asked that before.

He said something then, but it was quite lost in the rattle of the wheels and the pounding of the horses' hooves.

"What was that?"

He put his face to my ear and shouted: "It was me—but the girl—I an't sure of her name—she was also there."

"You mean Clarissa?"

"Aye, that's her. We was out—" He broke off and nod-ded ahead, reaching out at the same time to ease back on the brake. Then, taking the reins in both hands, he hauled them in. As we slowed sharply, I recognized the turn into the driveway just ahead. He made the turn with room to spare.

Clarissa! I reflected. Now, that was an astonishment. Had I but accepted Will Fowler's invitation to tour the house and grounds, I would almost certainly have been present at the discovery of the body. Indeed, I might even have been the one to find it, rather than she.

"You'll hear all about it, I'm sure," said he to me.

"I'm sure I will."

Then, of a sudden, we came round a bend, with a meadow on our right, a fenced wood upon our left, and a male figure did leap from the wood into the road and begin waving his arms at us rather frantically. Fowler pulled back hard upon the reins, slowing the horses, and almost simultaneously gave another hard tug to the brake. Though it looked for a moment as if we might run the poor fellow down, we did manage to come to a halt just in time to save him (though I, reader, was nearly catapulted forward onto the neck of one of the lead horses).

"You all right?" asked Fowler.

I assured him I was. "But . . . but what is the meaning of this? Who is this man?"

"I know not," said he with a shake of his head.

Then did two more men emerge from the brushy wood; one of them I recognized as Sir Simon Grenville; the other was quite as unknown to me as the man in the driveway.

"Those two men with Sir Simon," Fowler muttered to me, "they're part of that new crew, like the man who was killed."

"Will," Sir Simon called out, "Will Fowler. Had you forgotten completely where you found the body? You, of all people!" Then did he let go a low, chuckling laugh, as if to assure his man that he meant what he had said merely as a mild reproof.

Yet Fowler was clearly confused: "I . . . well, I suppose I did, sir. Do forgive me."

"Nothing to forgive," said his master magnanimously. Then did he call out: "Sir John, Mr. Sarton, if that wild stop did not kill or cripple you, come along and I'll show you what you were summoned to see." He seemed oddly jovial.

At that, I scrambled down to the ground to assist them. I

opened the door to the coach and presented my hand first to
Mr. Sarton, who hopped down with no difficulty, and Sir
John, who exited a bit laboriously.

"Are you all right, sir?" I asked him.

"I believe so. No broken bones, in any case. Here, give
me your hand and a stiff arm to lean on. I won't risk jumping."

Thus he made it down, step by step, panting slightly
from the effort. Holding my arm, he limped along in a
rather tentative manner. I wondered if he were perhaps in
pain.

"This way, gentlemen," said Sir Simon, beckoning us
into the wood.

"Is there no path?" asked Mr. Sarton.

"I fear not. And the undergrowth is rather thick just
here."

"Perhaps it would be better, Jeremy," said Sir John, "if
you preceded me."

And so we arranged ourselves in single file—Sir Simon
leading the way, followed by the magistrate of Deal, then
myself, and Sir John last of all. As I passed them, I gave a
good, thorough examination to the two that Fowler had described as belonging to "the new crew." They were a hard
sort. I had seen their kind in London, in and around Covent
Garden—on Bedford Street specifically. And when I saw
them there, I usually had the good sense to give them a wide
berth. But having thought of Bedford Street, my mind went
swiftly to Mr. Perkins, who had mentioned it earlier that afternoon. With such as those two around, staring after us, I
found myself wishing that he were here. I always felt safer
with Mr. Perkins close by.

Sir Simon seemed to know just where he was going. We
followed as he tramped on through the dense brush for a
good twenty yards or more.

The trees hereabouts were grown so close that the leaves
above masked the greater part of the afternoon sunlight.

The light did thus come through only in patches. We moved from sunlit patches to patches of darkness, and then back into sunlight. It seemed oddly fitting that the corpus, when at last we came upon him, lay completely in the dark.

The body was that of a young man, one in his middle twenties at most. And though still young, he was thick through the chest and legs in a way which suggested he had done a good deal of physical labor in his short life—a farm lad perhaps, a plowboy. He had a beard of a few days' growth which was nevertheless thin and patchy. Dressed quite ordinarily he was, except that he wore no hat; perhaps it had fallen from his head and was beneath him. He was on his back, arms thrown out to each side. The ugly wound that had killed him was exposed to view. It followed the line of his chin some inches, perhaps just two, below it. Though bloody still, the red had dried black upon his throat, indicating, to me at least, that he had been dead a good many hours. I saw no sign of a weapon of any sort.

I described the corpus in words quite like these to Sir John. He listened closely, nodding his understanding as I talked on in a mere whisper. While we were thus engaged, Albert Sarton was bending close to examine the body, though not closely enough to suit him: Before he was done, he was down upon his hands and knees, spectacles upon his nose, looking at the wound, at the hands and fingers of the deceased, and even at his shoes. Finally, and most peculiarly, he looked carefully at the ground all round the victim.

Looking on, Sir Simon seemed at first amused and somewhat puzzled by the magistrate's strange behavior, then finally, openly annoyed. Why he should be annoyed, however, I could not fathom.

At last, Mr. Sarton rose from his hands and knees to his full height (which was not great) and announced: "He was not killed here." This was said with great certainty. "No doubt he was moved to hide him."

"How can you be so sure?" Sir Simon demanded.

"Easily enough," said the magistrate of Deal. "There is no sign of a path in the surrounding area, and so he would have to have come to this spot in the same way we did—that is, from the roadway. But look at the soles of your shoes, and you will see that they are clotted with humus—moist, dark dirt with bits of decomposing organic matter therein." He held up some to show Sir Simon. "This bit here is specially moist, almost like mud."

"That proves nothing!"

"Not alone—no, of course not. Yet if we look at the soles of the shoes worn by this poor individual, we see no sign of humus. What we find instead is something very interesting: chalk."

"Chalk?" echoed Sir John.

"Yes sir," responded Mr. Sarton, "*chalk*. It's quite common in these parts—whole cliffs of the stuff, as I'm sure you've heard."

"So I have."

"Come all of you who wish, and take a look at these soles—almost completely whitened with chalk dust. And see, too, his clothes are dusted all over with chalk dust. He could not have picked it up here. Sir Simon, do you know of a place in your vast holdings where a man might whiten the soles of his shoes from an abundance of chalk on the ground?"

"No, I know of no such place." His response came so quickly that it seemed he had anticipated the question. Yet perhaps thinking better of it, he added, "Though there may be such. After all, I know not every nook and cranny of what you call my 'vast' holdings."

"I meant no offense."

"None was taken."

"Good, for I have a few questions regarding him. First of all, who is he—or, lamentably, who *was* he?"

"I know not his name, but he has been in my employ for

the past four or five months. No doubt one of the other men knows who he is."

"His next-of-kin should be notified, after all."

"I'll find out."

"Good." Mr. Sarton rubbed his chin, as if in thought. "Now, this poor fellow's body is already quite stiff, which means he has been dead a good long time. My guess is that he was killed sometime during the night. What was he doing out, say, well after midnight? Just out on a nocturnal ramble? Or had he some duty to perform?"

"No doubt," said Sir Simon, "he was out as a guard. I had left orders that guards be posted."

"For what purpose? What were they to guard against?"

"Against poachers."

"Oh? Are they such a problem?"

"I've lost a good many deer. I fear I shall have to lay traps."

"Man traps?"

"Yes, of course."

"I've seen what they can do," said Mr. Sarton. "They are truly terrible things."

"Is not the murder of a man a worse thing?"

"Oh yes. Yes, of course. I did not mean to say . . ." He allowed the sentence to go unfinished. Yet though that quietened the young magistrate for a moment, it did not end his questions. "Who found the victim? Was it you, Sir Simon?"

"By no means. I, in fact, was off some distance attending to a business matter near Sandwich. Mr. Fowler found the body just here and sent for me. Then he drove off to Deal to fetch you. I had arrived only a little before you myself."

"Then it was he who brought us here who found him?"

"That's as I said."

"Strange that he did not tell us that."

"Well, you must take that up with him," said Sir Simon.

"Now, however, if you have no more need of me, I must return to Sandwich to conclude my business there."

Without waiting for an answer, he did then gesture that we were to follow and started back through trees and into the underbrush along the way we had come. Having little choice in the matter, we trailed him as before, though this time Mr. Sarton took up the rear, reluctant (it seemed) to leave the body.

When we arrived at the driveway, we found to our general dismay that Will Fowler was nowhere about. His place in the driver's seat had been taken by one of the two new men, him whose frantic waves had persuaded Fowler to stop. Sir Simon, I noted, was conducting an earnest conversation with the second of them. He concluded with him and came over to us.

"Mr. Sarton, I regret to say that Will Fowler has gone off to attend to his regular duties. I did not tell him to remain because I, like you, supposed he had told you all that he knew before bringing you here."

"Ah well," said Mr. Sarton, "it seems then that we are both deceived."

"So it seems. I'll see that he talks to you tomorrow."

"I should greatly appreciate it if you did."

"Well then." With that rather unceremonious goodbye, he took his leave of us and began trudging up the hill. The manor house was no more than a hundred yards ahead.

"Into the coach, gents, and I'll take you to the house," called the new driver.

"No," answered Mr. Sarton, "I've a wish to talk with Sir John. Take the coach up to the house, and turn it round. Then you may drive me back to Deal."

"As you wish, sir."

And so saying, he started the team up the driveway, and in a few moments he was out of sight. Only his companion, whom first we viewed emerging from the wood with Sir Simon, remained behind; and he, it seemed, was returning to that spot in the wood where we had been but minutes before. No doubt he had been told to keep a vigil over the body.

Sir John kept his right hand upon my left arm, which I held bent at the elbow. And beyond him, on his left side, walked Mr. Sarton. Thus we went three abreast up the rise along the circling driveway. I was eager to hear what the two men would say one to the other about the scene in the woods, for by that time I had formed impressions and opinions of my own. For a moment or two they seemed to hold back; each seemed to be wishing the other would start. Yet in the end, of course, Sir John initiated the conversation. He never was one to stand upon ceremony.

"I must congratulate you, Mr. Sarton, upon your observations regarding the corpus. It was both sound and clever the way that you proved—conclusively, to my way of thinking—that the victim had been murdered elsewhere and his body simply dumped where it was found."

"For that I thank you, sir. There is no man alive from whom I would rather hear such praise." The young magistrate hesitated: "But . . . well . . . I daresay Sir Simon did not take kindly to my suggestion. I don't know why. I fear I've lost a friend."

"Young man, Sir Simon is *not* your friend."

When Mr. Sarton heard that, the look that came upon his face was not one of anger or indignation, but rather one of terrible disappointment. He seemed quite crushed by Sir John's rather emphatic suggestion.

"It would seem," said he at last, "that I have not many left. But why? How did I offend him?"

"He was rather vague on that," said Sir John, "but it seems it all has to do with your unwillingness to take his advice and follow his tips on subsequent landings of the smugglers."

"That was on the advice of another—indeed, the same individual I hope to introduce you to on the morrow."

"Well, I shall look forward to seeing you then."

As Sir John realized with that sixth sense of his, we were quite near the entrance to the house. The coach had been turned round, and Mr. Sarton was about to take his leave of us. Therefore, Sir John's next words to the young magistrate had the sound and sense of a speech of farewell.

"Were I you," said he, "I should not worry overmuch whether or not you have the friendship of Sir Simon Grenville. The nature of our work is such that we are not allowed many friends, and those few we have must be those worthy of trust. I do not feel that Sir Simon is altogether worthy of trust, do you?"

Mr. Sarton sighed. "No, I suppose I do not. If I put great value upon his friendship and support, it is because he is a very powerful man in these parts."

"Well, it has been my experience that those who have power are most interested in keeping and increasing it. All their plans, all their activities, even their choice of friends—all are directed toward those ends. If Sir Simon once offered you his friendship, it was no doubt because he thought that you could be of use to him. You may take that from an old cynic such as myself, for it has thus far in my experience proven to be so."

Albert Sarton smiled a rather crooked smile. It seemed to give him a mischievous look. "I shall do that, sir," said he. "And I look forward to our meeting in the morning."

I saw this as my last opportunity to say to him something I felt needed to be said. Clearing my throat and lowering my voice (that the waiting driver might not hear), I said to Mr. Sarton: "Before you go, sir, there is something I heard from Will Fowler whilst riding beside him that I think you should know."

"Then tell me by all means, young sir," said he.

"I learned from him that he was not alone when he found the body. Mistress Clarissa Roundtree, who traveled from London as one of our party, was with him."

"She is our ward, more or less," Sir John interjected. "Lady Fielding employs her as her secretary."

"I see," said Mr. Sarton. "Well, by all means bring her along. I should like to hear her version of the event." He paused then just long enough to bow a proper bow to Sir John and me. "I thank you both," said he. "Until tomorrow."

And with a wave of his hand, he was gone.

Though greatly interested in my meeting with Dick Dickens, and of all that Constable Perkins had to say of his former employer, rather than discuss it at length, Sir John chose to retire to bed for a nap. He admitted he had tumbled to the floor of the coach when Will Fowler had made that wild stop, but he insisted that he was in no wise crippled by the fall.

"You, as I," said he, "must allow that as I grow older my body seems to need greater rest."

"Nevertheless, I do believe, sir, that you have pain in a particular place. Now, where is that?"

"Oh . . . my hip, if you must know, my left hip. It was there I hit the floor of the coach."

"Well then, I agree that a rest is in order—and perhaps later, a doctor should be summoned to have a look at you."

"No doctors," said he, "no surgeons, no provincial saw-your-bones. If I have need, I shall wait till we return to London and put myself at the mercy of Mr. Donnelly. He's the only doctor I trust."

And that, reader, put an end to the discussion. There is a certain tone of voice adopted by Sir John when he wishes to make it plain that he will brook no argument, and that last, "provincial saw-your-bones" speech was spoken in that tone. I said nothing more, helped him undress, and assisted him into bed. Then, remembering to take with me Laurence Sterne's *Sentimental Journey*, I tiptoed out of the room, convinced that he was already asleep. Then did I most quietly close the door behind me.

The room across the hall, which I recognized as Clarissa's, had attracted the attention of a maid at the time I accompanied Sir John to our door. She was just finishing up with her broom when she spied us. Of a sudden she did drop her broom and deliver a curtsey with a brightly spoken, "Good day to you, sirs."

So taken aback was I by this that I could only think to say, "Good day to you and . . . carry on."

Having said that, I did throw open the door to our room and show Sir John the way inside.

I had all but forgotten the incident when I stepped out into the hall. I was reminded of it only in noting that the courteous maid was no longer about. My original intention was to go to the library where I might read for an hour or two before looking in on Sir John. But having noted Clarissa's door, I wondered if I might not visit her and hear her story of the discovery of the body. There could be no harm in it, I told myself, so long as there was no such foolishness as last evening's kissing games.

Assuring myself that there would be nothing of the kind, I knocked softly upon her door. For some several moments there was no sound beyond the door. It occurred to me that she, too, might have taken it into her head to go down to the library. But no: there was a sound and another and another. Clarissa was inside, right enough, and she was coming to the door.

"Who is there?" she asked. But was it Clarissa? The voice I heard seemed lower, huskier, than hers.

"It is I, Jeremy," said I and waited—yet there was no move to open the door. "Let me in."

"I cannot," said she.

"What do you mean? Why not?" Was she ill? Not properly dressed?

"The door is locked." It was suddenly rattled from the other side. "There, you see?"

I grabbed the latch and tried the door myself. It did not budge. I rattled it, and it still did not budge. Yet between us we had loosed the key from the keyhole. Big as it was, it dropped with a clang to the floor.

"Wait a moment," said I. "There is a key."

"Well, use it, you dolt!"

Sharp-tongued as ever. I'd a notion to drop the key in my pocket and walk away, leaving her to shift for herself—but I did nothing of the kind. No, I jammed it into the keyhole, turned it, and threw open the door. As it opened inward, I managed somehow to bestow a bump upon her forehead. (Thus, without quite willing it so, I had my revenge upon Clarissa.)

"Ow!" She clapped a hand to her head.

"Sorry! Truly, I am sorry!"

"Such twaddle! If you were *that* regretful, you would come up with phrases that would comfort me more."

"Such as?"

"Oh, I don't know. It's not my place to think them up. Men are supposed to have such phrases always upon their tongues." Such notions came from her constant reading of romances. "Why don't you?" she demanded.

"Because I do not read the same books as you do," said I proudly.

"No, I suppose you don't. Well, the least you can do is throw your arms about me and comfort me with a few gentle pats upon the back. I've been weeping, you know."

Kicking the door shut, I stepped close and took a good look at her face. Ah yes, her eyes were red and a bit puffy; her nose was sniffly; and her voice had, as previously noted, grown husky.

"So you have," said I. "But why?"

"*Why?* The heroine always weeps when she is imprisoned."

"You weren't imprisoned," said I. "Someone simply turned the key in the lock by mistake—probably that little maid who was so well-mannered."

"What *are* you talking about?"

"Oh, never mind. But here now, this is all the consolation you'll get from me."

So saying, I wrapped my arms awkwardly about her and delivered a few perfunctory pats. As I did so, I happened to look over her shoulder at the carpet upon which we stood. Its dark pattern was interrupted by crisscrossing marks of white. I had stared at them curiously for a bit until I realized that the marks were, in fact, footprints, and the white was the same chalk white which covered the soles and heels of the dead man's shoes in the wood. Releasing Clarissa, I turned her round and pointed down at the carpet.

"Are those your footprints?"

"Yes, they are. I'm afraid I've made a mess here. It's chalk, you know."

"Indeed I do know. Mr. Sarton, the magistrate here, pointed that out to us when we viewed the remains of the victim. Chalk was all over the shoes of the poor man. Yet the odd thing was that there was no place thereabouts that he could have picked up the chalk on the soles of his shoes, and so he came to the conclusion that the body had been moved."

"But that's nonsense," cried Clarissa.

"No, I thought it was quite reasonable, and so did Sir John."

"Yet it is only so if you did view the body in another place from that where I found him."

"*You* found him? You mean where you and Will Fowler found him, don't you?"

"No, I found him first, and then I took Mr. Fowler to see."

"Just a moment," said I, "perhaps, Clarissa, you had best tell me the story from the beginning."

"But where shall I start?"

"As I said, *at the beginning*." I fear that the exasperation I felt at her higgledy-piggledy lack of all sense of logic was made much too plain by my tone of voice. Yet I recovered sufficiently to suggest that she might start at the point where I left her and her guide, Will Fowler, and headed for the library.

"Oh, well enough, well enough," said she, "now let me see. When you went off to the library, Mr. Fowler took me to a room that is kept as a kind of picture gallery. Oh, you should have stayed with us, Jeremy. Some of the paintings were *quite* wonderful, especially those of an artist named George Stubbs—all sorts of animals. A zebra! Can you imagine? He painted the most *wonderful* picture of a zebra. Can he have gone to Africa to do that?"

"Really, Clarissa, I have no idea. Do get on with your story, won't you?"

She sighed. "Well, all right. Oh, but whilst we were there in this gallery room, Mr. Fowler began to tell about the ghost. You remember? Sir Simon talked about him at dinner? Well, Mr. Fowler's version was much more complete. For one thing, the spirit which haunts this house is that of the first Baronet of Mongeham, Sir Roger Grenville, who received his title over a hundred years ago! There was something familiar about the features of the face in the portrait."

"Please, Clarissa, get on with it."

Well, obviously her way of telling a story is not my own. If there is a byway or a digression in sight, then she will take it, no matter where it leads. And indeed, in spite of my urging that she get on with her tale, she supplied all manner of extraneous detail on the arrogant cook, Jacques Dufour, and his most impressive kitchen belowstairs; then, too, she gave me Will Fowler's account of Sir Simon's courtship of the present Lady Grenville, which was presented down to every last particular. And so on.

Since I am sure, reader, that you would prefer that I dispense with all such minutiae, I now offer you my version of the discovery of the body purged and abridged of all but what is relevant to this narrative. Let it begin with Will Fowler's offer to show her about the grounds upon which the house was situated.

Having given her a good look at the kitchen, he showed her out the rear door of the house and into the garden. (This did surprise me, for I did suppose that in order to reach the place where the murdered man had been found, they would have exited by the front door.) In any case, Mr. Fowler did show her about the garden, proving himself knowledgeable regarding the varieties of flowers and other plants which were laid out in the space in chaotic profusion. They walked the garden path which led out past some outbuildings and ultimately into the thick woods which surrounded the house on three sides. She asked Mr. Fowler where the path led, and he said that there was an old, deserted chalk mine higher up the hill and nothing more. Just then Mr. Fowler was hailed from the house by the cook, Jacques, who demanded that he return to settle a disagreement with one of the porters. Reluctantly, he made to go, but Clarissa asked if she might not stay on there in the garden, and he, thinking it would take but a short while to settle the matter, granted her wish and suggested that should she grow weary of the garden and wish to rest, she might sit upon the bench near the brook, "a favorite place of Lady Grenville's."

As it happened, Mr. Fowler was detained longer than expected. Clarissa grew bored with inspecting flowers; and not one to rest content sitting in one place, she chose rather to follow the path which led out of the garden and up the hill. The out-buildings which she passed were quite unlike the stables which lay off to the far side of the house: they were intended for human occupancy and were evidently indeed occupied; she heard rough, male voices issuing from one and moved swiftly and quietly past it that she might not be detected.

Once beyond, she turned and looked back at the house, half hoping that she might see Mr. Fowler below, beckoning her to him. Yet, not seeing him, there seemed naught to do but plunge onward up the path and into the woods. Glancing down, she happened to notice a peculiarity in the pathway: it was heavily dusted with white, and there were many footprints. It was not so below in the garden—of that she was certain. But then she recalled that Mr. Fowler had said there was a chalk mine up on the hill, but he had described it as a "deserted" chalk mine. Evidently he was wrong about that. Apparently the men who lived in those buildings worked in the chalk mines. But surely Mr. Fowler would have known about that, wouldn't he? After all, he seemed to act as a sort of majordomo in the Grenville household. She was puzzled, but fueled now by curiosity, she picked up her pace and made her way swiftly up the path.

She saw the entrance to the mine plain enough, though not until she was a scant ten yards away, so dark was it in that part of the wood. But having come so close, she noted that the chalk dust was specially thick in that space, and that there were all manner of prints to be seen in it—and not just bootprints. For, contrary to what Will Fowler had implied, the path did not end at the entrance to the mine; it led beyond and farther up the hill. But just before the entrance, it intersected a wagon track which led off to the right—that is, in the direction of the stables. There at the crossing, hoofprints and wagon tracks cut back and forth in the chalk dust. There could be no doubt that there had been a good deal of sustained activity in that wide space. It would seem that, far from being deserted, the mine was working briskly once again.

She was moved to explore the mine in order to confirm this. On the other hand, she was curious as to what lay above the mine and where the path she had followed truly led. And would it not be good to know where the wagon track terminated? Perhaps at the stable, where she had supposed; but perhaps, too, somewhere beyond it at some secret intersection with the main road. Yes, secret—all of this was most curious and most secret.

As Clarissa stood before the mine entrance, casting her eyes this way and that, trying to decide what her next move might be, her glance did fix upon something in the underbrush, something that looked, as near as she could tell, like a human hand. She was drawn to it immediately. Hastening to the spot, kneeling, though not touching the hand, she looked closely beyond it and saw, thank God, that it was attached to a whole body, one hidden among the plants and bushes that provided a kind of carpet beneath this mighty forest of oak and pine. She pushed the bushes aside and flattened the plants, and then she had a proper look at him. He was dead, of course. She expected that. A man does not climb in amongst the vegetation to take himself a nap. No, this was not the place for it. The young man's wound did give her pause, however. Looking down upon the cut in his throat, she saw that he had lost much blood. The lower part of his neck was quite drenched with it, though it had caked and darkened and looked more like dirt than blood. She shivered at the sight, quite in spite of herself. (It may have been that the nature of the wound brought back the memory of a time when a knife was held against her own throat, by that villain, Jackie Carver, and a threat was made to inflict just such damage, as you, reader, may recall from an earlier narrative.)

She had seen enough to know that there was no point in remaining there. Half-crawling to avoid the lowest branches of the pine trees, she left the body and turned back down the path toward the house. Just then, from far below, she heard Mr. Fowler's voice calling her name. She ran to meet him and told him what she had found. Quite shocked she was at the effect her news had upon him. He was not angered at her, as she thought he might be; he seemed, rather, to be quite terrified at what she had told him. Instructing her to wait for him on that bench by the brook, he hastened up the path without so much as a look back at her. Yet he surprised her by stopping at the out-buildings, banging on the doors, and rousting four men from them. Together they ascended the path and disappeared round a bend.

Though she waited long, this time she did not stray from that bench in the garden. She kept place for what seemed a century yet must have been near an hour. When Mr. Fowler returned, he came alone. She reflected that perhaps the four who had gone up with him had remained to bury their comrade—somehow she was sure that the dead man at the chalk mine was one of them. He advised her to go to her room upstairs, for he was off to inform Sir Simon of this terrible crime, and then he must fetch the magistrate from town. All this made perfect sense to her, and so she left him at the back door and went to the room, where he had sent her. She was so overcome by what had happened that when she lay down upon the bed to rest, she fell asleep. When she awakened, she found that she had been locked inside. No matter how loudly she called, and no matter how fiercely she rattled the door, there was no response.

"Was that when you began to weep?" I had asked her then.

"You'd weep, too," said she, "if you were locked up for three or four hours."

"It is not in my nature to weep," said I, which was both a lie and a rather priggish thing to say.

"Well, that is just one of the many ways in which we differ."

"It was all probably done in error, anyway. The little maid who cleaned the carpet before your door seemed most mannerly, but she may simply have been careless and turned the key by mistake."

"Are you trying to tell me that none of this is out of the ordinary? A murdered man? His body moved from where it was discovered? The finder punished by imprisonment?"

Clarissa did have a way of putting things in the most dramatic way possible—"punished by imprisonment," indeed!

"Well . . . no, of course not. It's all most extraordinary." I paused to give the matter some thought. Yet after turning the matter this way and that in my mind, I could but pose a question: "Why should they have moved the body? I rode next to Will Fowler on the trip from Deal, and I daresay he was *most* surprised when he was informed that the body which had been in one place was now in quite another. Why should they have moved it?"

"Well, it seems clear to me," said she. "Since I found the corpus practically at the entrance to the chalk mine, Sir Simon wished to keep visitors away from it. If they were to see it, they might well wonder what went on in there and might start asking questions."

"Yes," said I, "Sir Simon denied to Mr. Sarton that there was anyplace in all his property where the dead man could, while alive, have managed to cover himself, his clothes, and his shoes so thoroughly with chalk dust."

"He denied it? Well, there's your proof right there on the floor." She gestured to the chalk-covered carpet upon which we were standing.

"I should like to get up there and see for myself just what is in that old chalk mine."

"So would I," said she. "It must be something more valuable than chalk, something worth guarding."

"Guarding? What do you mean?"

"Oh, didn't I tell you? The fellow was simply bristling with arms of every sort. The poor man was obviously guarding something. He was a sentinel, a guard. He had a pistol tucked in his belt, as well as a dagger, and a great long musket by his side."

"You mean there beneath the bushes and the trees? I wonder whoever killed him didn't take them as a prize of war."

"Whoever killed him must have had a lot to carry away," said she.

"By the bye, you said nothing of pistols and muskets when you told me all this the first time."

"I didn't? Just an oversight, I assure you."

"Be sure you include it when you tell your tale to Sir John."

As it happened, that did not take place until a good deal later. Fearing that Clarissa might suffer a relapse and begin behaving oddly once again, I made my excuses to her and slipped out of her room as swiftly as decently possible. I took a moment to listen at the door to the room shared by Sir John and me, and I satisfied myself from the sound of his snoring that he slept soundly still. Then did I make my way quietly downstairs to the library where, for over an hour, I read uninterruptedly in *A Sentimental Journey*. Perhaps my interest in the book flagged, or perhaps I thought it time to go back upstairs and listen at the door to our room once more. In any case, I left the library and ascended to the first floor where, to my surprise, I found Will Fowler in the corridor between our two rooms. He was moving briskly in my direction.

"Ah, there you are," said he, having obviously recovered his assurance. "I've been looking for you. I tapped upon your door and, getting no answer, I stuck my head into your room and saw Sir John sleeping. I hope I didn't disturb him."

He seemed to be talking with greater animation than was necessary, and a bit more rapidly, as well. I wondered what errand had brought him up to this part of the house.

"What will you, Will?" I was not punning upon his name, reader. It simply came out so.

He cleared his throat and spoke forth in his grand manner: "I wish to inform you and all of your party that much as Sir Simon would like to have your company upon this evening, he has been detained in Sandwich by certain affairs of business. He cannot dine with you at seven, but he trusts that Jacques will do as well for you tonight as he has ever done in the past. Will you be good enough to pass this on to Sir John and to the young miss, as well?"

"You may consider it done," said I to him.

Then did he add in a somewhat nervous manner: "And do please pass on to her my hope that she is well recovered from her shocking experience of this morning. Has she talked of it?"

"I shall tell her, right enough," said I, "but she is a brave girl and made of stronger stuff than you might suppose."

Then, thanking me, he took his leave and made for the stairs. I watched him go, wondering what it was made him uneasy. He seemed a decent sort of man. Dissimulation did not come naturally to him.

I listened at our door, and hearing none of the sounds of sleep, entered the room. Sir John, still in bed, did rise up beneath the mound of covers, his hair tousled and his jaw set pugnaciously. He called my name.

"Yes sir, it is I, Jeremy."

"You're the second who has come in the last few minutes. And neither of you had the decency to knock upon the door first. I feigned sleep to find out what he might do—nothing, so far as I could tell. Yet he stayed an unconscionably long time. He seemed to be looking for something, though what it might have been I cannot suppose."

"Nor can I," I declared.

As I helped him dress, I informed him that Will Fowler had been the intruder, that I had encountered him in the hall, and told of the announcement he had made regarding dinner. I also let him know a bit about Clarissa, yet I did not attempt to tell her story. I did mention, though, that for some reason, someone seemed to have locked her in her room.

"Locked her in?" exclaimed Sir John.

"Yes sir."

"All this seems to be much too mysterious and threatening. I'd thought we might enjoy some pleasant country air out here in Mongeham. Yet now we have a body turning up then moving about—not on his own, I'm sure. Clarissa is locked in her room, and somebody comes snooping about in ours. No, I don't like this a bit." He paused, then asked, "Is it still light out?"

"Yes, but not for much longer."

"As soon as you have me looking fairly presentable, go across to Clarissa's room and see if she would like to take a stroll with us and tell us her tale. I'd like to loosen up this hip a little. We should be able to work that in before dinner."

And that was how it was done. Perhaps intimidated by Sir John's official manner, she restrained herself from digressing quite so often as was her usual. What had taken her half an hour to tell me, she told him in half the time. A good thing, too, for we were back in the house and seated at table by seven.

No doubt Jacques did just as well preparing the meal for us three as he had the night before when his master was present. It is simply that, because of all that had happened that day, I remember it not quite so well. Nor do I remember the same plenitude of wine—simply a good claret for the meat and a white wine of some sort for the fish: a bottle of each to share among the three of us.

So we were all sober, at least, when we climbed up the stairs, having spent no less than two hours at table. Sir John suggested we adjourn to Clarissa's room that we might review our situation. He had been quiet through dinner, indeed we all had been. Yet now he spoke forth and revealed what had been on his mind.

"I believe we must take defensive precautions. There is not much we can do, but we can at least lock our doors. Clarissa, you have the key to your room now, do you not?"

"Safe in my pocket," said she.

"Then you must use it. Lock it and stay inside till it be morning.

"I shall also want you to go with us tomorrow to the magistrate's in Deal. We have all been invited for dinner tomorrow evening, so we are to remain there the better part of twelve hours."

"So long?" asked Clarissa. "Whatever shall I find to do there?"

"Jeremy will show you Deal, a charming place, or so it was said to be at one time. You will be happy to do so, won't you, Jeremy?"

I sighed. "If you ask it, Sir John, it will be done."

FIVE

*In which plans are
made and a grand
feast is eaten*

Because we returned to Deal in Sir Simon's coach with its curiously limited capacity, I was once again forced to ride up top beside the driver, who was once again Will Fowler. If I had thought it difficult to extract information from him when last we rode together, it proved absolutely impossible on this occasion. In response to my questions regarding the identity of the dead man, the time of the discovery of the body, and Clarissa's reaction to the event—I studiously avoided all mention of the chalk mine—he would say nothing, nor would he so much as shake his head, yea or nay. He ignored me. Yet the expression upon his face answered me far more eloquently than any verbal response he could have made: he appeared frightened quite out of his wits. I knew that, since I rode with him last, he had received a severe dressing down from his master for allowing Clarissa to go off discovering on her own.

I had witnessed Sir Simon's return somewhere round midnight. The barking of the dogs had wakened me. I went to the window, which overlooked the front of the house and witnessed, by the light of the torches burning on either side of the front entrance, the arrival of three horsemen. The one on the proudest mount was Sir Simon. He handed the reins to a stable boy and hopped down from the saddle. A man whom I recognized from above as Will Fowler came out to meet him, and immediately Sir Simon fell to up-braiding him most aggressively. Though the window was shut, and I was thus prevented from hearing the words he used, he made his anger plain with his sharp gestures. First he pointed at poor Will as he moved toward him, then shook his finger at him, and finally shook his fist so vigor-ously under his nose that I felt sure he meant to strike him. Yet he did not go so far as that—not in my sight, in any case—though I cannot say what may have come to pass in-side the house. This alone would have frightened the fel-low. Who could say what verbal threats were made?

Fowler drove even faster than on our past occasion. I held tight to the seat as before, but twice, as we leaned round curves, I feared I might lose my grip and go hurtling off into the ditch which seemed to run along every road in Kent. Yet I managed to hold on till at last we went charging down Middle Street and came again to a halt at Number 18. We three assembled on the walkway before the magis-trate's house. Before ever we could move to make our pres-ence known to Albert Sarton, he threw open the door, all smiles, and welcomed us as friends. Clarissa was presented to him by Sir John. And agreeably, he even shook the hand which she thrust out at him.

"I shall look forward to interviewing you, Miss Clarissa," said he. "But just now I shall talk to Mr. Fowler. Perhaps all of you would do well to wait for me in my courtroom. It is the large chamber to the right and across the hall from my study."

"We shall be happy to do so, Mr. Sarton," said Sir John. "I welcome the opportunity to witness you in this role, as well."

"I have but one case," said Mr. Sarton, "involving four men, a misdemeanor."

"Just as well, for I think you'll agree that there is naught so boring as a whole morning spent in court on misdemeanors."

At that Mr. Sarton burst out laughing. "You're quite right, sir. Many times have I thought it, yet until you spoke up just now, I had not the courage to say so."

It was at that moment I decided I really liked the man quite well. He left us with a wave of his hand, scrambled up to the top of the coach to the place I had as my own until some moments before, and faced Mr. Fowler.

"Well, let's inside, shall we?" said Sir John. "Jeremy, give me your arm. You won't mind bringing up the rear, will you, Clarissa?"

And so, in the order described by Sir John, we made our way into the large room used by Mr. Sarton as his courtroom. There were sufficient chairs to accommodate about a dozen visitors. They faced a plain deal table not unlike the one Sir John himself used at Number 4 Bow Street. A man whom I took to be Mr. Sarton's court clerk sat at the table next the empty chair which awaited the magistrate. To one side sat the prisoners in the charge of a constable. We were just sitting down when I noticed something quite striking about the prisoner farthest from me: he had but one arm. How many one-armed men could there be in Deal, after all? That is, how many could there be besides Constable Perkins? It was curious how much, in general, the prisoner otherwise resembled Mr. Perkins; his clothes, for instance, were quite like those in which the constable was dressed when last I had seen him on the day before. And there was something about the way he held his head . . .

Good God! It *was* Mr. Perkins!

It could have been at just that moment—that, in any case, is how I remember it—that Clarissa fell into a fit of coughing. I glanced over in her direction, but then my glance was held by her, for I saw most immediate that she had loosed the chorus of coughs simply to get my attention. Now that she had it, she was signaling wildly, pointing ahead toward the prisoners, rolling her eyes in consternation, then gesturing toward Sir John as she heaved her shoulders in a great shrug. She was asking, in effect, if we should tell Sir John of the unfortunate situation in which Mr. Perkins found himself. All I knew to do was shrug back to her in response. How had he gotten into such a pickle? I looked back at our constable and found him staring at me. I pointed at Sir John. Mr. Perkins hesitated a moment, and then nodded most soberly. Thus he urged me to tell Sir John of his predicament.

I know not if he then expected the response he got from his chief when I whispered all—*I* certainly did not. It did not take long to tell Sir John, yet even before I had quite finished, he had begun to giggle. The giggle turned to laughter which he tried to suppress, yet without success, for in a moment more he had thrown back his head and was laughing in great guffaws. I turned to Mr. Perkins, hoping to signal to him my confusion and helplessness, but I found him in the same state as Sir John—unable, that is, to stifle the laughter within him. The other prisoners, seeing no humor in their situation, exchanged puzzled looks at his behavior. The Deal constable liked Mr. Perkins's behavior not in the least and came over to him and admonished him sternly.

This then was the scene when Mr. Sarton entered his courtroom and his clerk did solemnly order: "All rise." And all the rest of us did scramble to our feet.

(Sir John had long ago dispensed with this bit of ceremony at Number 4 Bow Street, and so I was taken somewhat by surprise, though no more than by what followed.)

Once Mr. Sarton was firmly settled in his seat at the table, the clerk urged all to be seated, and the session was begun.

It seemed that the charge against all four of the men was public drunkenness and brawling. All four were obliged to give their names, then the three prisoners who were unknown to us chose one of their number to speak for them. His name was the only one of the three I now remember. It was Samson Strong, a difficult one to forget. He did, in a sense, live up to his name, for though not tall, he was thick through the shoulders and chest—but no more so than his two companions. He did not present a trustworthy appearance.

"Where did all this difficulty take place?" asked Mr. Sarton.

"In Alfred Square, m'lord."

"I am but a magistrate and do not deserve so august a title. Call me 'sir.' That will do."

"Yes sir, m'lord . . . sir."

"Hmmm, well, where specifically did it take place?"

"More or less at the Turk's Head, sir."

"I might have known. Most of the trouble in Alfred Square begins or ends there. I've a notion to close that place down as a public nuisance."

"Yes sir."

"Tell your story."

"Well, we three, who are old friends and well known each to the other, we was sittin' together at the Turk's bar, havin' an ale together when this fella here—"

"Just a moment," said Mr. Sarton, interrupting the prisoner. "How long had you been there? How much ale had you drunk?"

"That's a little hard to say, sir. What's today? What day of the week?"

"Why, it is Thursday." Mr. Sarton turned to his clerk. "Is it not?" The clerk muttered something in the affirmative.

"Well, if it's Thursday," said the spokesman for the three, "then we was in there since Tuesday."

"*Tuesday?* You mean you were drinking ale in that place for *two* days?"

"Aw, it wasn't so bad. Every once in a while they'd come through and sweep it out, and if we needed a lie-down, there was always a whore to oblige. You can ask the innkeeper if it wasn't just so. His name's Harley."

Mr. Sarton, taking note of Clarissa's presence beside Sir John, gave him a warning: "I shall ask you, Mr. Strong, to watch your language, for there is a child present in the courtroom. That is the only warning I shall give. If you err again in that way, I shall hold you in contempt of my court. Is that understood?"

"Yes sir," said he.

"Continue."

"Well, in comes this one-armed cod, and, without so much as a by-your-leave, he sits right down at the bar. And then he—"

"Let me interrupt," said Mr. Sarton. "There was an empty place at the bar?"

"There was, yes sir."

"And you expected him to ask your permission before he took it?"

"Well, an't that the proper way? I mean, there was an empty place at the bar, true enough—in fact, there was more than one—but there might not've been. There mighta been one more of us and him gone off to take a—" He caught himself just in time. "To answer one of nature's calls, if you get my meaning, sir."

"Indeed I do. Continue."

"Well, he was friendly enough in his way, I s'pose. He

offered to buy a round of ale for us, and we accepted his offer. He said he'd come to Deal lookin' for work, and then he began askin' all these questions."

"Such as?"

"Oh, he wanted to know such things as, who were we, and what did we do, and did we think there was any chance for a job in our line of work. And we didn't like it."

"Why not? Those seem innocently enough intended to me."

"Maybe so, sir, but it wasn't what the questions were as how he asked them."

"And how did he ask them?"

"Well, he asked them in such a way like he really expected an answer."

"Isn't that how it's usually done? Isn't that how I am putting questions to you now?"

"Yes sir, that's just it, y'see. He was askin' questions like it was our duty to answer them, just like it's our duty to answer your questions now."

"I understand. Continue."

"Well, sir, we just decided we'd go and leave him alone with all his questions. We drank up, and we left."

"Then how did this great brawl occur?"

"I was gettin' to that. We were standin' round outside, the three of us, when out comes this one-armed cod, and he was just askin' for a fight."

"You mean that literally? He *asked* to fight you three?"

"No sir, he wasn't even that proper about it. He just up and attacked us."

"He attacked all three of you?"

"You might say so, sir. Anyways, he didn't fight fair. He did a lot of head-butting and kicking and suchlike, not the kind of fighting I'd call fair. And . . . well . . . that's our story of how it happened. An't it boys?"

He looked round him at his two companions. They grunted, nodded, and gave their assent.

"All right, Mr. Strong, you may be seated," said Mr. Sarton. He turned to his clerk and asked a whispered question. In return, he received a response spoken just as quietly. "Now, Mr. Perkins, if you will please, give us your side of the matter."

Constable Perkins rose and came forward so that he stood just opposite Mr. Sarton with only the table between them. He took a deep breath and began:

"In its general outline, sir, I cannot take exception to what you have heard from Mr. Strong just now. Yet it's in the details that my version differs. Let me say, first of all, that I'm a native of these parts. I grew up here and worked on farms hereabouts till I was enlisted in the Army. I saw service in the American colonies during the war with the French after which I've gone through life with but half an arm here on the left side. This has made it hard for me to get and keep work. I tried London. I thought I might try where I was born in."

At this point he paused, apparently to organize his thoughts. Mr. Perkins had a good head upon his shoulders, and when called upon, could deliver testimony as well or better than any of the Bow Street Runners. Here he was called upon to testify in his own behalf. So far he was making a good job of it.

"Now that you have explained your presence here in Deal," said Mr. Sarton, "let us go quickly to your entrance into the Turk's Head and your meeting with the three men seated behind you."

"As you say, sir. I had been asking about work at every inn in town. I had heard that Alfred Square was a most lively part of town, and the Turk's Head, I'd heard, was the liveliest place of all. So I come to Alfred Square—oh, about eleven o'clock it must've been, not yet midnight, anyways. Though I'd drunk a little ale, asking at one place and then another, I was still sober. You may take my word on that, sir. I headed into the Turk's Head, and I saw that all the tables were filled up, but there was plenty of room at the bar—just these three behind me sitting there. There were plenty of empty places there. Now, I should've taken that as a caution, shouldn't I? If these three were sitting all by themselves like that, must be because nobody wanted to be near them. I should've taken a hint that they were troublemakers—but I didn't.

"Instead, I took a place right nearby, ordered an ale and asked if I might buy them another of what they were drinking. They were willing enough to accept an ale from me but not to answer my questions—or so it seemed to me. For when I asked how it was they earned their bread, a common enough question amongst those wishin' to have a bit of talk over their ale, there was a bit of wrangling over how it should be described. Finally, him who addressed you, sir, came up with a phrase that seemed to satisfy them all. He said, 'You might say we was casual laborers.' I said they seemed to be doing well at it, for they had already boasted they'd been drinking at the Turk for two days running. 'But,' I put it to them, 'in what trade are you casual laborers? Would there be work for me in it?' At that they commenced to laughing most uproariously. When I asked what I had said that struck them as so funny, this man, Samson Strong, he told me they was in the owling trade, and he asked me, did I know what that was. I told him being from round Deal I had a pretty good idea. Then he offered me what I can only call a sneer, and he asked if I really thought there was likely to be any work for a one-armed man in the owling trade. Then one of the other two—I cannot say which—he told me, 'Try again when you finished growing that other arm.' That struck them as the funniest thing that had yet been said. To be honest, sir, I do not take kindly to such remarks regardin' my disability. And so I fear I made some hasty remarks which I would rather not repeat here."

"And why would you rather not?" asked Mr. Sarton.

"Well," said Mr. Perkins, "you already cautioned the

other fella about usin' improper language in this court because of the presence of children and all. I'm afraid all of what I had to say to them was in suchlike language."

"I see, but give us some idea of it, will you? What—without being exact—did you say approximately?"

"All right, sir, I would say that the burden of it was that I, with my one arm, was a better man than any one of them—no, better than all three of them."

"Was this issued in the way of a challenge?"

"I don't think so, sir. It was more like a statement of fact."

In spite of himself, the magistrate smiled at that. "Continue."

"Well, right then the three of them put their heads together and commenced to whispering amongst themselves. Then, making a few nasty remarks and a lewd gesture or two, they walked out of the Turk's Head, and I thought to myself, 'Good riddance!' Well, I sat about long enough to finish my ale and decided it was time to leave. Well sir, I get outside, and I find them waiting for me. One of them says, 'We'll just see if you're as good as you think you are.' And in all modesty, sir, I do believe I proved myself to them. Just one more thing: I suppose I did not fight fair—or let's say I did not fight usual. But not havin' but one arm, I believe I'm entitled to a little leeway in that way. Yes, I did butt, and yes, I did kick—in truth, I'm quite good at kicking—but there was three of them and just one of me."

"You may sit down, Mr. Perkins. Constable Trotter, will you come forward, please?"

The constable did as his chief bade him to do; he took his place before him, his feet well planted, his hat tucked under his arm.

"Will you give me your account of it from the time you came upon the scene?"

"Yes sir." He cleared his throat and began his tale. In truth, he had not much to tell, for by the time he had come along, the three troublemakers from the Turk's Head were all down upon the pavement, moaning in pain or senselessly silent. In fact, Constable Trotter might have taken Mr. Perkins to be one of the crowd of onlookers who had gathered outside the Turk's Head, except that when one of the trio shifted and attempted to rise, "the one-armed man" (as the constable described him) stepped forward and delivered him a swift kick in the backside. Having seen this, he seized Mr. Perkins by the shoulder and, his club at the ready, asked him if he were the party responsible for this.

Now to quote Constable Trotter: "He cheerfully responded that he was, and that he'd been keeping them quiet, just waiting for me to come along. He also offered diverse weapons which, he said, he had taken from them: knives, iron knuckles, and suchlike. These I've shown you, and you have before you now."

"And so he gave you no trouble?" asked Mr. Sarton.

"Oh no, sir, none at all—quite the opposite. He got them on their feet so's I could put the hand-irons on them. I only had two sets with me, so I cuffed them each-to-each, and told him to come along, too. And he did—without so much as a word in argument."

As it developed, all were marched off to the Good King George, which served the magistrate as a gaol, when needed. I later learned that the inn had been put to this use since the old gaol had burned down near a year before. The town fathers had not yet found money to build another. The three from the Turk's Head were locked up in a single room; since Mr. Perkins was already a registered guest, he simply retired to his assigned room and slept the night in the bed he'd grown used to. And here he was now before the magistrate, about to be judged along with his victims.

Mr. Sarton dismissed the constable and instructed all four to come before him, which they did. "Now," said he, "as to the charges against you three, by your own admission you were drunk—nor should I wonder at that, for after all, two days of continuous drinking will indeed produce such a result! And so I fine you ten shillings each on that charge. As for brawling, certainly you are guilty of it. Nonetheless, you suffered so by your wrongdoing that it would be excessive to fine you in addition to what you have already paid in bruises and bumps. So if you will step over and pay the court clerk to the amount of ten shillings each, you may then leave."

The three exchanged glances. Clearly, they were pleased by what they had heard. They hastened to the clerk, and each made a separate pile of coins before him. By the time I might have counted to a hundred, they were gone.

"Now, Mr. Perkins, if you will step forward, let us discuss your case. I am here in rather an awkward position. I tend to believe your story in its details and not the one told by Mr. Samson Strong. You see, my usual method is to listen to both sides and make a reckoning somewhere between the two. I have never supposed that when two stories were told me which covered the same events that one was completely true and the other completely without truth— that is, until now. I tend to accept your version of it absolutely—and that for a couple of reasons. First of all, I know those men are capable of just what you describe. I have heard it said often that they were in the owling trade, as they told you. And drunkards they may be, but they are dangerous men, and you had best keep an eye out the back of your head for them, for at your back is where the next attack will come." At that point he paused.

"Yes sir," said Mr. Perkins. "I'll do that, sir."

"And secondly, I tend to accept what you tell me because it is you doing the telling."

"How's that, sir?"

"Simple enough. I consider myself a fair judge of character, and yours impresses me. I should be very surprised if I were to find that you had lied to me in the details, as you call them—and disappointed, too. In short, I like the way you conduct yourself. And so, Mr. Perkins, I dismiss the charges against you. You gave me your word that you were not drunk when you entered the Turk's Head, and I accept your word on that. And as for the charge of brawling, what you told me—and what I heard from Constable Trotter—convinces me that you were defending yourself against an unprovoked attack. And so, sir, you are free to go. But before you do, I wonder if you would mind stepping closer that we might discuss a confidential matter."

Mr. Perkins hesitated, perhaps as puzzled by the request as I was, but then he came forward and leaned across the table. What passed between them then came to us only as unintelligible murmurings. Their conference did not last long—a minute or two at most—and when it concluded, Mr. Perkins came erect once more and bobbed his head in a little bow, which was for him quite unusual. He turned round then and started for the door, but as he passed near to us, he rolled his eyes, indicating (to me at least) that he had just been given a great surprise.

I leaned to my left and whispered this into Sir John's ear. He, in turn, gave a rub to his chin, and whispered to me, "Catch him up and tell him to wait until I arrive. Then come and fetch me."

I scrambled past Sir John and Clarissa and to the door—then into the hall and out the door to the street. I need not have hurried so, for I found Mr. Perkins just beyond the door.

"Ah, Jeremy lad, have I something to tell you!"

"And I want to hear it, but so does Sir John. Wait for us."

He nodded his assent and moved out of sight of the windows.

"We'll be back soon as ever we can," said I to him.

Re-entering, I found Sir John in conversation with Mr. Sarton. Clarissa stood close beside them. I perceived after a moment that Clarissa was about to be interrogated by Mr. Sarton regarding her discovery of the as-yet-unnamed corpus. Sir John was taking his leave, promising to return within the half of an hour.

"Jeremy has promised to take me for a walk," said he, "that I might smell the sea air. Nothing clears a man's head like the smell of the sea. Don't you find it so, Mr. Sarton?"

"In half of an hour then, sir. Our guest should be coming along at about that time."

I wondered at that, but so eager was I to learn Mr. Perkins's secret that I did not trouble Sir John once we were outside. Having spied our friend at the end of Middle Street, where he had withdrawn, we hastened to him. Yet I noticed that Sir John was having a bit of difficulty keeping up the pace he himself had set.

"Is your hip troubling you, sir?" I asked him.

"A bit, but that is my affair, Jeremy. I'll not have you nagging at me like Lady Kate."

"As you say, sir."

We met Mr. Perkins at a point halfway to the corner of the street. He was as eager to tell Sir John as he had been only minutes before to tell me.

"I've no intention of guessing, Mr. Perkins, for you will surely tell me."

"He offered me a job."

"He *what?*"

"Mr. Sarton offered me a place as constable here in Deal."

"Well," said Sir John, "what did you say? Did you accept?"

"I said I would have to think about it. He said that he understood that, right enough, and if I wished to talk about it, he would be available from nine o'clock on. I told him again I'd think about it."

"Why did you say that? What did you mean?"

"I had no way of knowing what *you* would want me to do."

Sir John's forehead wrinkled in a frown as he considered

the matter for a moment. "In all truth, I do not understand you, Mr. Perkins. You are one of the best, if not *the* best, of all my constables. I would say as much to any who asked me. Yet I can certainly understand that you might wish to return to these parts since you grew up here. I would in no wise hinder you in that."

"But that an't it, sir. That an't it at all. When I said I didn't know what you'd want me to do, I meant I didn't know how it would fit into your plans. After all, you sent me out to gather some information on the owling trade hereabouts. I thought you might want me to keep on finding out what I could, or if not, maybe you'd like me to start acting as your bodyguard, as was originally discussed by us."

"I must admit," said Sir John, "that things have changed a bit."

"In what way?"

"Well, in a number of ways. Much has happened since you met with Jeremy yesterday noon. What say, lad?" said Sir John to me. "Shall we bring Mr. Perkins to date?"

Together we tried. Sir John provided the framework, and I filled in the details. We told first of the examination of the body by Mr. Sarton, and of the clever deduction he had put forth regarding the chalk, which proved, to our satisfaction, that the body had been moved from some other place. Then did I provide Clarissa's tale of the original discovery of the body near the entrance to the chalk mine.

"Ah," said Mr. Perkins, "I'd like to see what's in that mine."

"So would we," said I.

"Most curious of all," said Sir John, "it seems that they locked Clarissa in her room. I can only suppose that it was done to keep her away from Mr. Sarton after they had moved the body from where she had found it. They do seem to be trying to keep that chalk mine a secret."

"But of course at this very moment," said I, "Clarissa is

telling all she knows to Mr. Sarton—and much of what she suspects, as well."

"It is all quite puzzling," said Sir John.

"Well, if you'll pardon me for saying so, it an't just puzzling; it sounds to me like it's gettin' downright dangerous for you people there in the big house. I think you could use a bodyguard, Sir John. I don't think that I've been all that successful as a spy, anyway."

"Perhaps you're right. Still, it is possible you would be even more useful to Mr. Sarton. You see, we're planning a little something on the order of the enterprises we've undertaken in London."

"The Bow Street Runners?"

"Exactly. Yet the Runners number over a dozen and Mr. Sarton has but two constables at his command. Even if Mr. Sarton himself participates, the enemy will still outnumber us. I may be forced to volunteer Jeremy for service, though I have not yet spoken to him of it."

(Indeed he had not, reader. I quickened at the notion of participating in such a venture.)

Mr. Perkins nodded and took a moment to reflect upon what he had just heard. "On whose information have you planned it?" he asked.

"Mr. Sarton has a source in whom he puts great trust. I have not yet met the fellow, but I shall later on today."

"And you feel that he needs me for this?"

"Yes, I do. He is a very young man and needs the sort of guidance you can give him. You may tell him . . . oh, that you would like to try it out for a period of time. That might work, eh?"

"Well, it might, but I hate lying to the fellow—him having such a high opinion of me and all."

"I can understand that, but I shall make it right with him. I must eventually explain all to him."

"All right, sir," said Mr. Perkins, who clearly had yet some misgivings, "since it's what you wish, I'm for it. I'll drop by his place later today and tell him I've decided to accept his offer."

"Perhaps you'd best make that tomorrow morning. I intend to keep him busy the rest of the day."

As they had talked on so intently, I had guided Sir John in the direction of the sea. It was not long till we were walking along Beach Street, braced by a good, stiff breeze from off the Channel. When we reached Broad Street, I thought perhaps we had gone far enough. Sir John wished to be gone but a half of an hour. A resolution had been reached in their discussion. It was time now to part company with Mr. Perkins and return to Number 18 Middle Street. I halted Sir John.

"Time to go back?"

"Just so, sir."

We took our leave of the constable and walked back the way we had come. For the most part, Sir John was silent the entire length of our journey. I can recall but one remark made by him.

"You know, Jeremy," said he, "all those grand things said by Mr. Sarton about Constable Perkins?"

"Yes, Sir John?"

"They were all quite true."

Upon our return to the magistrate's court and place of residence, I gave three or four sound thumps upon the door with the knocker, and then did we wait. I had noted the door was never opened unless Mr. or Mrs. Sarton was quite sure who it was stood on the outside. Yet they could not know *every* visitor who knocked. What about those who wished to attend his court sessions? What about witnesses? But I saw what I had not before noticed: just above the knocker, which like so many was cast in the form of a hand, was a spy hole which blended so well into the wood of the door that it was near invisible.

As all this did pass through my mind, my ears told me

that there approached from the far back of the house a determined and steady beat of footsteps down the long hall. Then the footsteps halted, and a challenge came from beyond the door.

"Who is out there, please?" The voice was that of Mrs. Sarton.

"It is John Fielding, and with him is his assistant, Jeremy."

The door came open, and there she stood, a broad smile upon her face. Though her hands were dusty with flour, and a stray lock of her red hair dangled down over one eye, she was not near in the state she was when we interrupted her the day before.

"Do come in," said she. "I've just made the acquaintance of your lovely daughter, Clarissa, as fine and intelligent a girl as I've ever met."

As we stepped inside, Sir John sought to correct her: "Well, madame, I quite agree with you that she is lovely, fine, and intelligent. Clarissa is, however, not my daughter."

"Truly not?" said she. "And I even thought that she looked a bit like you! And are you going to tell me that this fine lad is also not of your blood?"

"Alas no, and Lady Fielding and I are the poorer for it. Clarissa and Jeremy are the family we have—and they do quite nicely for us. We could not want for better."

"Come back to the kitchen and see. I've got her mixing dough for the dainties for this evening's dinner." She led the way down the long hall.

"Ah," said Sir John, "I can hardly wait."

She turned back to me. "You, young man, you'll be taking her for a walk round Deal, or so I heard from her. Be sure to take her out the pier, and show her the castle. You've not been to Deal unless you've seen the castle."

"Oh, I've seen it."

"Well, she hasn't. And when you've done seeing the

sights, you might take her to the tearoom in High Street, just at Broad."

"Yes, ma'am." She'd planned a complete itinerary for us, had she not? I would gladly remain, so that I might be privy to the plan Sir John was hatching with Mr. Sarton and his unnamed informant.

"There's a widow lady who runs it," she continued, "a Mrs. Keen. Just tell her Molly sent you, and she'll treat you right—if she knows what's good for her!"

She had a somewhat rowdy manner but was altogether direct and quite good-natured. I liked her—as evidently Clarissa did also. I had not seen Miss Roundtree smile so brightly since we went out a-walking that day in Bath. It was evident that Mr. Sarton had not made her interrogation a difficult ordeal.

She greeted us most happily and ran off to wash the dough and flour from her hands.

"Has she been with you long here in the kitchen?" Sir John asked.

"About the quarter part of an hour," Mrs. Sarton responded.

"Then the mysterious visitor should be coming along soon."

"That I wouldn't know, sir. I do the cookin' and the cleanin' and leave the magistratin' to him." She cocked her head then in an attitude of listening. "But unless I'm mistaken, I hear Berty moving round where he keeps his papers upstairs. He went up to find something for you, sir."

"Oh?"

"Yes, he should be down soon."

Clarissa came back, wiping her hands upon a towel, announcing that she was ready to be taken for a tour of the town. Well, as her guide, I took my leave of Sir John, and in company with Clarissa, allowed myself to be taken back down the hall to the door by which we had entered. Mrs.

Sarton insisted on letting us out that she might again turn the locks from the inside.

As we departed the house, she waved us an enthusiastic goodbye. "The town's got itself a bad name from all the smuggling done here. But there's much pleasure to be had in Deal. Enjoy yourselves, both of you."

Then did she shut the door behind us, turn the key, and throw the bolt.

"Isn't she wonderful?" said Clarissa to me.

"Why yes, I suppose she is," said I. "You certainly seem to have come to know her well in a very short time."

"That's the sort of person she is. I feel as if I had known her all my life."

"Hmmm, well, I see."

"Why, oh why, must you be so . . . so . . . *tepid*?" said she in utter exasperation.

And I? Well, I shrugged in answer, indicating, I suppose, that I did not know why, nor did I think it a matter of great import that I did not know. We had reached an impasse of sorts, one which had far more to do with the differences in our personalities than with anything of a material nature. It was often so with us.

We had walked but a short distance and were near to the corner of King Street. A man who looked quite familiar came round the corner. I studied his face as I tried to decide where it was I had seen it before. Then, of a sudden, I knew: he was Dick Dickens, to whom I had been introduced by Mr. Perkins; Dick Dickens, the smuggler turned customs officer. He passed us with no more than a wise nod. I, not knowing how else to respond, nodded back to him. What was he doing here? To me, it seemed quite evident that he was on his way to a meeting with Albert Sarton and Sir John Fielding. Dickens, it was, who had become the source of information about the owling trade. Could he be trusted? Though I had my doubts, Mr. Perkins seemed to take him as he presented himself. Well,

I had in a sense been invited to stay away from their meeting with him. Let them do without me and my misgivings, thought I.

"Don't you want to hear about her?" asked Clarissa.

"About who?"

"Why, about Mrs. Sarton—about Molly. Who did you suppose I meant?"

"Certainly, I'd like to hear more, if there's more to know. I fear my mind was elsewhere."

"Obviously," said she. "But now that I have your attention, I'll tell you a thing or two that you don't know. First of all, Molly was cook at the house of Sir Simon Grenville until that arrogant fellow Jacques came over from France and robbed her of her position. Lady Grenville insisted that she must have a French cook, and so there it was, practically a condition of the marriage. She would brook no argument in the matter."

"When did all this come about?" I asked, interested now, almost in spite of myself.

"A little over a year ago. That was when Sir Simon wed the beauteous Marie-Hélène, and it was also about the time that Mr. Sarton came to Deal as the new magistrate. That was how they happened to get married."

"I don't follow you," I said, "not at all."

"Well, it's simple enough. Cut loose as she was, with nowhere else to go, she presented herself to the new magistrate and asked if he needed a cook. Well, she knew very well that he did—for he himself, being a man, knew not the first thing about cookery, of course. But Mr. Sarton— 'Berty,' she calls him—was quite smitten by her, red hair and all, and so he hired her on the moment. Six months later they were to be married—and that caused a great many problems."

"Of what sort? I'd not heard of any of this."

"Didn't I tell you it would all be new to you?" said she smugly. "Well, there was trouble on his side because his father and mother had hoped and expected he might marry the daughter of a rich man, who would herself bring a considerable fortune into the marriage, money that might be used to provide him with an entry into genteel society."

"Well, there'd be little chance of that, I suppose."

"Little chance indeed! She'd been living under the same roof with him as his cook. That was cause for scandal."

"But they hadn't actually been . . . that is . . ."

"Well, she didn't go into that—but after all, they were in love, weren't they? But it did bring them down a bit round town. A magistrate simply does not go about marrying his cook, you know. The bishop was reluctant to let them be married in St. George's, which is, of course, where the magistrate of the town should be married. And of course Sir Simon could not play host to them."

"But why not? He was more or less Mr. Sarton's sponsor here in Deal."

"He and Lady Grenville could hardly set a table for their former cook, could they?"

"I suppose not," said I as I thought about it for a moment. "It does account for a lot, does it not? They did eventually marry, though?"

"The wedding was held in a little side chapel and snubbed by all the best people in Deal." Clarissa sighed. "Isn't it a beautiful story, Jeremy? Love conquers all! I do believe I shall use it as the plot for my first novel. I wonder if she would mind?"

Again she sighed. Actually, she sighed quite a number of times during the telling of Molly Sarton's tale.

"Indeed," said I, "you certainly got a lot out of her in a short time."

"It's true, isn't it? But you know, I believe she's lonely. She seems to have no one to talk to. I came along, eager to hear, and she simply came out with it."

Then did Clarissa stop of a sudden and look about her, as if noticing her surroundings for the first time.

"Dear God," said she, "it is the sea, isn't it?"

Indeed it was, for we stood on Beach Street quite near the pier, where a few fishing boats of differing shapes and sizes jittered in the glittering water.

"You may call it the sea or the Channel, whichever suits you best."

"I'd no idea we were so close."

"Didn't you smell it? Nothing quite like the smell of the sea. But come, let's walk out on the pier and look at the boats, shall we?"

And that we did, finding much to laugh at as we went upon our way: at the gulls, for instance, which seemed the most pompous of birds as they strutted about boat and pier; and at rest, they seemed to strike heroic poses as they stared out over the sea in the direction of France.

In general, I led Clarissa along the route I had traveled the day before. The difference, of course, was that together we traveled at a more leisurely pace, thus finding more to see, more to notice, along the way. It was in that way far more enjoyable than yesterday's brisk race to the castle and back.

At the fish market, Clarissa exclaimed over the variety of seafood which was on display. She pointed to the mussels, the skates, and the ugly eels and crabs.

"Do people really eat such?" she asked.

"Oh, they do indeed," I assured her, "and live longer for it—or so I hear."

And then did we travel on along the sand, examining closely what the sea had left at the waterline. And on to Deal Castle, where the great cannon pointed out toward France. We walked carefully round the moat, daring only to peek down at its murky depths, which seemed more frightening than the sea itself.

On our return I guided us down High Street, where Clarissa shopped in every window either side of the street. She had a talent for it and high standards, as well: though her interest was easily captured, in the end nothing she saw—neither frock, nor locket, nor shawl, nor armoire—satisfied her completely. Thus was she saved the embarrassment of attempting to pay for any of these items with an empty purse.

The tearoom was the happiest surprise of all in our tour of the town. We had passed a coffeehouse on the way, and I looked longingly inside, for as was well known even then, I much preferred coffee to tea. Yet coffeehouses, in Deal as well as London, were of the male province; except for servers, I had never seen a woman inside such a place, nor have I since. Yet as we sat down in our chairs at a table quite near the window of the tearoom, I looked round me and saw that there were women aplenty scattered through the place; some were in the company of men; at other tables there were ladies only; and one brave soul, a woman of apparently limited means, had a table all to herself. The server, a woman of about thirty-five, presented herself and asked our order.

"We should like a pot of your best tea," said I.

"Oh, well, all our tea is the best, sir. What sort would you like? We've Chinese green tea, Indian tea, even Persian."

Not wishing to seem an utter numskull in matters of tea, I sat for a moment and pondered the matter.

"I understand," said I, "that Darjeeling is quite good. It is an Indian tea, is it not?"

"It is indeed, sir, and among the best. I might say that it is the best of the best."

"Then a pot of that, please, and as for something to accompany it . . ."

"We have all manner of cakes and dainties, sir."

"Might I perhaps speak with Mrs. Keen on the matter?"

She assented with a curtsey and disappeared through the curtained entrance to the rear of the shop. It was not much more than a minute later when a woman somewhat older than Mrs. Sarton (but otherwise quite like her) appeared from the rear and came straight to our table. Clarissa and I rose, curtsied and bowed, and introduced ourselves to the woman who offered herself as Mrs. Keen.

"You asked for me?"

"We bring you greetings from Mrs. Sarton," said I. "She would not have us pass through Deal without visiting your tearoom."

"Ah, she wouldn't, eh? Sounds like her, so it does. How long have you known her?"

"We've just met," said Clarissa, "and she seems quite the most wonderful person."

"She is, bless you, and also quite the most wonderful cook in Kent. Indeed I should know, for I was her pastry maker for three years—that is, before both of us was turned out to make room for the new crowd. We're both better off for it, but poor Molly had to put up with a lot from this town before she and her magistrate were married. Ah, the snubs and the gossip—it was disgraceful."

Most of this last was whispered, yet there was conversation aplenty in the tearoom; none seemed to be listening.

"But sit down, both of you. I know why Molly sent you here. It was to have a sample of my best. And as it so happens, I just pulled a pan of my best out of the oven. It'll be here with your tea."

And it was. Her "best," as she called it, was a whole plate of sugar cakes of such a taste and quality as I had never experienced before—nor, for that matter, since. Clarissa and I ate them all, right down to the last crumb. It was, for us both, a most joyous experience of gluttony. (The tea was also good.)

We wandered the length of High Street, but when we came to Alfred Square, with its notorious inns, its drunks staggering about in the daylight hours, I thought it best that we circle round it and avoid it altogether. Thus we returned to Beach Street and to the sea. As we did so, I spied a stretch of sand beach ahead of us which was, in its way, quite mysterious. I had no trouble persuading Clarissa to visit the place with me.

What had attracted my eye at some distance was the unexpected sight of a mast—no, two of them—rising up from the water, bare of sails. As we came closer, I saw that there was even a bit more of the ship to be seen there: the forward gunwales were also barely visible, giving the impression that it was rising from the sea of its own power, like some great monster of the deep. Yet there were no depths where the masts rose up—only shallows. We stood together looking out at it. I, for one, felt something more than curiosity and something less than awe, and yet a bit of both.

"How do you suppose it got there?" Clarissa asked.

"It ran aground," said I. "Perhaps it was bad navigation that brought it to such an end. Or it may be that it was driven there by a storm."

"It looks old. I wonder how long it's been here."

"I couldn't say, though I'm sure there are those in town who could tell us with fair exactitude." I studied its position in relation to the waterlines in the sand. "At lowest tide it might be possible to walk out to it or wade there from the shore."

"Possible for you perhaps," said Clarissa, "though not for me with these great skirts I must wear. Sometimes, Jeremy, I simply loathe being a girl." She gave that a moment's thought, and then added: "And sometimes I quite enjoy it."

Returning to Number 18 Middle Street, we were both surprised to learn that it was well into the afternoon—near three o'clock, as I recall. The meeting (to which I had not been invited) had concluded less than an hour before, and Sir John had asked if there might be a place, perhaps upstairs, where he might take a nap. He was accompanied to the small guest bedroom by Mr. Sarton. Sir John assured him that he was not ill, simply tired. This was heard from Mr. Sarton himself as he prepared to leave on an errand.

"He's resting very well up there," said he to me. "Molly's working at dinner, and Clarissa is doing what she can to help. How can we entertain you until dinner, Jeremy?"

"Oh, I need not be entertained, sir. So long as I have something to read, I'll be well satisfied."

"And have you something to read?"

"Well . . . as it happens, I don't."

"Come along then," said he, and led me to that small room near the street door which served him as a study. He waved inside. "Such as it is, my library is here. You are free to browse and read what you find. I must, however, ask you not to disturb the books or papers on the desk. They are part and parcel of something I'm writing—or hope to write."

(Ah-hah, I had guessed correctly!)

"I shall certainly do that, sir. And I thank you, sir, ever so much."

With that, he took his leave.

I entered the study and began searching through the nearest shelves. They were better-stocked than he had given out. I did not find what I hoped to—a copy of *A Sentimental Journey*, that I might resume where I had left off in the library of Sir Simon Grenville's manor house. Nevertheless, I did find a thing or two to interest me in the shelves along the wall. There was a copy of Dean Swift's *Gulliver's Travels*; and tucked away in a far corner, I found a battered and dog-eared copy of a Latin grammar. It was so old and ill-used that I thought it must be Mr. Sarton's first book of Latin.

I moved round the desk for a better look at the books in the case below the window. Yet as I did, my eyes fell upon a paper that had been left upon the desk. It was a map, rather crude but clearly drawn, of that stretch of sand beach which Clarissa and I had visited a good deal less than an hour before. There on the right was a rectangle, which was labeled "shipwreck"; below it, the shoreline; and above and all around it, a shaded area indicating the size and shape of the sandbar which had trapped the ship. Significantly, the sandbar did not stretch the length of the beach: There was a channel marked, a clear passage from the open sea to the shoreline. Distances were noted in yards or feet.

This I found most interesting. I would wager that the map was the work of Dick Dickens. Had he brought it with him or drawn it on the spot? Well, little it mattered, for I daresay that Dickens knew the surrounding area so well that he could have drawn any number of such maps from memory. And if I were not mistaken, Mr. Sarton was now on his way to that sandy beach to study the lay of the land and the look of the sea. Or he might even, at that moment, be surveying the scene from the bluff above the beach, comparing it to the map whose image he now had fixed in his mind.

I could be sure now what was discussed at their meeting. More important, I even had a good idea where the operation which Sir John had mentioned to Mr. Perkins would take place. It occurred to me that after Mr. Sarton had returned, I might go for another look at the beach myself. With that in mind, I resolved not to weight myself further with books. I took the two I had chosen and stepped across the hall to the large parlor which served him as a courtroom; there I would hear the magistrate's return; there I could read without fear of interruption by Clarissa. I browsed through the Latin grammar and found it not near so difficult as I had expected; I resolved to buy one like it as soon as we got back to London. I put it aside and picked up *Travels into Several Remote Nations of the World*, by Lemuel Gulliver, which all the world knows as *Gulliver's Travels*. I had read the book when I was but twelve, and I thought it quite funny but little more than that. I had come

lately to realize that I had missed much of its meaning and
made up my mind to reread it at my earliest opportunity.
And so I began it and was well into the second chapter,
wherein Lemuel Gulliver learns the language of the Lil-
liputians as a squad of the little people enter his pockets
and make a survey of their contents. Thus far did I go—and
no farther—for at that point did I fall fast asleep.

It was Molly Sarton who woke me. She came blustering
in, table linen in hand, and began preparing the deal table
for dining, the one at which her husband had sat during his
morning court session. She looked across the room at me
and chuckled.

"Ah, so this is where you went to hide!" said she.

"I wasn't hiding, I was reading," said I quite defensively.
Then I added, "Is it late?"

"Late enough. We'll be eating soon as Clarissa and I can
get things on the table. Should be about a quarter of an
hour, or not much longer."

"May I help?"

"You can help by going upstairs and attending to Sir
John. He's been making waking-up noises for the past five
minutes, and it's time somebody looked in on him."

And I, of course, was that somebody. I ascended to the
floor above and had no difficulty in finding which of the
two rooms he had situated himself in. It was the door from
which issued a medley of coughs and throat-clearing
sounds. I opened it and found that he was having his usual
difficulty finding his way into his coat. He signaled for his
kerchief, which had fallen to the floor. Once he had it in
hand, he blew his nose, sneezed, blew his nose again, and
thanked me.

It was not long before we were both ready to sup in polite society. I guided Sir John through the door and down
the stairs, and then into the courtroom where all but Mrs.
Sarton awaited us. Mr. Sarton was engaged in reducing a
magnificent haunch of beef to portions of slices, chunks,

and chips. Indeed, he had carved so much from it that it was evident he had great confidence in the capacity of his guests. Clarissa looked across the table at me with something akin to fright. At about that time, Mrs. Sarton came into the room, beautifully dressed, her hair nicely coifed with no more than touches of rouge upon her lips and cheeks. She had transformed herself completely.

"Oh, Berty," said she, "that's quite enough, I think."

"I'm never quite sure. After all, there are five of us."

"No, that will be fine for the time being. Just dish out the pudding, and serve the wine, and we'll be underway."

With that, she smiled and took her place at the foot of the table, whence she presided over the carrots, sauce, and all those condiments and additional pleasures that can make a good meal into a great one.

Reader, I know not how you stand on matters of cookery. There are some, it is true, who hold that the French cooking is the best in all the world. We had had a fair sample of it the past two evenings, with its plenitude of small courses, wines with each, subtly spiced sauces with all. And I admit that I thought the strangeness of it quite grand.

Nevertheless, to my mind there is naught that can compare with a good English dinner for hearty flavor, abundance, and pure satisfaction. Be it beef, mutton, pork, or whatever, when cooked to perfection in the English manner, it cannot be equaled. And there could be no question but that Molly Sarton cooked that haunch of beef to perfection. Sir John and I asked so often for more that Mr. Sarton had unexpectedly to carve a bit more. And the Yorkshire pudding was as I had never had it—crisp and buttery, and subtle to the taste. There was but one wine, an excellent claret, yet it was abundantly available—bottles of the best. We were silent through the main course, so absorbed were we in the eating of it. We sighed contentedly through dessert (a fine apple tart), and only when the plate of cheese was brought out did we begin to talk in our usual voluble manner. The Sartons were eager to draw us out, and they questioned Clarissa and me direct on our tour of their town. Mr. Sarton gave forth on the history of Deal Castle; and afterward, I asked him rather pointedly about the shipwreck which was mired in the ocean sands just off the beach and not far from this very house: Did he know how long it had been there? What were the circumstances that had put it there? He had no real information to give, but the odd look that he gave me told me what I wished to know: owlers.

There was an awkward lull thereafter. Sir John saved the moment, however, by putting to Mr. Sarton a question, one which had troubled me as well.

"Sir," said he, "I've noted that you and your wife are very careful to whom you open your front door. Understand me, I believe you both act prudently in this. Nevertheless, is it not difficult to manage such a degree of security when your court is in session?"

"Ah, well," said Mr. Sarton, "there you've put your finger upon it, sir. Our house must be more or less open to the public during court hours. If it were left to us, we would keep the door locked and bolted during those hours, as well. As you may have heard, Sir John, our town jail burned down some months past—with no loss of life, I hasten to add. So far, they have not yet found the money to build another. When they do, I requested that they build it large enough so that the court may be convened there next to the cells with perhaps no more than a wall between."

"We have a similar arrangement on the ground floor at Number 4 Bow Street."

"The problem will be solved then," said Mr. Sarton. "We can keep our place in Middle Street locked up just as tight as a drum."

"Why do you feel it necessary to do so?"

"I should think that would be obvious. It's because of what happened to my predecessor."

"Oh? What was that?"

"You were never told?"

"Not a word. I assumed he had died of natural causes. He was of an advanced age, was he not?"

"Sixty-four. Since you were not told of any of this, you may not even know his name. It was Herbert Kemp. He held the post here for many years, married, had children, brought them up in this very house. His wife had died a few years before, and he lived alone here. A woman from town came in each day to do the cooking and cleaning. Aside from a peculiar tendency to be more stringent in his application of the law in his rulings, he seemed not to have changed in any way from the man who had been magistrate for so many years before.

"Nevertheless, on a certain night, long after the hour when there were possible witnesses roaming about the streets, a knock came upon his door and he opened it, and he was promptly shot dead by him who had knocked. That, in any case, was what was later supposed to have happened, for there were none about to see what had happened, and naught left by the murderer but a body in the open doorway, which was not found until the morning. Strange, is it not, that these houses be so close together, yet none heard the shot fired. Or, having heard, came down to investigate."

Sir John shook his head in a manner which seemed to indicate his bewilderment. "And despite all that, you accepted this post?"

"Despite all that," said he.

"Were I you, I do not believe I would have done."

"And that's just what I told him, as well," said Molly Sarton. "Yet if he had not come, we wouldn't've met, and my life would have been much poorer for it." And she smiled solemnly at her husband across the length of the table.

Following Mr. Sarton's story, it became rather difficult

to recapture our former mood at table. All the lightness had leaked out. It was not long before Sir John shuffled his feet politely and said that perhaps we had better be getting on.

"I've provided for your trip back," said Mr. Sarton.

"Oh? And in what way?"

"We've a most dependable hackney coachman here in Deal, perhaps the only *dependable* one among them. I asked him to come by when things slowed down in the evening, and I do believe I heard him draw up at our door but a few minutes past."

And so we organized ourselves for our return. Molly Sarton firmly declined our offer to help her clear the table and do the washing up. Mr. Sarton then led the way outside and introduced us to Mick Crawly, an easy sort of fellow, yet at the same time, he seemed good and responsible.

"How did you know when we'd be finishing up?" Sir John challenged the driver.

"Ah, how did I now?" Crawly asked himself. "Knowing Mrs. Sarton's reputation as a cook, I was sure that it would take two hours of eating to do justice to any dinner of hers, and to that I added another half of an hour, for you've quite a reputation as a talker, sir."

"Even here in Deal?"

"We're not so distant from London as you might suppose, though it may seem we are."

"Indeed it often does."

Happy was I to note that Mr. Crawly's hackney was of a size and shape comparable to those in London. I would not, in other words, have to ride atop the coach and hang on in fear as we rounded those tight corners which led up to great Mongeham. I climbed in last of all and found the interior quite spacious. All three of us were thus able to sit huddled together against the cold night air upon the same padded bench. It took but a moment to get us settled, and in a moment after that we were underway. Mick Crawly did not drive his team with the same merciless abandon as Lord

Mansfield's man, nor even Will Fowler's lack of proper concern. He kept his horses moving at a reasonable rate up the narrow roads—no faster than was necessary. As we went, the gentle rocking of the coach soon put Clarissa to sleep.

Unexpectedly, Sir John turned to me and said, "I met your Dick Dickens today, or perhaps Dickens belongs more properly to Mr. Perkins. In any case, I met him, and I was quite impressed by him."

"Favorably?"

He chuckled at that. "Ah yes, you plainly had doubts as to his conversion to the side of right."

"In fairness," said I, "Mr. Perkins seems to have no such doubts. At least he voiced none after I was introduced to his Mr. Dickens."

"Perhaps that is because the constable successfully underwent a similar conversion—or have you any reason to doubt its sincerity?"

"None at all."

"Well, there you are." He hesitated, then went on. "I'm inclined to accept Dickens as he presents himself because he is in possession of a great deal of information and has been quite generous with it. He is most resentful that he and his troop of customs men have been kept inactive by that dreadful fellow, Eccles, whom we met at Lord Mansfield's. By the bye, have you any idea why he has stopped all efforts on the Kent coast and blamed Mr. Sarton so unjustly?"

"None whatever," said I, "and I have sought some such reason without success."

"Well, he hopes that by presenting the efforts of the customs and excisemen as fruitless and painting the darkest picture possible, he will get the Army to loan him a detachment of soldiers, cavalry preferred. He is a fool if he believes he will command them. Rather, some fool of a lieutenant will be commanding *him.*

"But that is all in the nature of a digression," continued Sir John. "What I wished to say is this: Mr. Dickens has not sat idle as his chief would have him. No, indeed. He has assembled a most excellent network of spies and informants in the smuggling trade or at the periphery of it. He told me more in a morning than I would have thought possible. He has promised to return tomorrow and tell me even more. Then shall we begin our planning. I do believe that with Mr. Perkins's help and yours, we shall be able to make it work."

SIX

*In which a battle
is fought to a
shocking conclusion*

I had no exact idea of the time, though I was sure that it was quite late at night. The moon had gained its apex and had started its downward transit. Yet it shone down upon the beach, seemingly as bright as it had only an hour before. Mr. Perkins and I were halfway up the bluff and well concealed behind a grassy hummock. We had successfully evaded detection half an hour earlier when a party of four men with two horses had passed no more than thirty yards away. They were now waiting, down on the beach, just as we were above. Unknown to them, two of Mr. Sarton's constables also waited quite nearby; yet on that stretch of open beach, the constables were as near invisible as could be, for they had taken shelter beneath one of a number of fisher boats that lay up-ended upon the sand. We were all well armed. Two pistols and a cutlass had been issued by Mr. Sarton to each. And though there were but four of us, we would at least have the advantage of surprise.

There was a ship offshore. I could see it plain enough. It had the appearance of a sloop but was probably what I had heard called a "cutter" there in Deal. When it hove into view, someone aboard sent up a rocket from a flink pistol. And one who seemed to be in charge of the party on the beach lit a spout lantern and aimed it at the cutter, thus showing that they were ready on the beach to receive the landing party. It had been planned a full three days ago that when the boat from the cutter came, and the four men constituting the landing party were involved in beaching it, the constables were to emerge from their hiding place and rush the smugglers, threatening to shoot any who resisted. Mr. Perkins and I were upon the bluff to stop any that might escape the constables below.

It was a good enough plan and might have worked just as Dick Dickens and Mr. Sarton intended it to, but for one matter. There were too many of them and not enough of us. What was unknown was how many men would arrive in the boat and how well they would be armed. Mr. Perkins, newly appointed as a Deal constable, grumbled about this to me unceasingly and had cautioned me early on not to be surprised if he were to improvise a bit when the time came.

Well, the time had come. The boat was now visible, pushing through the channel which cut through the sandbar. There were but three in the boat: two oarsmen and a passenger. Presumably, there was also cargo of some sort aboard—though I had no idea what could be so small yet of such value that it would make worthwhile the voyage of a cutter across the Channel from France. Two men of the four who had arrived with the horses waded out to the boat.

"Jeremy!" he whispered urgently.

"Yes, Mr. Perkins?"

"Do you reckon you can take care of any who flee up this little hill?"

"You may be certain of it."

"Remember to shoot to wound and not to kill. And now, if you'll excuse me, I'm going to go a bit mad."

What did he mean by that? I'd no idea until he jumped up from our safe cover, drew the cutlass from its sheath, and let out a scream the like of which had surely not been heard in England since the days when the wild Picts came down from the north to murder and pillage the poor Anglo-Saxons. Then did he begin the run down to the beach, continuing to emit terrifying shouts as he whirled the cutlass above his head like a Musselman in the throes of some murderous dementia.

I rose from our place upon the bluff that I might see him better—yet still better did I see those round the boat. The effect upon them of Mr. Perkins's performance was like that of poor brutish creatures who stand in frozen awe when the lion attacks. Each of those who stood in the shallows now had in his hands a box of some dimension—the cargo. The horses, whose reins were held by one of the quartet, did not like those chilling screams of Mr. Perkins—no, not in the least; they stirred and pranced nervously and became altogether difficult to hold in check. Only the fourth of them managed to act: he drew from his belt a pistol and leveled it at Mr. Perkins; yet before he could fire, another pistol was fired at him—that of one of the constables; he staggered, wounded.

"Drop your weapons! This be the law!"

Then was all set in motion at once: the horses reared; he who held the reins kept tight hold, yet was thrown to the ground and dragged a bit in the sand; one of the oarsmen drew a pistol and attempted to return fire at the constables, but the powder flashed, fizzled, and failed to fire; the second oarsman and the passenger jumped into the water and began pushing their boat back out to sea in a most desperate manner; the two cargo handlers dropped the boxes they had taken from the boat and ran in opposing directions. So was it when Mr. Perkins arrived, and he was still whirling the cutlass above him as if he meant to lop off a head or two.

So intently was I watching the scene below on the beach that I nearly failed to notice that one of the cargo men had circled round and started up the bluff. He had not yet noticed me, because I was partly hidden by the high grass of the hummock and had not moved for a minute or more. It was now time to move, however. I knew I must head him off ere he reached the top of the bluff, and I lose him completely among the houses and the winding streets at this edge of the town. I ran to intercept him.

He was a big man, half again as large as I, but he lumbered unsteadily up the little hill in such a way that I knew I should have no difficulty in overtaking him. But then what? Short of shooting him in the leg, what could be done to stop him? He had glimpsed my approach, so there could be no question of catching him by surprise—and so I simply stopped. Yes, stopped and drew from its sheath the cutlass I had been given, and from its holster I took one of the pistols. With the sword in my right hand and the pistol in my left, I resumed my run, and in seconds I caught the big fellow up.

"Halt," said I.

Yet he did not halt; he kept straining up the bluff, his feet slipping in the dry sand, so that he found it near impossible to make any upward progress.

"Halt," said I again.

To no avail. He pumped his legs still more vigorously, and so I gave him a swift jab in the buttocks with the point of the sword. He let out a proper scream. I knew that I could not have hurt him quite so much as that. It must have been that he was taken by surprise.

"Would you like another?" I shouted at him.

His legs at last had halted. He turned round, and I saw in his wild eyes an unspoken threat. He seemed to be weighing his chances. I raised the point of the cutlass so that it was less than a foot from his sagging belly. I brought up the pistol that he might reckon it also in the odds against escape.

"Go ahead," said I in a suitably nasty tone, "and if you do, I'll skewer you on the sword and finish you off with the pistol. And do not suppose I lack the stomach for it."

I should like to think, reader, that it was my threatening tone persuaded him—and perhaps it was—but I believe it more likely that the poor fellow, panting with exhaustion, was simply too tired from the efforts he had made thus far, to consider any course but surrender.

Reluctantly, he nodded, and I stepped aside and pointed the direction with the sword.

"This way," said I. "Down there with the rest."

And down the bluff we went. There was nothing more for me to say to him, and so I said nothing. Upon our arrival, I found the rest had been disarmed and were in a similar state of sullen compliance. One of the constables had with him a considerable length of rope and was occupied in binding the prisoners each to each; the second held them where they stood with pistol and cutlass. Mr. Perkins brought the horse-handler back to his fellows, urging him on from the saddle with the flat of his sword. I noted that the wounded man had had his shoulder bound after a fashion; the bleeding had, in any case, been stanched with a tourniquet.

With my prisoner added to their number, we had taken four. Not a bad haul except that three (the second cargo-handler and the two in the boat) had escaped our trap. Still, none of our fellows had been so much as scratched. We could count this a certain victory.

In all, it took about ten minutes to attend to matters before marching the prisoners off to the inn where they would spend the night. We marched them up toward the bluff, with the constables at the head of the column and Mr.

Perkins and I bringing up the rear, leading the two horses. Along the way, he mentioned a matter in which I had considerable interest, as did Sir John later on.

"You know, Jeremy," said he, "something struck me as strange whilst I was putting on my show back there."

"Oh? And what was that?"

"Well, when I got down amongst them and everything started happening at once, I could just swear that one of them who pushed the boat out and manned the oars—the passenger, I guess you'd say—"

"Yes?"

"Was wearing skirts. Could you tell better from where you were?"

"Why, I don't know. Let me think about that a moment." I sought then to call to mind exactly what I had seen. Yet all that came was a picture of confusion. At last, giving it up, I shook my head. "I really can't say," I declared. "As you yourself put it, everything was happening at once. But it would indeed seem strange if it were a woman."

He nodded, then fell silent, though not for long. "Another thing," said he, "these two horses."

"What about them?"

"Well, that one you're leading, he was meant to be led, no question of it. He's big and strong and meant to carry cargo. In short, he's a packhorse. That's why we loaded him up with those boxes that came off the boat, whatever's in them. An't I right?"

"Certainly you are, but what is your point?"

"Just that this one I'm leading is a saddle horse, pure and simple, and a damn good one at that. She's nervous and temperamental and just a bit headstrong, but those are all signs of a good animal. Now, she was all saddled and waiting there for the passenger that came off that cutter. But you know what I found out when I went to ride her? I found out she had on her a sidesaddle, a woman's saddle, if you please. Now, what do you think of that, Jeremy?"

"I'd say it proves your point beyond argument," said I, laughing. "Now why didn't you—"

I never quite finished that sentence, for behind us a great roar sounded, then above, a moment later, came a great whirring noise.

"Duck!" shouted Mr. Perkins, and duck we did. A good thing, too, for the great shower of sand that fell upon the four prisoners and two constables did miss us altogether.

"Better run for it, gents," yelled Mr. Perkins. "That ain't a musket they're shooting at us!"

"What is it, then?"

"A cannon, and that was a cannonball landed just to the north of us."

Hard as it was to find proper footing on that sandy bluff, the entire party managed, nevertheless, to make their way to the top of it in impressively short time. The horses, too, alive to the sense of panic in the men, heaved their way up through the sand in great, bounding leaps, racing them to the summit.

Once up and over the crest, prisoners and captors stood, resting as if out of range, wheezing and coughing. But Mr. Perkins would have none of that.

"Better move it on, gents," he urged them. "Next time might come closer."

There was no next time, as it happened—not on that night, in any case. The cutter fired but once, perhaps more in pique than with a true intention to destroy: the prisoners were, after all, their own people. One of them was greatly disturbed by these events. The oarsman whose pistol had misfired seemed to be praying in the Romish style, blessing himself repeatedly. But listening carefully to him (he was quite near us), I found that it was not Latin but French he spoke, and that those were not prayers but curses he raised to heaven.

• • • •

A surgeon had to be roused to remove the bullet from the wounded prisoner's shoulder. Mr. Perkins was sent by the senior constable to fetch him. I volunteered to accompany my friend, for there was yet much I wished to know. There had been little opportunity to talk while on our way to the Good King George. The constables had unwisely marched the procession through Alfred Square, perhaps eager to show off what they had accomplished in their night's work. While they received all the attention they might have wished, even then it seemed to me to be attention of the wrong sort. At our first appearance in the square, the patrons had poured out of the Turk's Head and the other inns, alehouses, and dives to jeer at the luckless captives. The prisoners were greeted with laughter, hoots, and cries of derision. The tenor of these calls seemed to be that the mighty had fallen, that they were finally to get what they deserved. Oddly, it had not occurred to me until then that there might be more than one party in the smuggling trade there in Deal; there might be two, three, or even more; and all might be in mortal competition, each with the other. And why not? The robber gangs of London were in such a state, were they not? Upon one fabled occasion, two gangs had fought a pitched battle in Bedford Street over the question of which of them "owned" a certain territory below Holbourn and above the Strand.

The crowd from Alfred Square had followed us down Middle Street, creating noise and confusion all the way to the house at Number 18. We—Mr. Perkins and I—were much annoyed by these who trooped after us, most of them drunk, all of them ill-behaved. Yet far more than we, the horses we led resented their presence—and the mare, led by Mr. Perkins, most of all. She pranced and danced, so that she was difficult even for him to hold. And at one point, she planted her front hooves and kicked back with her rear. Yet she made no contact with man nor woman, which was just as well, for Mr. Perkins had told me that he had known of people who were crippled for life from the kick of a horse.

Mr. Sarton, no doubt troubled by the noise of the crowd, seemed to take a specially long time to unlock the door; he had insisted upon hearing from both his constables before showing his face. When he did, I saw Sir John to his rear, listening closely to all that was said.

And what had been said? Mr. Trotter, the senior constable, stepped forward and gave to Mr. Sarton a full report, including the number captured and the number escaped, and the fact that one of the prisoners had suffered a gunshot wound.

"Well then," Mr. Sarton had said, "you must get a surgeon to treat it."

"Soon as we've got them put away at the inn, I'll send off for Mr. Parker."

"Yes, the inn," Mr. Sarton had said in dismay. "Ah, for a proper jail, eh, Mr. Trotter?"

"Aye, sir. Quite right, sir."

So it was that Mr. Perkins, as the junior of the Deal constables, came to be chosen to search out and bring the surgeon, Mr. Parker, to the Good King George. They could have chosen better. Though Mr. Perkins was given an address and rough directions, he had not been in the town of Deal for a dozen years or more. He found the place much changed. And I, of course, could be of little assistance, for I was but a visitor.

The address he had been given was one in St. George's Road. Yet in giving directions, Mr. Trotter carelessly pointed us south instead of north, starting us off in the wrong direction. Thus we began wandering about the town, looking for Mr. Parker's surgery precisely where it was not.

Mr. Perkins was quite exasperated by the time we had searched near half an hour and found naught nor no one to show us the way. It was by now far too late to find anyone on the street in that part of town.

"Now, this is damned annoying, Jeremy, old chum," said he. "I listened careful to him. I could practically repeat what he told us word for word."

"Little good it would do," said I, "for he clearly misinformed us. You don't suppose he did it a-purpose, do you?"

"No, not a bit of it. I fear it's just that our Constable Trotter an't too bright."

"We must have walked up and down every street this side of Deal." I sighed and sought to think of something which might engage him more than my comments upon our fruitless search. Surely there was something I might ask to divert him. Then I remembered the question which had been paramount in my mind when we began this bootless enterprise.

"Mr. Perkins, I've a matter at which I've wondered ever since you jumped up and ran down that hill of sand and began yelling and shouting at the smugglers down at the water."

"Well and good," said he. "What is it had you wondering?"

"Why did you do it, first of all?"

He chuckled. "Why indeed," said he. "I daresay you remember my grumbles and my protest to Sir John that the plan they had devised *might* work, but that we had not enough men to be *sure* that it would work."

"I remember. And you did then say you might do a bit of improvising when the time came."

"So I did. And what did you think of the show I put on?"

"It was quite . . . quite . . . impressive. Not something I'll be likely to forget. How ever did you think of doing that?"

"Back when I was fighting in what they called Pontiac's War—'twasn't but an uprising, really, but it had its frights—they'd send us out on picket duty to guard the encampment. That made for some pretty wild nights because the Chippewas had a practice of sneaking up close as they could, then jumping up and yelling the awfullest war cries, then running at our picket line and throwing one of their hatchets at the handiest target, then disappearing from sight. They didn't do all that much damage, but they sure scared the devil out of us."

"So you were trying to scare them?"

"No, more than that. I was trying to catch their attention and keep it. Y'see, those boats on the shore gave our fellows good cover to hide under, but it's damn difficult to get out from under them. See what I mean? I gave them time to get out from under by getting the attention of the owlers, creating a diversion, y'might say."

"You certainly did hold them," said I. "They stared at you like you were an Indian yourself, just suddenly come to life in Kent."

He laughed at that. "Yeah, they did, didn't they?"

At least I had succeeded in raising his spirits a bit. "Did the two constables have anything to say about that?" I asked.

"No, but between them they gave me some mighty queer looks." Again, he laughed, but suddenly he stopped. Clearly, something had occurred to him. "Jeremy," said he, "do you remember the name of that church at the other end of High Street?"

"Well . . . no, I fear I didn't give it proper attention."

"Nor did I, but . . . could it have been St. George's?"

"Certainly it could, and St. George's Road would likely be found near it," I suggested.

"We can only hope."

It took us no time to find our way to the church and thus to St. George's Road. Waking the surgeon, however, was quite another matter. It seemed to take minutes of beating upon the door and calling out his name before his head appeared, thrust out of an upper-story window. There were then more minutes until he appeared dressed, after a fashion, with his bag of tools in hand. As we three walked along swiftly to the inn, we found little to say. The only sound was that of our footsteps upon the cobblestones and the menacing rattle and clank of saws and knives inside the surgeon's bag.

Upon our arrival, Mr. Perkins gave a stout single knock upon the door of the inn. He might have beat longer and louder upon it, but it was hardly necessary, for the door unexpectedly flew open. There was only silence from inside. Mr. Perkins and I exchanged looks of concern. He drew his pistol as I did mine; Mr. Parker, the surgeon, shrank back.

Then, as near together as was possible, we leapt into the darkened taproom, diving to the floor on opposite sides of the door. Then did we wait tensely for some sign of what we might expect. It soon came. The long barrel of a fowling piece pushed its way over the bar and seemed to be pointed in my direction. Or was it? Perhaps it was simply aimed at the open door. I wanted to move, but I was fearful that if I did so, I would certainly make plain my location.

"All right," came a voice from behind the bar, one husky with fright, "I know where you are, so you better just get on out of here. I don't know why you come back, but if I pull this trigger, you'll be sorry you did."

"It's me, Oliver Perkins," came the response. "I'm stayin' here at the inn. You know me, don't you?"

Silence; then: "Well, maybe I do. What room you in?"

"Number six on the second floor. It's kind of an attic. Only one other room up there."

"Well, I suppose that's right."

"And I just started on as a constable here in Deal."

"Oh, I guess I did hear that." Then, reluctantly, he said, "All right, get up and come ahead slow."

Tucking away his pistol, Mr. Perkins rose with exaggeratedly deliberate movements. He came forward with his hand open, showing that he had no weapon.

"I was sent out to fetch a surgeon," said he.

"That's good. We've need of one."

"You mean for the wounded prisoner?"

"Oh no, he's gone with the rest of them."

The innkeeper raised himself and placed the great, long fowling piece upon the bar. At the same time, I holstered my pistol and got up from the floor.

"Wait a bit," said the innkeeper to me, "who're you?"

"Never you mind that," said Mr. Perkins. "What's this about 'gone with the rest of them'? Mr. Parker, come ahead. He says there's need of you."

The surgeon put his head timorously through the doorway and, seeing there was no danger, entered cautiously.

Mr. Perkins turned back to the man behind the bar. "Now, tell me what happened."

"Well, they just crashed in here so fast. I thought they was you two returning with the surgeon. They held a gun to my head and threatened me. I didn't have any choice at all. I had to tell them what room the prisoners were in. No choice at all."

By the time the innkeeper had exonerated himself of all blame in the matter, Mr. Perkins was running for the stairs and pulling the surgeon after him. I followed, and the innkeeper, grabbing up his fowling piece, trailed along behind.

The scene which greeted me on the next floor was surely one of the most dismaying that ever I have viewed. Mr. Trotter, the senior constable, knelt by the other constable (I blush to say I never learned his name), supporting him at the shoulders, thus providing what comfort he could. If not dead already, the poor fellow on the floor would soon be gone: he had a great gaping hole in his chest which certainly could not be mended. Constable Trotter, far from unscathed, held his free arm at such an awkward angle that it was evident that he had taken a bullet there, one that had probably broken his arm, as well. There was a good deal of blood upon the floor, yet it was not easy to tell from which of the constables it had come; perhaps from both. The surgeon gave his attention to Mr. Trotter. When the senior constable sought to persuade Mr. Parker to treat the other first, he seemed unable to speak above a whisper—probably weakened from loss of blood. In response to Mr. Trotter's urging, the surgeon simply shook his head: his meaning was clear—the man was beyond saving. He said something over his shoulder to Mr. Perkins, who passed the order on to the innkeeper:

"Get us a bottle of gin, and be quick. We've got to get this man drunk right away."

The innkeeper ran downstairs, apparently eager to do as he had been told.

"We must have him in a bed if I'm to get that pistol ball out and his arm properly set," said Mr. Parker. "You, lad," said he to me, "grab his feet. I'll lift him beneath his arms, and you, constable, hold his arm steady, but be careful with it. I'm sure it's broken above the elbow."

Thus we managed, with a minimum of pain to Mr. Trotter, to move him through the open door and onto one of the two beds in the room wherein the prisoners had been held. Just about then, the innkeeper returned with the bottle of gin.

"I could use a drink," said Mr. Trotter in a choked, husky voice.

"Take as much as you're able. It'll dull the pain."

The innkeeper pulled out the cork and passed the bottle to the constable. Trotter took it and drank a dram-sized gulp. He came up panting.

"Go ahead, take another," said Mr. Parker, and the constable obliged. And then to me and to the innkeeper: "All right, you two, get out of here now. The one-armed constable will give me all the help I'll need. Your name's Perkins, is it not? Show them out, Constable Perkins."

Once sure that he would not be made a target, Mr. Parker

felt in his element. He organized things well and gave orders in a crisp, authoritative manner that proved that at least he was now fully awake. I wondered if perhaps he had a naval background.

Mr. Perkins herded us to the door and out into the hall.

"See what you can do to get this poor fellow's body out of the hall, would you?" said he to the innkeeper, indicating the dead constable. "Put him up in my room, if you must." And to me he whispered: "Jeremy, find out what you can from him about what happened here. You're going to have to make a report of some sort to Sir John and to Mr. Sarton."

And so as we temporarily disposed of the body in the hall and mopped up the blood from the floor and washed it down, I questioned my coworker in detail regarding what had happened. His answers, together with what Constable Trotter later told us, provide the basis for the account which I provide below.

After Mr. Perkins and I had been let out to fetch the surgeon, Mr. Trotter returned to his place outside the room where the prisoners, still tied each to each, had in addition been secured to the bed. As he left the taproom, he advised the innkeeper that we would be returning soon with help for the wounded prisoner.

Thus the innkeeper did not hesitate to open the door when a group of men appeared shortly after our departure, for he thought them to be we two come back with the surgeon and a surgeon's helper. There were, in any case, four at the door when he threw it open to let them in. He did not notice until they swarmed upon him that all wore masks of one sort or another. A pistol was put to his head and cocked, as he had told, and he did indeed tell them where they would find the prisoners and their guards. This brief interrogation was conducted in whispers, and though he recognized none because of the masks, two of the four had voices that he was sure he had heard before. (And another detail: the leader of the gang took them directly to the stairway to the floor above, though it was not immediately in sight; he clearly knew his way about the inn.) They forced the innkeeper to accompany them. When the two constables above became uneasy at the sound of so many footsteps in the taproom, they called down to him asking who was with him there; he answered them reassuringly, even told them that the surgeon had come to care for the prisoner. That last, reader, seemed inexcusable to me.

Yet the two constables were sufficiently suspicious that, in spite of the innkeeper's assurances, they had drawn their pistols and cocked them, expecting the worst—and the worst was what they got. As the masked party reached the top of the stairs, they immediately began shooting. The constables returned their fire. One, hit in the chest, fell immediately. Mr. Trotter shot off his two pistols and inflicted a wound on one of the attackers before he, too, fell wounded—though not mortally.

After that, there was nothing nor no one to keep them from the prisoners. They threw open the door to the room, cut the bonds that held them, and made ready to go. Yet before they did, the leader of the masked band walked over to Constable Trotter in the hall and gave him a kick in his bleeding arm. He then said coldly, with an unmistakable threat in his voice: "You may tell them all that *we* run the owling trade in Deal. There will be no more doubt of it when we finish tonight."

Not another word passed between them. Quick as they had come, they went, though it was later learned that they had reclaimed the cargo carried by the smugglers' boat. The innkeeper promised that he would somehow find help, but once he was downstairs and behind the bar in the taproom, it seemed to him necessary to have a bit of rum to fortify himself for the journey. He was just finishing it, ready to pour another, when Mr. Perkins knocked once upon the door, and it swung open.

Whilst the tale was told me, there were a few cries of pain from within the room, but when Mr. Perkins emerged, he said that Constable Trotter had done well.

"'Twasn't taking the bullet out that hurt him so," said he, "but setting his broken arm—that's what set him going. The gin didn't help much there."

Mr. Parker had abundant instructions for the care of Constable Trotter. The question was, who would stay with the patient to carry out the instructions? When the surgeon put the matter to the innkeeper, the latter insisted that, much as he would like to nurse the constable back to robust health, he must be free to run the taproom below.

"There is a possibility, however," said he after giving some thought to the problem. "Perhaps the dull-witted girl who sweeps and mops the place in the mornings might be persuaded to sit with him through the rest of the day."

"But you call her 'dull-witted.' Would she know enough wit to change the bandage each day and to administer a chemist's potion at regular intervals?"

The innkeeper scratched his head. "Probably not."

"Sir," said I to the surgeon, "I know of such a girl. She is able and dependable." I had Clarissa in mind, of course.

"Yes, but she is not here now. How am I to instruct her? Can she read?"

"She would spend all her time with books, if given the chance."

"Ah, well then, innkeeper, if you will provide pen, ink, and paper, I will write out what must be done."

Mr. Perkins stepped forward. "And I'll remain here with Trotter until she comes," said he. "The lad must be off to make a report of all this to the magistrate."

"Well enough then, do it as you like. All that matters is

that he be given proper attention. He'll be going into fever by the end of the day."

Mr. Perkins gave me a wink and a nod, which I took to mean that I might leave now. I answered with a nod of my own.

"If you'll excuse me," said I to Mr. Parker, "I'll be on my way."

With that and a bobbing bow, I left the room. It so happened, though, that the cowardly innkeeper was below, assembling the writing materials the surgeon had called for. He raised a hand to me, beckoning me to him ere I walked out the door. I went to him. Apparently he wished to tell me something, but knew not quite how to do it. He made a false start or two.

"Perhaps you could . . . I would like to explain . . . that is to say . . ." Then did he stop altogether and collect himself before proceeding. "I would ask, lad, that you not judge me too harshly. What I told you is the truth, no less than if I'd given it under oath. Mind, I'm none too proud of my behavior, as I've described it to you. Nevertheless, I'd have you know that I was afeared for my very life. I vow that I've never been so close to death before. You do understand, don't you?"

I knew not what to say. If he were asking for my approval, I would certainly withhold it. If he were asking for absolution—forgiveness—as those in the Romish faith are said to ask it of their priests, then I could not grant it, for such power had not been given me. Yet the innkeeper was asking for much less, was he not? He wanted only my understanding, and that much I could certainly offer him.

"Yes," said I, "I do understand."

Then did he look me in the eye for the first time since he had beckoned me over. And quite at a loss for something more to say, he simply nodded.

Outside, I saw that there was light in the east and realized I had labored in a good cause the whole night through.

I wondered at the sense of exhilaration which I felt. Whence came it? It had been near twenty-four hours since last I slept—or perhaps even longer. Why was I not tired, exhausted by all I had seen and done? How long could I thus continue as fresh as I might feel had I just rolled out of bed? Though day was breaking, there was yet no one to be seen upon the street. So, since there was neither man nor woman to be seen upon High Street, I gave full rein to these exuberant feelings and began running down the street, my footsteps clattering down upon the cobblestones, my reflection appearing and disappearing in the windows of the finest shops in Deal. Then did I turn down King and up Middle Street. And of a sudden came the feeling that something was terribly wrong. Nay, it was more than a feeling, but rather an awful, frightening certitude. I slowed to a fast walk that I might hear better. And what was there to hear? Naught in that first hour of daylight but a woman's voice, moaning and softly wailing. I went directly to Number 18, for there was not the slightest doubt but that these sad sounds did come from there. What I saw would be enough to rend any stout heart in two.

The door to the house was wide open, yet the space was filled by the body of Albert Sarton—plainly he was dead. Kneeling above and hugging his inert form to her as best she could was Molly Sarton; she sighed and sobbed in a manner so resigned that it seemed she might never stop. Sir John bent over her, his hands upon her shoulders. Supporting her? Certainly. Attempting to draw her away? Perhaps. I approached them slowly and uncertainly, oddly unwilling to let them know of my presence. It came to me then that, quite unexpectedly, I felt quite tired—truly exhausted.

SEVEN

In which I see
Sir John in full fury
for the first time

For the most part, during the years I had known him, Sir John Fielding had been a man of placid disposition. Oh, he had bad days, of course, as any man will. He could grow cross or tetchy, or occasionally take offense when none was intended. Nevertheless, I insist that for a man of his position and time he was remarkably even-tempered.

The only true exception I must make to this is that period in Deal, of which I now shall write. From the time of Mr. Sarton's murder until our departure from the town, Sir John seemed to be in a state of extreme anger. Even in his relations with Molly Sarton, the widow, which were of the most kind and cordial nature, there seemed some part of him beneath the surface which seethed with rage. It was as if he had on his mind one matter and one alone. He would break long silences with remarks such as this: "An attack upon an officer of the court, even one so lowly as an ordinary magistrate, is an attack upon the law itself, which is the very structure which supports our society." (I recall that being said in the course of the long coach ride from Gravesend, of which you will hear anon.) And he spent more than one sleepless night ruminating at length and aloud upon the perfidy of the ordinary people of Deal, that they would happily tolerate the smuggling trade and its attendant crimes so long as they shared materially in its benefits. Or, another favorite topic during these nocturnal rants: the evil of our immoral age, in which human life was given so little respect and taken with so little regard. "Was it always so?" he would say. Then would he answer, "Yes, alas, it was always so."

He would boil over. He would fulminate. And in between such eruptions and explosions, he brooded furiously. His only remedy was work. It was by doing what had to be done—and more—that he managed to maintain some degree of equanimity. And only when, through cunning and clever planning, his work succeeded did he become, in some sense, his old self.

Putting aside the matter of comforting the widow, who was so utterly distraught that I thought for a moment she might never regain her composure, there was much of a practical nature which should be attended to by me. Sir John managed to persuade her to come away from the corpus so that I might move it and close the door.

"Go to the kitchen," said he to her. "I'll join you there as soon as I am able. Please, Mrs. Sarton, it is the only way under the circumstances. You must see that, do you not?"

Reluctantly she rose and—in a voice husky with tears—managed an affirmative reply of some sort. Then, even more reluctantly, she started down the long hall. Unable to turn her back upon the dead body of her husband, she kept turning round as she went, as if to convince herself that what she had seen were really so—and yet hoping it were not.

Soon she was out of earshot. Sir John turned to me then, his face contorted by extreme emotion. Feeling for my hand, he found it, and squeezed it with such strength I near cried out in surprise.

"Now, Jeremy, you must describe to me the condition of the body whilst still it lies as it fell."

That I did, beginning with its position, which was much further out upon the doorstep than I would have expected, face down, bent at the knees, with arms outstretched. Had he meant to attack his killer?

"His hands are empty?" asked Sir John. "He has no weapon?"

"No," said I, "no weapon of any sort."

"Look about the body to be sure."

I did as he told me. "No, nothing."

"How is he dressed? For bed?"

"Oh, no, he's dressed as he was when last I saw him— when we brought by our prisoners and informed him of the success of our operation." Only then did I remember what I had come to tell. "But Sir John, I came to inform you of the terrible—"

"*Later,*" he snapped. "I must concentrate upon this poor fellow now. What would you say? Is he dressed for the street?"

Somewhat chastened by his reproving tone, I lowered my voice. "No, sir. He is in waistcoat and shirtsleeves."

"I take it there is a candle burning in the small room to our right?"

"There is, yes."

"You have been in that room a number of times," said he to me. "Tell me, is it possible to see who is at the door from inside it?"

"No, it would probably not be possible—from the window behind the desk—unless the visitor wished to be seen."

"*Ha!*" He let forth a single ironic cackle. "In this case, Jeremy, we may rest assured that his visitor wished it so."

That confused me a bit. "But *why* should he wish to be seen?"

"Never mind that. Look now at his wound. Turn him over, if need be."

The exit wound was so large that one might claim, without too much exaggeration, that Mr. Sarton had had the back of his head blown off. What more could the entry wound tell us? Nevertheless, I turned the body over—and got quite a surprise. I must have exclaimed involuntarily at what I had seen.

"What is it?" demanded Sir John.

"Well," said I, "the ball entered approximately where one would expect, right between, and just above, the eyes. But . . ."

"Yes? Go on."

"I've never seen a wound so sooted with gunpowder. His whole face has been blackened."

"There! You see?"

"No, quite frankly, sir, I don't."

"Well, it should be evident. I can give you the last minute or so of Albert Sarton's life from what you've told me. He was sitting at the desk in the room, working by candlelight. I daresay that if you were to look at the desk you would find a book open, or some sentence left unfinished, to prove that he had been interrupted. What then? He hears a tapping upon the window behind him. Would he then have opened the drapes to see who it was at the window? Not likely, from what we have earlier seen of him and his elaborate identification of all callers who come to the door. No, something was said by his visitor through the window glass—something that gave him reassurance that it would be all right to open the drapes. When he did, he was reas-

sured further by the sight of his visitor that it would be safe
to open his door to him, which was evidently what had
been requested. He then went to the door and opened it
without the usual request for identification. There was no
need of it. After all, he knew who was out there, didn't he?
As soon as the door came open, the pistol was put close to
his head, the trigger was pulled, and along with the ball
which passed through his brain, an inordinate amount of
black powder was discharged upon his face. Thus is it
proven that Mr. Sarton not only knew his visitor, he also
trusted him sufficiently to throw his door open to him without further ado. And this restricts the number of possible
suspects considerably."

Put thus, it did seem evident, truly enough. There was
yet a detail or two that troubled me. I decided to challenge
Sir John on at least one of them.

"Sir," said I, "would not the opening of the drapes have
provided the visitor with all the opportunity he would
need? Could he not have shot through the glass?"

Taking a moment to consider the point, he rubbed his
chin thoughtfully. "Yes, why didn't he?" said he. "It could
be simply that Mr. Sarton did not present as sure a target
this side the window. For after all, his first impulse upon
catching sight of a pistol would be to let fall the drapes and
duck back away from the window."

"I can see that," said I. "The visitor felt he had to have a
sure shot, for recognition during an unsuccessful attempt at
murder would have been simply disastrous."

"Yes, well . . . but what about this? Let us suppose that
there was not one visitor but two. The first we have discussed, one who would instill such confidence in Mr. Sarton that he would throw open the door without hesitation,
and the second to do the shooting. Why a second? Perhaps
because he is used to such ugly work—a practiced killer.
And perhaps because the visitor, the man whom Mr. Sarton

recognized, was himself too fastidious to commit such an act."

When Sir John had completed his study of the corpus and its surroundings, I informed him of the disastrous events that had taken place at the inn. I feared my news might crush him altogether, yet he took it quite stoically, as if so much had already gone so terribly wrong, that further calamities were of no real consequence and almost to be expected. Ultimately, the story of the unexpected failure of our operation against the smugglers, and the loss of the cargo, as well as the constable's death, did naught but provide more fuel for his anger.

I concluded my report by confessing that I had more or less volunteered Clarissa for duty as nurse to Constable Trotter. He took it well and seemed to approve this new role for her.

"Just so long as it does not involve her for too great a time. Another must be found to help. Clarissa will be needed to act as companion to Mrs. Sarton, for the two get on well. She can help the poor woman through this crisis."

"She will stay here, then?" I asked.

"We shall all stay here. This will be our new headquarters, if Mrs. Sarton will have us. I shall be particularly glad to have Clarissa out of that environment. Imagine locking a girl of her age in her room! On whose orders, I should like to know! And to what purpose?"

"What then with our baggage, Sir John?"

"Collect it all," said he. "Perhaps it might be best if you were to find that coachman, Mick . . . Mick Crawly is his name, I believe. He'll take you up there. You can collect the baggage. Crawly will load it on the coach, then take you and Clarissa back to town."

"Very good, sir, I'll attend to that immediately."

"No, I rather think that first we had better move Mr. Sarton's body as best we can. Then you must call at the surgeon's and ask him to come by. I have questions about the wound in Mr. Sarton's head and the condition of the body that only he can answer. And lastly, you must visit the mortician and ask him to come at the end of the day to collect Mr. Sarton's body and prepare it for burial." Having said all that, he sighed, as if unwilling to continue. But, having sighed, he filled his lungs again, straightened his shoulders and suggested that we move the corpus. "I may be blind," said he, "but if you take the lead, I should be able to follow."

"No, you'll do no such thing." It was the unexpected voice of Molly Sarton, loudly preceding her as she came down the hall from the kitchen, her arms filled with rags and a pillow. She was much changed from the weeping widow I had seen kneeling over her husband. Clearly, she had got herself under control and was now determined to play her part in these sad, postmortem events. "He was my husband, after all," said she, "and the least I can do for him is see that he's given a proper burial. So you take him under the arms, Jeremy, and I'll take his feet, and we'll bring him into the big room here, and lay him onto the sofa."

She nudged Sir John aside and tossed the pillow and rags down upon the middle of her husband's body.

"Take a cloth or two and wrap it round his head," said she, "for if you don't, you'll have blood and brains all over that fine green coat of yours. I'd do it for you, but . . . but I can't. In truth, I just can't."

I did as she directed, wrapping his head tight in the rags, using a third and then a fourth, until there were no spots of blood leaking through the layers of cloth. I could not but notice that all the time that I was thus occupied, she kept her gaze averted.

When the task was done, she asked if I were ready. I nodded, and she lifted his feet by the heels. I heaved him up by the armpits and wondered at how heavy he seemed for such a small man. Then did I recall the phrase "dead weight," and understood its origin and true meaning. We had not far to carry him, and indeed could not have carried him much farther. As I passed Sir John, he put his hand lightly upon my shoulder and in this way followed close behind me into the room, which they had ever used as a courtroom. Mrs. Sarton placed his feet upon the sofa, and I followed, situating his body in such a way that it rested easily upon the length of the piece.

"You had best tuck the pillow beneath his head," said she to me, "for the wound will likely leak further."

Again I did as she told me, without question or comment. Sir John, who like me had said nothing since her sudden appearance, at last cleared his throat and made to speak.

"Your resolution is admirable, madame," said he, "but would it not be better if you were to take a rest? You have had a terrible shock. You ought not strain yourself overmuch in such a situation."

"I thank you for your advice, Sir John, and though I know it be well meant, I'll not take it."

She looked down at her husband's body there upon the sofa. With his head wrapped as it was, his face was barely visible, and what could be seen of it was so blackened by the pistol·shot that the features were hardly discernible.

"Dear God, I did love that man," she continued, "but there is naught I can do to return him to life, and so I must get on with my own. I'll bury him well, and in my heart I'll mourn him." At this point I remember well that she sighed and shook her head before concluding: "But I can't bring him back."

"True enough," said Sir John, "but do you not suppose that—"

"In this alone I'll have the last word. 'Tis I will summon the surgeon and notify the mortician. These be matters which have to do with putting Berty safe underground. Let Jeremy go now and collect your baggage and return with

Clarissa, as well. I'll be happy to have you all here—and Clarissa not least."

In this way it came about that I rode in the place beside Mick Crawly on my way out to Great Mongeham and the manor house of Sir Simon Grenville. I liked the man and his ready manner well enough, but his curiosity threatened to become an impediment to good relations between us. It seemed that he had learned something of the hectic and deadly events of the night before, and he wished to learn more. I guessed that the innkeeper was the source of his information. That meant that in little more than an hour, news of our victory-turned-defeat had spread across half the town. This in itself was not surprising when one considered the extent to which Deal depended upon smuggling as its leading local industry. No doubt it would take no more than another hour for the whole of the sad story to be spread cross the rest of the town. Yet if he were to learn more, it would not be from me.

We bounced along at a good rate of speed out the Dover Road and then up the hill. The horses were fresh and well fed and full of life, so that Mick Crawly had all he could do to hold them down to a trot. Nevertheless, that did not stop him from hinting broadly, giving a wink or two, and putting forward a few indirect queries. He would shoot me a glance, smile, then come forth with a question so innocently framed that one could in no wise object to it.

As an instance, he asked, "Heard you fellas had a bit of trouble last night. Anyone hurt?"

Then I, thinking to give him as little information as possible without actually lying, said: "There were casualties on both sides."

"Ah, no doubt there were," said he. He could not fault me for my ready response, and that did, in a sense, end discussion.

Yet there were two or three more attempts by him to

draw information from me—or so it seemed to me. The most obvious was surely his rather direct inquiry: "You people going to stay around here much longer?" (This, by the bye, was delivered with a wink.)

My reply: "A bit longer, I should think."

That ended it between us, for by the time it was asked, and my answer given, we were trailing up the driveway to the manor house, just passing the point where Will Fowler had been forced to pull his team to a swift stop, when a man bolted from the trees to our left, waving his arms and frightening the horses.

But then we were past it, pulling up to the entrance to the great house, looking to the door from which Mr. Fowler himself emerged to welcome us. I instructed Mr. Crawly to wait where we were. There would be baggage to bring down to him, and a passenger to take back to town—as well as myself, of course. He nodded his understanding, and I climbed down from my perch, happy to receive Mr. Fowler's friendly greeting. Though there was no speech of welcome, as he had given when first we arrived, he did seem truly glad to see me. His smile did fade, however, when I asked after Clarissa.

"How is she?" I asked. "I'm moving her into town. We'll be located a bit more conveniently there for our further inquiries."

"Ah yes, of course," said Mr. Fowler, "and perhaps it's just as well. Clarissa, poor girl, has had a bad night of it, I fear."

"Oh? What sort of bad night?"

"Truth to tell, it was all bad dreams. She believes she saw the ghost—*our* ghost, you know—and then it seems she took off on a sleepwalking adventure."

"Truly so?" I asked. "That doesn't sound like her at all."

I found Clarissa ready to pack. She had no wish to remain another night in the manor house, but would say nothing of what she had endured until we were underway.

When I told her of all that had happened—the battle on the beach, the deadlier battle at the inn, and the murder of Mr. Sarton—she was quite overcome by the drama of it all. Most of all, she declared, her heart quite ached for Molly Sarton.

"I'll be happy to do what I can for Constable Trotter," said she, "and I'm ever so flattered that you thought I should be the one to minister to him, but my proper place is with dear Molly. She needs me, I know."

Then did Mr. Fowler appear at Clarissa's door and volunteer to bring her portmanteau down to the hackney coach. As he hauled it away, we two crossed the hall and hurriedly packed Sir John's portmanteau and my valise. It seemed but a minute or two before he had returned and taken them down as well. We followed him and watched Mick Crawly securing the baggage at the top of the coach. Mr. Fowler nodded his approval as the coachman completed the job.

"All ready?" I called up to Crawly.

"Whenever you are," said he.

"Then let us be off." We hopped inside, waved goodbye to Will Fowler, and were thumped back in our seats as the team sprang forward at Mick Crawly's urging. Then did Clarissa turn to me with a frown and a shake of her head. What could they mean?

"I feel sorry for him," said she, as if that would explain all.

"Feel sorry for whom?" said I.

"For Mr. Fowler. I don't believe that he's like the rest of them."

"What rest of them? What do you mean?"

"Why, the rest of the servants," said she rather airily. "It could not have escaped even *your* notice that things are not near as they should be hereabouts."

"Of course not. A man was murdered just a few nights ago."

"Well, that's . . . that's certainly a sure sign that something's wrong. But apart from that—perhaps I should say, *along* with that—there are so many things that are not as they should be—well, you take last night, for example."

"All right, indeed, what about last night?"

Yet she evaded me still: "What did Mr. Fowler say about it?"

"He said that you'd had bad dreams, that you'd seen the house ghost, and gone sleepwalking."

"He must have been told to say that."

"Not true?"

"Oh, a little of it, I suppose. For instance, I did say that the entire experience was *like* a bad dream. I didn't say I'd *had* a bad dream."

"And the ghost?"

"That? Well, that was the silliest of all. He wouldn't have fooled anyone."

"Perhaps you'd better start at the beginning."

"All right, I'll try."

(And try she did. She had, in fact, improved her storytelling so much since last time that I have simply quoted her entire as best I can from memory. There were few, if any, deviations from the narrative line, and no digressions to tempt her away from the course of the tale she had set out to tell. A few of her comments seemed then, and seem yet today, to be quite pertinent, and therefore I shall quote them entire.)

"I was wakened at a time which seemed to me well past midnight. A great hurly-burly had disturbed me, the sound of men and horses and barking dogs. I jumped from my bed to see what it was had caused such a commotion. I looked out just in time to see a troop of men of no small number ride off at a gallop in the direction of Deal. At their head was Sir Simon Grenville, of whom I had seen very little in the past few days.

"What then? Well, I was awake, wasn't I? So I put a

wrapper round me and found me my slippers. Then, very quietly, did I unlock the door to the hall and step out of my room. In a big house, such as that one, it's seldom that you have the feeling that it is empty. But this was one of those times. There were no sounds from belowstairs; the dogs barked no more; even the big clock near the door ticked muffled time.

"And so I saw this as an opportunity to go exploring. It seemed to me that I had not been completely on my own— which is to say, unsupervised—since the day after our arrival, when I had discovered a dead man. Did I wish to find another? No, but I had an overwhelming desire to see what was in that chalk mine. Yet first, I told myself, there were corners of this huge house I had not yet explored, rooms whose doors I had not opened.

"In this way I did begin, driven by curiosity, which is in so many of us a great incentive to action. I opened doors up and down the upstairs hall. Most of these led into closets of one kind or another and were altogether disappointing. There were additional guest bedrooms which were, of course, empty; and at the far end of the hall, beyond the great stairway, were the bedrooms of Sir Simon and his dame. They stood across the hall each from the other and must indeed have been very large. As it happened, however, I never managed to find out. The reason for this remained vague in my mind; in any case *how* it came to be was uncertain."

(If this seems confusing to you, reader, so does it also still to me.)

"I remember that I was crossing the great open space at the top of the stairway," said she, "when of a sudden my attention was drawn down the wide stairs to the ground floor—by a noise of some sort, probably. Since it was the absence of noise in the house that had drawn me out of my room, a noise of the wrong sort might well send me scurrying back into it. I had no wish to be caught out. And so I stood quite still and waited, listening and staring down into the dark. I must have stood so for well over a minute, more likely two or three—for a very long time, anyway—until I was at last satisfied that I might go on. During that long wait, I had decided that I should just take a peek inside the two rooms and then be out the front door and up the hill to the chalk mine. That was what I wished to investigate; there was some purpose in that; what I had been up to until then was nosiness, pure and simple. Yet when I turned back to proceed toward the far end of the hall, I saw something I'm still a bit uncertain as to what it was—though I've a good idea.

"It was at the farthest end of the hall—just movement at first, but then it seemed to come closer, for it seemed to take shape before my eyes. How would I describe it? Well, it was a man, right enough, but he was dressed very odd. He wore great baggy trousers and big boots, and upon his head was a round hat with a wide brim. Taken in total, he looked like one who had stepped right out of the last century. There was the brimstone smell, too: that of sulphur, which gives a proper stink. It was the Grenville Ghost, right down to the last detail—and that made me suspicious. It was all a bit too perfect—or so it seemed to me—and there was one other matter which did not quite tally: the ghost looked a bit too much like Will Fowler—same general appearance, and in the face, well, in spite of the awful chalky paint he wore, I saw Will Fowler's features. I believe he had dressed up in that outlandish garb just to frighten me back into my room. And so what did I do? I ran—but not back into my room—oh, no. I ran fast as I could down the stairs and out the door. I would not be kept any longer from that chalk mine!

"Circling the house, I passed the stable, which was so quiet that I was quite certain that every horse in it had been saddled and ridden out in company with Sir Simon. From there, I found my way to the garden and the garden path, which led upward to the chalk mine. I shivered a bit as I worked my way up the path; nor was that surprising, for the wrapper I wore was never intended to keep me warm in the cold night air, and it covered naught but a cotton nightgown. As I approached the out-buildings, I slowed and attempted to walk as soft as my slippers allowed. What I had seen of the rough sort of men who lived in them was enough to tell me that I wanted nothing to do with them. Yet I continued to climb the path, even as it penetrated the wooded area above the out-buildings. There it became deep dark and most frightening to me. Were it not for the abundance of chalk that filled the path and caught the light of the moon, I might have lost my way entirely. Still, I did not, and as I continued, I saw ahead of me a flickering light of no great intensity, which drew me on. As I drew closer, I saw that it marked the entrance to the mine. There was no candle placed in front to give to all a warning. But just within the tunnel which led into the hill of chalk, a candleholder had been placed and a candle burned brightly. To my eye it seemed to have about an hour left upon it. I proceeded cautiously, listening at every step for any sound that might carry with it the threat of discovery.

"Perhaps I listened too carefully and did not watch close enough. In any case, I moved ahead with my attention upon the night sounds about me and my eyes fixed upon the entrance to the mine just across an open space about two rods wide. Therefore was I most astonished when, from my right, a dark-dressed figure leapt from behind a tree and grasped me by my shoulders and head. At first I thought I had been attacked by a wild animal of some sort—and at that I let out as loud a scream as ever I have screamed. Then a hand covered my mouth—and in a way I was glad of that, for it was a hand after all, and not a paw. What was I to do? Whoever it was who held me was much stronger than I was. I had only to struggle a bit to be certain of that.

And so I attempted a clever maneuver that is very popular with all the ladies in the romances: I fainted.

"I've no idea how long I was unconscious, nor in all truth just how unconscious I was. Though I saw nothing, I was vaguely aware of voices—male voices—and a strange smell that seemed to permeate the air round me. It was a most remarkable smell: sweet and heavy, as a whole wagonload of flowers. I could still smell it when I became conscious."

"And where was that? Where did you become conscious?" I asked, interrupting her story for the first time. "Were you in the tunnel? What did you see?"

"Oh no, not in the tunnel, not in the mine—though I had the feeling I had been there." She sighed. "I'm afraid I did not come to myself until Will Fowler had me halfway to the house."

"He was carrying you?"

"Well . . . yes. You did that once, or don't you remember?"

"But you were younger then."

"And so were you." She was about to say more but held her tongue, looked at me queerly, and returned to the subject at hand: "He's quite strong, you know. Will Fowler, that is. Nevertheless, I insisted that he put me down."

"That's good," said I.

"I assured him that I was quite capable of walking on my own two feet. He seemed to doubt me, but I assured him it was so, and reluctantly he let me try my feet on the path. It was odd, though. I wasn't near as steady as I expected. I seemed to need his support all the way to the house."

"Oh, you did, did you?"

"Which was rather annoying, after all—though not near as annoying as hearing from him that I'd been sleepwalking, and that he'd found me collapsed upon the garden path. That *he* should tell me that! He, who had dressed as the Grenville Ghost and tried to frighten me back into my room!"

"Think now," said I, "did he wear still any bits of the ghost's costume? Did you detect any of that white paint he wore upon his face?"

She gave but a moment's thought to it and decided he had not. "No," said she, "I would have noticed those baggy trousers and those floppy boots, right enough. And as for that chalky stuff he wore upon his face, it would surely have glowed still as it did in the house. He managed to change his costume and wipe his face before he rescued me."

"Rescued you? Do you feel you were in any real danger?"

"Why, how am I to know the intentions of that ill-mannered man who jumped out at me from behind that tree?"

"Mr. Fowler must've changed his clothing very quickly."

"Hmmm. Yes," said she, "he must've."

"Or you must've been unconscious far longer than you seem to think."

"I see what you mean." She hesitated. "Yes, well, I must think about that."

And so saying, she lapsed into silence.

Even with Clarissa's tale-telling and the talk between us that followed, it seemed that we had only just reached the outskirts of Deal. Having then little upon which to concentrate my attention, I promptly fell asleep. And why not? By my own reckoning, never had so much happened in so short a space of time—not to me, in any case, nor even to those round me.

I did not wake till given a gentle shake by Mick Crawly.

"We're here, lad," said he. "Right here in Middle Street—Number Eighteen."

I blinked my eyes and saw that Clarissa was no longer in the coach.

"Where did she go?" I asked.

"The young miss? She had me let her off at the inn—the Good King George in High Street. She said you'd be going on to this address in Middle Street. Did I get it right? This is where I picked you up the other night, an't it?"

I nodded and struggled from my seat and out the door of the coach which he held for me. Then, sighing, coughing, still only half awake, I managed to count out the trifling sum he requested and included a bit extra for an ale or two. Then did I look up at the door and see our baggage had been set out upon the doorstep and added another copper to his payment, for which he thanked me.

"I'll be ready to serve you just anytime," said Mr. Crawly. "You know where to find me. And I won't ask so many questions next time."

With that, he bobbed his head, gave me a wink, and climbed back upon the driver's seat. Then, with a wave to me and a crack of his whip, he set his team of horses off down the street.

I knocked hard upon the door, unsure who would come to answer. I was prepared to wait a bit, if wait I must. Still only half awake, I wanted little more than to get back to sleep. For a moment, I seriously considered sitting down upon the doorstep, leaning against the fattest of the portmanteaus, and continuing my doze right there. Yet I was surprised to hear a quick response to my knock—sharp footsteps coming down the long hall—a woman's step if I was not mistaken, though not Mrs. Sarton's. The door opened, and I was face to face with Mrs. Keen, proprietor and chief pastry baker at the tearoom in High Street.

"Ah," she said, "it's you. And where's your young friend?"

"Off nursing our wounded constable. And how is Molly Sarton holding up?"

Mrs. Keen shook her head and shivered in a gesture

which seemed to express both sympathy and revulsion at the same time.

"The poor woman," said she, "as if she hadn't suffered enough! And the two of them so much in love! But she's braving it through. Just asked me to come by to mind the house and"—she lowered her voice to a whisper—"help the blind man. She said you'd be coming by soon."

"I fetched our baggage from the Grenville house," said I.

"Come along then, let's get it inside, shall we?"

And she wasted no time in grabbing the fattest portmanteau and hauling it inside. I took my valise and the remaining portmanteau (Clarissa's) in hand and wrestled them through the door, then kicked the door shut behind me.

"Jeremy? Is that you?" Sir John's voice came from the small room just inside the door—Mr. Sarton's study.

"It is, sir."

"Come see me here when you've done moving the bags up to the bedrooms, will you?"

"I will, sir."

Then down the long hall and up the stairs, pushing the valise ahead and pulling the portmanteau behind. Mrs. Keen had preceded me and deposited Sir John's big bag in the guest bedroom, where he had been napping. I put my valise inside and looked longingly at the bed—but that, it seemed, would have to wait. By this time, Clarissa's bag had been tucked inside the master bedroom.

As we two descended the stairs, it occurred to me to ask after her tearoom: "Who's minding your shop, Mrs. Keen?"

"No one," said she. "I put a notice in the window which said that due to a death in the family, the tearoom would be closed for the day. Molly may not be family, strictly speaking, but she's all the family I've got. She'll have so much to do today—too much. Believe me, I know. I went through it all when my Neddy died."

"Well, with your permission, mum, I'll leave you now and find out what Sir John has to tell me."

"Oh well, go, surely. But when you're done, come back to the kitchen, and I'll have something for you."

We did then part company, and I started down the hall. I remembered as I went that Mrs. Sarton—Molly—had first mentioned Mrs. Keen to us as a "widow lady," and I wondered when it was her Neddy had died—and how. I had no idea how I might find out. Yet perhaps it might be best not to know. I had the uneasy feeling that if I were to inquire, I would discover that his was another life in the smuggling trade which ended violently.

When I entered the little room just inside the door, Sir John turned in my direction and bade me take a seat. He himself had chosen the place behind the desk where Albert Sarton had sat his last. Others would not have picked it— would have supposed it the unluckiest of places. Sir John, however, had never shown himself to be in the least superstitious, so far as I knew. He did not seem to believe in luck, neither good nor bad.

"I have had a report of bodies found upon the beach," said he. "From what was told me, it seemed to be the very same beach on which you apprehended the smugglers. I took it that none were killed in the course of your battle with them?"

"No sir, none killed. Only one man—one of theirs—was even wounded."

"Well then, it seems that we have three new murders to account for. The man who came with the news was a crusty old fisherman. He would have naught to do with me at first, for he insisted on telling 'the young magistrate' about it and only him. I finally managed to convince him that Mr. Sarton was indisposed, that a doctor would be coming soon to visit him—a surgeon, in any case—and that I was handling matters for him temporarily. Though he was not comfortable with it, he gave in at last and said that there were bodies out there on the beach. He said they looked familiar, but he couldn't put a name on any of them. He promised to wait a bit. Will you go, Jeremy? I know you must be tired, but . . ."

I sighed. "Certainly, Sir John."

"Good lad," said he. "I'd go with you, but I feel I must wait here for the surgeon." He screwed his face in annoyance. "He should have been here by now."

At least when I departed the house this time, my coat pocket was well filled with sweet cakes. I know not how many Mrs. Keen had given me, for I did not bother to count as I ate them, but I do know that they brought me strength when I feared that my store was near exhausted.

It was full daylight by the time I reached the beach. Just as before, I saw the ghostly masts which rose from the water well before I saw the beach proper. Then at last I stood on the bluff and looked down upon the wide strip of sand whereon we had fought our battle less than twelve hours before. From that vantage I saw that all the boats that had last night been pulled up on the beach were now gone—all but one. That one, now near the waterline, was being loaded for departure, lines, nets, oars, bait. He who did the loading was a short man of over fifty years; he worked with a kind of plodding efficiency, evidently determined to be off soon.

He would not be detained much longer, and so I hurried down to him, kicking sand as I went. Looking up suspiciously as I approached, he then returned to his methodical preparations.

"You reported three bodies here upon the beach?" I asked. "I've come to view them."

"The blind man said he'd send a constable. Are you a constable?" He seemed dubious.

"Closest thing to it."

"What's that mean? That you'll be a constable just as soon as you grow up?"

"No, it means that I'm close enough to a constable to be a pain in the arse to you if you do not choose to cooperate." I kept my eyes steady upon his.

"Oh, it's that way, is it?" Then did he surprise me by bursting into laughter—and a booming laugh it was for one of modest size. "So? You got some sand in you, do you? Well, I like a lad who'll show some pluck," said he. "So indeed I'll tell you all I know, which an't much. When I come down to start my day, all the fisher lads was up there"—he pointed up the bluff—"lookin' at something. So naturally, I goes up and takes a look, too, and I see it's three dead men—each one with a bullet through the brain. 'What's this?' says I to the fisher lads. 'What's it look like?' says they to me. Then one of them says he heard shooting and even a big boom like a cannon last night, and these three dead ones must be the result of it all. Then says I, 'Somebody ought to go up and tell the magistrate.' Then they come back at me, sayin', 'If you think that, then you're the one should go.' So I went and told the blind man, and when I got back, the fisher lads was all gone. I've been beat out to the shoals where the herring swim for my good deed. Satisfied?"

"That all you've got to tell?"

He began pushing his boat out toward the water. "That's all."

"Could you point out where to look for the three bodies?"

"Up there." Standing and pointing. "See? Just this side of that bushy, grassy place, you can see a leg sticking out."

The place he pointed out was the very same spot whereat Mr. Perkins and I had spent hours of last night waiting for the smugglers to appear.

"Oh yes," said the fisherman, turning back to me, "there was one more thing."

"And what was that?"

"Those dead men up there, I never knew them, but I saw one of them about town. One of the fisher lads seemed to know who they were, though. He said they were in the owling trade."

Having said it, he pushed the boat out into the sea, and with a quick, spry movement, he jumped inside it. He was then far too busy with the oars to bother further with me.

I turned round and started up the sand bluff. As I climbed, it occurred to me that I should have asked the fisherman the name of him who knew the three up ahead as smugglers. Would I ever learn?

As I came upon them, the three seemed to me to lay together where they had fallen. There was no sign that they had been moved. And though there were footprints aplenty in the soft dry sand, they were not the sort that would give a distinct and separate trace. It did appear, however, that a good many men had left the site, as many as ten—though there was no way to be exact.

I bent down and examined the bodies more closely. Immediately I saw that the wounds each had received were quite like the one which had felled Mr. Sarton. Judging from their size, they might well have been inflicted by the same weapon, or at least three weapons of the same bore and weight. The wounds were also placed similarly—that is, between and just above the eyes. And the faces of all three men had been blackened by the discharge of powder. All this was enough to tell me that the murder in Middle Street had likely been committed by the same man—or by one of the same men.

I grasped the cold hand of one of the victims and moved his arm, feeling no resistance or rigidity. What Mr. Donnelly named "*rigor mortis*" (Latin, I was certain) had not taken over the limbs of the corpus. I repeated this with the other two and had the same result—as expected. But I happened to look more closely at the face of the third, and I noted that there was something familiar about it. What was it? Where had I seen him before? The identity of this man did, of a sudden, take possession of me. The question of *who* he might be took on great urgency.

I went so far as to whip out my kerchief, which was reasonably clean, run down to the waterline with it, and dip it. I ran back, holding it, dripping water all the way. Then, returned, I rubbed at his face with the wet linen, removing the layer of gun-soot from it, rubbing it until at last it shone clean enough there in the morning sun. And who should appear before my eyes but Samson Strong, who had testified in his own defense and that of his fellows regarding their misadventure with Mr. Perkins. And these other two—could they be those who had appeared with him before the Deal magistrate? Indeed they could, though I had not seen them well enough from where I sat to be sure of it. What had these three done to deserve such a punishment?

EIGHT

*In which I journey
to London and
voyage back by ship*

Upon returning to Sir John, I gave my report and offered to notify the mortician that the bodies on
the beach might be collected and prepared for burial. Yet he
declined, saying that the surgeon, who had been to the
house in Middle Street and gone, had volunteered to attend
to it. Sir John ordered me to bed in the guestroom above.
Never did I obey an order of his with greater pleasure. So
great was my pleasure, indeed, that I came near to sleeping
the clock round—and perhaps I would have done just that,
had I not been wakened early in the morning by Clarissa,
who informed me that I must arise and catch the first coach
to London.

"To London?" said I, all surprised. "Are we to leave with
so much unresolved?"

"Not *we*," said she, "but *you*. You are to carry and deliver a number of letters there."

"What sort of letters? To whom?"

"Sir John will explain all as soon as he wakes."

"Wakes? Where did he sleep?"

"Why, with you, part of the night. Have you no memory of it? Just now he is dozing at the desk in that little room by the front door."

I grunted in response, rubbing my eyes, seeking full wakefulness.

"Come, Jeremy, you must get up," said she. "Mrs. Sarton is fixing a fine breakfast for you."

That was all the encouragement that I required. I ordered Clarissa from my room and leapt into my clothes. Indeed I was hungry, and who would not be after so long a sleep? Now that I was awake, my empty stomach sent up urgent messages that might only be satisfied by a considerable meal.

And that, reader, was what was given me. Mrs. Sarton was clearly determined to carry on, making herself useful, in spite of her evident sadness. To see her thus, so unlike the Molly Sarton we had come to know, was indeed disappointing; nevertheless, though it was true she did not smile, it was also true that except for those first minutes when she wept inconsolably over her fallen husband, I did not see her shed another tear all the time we were in Deal. And in that time she saw to her husband's burial, buried him, attended to certain matters for Sir John, and cooked for a small army. She was equal to all that was asked of her.

I shall not specify all that she put before me at that noble breakfast, for truth to tell, I do not remember. Let it suffice to say that I ate well and hearty enough to last me through a day of hard traveling. At the end of it, whilst I was lingering over my cup of tea, Clarissa came down the long hall to the kitchen and summoned me to a meeting with Sir John.

"Is it so near time to go?" I asked her.

"Soon," said she, "but Sir John would have a word with you first."

I nodded, rose, and followed her back down the hall. I noted—for the first time, I believe—that Clarissa's hips had grown (how shall I put it?) more substantial, more shapely, since last I looked. I thought that odd. Was this gawky girl becoming a woman?

As I entered the room, I expected Clarissa to accompany me. But no, she hung back at the door that she might call to Sir John to send me off in a few minutes' time.

Sir John pushed three letters cross the desk to me.

"Jeremy," said he, "these letters are important, among the most important I've ever asked you to deliver." He hesitated. "Are you armed?"

"Well . . . yes sir, I kept one of the pistols issued to me. It's tucked away in the pocket of my coat."

"Loaded?"

"Yes sir."

"It goes without saying that you're certainly not to use it, or even brandish it, except in the most extreme situation. What that should be, I leave to you."

"I understand, Sir John."

"Since these letters were dictated last night to Clarissa and are now sealed, I'll give you some idea of their contents. The first is to Lord Mansfield, the Lord Chief Justice. In it, I have asked him for temporary powers here in Deal. I shall be, in effect, the magistrate of Deal for a period not to exceed a month. This should be delivered direct into his hands, and the proper document should be given you to carry away. Find him, no matter where he may be. Do you understand?"

"I do."

"Very well. The other two letters are no less important, but they depend upon the powers to be granted me by Lord Mansfield, and so they are to be delivered after you have the document of appointment in your pocket. They are, in effect, invitations to Mr. John Bilbo and to constables Bailey and Patley to join us in Gravesend."

"Ah well, that should be pleasant," said I, not knowing quite what else to say—though why we should be going to Gravesend I could not surmise. "Seeing them all again, that is."

"For us, perhaps," Sir John replied sharply.

I knew not how I had offended. "Yes sir, will that be all, sir?"

He sighed deeply. "It should be. If all goes well, I should see you again in three days."

"So soon?"

"Just so."

"Sir John?" It was Clarissa, calling in from the hall. "He must leave now."

I stood and gathered up the letters from the top of the desk; then did I tuck them away safely in my coat pocket.

"Well then, sir, goodbye to you," said I to him.

"And Godspeed to you, Jeremy."

His face sagged. He looked quite exhausted. I wondered how much—or how little—he had slept. Yet I had not time to think long upon it, for well I knew that if I were to miss the coach to London, it would extend my absence for another full day.

Out in the hall, at the front door, I found Clarissa waiting for me. To my surprise, she held my valise in her hand.

"I packed your bag for you—two clean shirts and two pair of hose and two books."

"Two books?"

"*Gulliver's Travels* and a Latin grammar. That's what you were reading, isn't it?"

"Yes, but how did you know that?"

She shrugged. "I noticed—simple as that. But you must be on your way, Jeremy."

Then, throwing open the door, she handed me my valise, leaned forward, and quite unexpectedly kissed me upon my cheek. More of her girlish nonsense it was, but in truth, I liked it well enough that I gave her a grin as I planted my hat upon my head and ran out the door.

I was halfway to Market Street when I heard my name called, turned round, and saw Clarissa in the middle of the street.

"Jeremy!" she shouted loud enough for all the neighbors to hear. "Do not forget to wear a clean shirt and clean hose when you visit the Lord Chief Justice!"

I nodded and waved my assent. Then did I turn round and run fast as I could to Broad Street.

Of the journey by coach to London, there is little to say. During the short distances in which the horses were walked, and whilst at the rest stops along the way, I was able to read a little from *Gulliver's Travels*. For the most part, however, the rocking and bouncing of the coach made it quite impossible. The interior compartment was quite crowded, as seemed in those days always to be the case. Yet I had me a seat by a window and thus was able to study the countryside as it reeled by at galloping speed. This held my attention far better than I would have supposed, for a different route to London had been chosen, one which during its final stages followed along the south bank of the Thames. Thus, after many hours and a bit of fitful dozing, I arrived in London early in the morning.

Taking my valise in hand, I hurried from the Coach House to Number 4 Bow Street. I made the trip, it seemed, in a short time, for the streets were not yet crowded with the hordes on the march to their day's employment. In truth, I had taken to heart Clarissa's caution against wearing my soiled shirt and hose to visit Lord Mansfield. I entered by the door which led to the strong room and the Bow Street Runners' province—the area which Sir John referred to as Bow Street's backstage. Mr. Baker, gaoler and armorer, caught sight of me as I was about to ascend the stairs to our living quarters.

"Hi, Jeremy," he called to me, "is Sir John returned?"

"Uh, no, Mr. Baker," said I. "He sent me back on an errand."

"Going back to Kent, then?"

"Oh yes."

"Nice country, that." He hesitated. Then, with a wave: "Well, on your way, lad."

Waving back, I started up the stairs two at a time, but a thought held me, and I descended to call out to him: "Has Constable Bailey come in yet?"

"No, not yet, but he should be by soon."

"I've something to tell him. Would you ask him to wait for me? I shouldn't be long."

"As you will, Jeremy."

I thanked him, made my way up the stairs, and began my preparations for my meeting with the Lord Chief Justice. Indeed it did not take me long, though I washed and dressed more carefully than was my usual. When I had done brushing my coat and buffing my shoes, I went to Sir John's bedroom and studied my image in Lady Fielding's tall looking glass. Most satisfied was I at what I saw. Clarissa was right: a clean shirt and hose did indeed make all the difference.

As I descended the stairs, I heard the voices of constables Baker and Bailey raised in high hilarity. Mr. Bailey, it seemed, was giving forth with the voice and manner of a drunk in Bedford Street who had that night sought to prove himself sober by reciting the first chapter of the Book of Genesis. "He were never able to get to the end of it," said Mr. Bailey, "but I sent the poor fellow on his way since he made such a considerable effort."

Mr. Baker caught sight of me and pointed, and Mr. Bailey, still chuckling, did turn to me and nod.

"You've something for me?" he asked.

"Nothing much, but something," said I. "I thought to give you notice, though it cannot be done officially until Lord Mansfield gives unto Sir John certain powers."

"Well then, give it me unofficially."

And that I did, explaining that Sir John sought temporarily to serve as magistrate of Deal, taking over the duties of the late magistrate of the town.

"*Late* magistrate? How did he die?"

"Murdered."

"Murdered, is it? Well, if Sir John's in that sort of danger, then I'll be there, never mind what Lord Mansfield says—and you can count on that."

"And bring Will Patley with you?"

"If Sir John wants Patley, then he wants some proper shooting done. You want Patley to bring that rifled musket of his along?"

"That will all be in the letter, I suppose, but I must handle this as Sir John said and wait for Lord Mansfield's authorization. But I did want to give you some notice."

"You did right, Jeremy. It will take a bit of changing about to make this work proper. And I'll have to appoint someone to take my place—Baker probably."

Just as I had thought.

I took my leave of Mr. Bailey, went out into the street, and headed in the direction of Bloomsbury Square, where dwelt William Murray, Lord Mansfield, the Lord Chief Justice. There had I a long acrimonious history with Lord Mansfield's butler. "Acrimonious" might be too strong a term for our relationship. Nevertheless, there was no love lost between us—and precious little good feeling. I quite disliked everything about the man. His cold, aloof manner, and his secretive ways, were such that I never relaxed in his presence. Yet most of all I disliked his studied attitude of superiority. It was as if he were looking down at me from some great height and saw only the ragged boy who had first come to London, orphaned and alone, dirty-faced and desperate. I was no longer that boy. It was not just that I was four years older. I had in that time learned much of life. I was reading the law with Sir John Fielding, the Magistrate of the Bow Street Court. There was naught could be said against me, so far as I knew. Oh, not that I was perfect. (At this point, reader, I was reminded of that embarrassing matter of the coachman, Henry Curtin.) I had my faults, as I was most painfully aware. Nevertheless (I protested within) they were not such that I should be looked down upon by a butler—not even the butler to the household of the Lord Chief Justice.

Somehow I took courage in this lengthy conversation with myself—one no doubt much lengthier than what I have remembered here. In any case, whether because of it or because of the intrinsic importance of my mission to Bloomsbury Square, I felt a considerable surge of power as I knocked upon the door of Lord Mansfield's residence. This time, I swore, I would not be shamed, not even bested, by the butler. The door opened. That familiar cadaverous face appeared, distant and unamused, near a foot above me. (He was indeed a tall man.)

The face spoke: "Ah, it is you. What will you today, boy?"

"What I always will," said I, "an audience with your master."

"Ah, my master? Well, this day, as so often happens, you have come too late."

"But it is early," I protested. "It could not yet be eight o'clock."

"Nevertheless, Lord Mansfield has left for the day. I take it you have a letter from the blind fellow. You may either leave it with me or come back at the end of the day. I'll not have you hanging about the door all through the day like some beggar. So—what is it? Which will you?"

"Neither."

He stepped back. I could see that he was about to shut

the door. I tried vainly to jam my shoe in that I might block it, keep it from closing.

"Where has he gone?" I shouted. "Where is he?"

"Where do you suppose? Now *go away!*" The latter part of this rude response was shouted through the door.

I stood there upon the steps, listening to myself sputter with indignation as I fantasized some wild scheme of revenge. Yet gradually my temper cooled, and I realized the foolishness of such efforts. I put my mind on the far more important matter of finding Lord Mansfield. What was it that the hateful butler had said? I had asked him where his master had gone, and he responded, "Where do you suppose?" Well, I had not to think long upon that to realize that, of course, he had gone to court. He was, after all, a judge, was he not? The Old Bailey was, so to speak, his place of business. Though the hour was an early one at which to begin, it could well be that his docket for the day was so crowded that an early start was demanded of him. I turned about and hastened off in the direction of Old Bailey.

Perhaps the most objectionable thing about the Old Bailey was—and is—its nearness to Newgate Gaol. Only a street separates them, and there is a smell which emanates from Newgate, about equal parts sewer odors and the stink of human misery, which seems to penetrate the walls of the courts, as well. Once in Old Bailey, one could not forget that Newgate was near, nor that Tyburn Hill was not too far distant.

Indeed I was correct in supposing that the press of cases to be tried was such that Lord Mansfield had been forced to begin early. When I at last was admitted to the main courtroom where he presided, I heard from my seat companion, a richly dressed woman of near forty years, that three had already been tried that morning.

"With what result?" I asked.

"You dare joke with me, do you?"

"No, no, I assure you that—"

"—me, who's come for one last glimpse of my son, Billy, before they hang him?" She spoke over me, interrupting, ignoring my attempts to apologize, determined to have her say: "There's none who comes as far as this can escape the rope—or so I'm told. The least I could do was come down and bring all my girls to see the darling boy off. An't that so?"

"I . . . I suppose so," said I, a bit uncertainly.

Her reference to "her girls" intrigued me. I leaned forward a bit and saw, to my surprise, that our pew was crowded with a bevy of gaudily dressed and generously berouged young women of uncertain virtue; there must have been seven or eight of them visible to my eye; two of them returned my gaze rather boldly, and one of them winked.

"Are all these young ladies truly your daughters?" I asked the older woman next me (somewhat disingenuously, I confess).

"La, young sir, they might as well be, but they an't. My womb an't near so generous. Billy's my only." She was, in her own way, a proper mother come to mourn, though her child still breathed.

Needless to say, our conversation took place "between cases," as one might say, whilst Lord Mansfield sat resplendent in his scarlet robes, conversing idly with his clerk, awaiting the next defendant to be called. That next defendant, as it happened, was William Neely. Thus I found that the woman beside me was the notorious brothelkeeper, Mother Neely. He was summoned loudly and appeared but a moment later in the dock. He was in chains, though otherwise quite presentable; his coat was of velvet, and his shirt was apparently of silk and newly washed. At a sign from Mother Neely, our entire row burst into a great fit of sobs and boo-hoos; kerchiefs were waved; a few of the boldest of "her girls" called out to him. This demonstration, which caused quite a commotion in the courtroom, brought an immediate call to order, complete with threats of expulsion, *et cetera*. For my own part, I sought to disso-ciate myself from my pewfellows by shrinking down and away from them. And as for the prisoner, he seemed to take great pleasure in all the noise made in his honor; he smiled broadly and nodded two or three times; and had his hands not been manacled, I feel sure he would have waved in re-sponse.

The indictment, when read out in court by the prosecu-tion, did shock me—and I, working for years with Sir John, was not easily shocked. It told of how William Neely had bound and tortured the members of a diamond merchant's family, that he might learn where gemstones were hid about the house. When he was satisfied he had them all, he mur-dered the entire family—or thought he had. One, a daughter, survived her stab wounds and was able to identify Neely as thief and killer from the witness box. Asked if he could say anything in his own defense, the accused shrugged and said that if they'd been a bit more helpful, it wouldn't have been necessary to be so nasty.

"Then you admit the crime?" asked the Lord Chief Jus-tice.

"Might as well," said Neely, with another shrug.

"Answer yes or no."

"Awright then, yes—*yass, yass, yass!*"

"Then," said Lord Mansfield, "it will not be necessary for the jury to adjourn, confer, and vote guilty or not guilty."

So saying, the judge donned the black cap and pro-nounced the death sentence. Then did he add with no more than routine piety his wish that God might have mercy upon the soul of William Neely. And having said it, he banged thrice with his gavel and called a recess to the court session. When the prisoner was led away, I expected a rep-etition of the earlier performance of the ladies, complete with crocodile tears, yet there was no such. Mrs. Neely stood, and her companions with her as I, too, made ready to leave the courtroom. I knew not what to say, and so I simply held my tongue, bowing silently and politely as they left.

"He weren't really so bad," said Madame Neely to me. "It was just that he was tryin' to prove he could make his own way. Boys is like that. They got to prove that they're grown up—when they really an't."

And saying no more, she led her bevy out and up the aisle. She who had winked at me winked at me again and said, "Come see us sometime. We're in Tavistock Street. So easy to find." Then she, like the rest, followed their leader out the door.

I, too, hastened to go, yet I left by a side exit, one which I knew would bring me nearer to the judges' chambers. Yet there I found my way barred by a court guard.

"Where you goin', young sir?"

"I have a letter for Lord Mansfield from Sir John Fielding which must be delivered. It is a most urgent matter."

"Give me the letter, and I shall present it to him."

"Much as I should like to do so, sir, I cannot. Sir John forbade me to let the letter out of my keeping, except it be to Lord Mansfield."

"Hmmm," said the court guard who, bless him, did truly seem concerned. "Well, I must say you look like a responsible lad."

"I am Sir John's assistant."

"Ah, indeed? You don't say! Well then, I shall take a risk with you. If you take my place at this door and turn away all who seek exit through here, I shall go to the chambers of the Lord Chief Justice and ask him if he wishes your visit." He gave me a sharp look. "Do you accept this offer? It is the best I can do."

"I accept it gladly."

"Well and good." And with that he departed, leaving me in charge.

I took my assignment seriously and turned back two or three during the few minutes he was absent. When he returned with a smile upon his face, I took heart that all was well with regard to my visit—as indeed it was.

"The Lord Chief Justice will see you," said the fellow, "for he assumes you would not trouble him were it not an urgent and important matter. You'll find him third door on your left."

I thanked him and ran to the door he had designated, beat upon it, and threw it open the moment I heard the invitation to enter.

"Ah, you, is it?" said Lord Mansfield, wearing his scarlet and regarding me in his usual skeptical way. "I thought it would be. What have you for me?"

"A letter explaining the situation in Deal, my lord."

"Well then, let's have it."

He took it from me, broke the seal, and read. As he did so, his expression changed from mild displeasure (which was his usual) to sudden concern, and on to absolute outrage. By the time he finished Sir John's letter, he was breathing fire and snorting smoke (I mean that figuratively, of course). He then asked me a number of questions to learn more of events which were no more than mentioned in the letter. Then did he conclude by sitting down at his desk and writing out the document of temporary appointment which Sir John had requested. In addition, he wrote a letter of his own to the Commanding Officer of the Tower, another old chum of his, said he to me with a wink—"actually a cousin."

"You must take this to Colonel Murray forthwith," Lord Mansfield continued, "and he will provide Sir John with a small contingent of mounted troops. Sir John may use them as he sees fit. That should help even things up a bit, eh?"

"Oh yes," said I, "that will help considerably."

• • •

The rest of the day was taken up with the delivery of the remaining letters, which entailed a good deal of racing about from one destination to the next. Colonel Murray provided no problem. He simply read through Lord Mansfield's missive, smiled, and assured me that the requested troops would be provided and should arrive in Deal sometime during the day after tomorrow—or upon that night.

"And where should they report to your fellow, Sir John?"

"To Number Eighteen Middle Street, sir. And if I might make a suggestion?"

"By all means."

"A daylight arrival and a ride down High Street might be best. A show of force would be in order."

"Very well, you shall have it."

Thus I left the Tower in a state of high elation—only to begin what proved to be the most taxing of the errands, which was the delivery of Sir John's letter to Mr. John Bilbo.

First, I set off for his residence in St. James Street. It was yet early in the day, and so I had every hope of catching him there before he left for his gaming club in Mayfair. Nevertheless, by the time I arrived, he had gone. Nor was Bunkins present to advise me on any change in plans his "cove," Mr. Bilbo, might have made for that day. All that could be said was told me by Mr. Burnham, Bunkins's tutor. According to him, both Mr. Bilbo and Jimmie Bunkins had left together for the club.

And so I went on to Mayfair to find them. By that time, it was into the afternoon. Upon my arrival, I found the crew of cleaners busy at work, preparing the place for its evening opening at seven. A dealer of cards sat in the main gaming room, performing feats of sleight of hand with the deck for his own amusement. I waited respectfully for his attention. When he withheld it, I could do naught but shout for it.

"Where's Black Jack?"

He stopped and looked me up and down. "You know him well enough to call him so?"

"I know him well enough—and Bunkins even better."

"Then you should know where the two of them spend most of their time these days."

"In Wapping at the dry-dock."

"Ah, then you do know a little something, don't you?" He gave me a smirk he may have meant for a smile. "Well, they've just left for Wapping, but the sloop is no longer in dry-dock. It's in the slip next on."

"Thank you," said I as I turned and headed for the door.

"Better see them today, if that's your intention. They'll not be about for long." He called it to my back. Turning, I saw that he had gone back to his amusements. I nodded and stepped outside.

I did not like the fellow. He acted entirely too pleased with himself. I wondered how long he had been in the employ of Mr. Bilbo—and how long he would remain so. He did not seem the right sort.

The prospect of walking to Wapping had little appeal. Footsore and bone-tired from my journey from Deal, I thought it right to travel to my next destination in style: I would take a hackney—one from that line there at the end of the street. Time also was a consideration. Having missed Mr. Bilbo and Bunkins twice afoot, I could not afford to miss them again. Thus, bolstered by logic, I rode.

It was, by any measure, a considerable journey. We hugged the river except near Tower Hill, where it was not possible. Peeking out at the crowded streets, seeing the waves of people pouring this way and that over the kerbs and sidewalks, I wondered how I might find my place among them. As I grew older, I found myself thinking more and more (and not always optimistically) about how I

might make my way in the world. It would not be long, after all, until such conjecture must be replaced by action.
Jimmie Bunkins and I often talked of this; he was as much
perplexed about the possible direction of his own life as I
was about my own situation.

In this way do such heavy thoughts often catch us un-
awares.

The last part of my ride, which was taken along Wapping
Dock, led past ships loading and unloading, fitting and re-
fitting. I looked sharp at the docks and slips along the way
that I might not be conveyed past the one which sheltered
the *Indian Princess*. Then, of a sudden, I spied the Bilbo
coach-and-four waiting next a dry-dock and supposed beside it was the right slip. I beat loud upon the ceiling of the
hackney that the driver might stop where it was proper. He
guided the horses over to one side and halted. Paying off
the driver, I ran cross the street and up to the slip.

Mr. Bilbo's sloop lay half in and half out the water at a
slight angle, ready to be launched into the Thames. All glistening and new-looking it was from the many coats of varnish it had received. I saw that the tempo of work had
increased markedly since last I visited. Where earlier
workmen had walked about in a manner near casual, they
now scrambled about from one end of the deck to the other.
And in the middle of all this stood Black Jack Bilbo, shouting directions and encouragement, reminding them, none
too gently, of their obligations.

"If you're lookin' to get paid tonight, gents, you'd best
finish the job."

Then did he give his attention to another group, one
which seemed not to be performing to his high expectations. "Work, lads," he hectored them, *"work!"*

And so it went. I watched, fascinated, for minutes as he
hammered away at them with threats, a few blandishments,
and occasional curses. Yet at last I reminded myself of the
business at hand.

"Mr. Bilbo," I called out to him. "Permission to come aboard!"

He turned round and looked in my direction, squinting a bit against the afternoon sun.

"Ah, Jeremy, it's you, is it? Permission granted."

I made my way carefully across the gangplank, finding that the slight slant of the deck made quite a difference when out on the board between slip and sloop. In any case, I made it across and found Mr. Bilbo waiting at the far end to steady me as I jumped down.

"Good lad!" said he. "How goes it down there on the east coast? Has Sir John come back with you?"

"No, he sent me back with letters to deliver. One of them's for you."

With that, I brought it out and handed it over. From some secret pocket he produced a pair of spectacles and carefully hooked them over his ears. Putting the sun to his back, he broke the seal and read the letter. When he had done, he folded it with a dark frown and tucked it away.

"It sounds bad," said he.

"It *is* bad."

"Well, as it happens, we'll be leaving here on the morning tide on a run down through the Channel, to Cornwall and return, just as a test voyage, as you might say. Sir John's asked that I bring you and a pair of his Bow Street Runners with us to Gravesend. I can do that with no trouble at all. He says that he'll meet us there, for he has something to discuss with me which he'd prefer not to commit to paper. Do you have any idea what that's about, Jeremy?"

"None at all," said I.

"Hmmm, well, I'll find out when we get there, I suppose. In the meantime, you'd like to talk to Bunkins, would you?"

"I would."

"He's belowdecks. Go find him. He'll show you round

the vessel. I do believe that he's as proud of the *Indian Princess* as I am."

I took my leave of him and went, as I'd been told, to search out Jimmie B.

Finding him offered no difficulty; keeping him was quite another matter. He was overseeing the finishing touches to be put upon the cabins belowdecks and seemed to be taking his responsibilities every bit as seriously as his cove. And so likewise did he use the same devices upon those doing the work. He railed at some and encouraged others, shook his finger at some and patted others upon the back. Yet it was all taken in good stead, and the work continued at the same furious pace below as on deck.

As Bunkins called the attention of one of the carpenters to a bit of indifferent sanding, I interrupted with a hand upon his shoulder. He whirled about, ready for anything (like the street boy he once had been), but then, recognizing me, he relaxed, laughing, and pushed my hat down over my face.

"Well, Jeremy, how's my old chum?"

"Right as rain," said I. "The cove said you'd show me round the boat."

"Ship, Jeremy, ship," he instructed me. "Vessel, you *might* say, but it's never a boat. A sloop's just too big to be called so."

"I stand corrected," said I. It was seldom that Bunkins had the opportunity to put me in the right on matters of proper usage, and it did seem to me that he was belaboring the matter a bit.

"That's as the cove says, anyways."

"Ah, yes, well . . . ahem," said I, waiting.

He looked at me oddly for a moment, but then the light in his eyes rekindled, and he gave a great, loud laugh.

"You're waiting for me to show you 'round down here, an't you?"

"Well . . . yes. That is, Mr. Bilbo said . . ."

"True, but he didn't know how much more we still got to do down here."

"Another time, then?"

"Whenever you're next aboard."

"That'll be tomorrow. I'm going to passenger down to Gravesend on the *Indian Princess* with a couple of the Bow Street Runners."

"We'll do it then, I swear."

And saying thus, he raised his right hand and placed his left over his heart, making it official.

He was as good as his word; that next day, he took me on a quick tour belowdecks immediately as I again set foot upon the *Indian Princess*. I had come, as I had promised, in company with constables Bailey and Patley. They, who had packed light, tossed the little they had into one of the cabins and went above to await our departure. It was then that Bunkins grabbed me by the wrist and began showing me cabin after cabin, far more than I had expected.

"We put in four extra," he explained. "That's what all that work was yesterday—trying to get them done proper before we sailed."

The gun deck, where the crew slept, was correspondingly smaller. But then, as Bunkins explained, not so many would be needed to man the sloop if it were to be used for pleasure. As it was, the crew which would take the *Indian Princess* on its test run was hardly more than it would take to sail a yacht.

"Just a few who sailed with Mr. Bilbo in the old days," said Bunkins. "They're off together on a lark."

It remained for me to inquire about the gun ports. I had noticed that they had not been sealed, but rather, had been fixed with hinged doors, so that they might still be put to their original use.

"That's a sort of secret," said he. "Keep a dubber mum, will you, chum?"

I promised that I would indeed keep a dubber mum.

There was a bit of a creak from below, another from above, and then there was a curious feeling of floating free; we were launched—afloat in the Thames.

"Come, Jeremy, let's up and out and watch all London go by!"

And that was what we did, hanging out over the gunwale, near the prow of the ship. A light wind touched our faces, giving to me the feeling that we were hurtling along at a very high rate of speed; whereas we were moving at little more than the speed of the current. Still and all, the buildings and roads on the shore along the way seemed absolutely to flash by at a rate much faster than that achieved by any horse-drawn conveyance.

A few watermen in their boats deigned to wave us a greeting. We waved back most enthusiastically. I know not why—perhaps it was no more than the face of one of the watermen which reminded me—but my thoughts were carried back in an instant to him I had met the day before in Mr. Bilbo's gaming club. I decided to ask Bunkins about him.

"Jimmie B," said I. "I chased about a good long while, looking for you and your cove. And the last place I looked before I came to Wapping was the club in Mayfair."

"Yes?" said he. "What about it?"

"Well, there was a cod there, he was helpful enough, told me where to go to find you, but there was something about him . . ."

"Something you didn't much care for?"

"Well . . . yes, that's right."

"That'd be Mr. Slade, and truth to tell, I don't care for him much myself."

"What's he doing there? Does he work for Mr. Bilbo?"

"No. You know the cove, he don't talk much about his business, or his plans for the future, or any such matters,

but he's let it out that this here Mr. Slade has made an offer
to buy the gaming club."

"To *buy* it? I didn't know it was for sale. I mean, what's
Mr. Bilbo say about it? Does he want to sell?"

"He says he's thinking it over." Bunkins sighed. "He
must take it pretty seriously, though. He's given him the
run of the club whilst we're gone, so he can see how it
works." He shook his head in a gesture of disapproval. "I'll
tell you, Jeremy, there's a lot going on that I don't understand, but I've got the feeling that there's some big changes
coming." He looked distinctly unhappy.

Neither of us knew his future, and that put a pall upon
the present. Even though it was great fun to see London
and its eastern villages scattered out along the riverbanks,
it did not seem enough to raise our spirits. Yet we entertained ourselves by pointing out each to the other various
oddities and curiosities viewed along the way. Thus we
passed our time during the comparatively short voyage
downriver to Gravesend. There the great river had widened
and deepened to the extent that it was possible for Mr.
Bilbo, who served as helmsman, to steer in close to shore
and drop anchor. Bunkins was called upon to oversee this,
and I realized what should have been clear to me yesterday:
that he had picked up a good deal of maritime lore and
practice and would probably learn more on this voyage and
on others like it.

Along the riverbank I caught sight of a hackney coach
thundering up the riverside road to meet us. The coach—or
perhaps the team of horses—looked familiar to me, as indeed they should have. Yet I could only be sure of who was
inside when it stopped and Mick Crawly climbed down to
assist Sir John from the interior of the coach. The magistrate jumped down, as he usually did, but Mick was on
hand to steady him and made sure he did not fall.

"Halloo, the *Indian Princess*! Permission to come

aboard?" Sir John's powerful baritone cry floated steady across the water to us.

"Permission granted!" Mr. Bilbo's response, which sounded even stronger, was returned most immediately and, it seemed to me, quite enthusiastically.

Then, almost as an afterthought, Mr. Bilbo instructed Bunkins (whom he addressed as *Mister* Bunkins) to lower a boat, and indeed Bunkins saw to it.

Constables Bailey and Patley, and I myself did climb down the rope ladder to the waiting boat. Of us three, Constable Patley had potentially the greatest difficulty because of the rifled musket he carried. Yet he solved his problem with a strap which ran from the bottom of the stock to the barrel. Using it, he simply slung the weapon over his shoulder, and thus had both hands free to use to descend the rope ladder. Neither Mr. Bailey nor I had any such problem.

The two oarsmen supplied by Mr. Bilbo had no difficulty ferrying us to the riverbank, nor was the bank so steep that it caused difficulty; steps had been cut into it. Once constables Bailey and Patley had ascended to the high ground, where they were greeted by Sir John, I climbed the stairs that I might assist him down them and into the boat. That much he allowed, but when I moved to climb in after him, he barred my way.

"It will not be necessary to accompany me, Jeremy. I take it you have with you a document from Lord Mansfield giving me a temporary appointment in Deal?"

"Right in my pocket, Sir John."

"Excellent. Then you accomplished all the tasks I gave you commendably well. I shall take over at this point, having offered you my thanks."

"But . . . but won't you need me to help you up the ladder?"

"Jeremy, I am quite capable of climbing a rope ladder by myself. I climbed hundreds of them during my time in the Navy."

"As you wish, Sir John," said I with a sigh.

"That is how I wish it."

With that, he took his place in the boat. The oarsmen pushed off, and in not much more than a minute, were there at the *Indian Princess*. As he had predicted, Sir John made it to the top of the ladder without incident, and there was met by Mr. Bilbo, who helped him over the gunwale and onto the deck. Then, for nearly half an hour, the two men parlayed as they walked every inch of the sloop's topdeck.

At one point, as I stood watching with the two constables, Mr. Patley remarked to us, "I wonder what Sir John is planning with that old pirate."

"Whatever it is," responded Mr. Bailey, "it's going to cause some smuggler one hell of a great lot of trouble."

NINE

*In which Mr. Eccles
returns just as the
horsemen arrive*

The afternoon drive from Gravesend back to Deal
was uneventful, save for the one incident which I
have described, wherein quite unexpectedly Sir John declared that an attack upon an officer of the court was an
attack upon the law itself. He broke what had been a long
silence to say that—yet silence, in this case, should be understood only in a relative sense. Certainly, there had
been naught said by the two constables for many miles;
having put in a full night marching about the unruly
precincts of London, they were naturally quite tired. They
promptly fell asleep as Mr. Crawly set his coach upon the
main road and headed for Deal. I remained awake, yet
though I sat next to Sir John, he showed little inclination
to talk to me. Nevertheless, he was far from quiet. There
were steady murmurings and grunts from him; he must be
either in deep conversation with himself, or in a troubled

sleep. All other signs—his erect posture in the seat, the swiftly altering expressions of his face—indicated that the former was the more likely.

I wished to ask him questions. Indeed I wished to know just what it was he and Mr. Bilbo had discussed at such length as they ambled back and forth cross the decks of the *Indian Princess*. Clearly, Sir John had a plan, one which included Mr. Bilbo and perhaps also his ship. And I had an important matter to communicate to Sir John as well: I had not yet had the opportunity to tell him of the detachment of cavalry which would soon be under his command. Nevertheless, I kept my peace. There was simply no getting through to him whilst he was in such a state.

I did make only one attempt to do so, and that was just following his sudden pronouncement. He had spoken out with such authority that he roused both the sleeping constables; they sat up in their seats, blinked, and waited for him to continue. When he did not, they allowed their eyelids to droop once more and soon were fast asleep just as before. For my part, I took a chance, and once it was clear that he would add nothing to what he had said, I decided to tell him what I had to tell.

"Sir John," I blurted, "I've an important bit of information for you."

"Can it wait?"

"Well, I suppose it can."

"Then later, please."

And having said that, he went back to his muttering. His conversation with himself thus continued.

As it happened, I had not the chance to tell him of the cavalry's impending arrival until much later that day; it was, in fact, well into evening when I did. After we had eaten dinner—and a fine dinner it was, prepared for us by Mrs. Sarton (Clarissa also had a hand in it)—Sir John met with his constables to acquaint them with the situation in Deal before Mr. Perkins took them out to show them the town. Only after they had departed did I take it upon my-self to knock upon the door to the little room which had served Albert Sarton as his study. Invited inside, I took a chair just opposite the one in which Sir John sat at the desk.

"Well, Jeremy," said he, "I believe you told me earlier that you had an important bit of information which you wished to pass on to me."

"That's right, sir, I do."

"I asked you then to hold it until later. Well, this is later, is it not? Let me hear this information."

Whereupon I disclosed that he would, in a day or two, have a small contingent of cavalry at his disposal.

"Good God!" said he. "This is terrible!"

Did he truly think so? But why? Actually, I thought it rather a grand idea, but I kept this opinion to myself.

"Whose notion was this?" asked Sir John.

"Lord Mansfield's," said I.

"Well, if it was his idea, then there's no sending them back, is there?"

"I suppose not," said I. Then, after a moment's hesitation: "He must have felt that the situation here, as you described it in your letter, was so desperate that you would need such aid to set it right."

"Hmmm, well, yes, I fear I did paint rather a grim sort of picture. Perhaps I should have been a little less . . . convincing."

"Can't you find some use for them, Sir John?"

He gave that some thought. "Perhaps I can. I just hadn't thought of such before. But . . . but . . . where shall I put them?"

There I could give him no help at all, and so I simply kept silent.

"I shall give it some thought." He nodded then, which I took as a sign that he wished to be left alone.

I rose, excused myself, and made to go. He had, however, one last word for me.

"Jeremy, I had neglected to tell you this, but the funeral for Mr. Sarton will be held tomorrow at ten. We shall all attend. Please wear your best. I trust you have a clean shirt?"

The services, which were held at St. George's church, were coldly formal, remarkably short, and sadly ill-attended. If a person were to have come in as a stranger (as I did), it would not have taken him long to perceive that the vicar had been no friend to the man in the coffin. Where he might have made remarks in praise of Mr. Sarton, he said nothing, even went so far as to call attention to the omission.

"At this point," he had said, "time is often taken to speak well of him whom we bury. We shall instead return to the Service for the Dead." And return to it he did.

Molly Sarton, sitting quite nearby, started up from her place and was restrained by Mrs. Keen and Clarissa, who were on either side of her. I do believe she meant to attack the vicar, and I, for one, would have thought her justified. This was explained *sotto voce* by Clarissa to Sir John, who sat farthest away.

Was all this evident animosity to the Sartons caused by the irregularities at the start of their marriage? The scandal of a single man and woman living under the same roof, *et cetera*? Had I not heard that at first the vicar had refused to marry them? Such a to-do over so little!

We pallbearers four—constables Bailey, Patley, Perkins, and I—sat off to one side of the church, from which vantage we had a good view of all in attendance. There were not many. Of the eight mourners present, I recognized only three: there was, first of all, the unnamed server in Mrs. Keen's tearoom; there was also Dick Dickens, once a smuggler and now an exciseman; the third, however, a late arrival, did surprise me completely when he appeared, for it was no less than Sir Simon Grenville.

At the end of the service, having heard the great amen, we pallbearers came forward and followed the vicar out to the churchyard as we carried the coffin between us. He continued reading aloud from the Book of Common Prayer, yet mumbling as though to himself. Following us were the widow, supported by Mrs. Keen; Sir John, shown the way by Clarissa; and finally, those of the mourners who wished to hear the final graveside prayers.

Not all of them came. Mr. Dickens, the server from Mrs. Keen's shop, and one other took that opportunity to absent themselves, so that there were but five trailing in the cortege. The little group fit comfortably about the gravesite. Yet it seemed that they had no more than ringed it round when the vicar, who had been droning on incessantly, tossed in the requisite handful of dirt and suddenly clapped shut his prayer book. Without another word, he turned and left the churchyard in the direction of the vicarage. There were gasps from the ladies at his sudden departure and grumbles from the gentlemen. Only one was heard to laugh, and that one was Sir Simon Grenville.

Upon hearing his loud cackle, Molly Sarton turned sharply to him and gave him a fierce look.

"You find that funny, do you, Sir Simon?" said she to him. She had no need to raise her voice, so near together did they stand.

"Not funny, no, Molly," said he. "I found it unconscionably rude, yet to see such rudeness displayed in a manner so open shocked me into laughter."

"Ah well, you've the words for it, I suppose," said she. "To me, it seemed childish and your response no less so."

"I meant no offense."

"And I'll take none from such as you."

"Jeremy." A female voice. I looked round and found Clarissa. "Sir John asked that you bring Mr. Crawly's coach round. We feel we must get the two separated before they come to blows." All in a whisper.

I nodded and set off immediately, back through the church and out the door. Sir John, Mrs. Sarton, and Clarissa had taken the hackney over to the church, though it was a journey of no more than a quarter mile. It was Sir John's thought that a ride out of town might do her well after the service. Yet surely he had not foreseen any circumstance such as this. I hastened to Mick Crawly, who stood by his horses muttering to them in friendly fashion as he waited. I explained to him that he was needed immediately round the corner, and immediately did he ascend to his place above and take up his coach whip. All it took, however, was a call from him, and the team surged forward.

I started to follow but happened to notice as I turned round two men who had been hidden by Mr. Crawly's hackney. They, who had been talking secretly and earnestly, were now exposed to view, and indeed they liked it not: they ducked and disappeared behind their own coach, which I recognized as Sir Simon Grenville's. And though I saw the two men only fleetingly, I was sure that one was Sir Simon's major domo, Mr. Fowler, and the other, Dick Dickens.

Taking no time to reflect upon it, I jog-trotted to the churchyard gate, where I saw Molly Sarton leaving in the company of Mrs. Keen and Clarissa. Mick Crawly scrambled down from his perch in time to give Mrs. Sarton a hand up into the coach. As I approached, I heard Mrs. Keen giving assurances to her friend that she would go straight to Number 18 Middle Street and be on hand to welcome any who might come by.

"Not that any will," came Mrs. Sarton's voice from the interior of the coach.

"Ah well, you may be surprised," said Mrs. Keen. "At least we're prepared for them."

"We've baked for an army."

"And that's the truth."

"Come along then, Clarissa. It may be that a drive in the country will do me some good."

But Clarissa hung back for a moment, just long enough

to whisper to me: "Sir John will need you. He's at grave-side talking with Sir Simon."

"With Sir Simon? Oh dear."

"Exactly. Goodbye then. I've no idea when we'll be back."

And with that, taking Mick's hand, she swung up and into the coach. Then in a trice, he was up again in the driver's seat. With another shout to his horses, they were off again. I looked round me for Mrs. Keen and found her already gone, near to the corner she was already. And so there was naught for me but to square my shoulders and return, hoping as I did so that Sir John had not managed Molly Sarton's release by assuming her adversarial role.

A number of the mourners had left. Sir John and Sir Simon stayed on, addressing each other to my relief in fair friendly fashion—one might almost say, as old friends might. As I approached, Sir Simon seemed to be accounting to Sir John for the hostile nature of the exchange which I have described in part.

"No, we were not always so," said he to him. "She was to me earlier a most satisfactory cook, no more nor less. My first wife chose her, and then after a few years my first wife died. Whilst I lived alone, briefly, she served me well enough. But then, as I believe I told you, when I married Marie-Hélène, quite understandably, she wanted a cook of her own choosing. The French take these things very seriously, you know, so there was naught to do but give Molly her notice."

"Then you took no part in this persecution of Albert Sarton and Molly, whilst they lived in the same house as master and cook? I understand there was a great show of moral indignation."

"Certainly not by me!" declared Sir Simon hotly. "I care not how the local magistrate and his cook comport themselves. It was to me a matter of complete indifference."

Then did the expression on Sir Simon's face alter to one

of sly speculation as he lowered his voice. "Or perhaps not *complete* indifference," said he. "I will confess I was quite interested in one aspect of it all."

"Oh?" said Sir John. "And what was that?"

"Well, I daresay that Molly hooked her fish, played him well, and landed him. I give her credit. She carried it off quite skillfully."

"Just what are you hinting at, sir? You seem to be saying that she seduced Mr. Sarton into marriage. Have you any proof of that? Is it your opinion?"

"Proof, I have none, and my opinion will remain my own. Nonetheless, I believe it significant that Molly was years older than Mr. Sarton, don't you? And ever so much more . . . well, experienced than he. The poor fellow was an utter failure as a magistrate. Surely you must agree?"

"I fear I do not," said Sir John firmly.

The few who had remained round the grave were now gathered in close to hear the two men talk. One could divine from whispers and unspoken responses that those who listened disapproved of Sir Simon's remarks and thought them particularly ill-considered at such a time and in such a place, as indeed they were.

"How can you not, sir? He did naught but offend the local populace—or at least those who mattered. And as for the smuggling hereabouts, he encouraged it by his inactivity. No, Deal is far better off without him."

"If that is your feeling, Sir Simon, may I ask why in the world you bothered to attend this funeral service?"

He fluttered a hand, dismissing the question. "Oh, in my position, I must attend a good many ceremonies which I should prefer not to attend. For appearances' sake, you understand."

"Oh, indeed I do."

"I've no idea who will take Sarton's place—a local man, no doubt. For a time we shall be without a magistrate, and I venture that none will notice."

By this time the grumbling from the listeners had grown ominous. Sir Simon, however, seemed to take no notice. He wore his indifference as a shield.

"I believe," said Sir John, "that I have a surprise for you, sir. Deal is not without a magistrate, nor is it likely to be."

Sir Simon's eyes narrowed. He stepped back and regarded Sir John in a suspicious, even hostile manner. Though he knew not what this blind fellow had in store, he seemed sure that it betokened little good for him. "What do you mean?" he asked at last.

"Why, I mean, sir, that *I* am the magistrate of Deal for such time as it may take to set things aright."

"*You?* What do you mean by that? On whose authority?"

Sir Simon was thrown into such disarray by Sir John's announcement that the shock he felt was written plain upon his face. Laughter was barely suppressed by those who had remained to listen; it emerged in snorts and giggles, which seemed to anger Sir Simon greatly. He looked about him as if ready to demand silence from all. Yet no such order came, for when Sir John cleared his throat and made to speak, all fell quiet.

"I meant by that, sir, just what I said. I am, by the order of your old friend, Lord Mansfield, given temporary powers as magistrate of the town of Deal and surrounding territories and waters. And as for setting things aright, that is precisely what I intend to do. I intend to discover the murderer of Albert Sarton and bring him to justice. Further, I hope to deal a killing blow to the smuggling trade, if only here in Deal. My authorization and empowerment in this is set out in a letter from the Lord Chief Justice. You may see the letter, if you care to, any time you drop by the magistrate's residence. Now, is there any part of that you would have me explain further?"

"No." Sir Simon appeared so taken aback by the speech from the heretofore nearly silent Sir John that that single syllable was all that he could manage.

"And if I may, sir," Sir John added, "I should like to introduce you to three of my Bow Street Runners—constables Bailey, Patley, and Perkins." And so saying, he waved a hand in the precise direction where the three stood together beneath a great elm tree. "They have come down from London at my invitation. Do make it clear, sir, to your servants and those who work for you, that these men speak for me in all matters to do with the law."

He bobbed his head, and at the same time touched his hat in a farewell salute. "Now if you will pardon us, Sir Simon, we shall take our leave of you. A good day to you, sir."

For the rest of the day and for all of the next, the Sarton house was humming with the making of plans and preparations. To what end was kept secret from me, though I was fair certain that it was Sir John's intention to strike that "killing blow to the smuggling trade" of which he had spoken to Sir Simon Grenville.

Endless conferences with the Runners who had come down from London were conducted behind closed doors. Another visit by that slippery individual, Dick Dickens, took place late at night and lasted well past midnight. And I was altogether astonished when, next morning, I was sent off to the heart of town to find Mick Crawly, the driver of the hackney coach.

"Find him?" said I. "What then?"

"Why, fetch him," said Sir John. "Tell him I wish to speak with him."

I started to go, but then did I stop and turn about, thinking that I might save a bit of time and trouble for myself and for Sir John.

"Perhaps I could take a message to him," I suggested. "If you wish to travel with him somewhere, just tell me where that might be and when you wish to depart. I shall tell him, and he will be here. He is, in that way, quite dependable."

"Jeremy, please, just fetch the fellow. The matter between us may take some discussion. It is not the sort of thing that may be handled with a message and a simple reply. Be a good lad, and do as I ask."

Yet still I hesitated. "What if he asks what it is you wish to discuss with him?"

"Then tell him he will learn that when he comes. Get on with you now. Do as I say."

And so, having little or no choice in the matter, I left forthwith for Broad Street. I knew the way quite well. Indeed, in the space of time we had been in Deal, I had learned the shape of the town so well that I could have drawn a map of its center and erred little more than in a detail or two. Yet, of the surrounding region I knew very little.

Even less did I know of the plan—or plans—that Sir John had made to trap the smugglers and put an end to the smuggling trade in Deal. In spite of hints I had dropped to the three London constables, I was coolly ignored. At the time, that did seem to me to be most cruel—particularly in that I counted two of the three among my close friends. And now it seemed that even one of the local hackney coach drivers was to know better than I just what was afoot. What was one to do?

I was to do naught but what I was told, apparently.

And so did I make my way along High Street in the direction of Broad Street—Broad Street, where the hackney coaches gathered in line to serve the travelers who arrived there from all points by post coach. Yet just as I arrived and spied Mr. Crawly's sturdy coach at the head of the waiting line, my attention was drawn by a sound of an unusual sort coming from farther down High Street: it was a tune played on a trumpet—nay, a bugle call—which came from a small troop of mounted men who were making their way up High Street in my direction. They were colorfully and yet familiarly uniformed.

Had I seen such before? Why, yes, indeed I had. They

wore the colors of the King's Carabineers and were the same mounted troopers who had aided Sir John in the apprehension of the Dutch ship, *Dingendam,* loaded to the gunwales with stolen treasures. The Bow Street Runners had challenged the ship's captain, and when he attempted escape, the Carabineers had pursued the ship down the Thames. I knew whence they had come and where they were headed, and I was certain that if we were to fall in behind them, our short journey to the house in Middle Street would take very much longer, for already a crowd of townspeople (which included a full company of children) was gathering round them, cheering them on. I had near forgot that the cavalry was coming.

I ran to Mr. Crawly, who stood, whip in hand, leaning against a wheel of the coach. I quickly explained the situation to him, and he responded by saying not a word, but by climbing up to his driver's seat swift as a cat might scale a fence. Only then did he call to me.

"Come along if you're comin', for we've not got a moment to spare."

Then was I up beside him, near as fast as he had got up there himself.

"Hold on tight," said he to me.

With that, he cracked his whip into the air, and the four horses leapt forward as one. Off we went, round the corner and onto High Street only a bit before the King's Carabineers themselves had arrived. There were fewer of them than I had at first realized—probably no more than the squad who had galloped down the Thames at Sir John's order in pursuit of the *Dingendam*; and at their head I saw the same Lieutenant Tabor, who had led them on that chase.

"Where are we headed?" asked Mr. Crawly.

"To Middle Street—the magistrate's house," I shouted my reply.

"That's to pick somebody up? Just to Middle Street an't much of a fare."

"No, Sir John asked to see you. He says he has some-thing to discuss with you."

"Discuss, is it? Sounds a bit hazardous. The last time a magistrate had a discussion with me, it cost me two days work and a five-shilling fine. That was the old magistrate, Mr. Kemp."

"Well, Sir John has no such intentions with you, I'm sure."

I noted that it was no longer necessary for me to shout. Turning round, I saw that the contingent of cavalry lagged considerably behind—had now, in fact, come to a halt somewhere near the Broad Street corner, so tightly sur-rounded were they by the enthusiastic citizens of Deal. As I watched, the bugler put his horn to his lips and played an-other tune.

Middle Street was as I had left it, empty of all but two or three pedestrians who could be seen in the distance. I tried to imagine just how this quiet scene might look with the addition of horses and red-coated cavalrymen; yet try as I might I could not suppose them there.

"Number Eighteen, is it?"

"That's right, Mr. Crawly."

And just then he pulled back on the reins, and as the horses slowed, he applied the brake. The judicious use of both brought us to an easy halt just at Number 18.

I bounded down from the top of the coach and, with a promise to return just as soon as I might, left him and was admitted through the front door by Clarissa, who had been watching through a window, awaiting my return.

"Is Sir John in that little room there?" I asked.

"He is," said she, "but he's with someone now."

"Oh? Who?"

"I've no idea," said she in a rather airy manner. "Never have I seen the man before. He's certainly an unpleasant sort, however."

I could not think who that unpleasant man might be.

Certainly we had met some in Deal who might fit that description, yet it seemed to me that Clarissa could put names to most of them.

"Did Sir John ask that he not be disturbed?"

"No, not so far as I remember."

"Well then," said I, "I'll chance it."

And so saying, I beat stoutly upon the door to the little room. Hearing something not quite understandable called from inside, I chose to take it as an invitation to enter and threw open the door. There behind the desk was Sir John, exactly where I had left him; the expression upon his face was such that I had no need to fear I had displeased him by my sudden entry. Yet there was displeasure aplenty written upon the face of his guest, who was no less than the Chief Customs Officer for eastern Kent—that is to say, Mr. George Eccles. Mr. Eccles had done little since last they met at Lord Mansfield's to endear himself to Sir John; the scowl upon his face made that plain.

"Ah, Jeremy, is it you?" asked Sir John. "You may recall our previous encounter with Mr. Eccles?" I bowed politely as Sir John continued: "He has been telling me of the sad outcome of his dealings with the Chancellor of the Exchequer. And I had just explained to him why it is that I sit here, rather than the duly appointed magistrate to the town of Deal. And he, I must say, seemed to dismiss the death of Mr. Sarton as a matter of little importance."

"Well, now," said Mr. Eccles in that same sharp tone which recalled itself immediately to me, "I did not say that exactly—no, I did not."

"And what did you say, sir?"

"I believe I said that sad as it may be to hear of a life cut short as Mr. Sarton's was, the town is no worse off for it. He was of little worth as a magistrate."

"I think it remarkable you should have said that, Mr. Eccles, for Sir Simon Grenville said much the same thing only yesterday. Tell me, sir, have you discussed this matter with Sir Simon?"

"I may have," said Mr. Eccles in a manner that could only be called hesitant. Then, in a more emphatic fashion: "Well, yes I have—and what of it? Only yesterevening I dined with him and we discussed these matters thoroughly. He told me of your intemperate remarks at graveside. Naturally, I hope you succeed in your declared intention to find the murderer of Mr. Sarton, and as for your wish to wipe out the smuggling trade here in Deal, of course I'm for you there, too, though I doubt you'll succeed. But let us be practical. Whether you do or don't succeed, eventually you will leave here, Sir John, and return to London. Then it will fall to the leading citizens of Deal to choose a successor to the late Mr. Sarton. And when that time comes, there can be one and only one choice to be made for the office of magistrate."

"And what choice is that?" asked Sir John.

"Why, Sir Simon himself, of course. He is the greatest landholder in this part of Kent. He can claim near a thousand acres. There are few in the county who have more."

"You feel that this qualifies him as a magistrate?"

"Indeed I do. How much law, after all, must a magistrate know? With all due respect, Sir John, I believe you would admit that the answer to that would have to be . . ." Mr. Eccles paused for effect. "Not a great deal."

"I daresay you're right there," said Sir John with an amused chuckle. "But do you feel that justice is best served when the rich sit in judgment upon the poor?"

"Why not? God has shown that he favors the rich by giving wealth to them. Why should he not also favor them with wisdom?"

"There are, I know, some who feel as you do in such matters."

"Let me tell you, Sir Simon would have been magistrate

here in Deal had not Lord Mansfield butted into the town's affairs. It had all been arranged."

"How interesting."

"Then came a letter from Sir Simon's friend, Lord Mansfield, asking his aid in securing that same appointment for a young fellow barely out of university. Of course he had no choice but—"

At just that moment, reader, came the not-too-distant sound of a bugle. The King's Carabineers were now quite near. Had Sir John heard the call? Of course he had. The shadow of a smile flickered across his face. As for Mr. Eccles, however, there could be not the slightest doubt that he had heard it clear. He leapt up from his chair and looked first at Sir John and then at me, as if one of us two had been the source of that unexpected tooting.

"What was that?" he demanded. "What was that sound?"

"Why, I be damned if it did not sound like a trumpet, sir. Now, who would be playing a trumpet here in Deal in the middle of the day? Have you any idea, Jeremy?"

"None at all, Sir John." That seemed an appropriate answer under the circumstances.

"But forgive me, lad," said he to me. "What was your purpose in knocking upon the door? As I recall, I sent you off on an errand, did I not?" (He knew very well on what errand he had sent me.)

"Ah yes, you did sir. You said you had business with a Mr. Crawly and sent me off to fetch him."

"And have you done as I asked?"

"I have, sir. Mr. Crawly awaits outside."

"Well done," said Sir John, rising from his chair. "Let us go and meet with Mr. Crawly, shall we? I'm sure Mr. Eccles and I have concluded our talk, have we not, sir?"

"If that is your view, sir, then I daresay we have finished," said Eccles in a manner rather sullen. "I would not take up more of your valuable time."

Sir John, who had learned the room with no difficulty,

squeezed round the desk and made it across the room to the door. There I offered him my arm, and we two waited that Mr. Eccles might exit before us. In truth, he had little choice.

At the door to the street Clarissa awaited us, quite beside herself with excitement.

"You've no idea what's out there," said she to one and all. "You'd not get it right with a hundred guesses."

Sir John put a forefinger to his lips, asking for silence. Clarissa assented with a nod. Mr. Eccles, having heard thus much, sprang to the door and, unwilling to wait, threw it open and gasped at what he saw.

"Good God," he cried aloud, "they're here! The Chancellor of the Exchequer granted my petition, after all!"

He was so transported by the congregation of horses and men just outside the door that for a moment or two all he could do was stand there in the doorway, his hands clasped before him, and gloat loudly, "They're mine, they're mine."

He did, in fact, speak so loudly that he attracted the attention of a group of soldiers nearby. One of them turned round and looked curiously at Mr. Eccles and Sir John. It was not, however, until he separated himself from the rest and started toward us that I saw that the man who approached was Lieutenant Tabor, who had played a role in the *Dingendam* matter. He gave a casual salute and proceeded to address Sir John.

"We are perhaps a little later than expected, sir. For that I beg your pardon most sincerely, but we—"

As this was said, Mr. Eccles began, subtly at first, to intrude himself into Lieutenant Tabor's line of vision. By the time I did notice, he seemed truly to be attempting to elbow Sir John aside.

"Young man . . . uh, lieutenant," said he, "I believe you've made a mistake. It's me you wish to address, if I'm not mistaken. My name—as you will see if you check your orders—is George Eccles. I am the Chief Customs Officer for eastern Kent."

"Oh no, sir, I fear not, sir," said Lieutenant Tabor. "I know my orders well, and they direct me to Sir John Fielding at this house in Middle Street—Number Eighteen."

"But—"

"And indeed I know Sir John well enough, for I assisted him in another matter quite recently, and so you see, sir, I have made no mistake."

"Now, don't be impertinent, young man."

"I was not aware of any impertinence on my part, sir."

"But you should be aware that I submitted a request to the Chancellor of the Exchequer, no less, for just such a mounted contingent as this one here. And so it stands to reason, does it not, that this must be *my* mounted contingent? Don't you understand? I need cavalry to chase the smugglers. I can only conclude that the orders you have been given were wrong. Mistaken. Misdirected."

All through this wrangle, during which Mr. Eccles grew increasingly strident in his representations, Sir John had listened with an amused smile upon his face, saying nothing. Yet during this last speech the smile faded. What seemed to offend was Eccles's assertion that because the lieutenant's orders were not as he would have them, then the orders must be wrong. This was simply too much for Sir John. It was, of a sudden, time to lodge a protest.

"Enough!" said he with a great shout, which silenced all. "Mr. Eccles, your argument is pure nonsense. You tell Lieutenant Tabor to forget his orders because they are not consonant with your desires. Well, that, sir, is nonsense and not near good enough. If you hope to have your way, then you must write to the Chancellor of the Exchequer, explain the situation, and get from him some written document that is endorsed by the Commander of the Tower which states that these particular troops are transferred to your command. Until you can present such, you are to trouble nei-

ther me, nor the lieutenant, nor any of his men further. Good day to you, sir."

Mr. Eccles did not respond to that, though it was not for want of trying. He stood rigid and red-faced, stuttering and sputtering, unable to complete or even begin a sentence. Thus did he for a minute, or maybe even two, as Sir John waited most patiently. At last, however, Eccles surrendered to circumstance, turned, and beat a swift retreat down Middle Street. Looking after him, the lieutenant permitted himself a smile. From his men, however, who had listened carefully to all that was said, a few chuckles and snorts were heard.

Sir John listened to Eccles's footsteps fade, then did he call out to the assemblage: "Mr. Crawly, will you please come forward?"

And so did the driver of the hackney work his way through the assemblage of men and horses to greet Sir John most respectfully.

"What will you, sir?" he asked. "Where can I take you?"

"Nowhere for now, though I do have a proper and important journey for you."

"From here to where?"

"From here to the residence of Sir Simon Grenville. I want you to lead this small troop of mounted Carabineers up there that they may pitch their tents upon his front lawn and water their horses in the brook that runs through it." He paused to think a moment. "I did hear a brook up there on our approach to his door, did I not, Jeremy?"

"You did, Sir John," said I.

"That should do nicely, don't you think so, lieutenant?"

"Oh, well enough, I'm sure," responded Lieutenant Tabor.

"Though I must ask you to remain here with me, whilst I explain to you our situation here. You may join your men later. And you, Mr. Crawly—"

"Yes sir?"

"I would have you return here once you have the Carabineers situated in Sir Simon's great dooryard, for we shall have further need of you, the lieutenant and I. We three have plans to make."

"Well and good, sir," said Mr. Crawly. "I have but one question for you."

"And what is that?"

"Does Sir Simon know that these army gents will be staying with him as his guests?"

Sir John smiled. "In all truth, he does not. Still, as the biggest landholder in these parts, he should not be surprised if, from time to time, he has official guests drop in. If he protests vigorously, just tell him that Lord Mansfield sent these troops down to help Sir John Fielding in the discharge of his duties. You may pass that word on to the troops."

This time I was privy to the plan as it was made. I sat and listened to Sir John outline it. I bent over the map with them as Mr. Crawly chose the best place for a roadblock. I heard Lieutenant Tabor's comments on the difficulty of following a train of wagons undetected. In short, I saw that as I had suspected, this was very likely the plan that Sir John had worked through with Dick Dickens late into the night before. How Dickens had come by the information upon which it was based I had no idea.

My suspicion that he was co-author and prime mover of the plan was confirmed when, at the end of the afternoon session, Sir John dictated to me a memorandum, giving all details, which was to be delivered into the hands of Dick Dickens only. Thus had I an opportunity to enter Deal Castle, which I had wished to do ever since first I spied it.

It was to my mind no proper castle at all, for it had neither turrets nor towers. It did, however, have a moat with a bridge across it which could be raised to make unwanted entry impossible. The bridge was down, as one might have expected, and I strode across it in a manner more confident than I felt. At the arched entrance I was challenged and halted by a soldier dressed in odds and ends—or one who was more likely a member of some local militia detailed to guard the castle against unauthorized visitors; he was, in any case, a man with a musket, and I thought it unwise to disobey him. I stopped, as ordered, and gave my name to him and told him whom I wished to visit. This information was passed on to another just inside the castle who ran off to deliver it to the proper place and person. I had no choice but to wait. Upon his return, he invited me to follow him and thus did serve as my guide through the narrow corridors and descending stairs which led ultimately to the office of the Customs Service.

"Why not wait for me?" said I to my guide. "I cannot suppose this will keep me here long." He was years younger than I, and appeared sickly. I saw no cause for him to tramp the stairs unneedful.

He nodded and took a place by the door which he had pointed out to me. I knocked upon it, and it was opened by Dick Dickens himself. Saying not a word, he beckoned me inside and closed the heavy oaken door after us.

"You know all about this?" he asked as I passed him the letter from Sir John.

"I do now," said I. "I was present while the details of the plan were fixed, and I took in dictation the letter you now hold in your hand."

"And do you think it will work?"

I was somewhat surprised by the question. What should it matter to him what I thought? Perhaps he was as unsure as I.

"I think it may if the information we've been given is correct; if the men in the wagons do not greatly outnumber us; and if Mick Crawly does not betray us." I said nothing of my uncertainty about Dickens himself.

At that he laughed. "You need not worry about Mick,"

said he, "nor about the quality of the information. I stand firmly behind both."

He then took but a moment to read quickly over the letter; then did he surprise me again by handing it back to me.

"You do not wish to keep it?"

"No, I have the contents firmly in mind. Better that you have the letter. It would not do to have it found here or on my person."

And so I took it and buried it deep in my pocket. Then did I bow my goodbye to him. I was out the door and, with the aid of my guide, out the castle in not much more than a minute.

We rocked easily in the interior of the hackney coach as the horses proceeded up the hill at a walk. There were five of us. Apart from Sir John and myself, I counted the three constables who had come down from London—Messrs. Perkins, Patley, and Bailey. Earlier in the evening they had made the rounds in Deal, giving special attention to Alfred Square, hoping to give the impression that there was naught different about this night. Now all had gathered together, mounted into the hackney, and rode in silence up through the highlands to the place Mr. Crawly had judged the best to stop the train of wagons on their way to London.

As Sir John had explained earlier that evening: "Smuggling goods from France—or anywhere else—can only be successful if you get the smuggled goods up to the market. And the best market is not down here in eastern Kent but in London. Whatever has been landed here must be brought up there for the job to be completed. We may either try to cut off the traffic as it is put ashore, or on the road leading to London. We have information of a large shipment—at least three wagons full—to be brought north. The shipment will be made up of the usual luxury goods—wine and brandy from France, and perfume, as well; tobacco from Turkey; and even fine linen and lace from Flanders. If we can stop the shipment, then we can deal a telling blow to the smuggling trade here—not perhaps the deathblow I would like, but one that will certainly wound."

And so it was to be a roadblock, one set up at some back-country crossroads of Mick Crawly's choosing. The idea was to halt them whilst the King's Carabineers rode up from their rear to cut off a possible retreat. How did we know the owlers' train of wagons would go up this particular road? And how could we be sure that they would not leave till after midnight? These were essential questions, of course. Yet they were questions I could not answer; nor was I even certain that Sir John could. In short, this seemed to me to be a good enough plan yet one based upon information of questionable worth—a sound structure built upon an uncertain foundation. I had hinted as much to Sir John upon my return from Deal Castle, yet I drew no response from him—no, none at all.

It should be evident from what I have written thus far that I was uneasy and somewhat agitated regarding that which lay ahead. What I felt was not so much fear as it was a heightening of the emotions, a quickening of the pulse, as I prepared myself for battle—or so I told myself. In any case, the slow pace of the horses pulling the hackney in no wise matched the racing of my heart. Oh, how I wished Mr. Crawly would drive the horses faster! Yet he had said as we began our journey that it would be best to go slowly, so as not to attract attention so late at night. All that was understood and agreed upon, yet now that we were beyond the town, must they plod as old plow horses? Unbeknownst to me and unintended, my left foot had been tapping at a quick, steady pace upon the floor of the coach. Indeed I knew not how long it had done so, for it seemed to have a will and a mind of its own. I was only made aware when Sir John placed his hand upon my knee until my foot was still, then put a finger to his lips, asking for silence. The three constables were quiet as could be. Mr. Perkins and Mr. Bailey, who sat across from us, rode along, bouncing and jostling with the movement of the coach. Their eyes were shut so that I supposed them to be nodding with sleep. But could they be praying?

At last we did reach the crossroads which Mr. Crawly had designated as the most likely spot to halt the owlers' caravan. I had to admit that it was well chosen. There, two country roads merged into a single high road which led northward to London. We climbed down from the coach, taking with us the musketry and cutlery which had been on the floor, wrapped in a blanket. In addition, each of us, except Sir John, wore a brace of pistols and carried powder and shot enough for a sustained battle. Once the coach was positioned well across the London road, Mr. Crawly, aided by Mr. Perkins, unhitched the team of horses and led them behind a copse of trees, to give them fair protection when the bullets began flying. Mr. Crawly and Sir John would remain there with them. Mr. Bailey took a place in good cover about three or four rods down the road where the owlers were expected to appear. Mr. Perkins took another on the other side of the same road about three rods beyond that. That left Mr. Patley and I to establish our position upon the roof of the coach. In a way, we were quite exposed. Because of that, we prepared a barricade there atop the coach—Sir John's portmanteau and my valise, each stuffed with bits and pieces of heavy clothing. In addition, there were two cloth bags filled to bursting with sand; these had been supplied by Mr. Crawly. We were to lie behind them. Constable Patley was to do the shooting with the two guns we held between us, and I the loading. I had practiced it in a prone position with him until I managed to do it (an accomplishment in itself, it seemed to me) in about half a minute. Try as I might, I seemed unable to manage it any faster. One of these weapons was his alone—a musket with a rifled barrel, with which, according to Mr. Bailey and others, Patley could hit a target a hundred rods distant.

It took a bit of doing for us to establish ourselves, and for that matter, we two were the last to settle into position, but eventually we were also ready. We had planned for a three-wagon train. Mr. Patley and I would be responsible for the first of them, Mr. Bailey for the second, and Mr. Perkins for the third; if there were a fourth or even a fifth, it would be the responsibility of the King's Carabineers. We felt we were ready for them.

We waited. Time passed slowly, so slowly that it seemed a very eternity since we had taken our positions. I wondered at that.

"Have you some idea of the time?" I asked Mr. Patley in a whisper.

"Oh, I don't know," said he. "I'd judge it to be about half past midnight, give or take a bit."

"Only that?"

"Well, let's see what my timepiece says." All the Bow Street Runners carried them as necessary equipment.

He rolled over upon his side and fished out of his waistcoat pocket a fat watch of German make. It opened with a button spring. He held it up and looked at it closely by the light of the moon.

"I misjudged by ten minutes," said he. "I have it here as twenty minutes to one in the ay-em. Keeps good time. Should be right."

I nodded, shifted my position, and waited longer. The moon was nearly full and very bright. In the gap between my valise and one of the sandbags, I looked down the road upon which the wagons were expected to come and was surprised at the clear detail I saw in the scene before me. Each bush, rock, and tree stood out as if in the clear light of day. In a sense, there was not much to see, for the road curved out of sight only about ten rods, or perhaps a little less, from where we were positioned.

"You'll hear them before you see them," said Patley.

"What will they—"

"Shhh! Listen! Here they come."

I attended closely but heard nothing—nothing, that is, of hoofbeats and creaking wheels; I caught only the sounds of the night—the breeze rustling the leaves of the trees, the call of an owl. Were Mr. Patley's ears so much sharper than mine?

Evidently they were, for in about a minute's time there came the sound of voices. I had not expected that. Perhaps I had thought the smugglers would be as silent as we. They were not. There was shouting and raucous laughter coming from beyond the bend in the road. I suspected that they had got at the brandy they were hauling and drunk deep of it. They must have contemplated the journey to London as one long drunken ramble.

Thus did they come. Just as the first wagon appeared, one who rode in it burst into song, and two or three of the celebrants joined him. I did not know the ditty, nor could I quite make out the words to it, but it had the sound of a sea shanty, or some sort of drinking song.

It was remarkable to me how close they came to us before noticing that there was something amiss. The fourth and last of the wagons had just appeared at the bend when the first of them at last pulled up no more than ten yards distant from us. It was close enough, in any case, so that I could tell that indeed there was something out of the ordinary about this wagon and team which led the smugglers' caravan. It was filled not with goods but with men—armed men, whose assigned task it was to protect the three wagons behind them. This they might have done well enough had they been sober, for indeed they outnumbered us four and were heavily armed. Nevertheless, their condition had the effect of making our respective circumstances even. And after all, we would soon have the cavalry galloping to our aid, would we not?

The first wagon had come to a halt so close to our teamless hackney that we could hear its occupants discuss this peculiar situation as they might a felled tree in their path or a flooded river.

"Here, now," said the driver, who seemed the most sober of all, "what's this large thing blockin' our way? Looks like a coach, so it does."

"Where?"

"Let's see."

"Right up yonder it is."

"I be damned if you an't right. It does look like a coach for fair, don't it?"

By then, all in the wagon were up from the wagon bed and looking at the hackney. One or two had bottles in hand, others pistols; some simply stood empty-handed and stared. There was general agreement among them that what stood before them, blocking their way, was a coach.

"But where's the team of horses that brought it there? How did it get there?"

"And why did they leave it—that's what I'd like to know."

"Well, I'd like to know, too," said the driver in a manner which seemed to be intended to put an end to such useless commentary. "But one thing I'm certain about. A couple of you—or maybe it'll take four—better climb down and move that thing because I can't get around it on either side. Trees are too thick and close to the road. Just push it over into the ditch, which is where it ought to be anyways."

The six or eight in the wagon set to arguing amongst themselves as to which of them were to push our hackney off the road. Having worked it out at last amongst themselves, the designated four clambered down from the wagon. Just at that moment a voice sounded forth deep and loud from among the trees; we recognized it in an instant as Sir John's.

"I am Sir John Fielding. I hold an appointment as magistrate of Deal. I order you to lay down your arms and climb down from your wagons with your hands raised, for you are all under arrest by my order. If you resist, or attempt to flee, you will be shot dead. This is your one and final order."

The driver of the wagon jumped down immediately and threw his hands up into the air. The four, who were at that moment the most exposed, looked wildly about. The others stood rooted in the wagon.

"Who was it? The magistrate? I thought he was kilt."

"Where'd that voice come from?"

"That copse of trees behind the coach."

Having heard that, one of the four drew his pistol from his belt and fired blindly at the trees. Mr. Patley returned fire, and the shooter fell dead. Then did all seem to happen quite simultaneous.

Patley passed the musket he had just discharged to me and took up the other. I set about to load the empty gun. Those in the wagon began firing up at us with their pistols; all shots flew overhead, save one which hit the valise with a *thunk*. Patley fired again and another dropped. I passed him the weapon I had just loaded.

But then—most alarming—we heard scrambling below and realized that three of the original four were below attempting to scale the coach with the intention of murdering us. I grabbed my pistols whence I had stored them, rolled over to the edge of the coach roof, and came face to face with an ugly owler; his pistol was half up, yet before he could discharge it, I brought mine down upon his crown, barrel-first, knocking him senseless. His eyes rolled in his head; he fell to the ground, knocking another down beneath him. I fired down at the sprawl, unsure which I had hit, nor whether I had hit either. Then, with my second pistol in hand, I looked about for the remaining villain. I found him behind me at the far side of the coach roof with his knee up and a pistol in his hand. Taking care to aim, I fired my own at him, and he fell back out of sight; I heard a thump as he hit the ground.

Then was all suddenly, deafeningly silent. Only the restive horses stomped and whinnied.

I saw Mr. Patley rise slowly to his knees from behind our makeshift rampart, his musket at the ready. I followed him up and set about purposefully loading my pistols. Before me and below, there were four men with their hands upraised. In the open wagon I could see one stretched horizontal across the floor—dead or badly wounded—and another close by, certainly dead. I could not be certain about the three at the foot of the hackney; whether they were alive or dead I knew not but would soon discover.

Then did Sir John's voice boom out once again: "Gentlemen, please make your reports. Mr. Perkins?"

"Two prisoners, sir."

"Mr. Bailey?"

"Two prisoners."

"Mr. Patley?"

"Four prisoners and two dead. Three are not yet accounted for."

"Jeremy? Are you all right?"

Before I could open my mouth to give assurances, Mr. Patley sang forth: "Jeremy's better than all right, Sir John. The lad's a proper soldier."

"All good news then?"

"Not quite," Mr. Perkins called out. "There were four wagons. The last of them got turned round and took off down the road they came up."

"We'll leave them to the Carabineers," said Sir John. "They've contributed naught so far to this operation, save for their presumed presence down the hill. And if we find that cocky young lieutenant has let that wagon get through and escape, I shall twist his ear for him."

Reader, I hasten to add that Sir John was speaking in jest.

TEN

*In which the
decisive battle
is fought and won*

Mr. Patley managed to embarrass me with his description of my part in the battle at the crossroads. "Not only did he load for me," said he to all, "he guarded my arse like it was the King's own. Kilt three of them, as I believe." I'm glad to say that he was wrong about that: I killed no one, though I wounded two. This we discovered in our final accounting, as we herded the prisoners into the open wagon, hands tied behind their backs. Him I had shot last had to be lifted with care onto the floor of the wagon, nor could he be tied, as the others were; yet so weak was he from the shoulder wound I had given him that he could scarce move there in the wagon bed. It did not please me to look upon him thus—though he would have happily murdered us, had I but given him the chance.

Included in that group of prisoners loaded into the open wagon were two taken by the King's Carabineers from that fourth wagon which had turned about and run, thinking to flee whilst our attention was elsewhere. Yet just as Sir John had predicted, they were caught and brought back by Lieutenant Tabor and his men.

All were together now, and ready to travel. Mr. Perkins drove the open wagon, and constables Bailey and Patley sat at either end, guarding the prisoners. Three of Lieutenant Tabor's troopers drove the remaining wagons, and we—Sir John and I—rode back to Deal in Mick Crawly's hackney coach. We went in caravan, Mr. Crawly leading the way, obviously relieved that neither his coach, nor his horses, had suffered a scratch during the encounter. All this took time, of course. It was about two o'clock when we set out on our return journey. Knowing that it would be near an hour before we reached Deal, I thought to learn more from Sir John of what lay ahead. I had, for instance, no notion of where, precisely, we were headed. Nor did I know what next he might be contemplating. To these and other like questions I hoped to learn the answer, and I was bold enough to believe that because of my conduct under fire (as it were) I was entitled to them. Vain expectation!

Once we were underway, I put that first question to him in the manner of a helpful warning. "I do hope, Sir John," said I, "that you do not intend to install all these prisoners at the inn. They would be easily rescued from there. Do, please, remember what happened when last prisoners were locked up there."

"I am not likely to forget, Jeremy," said he to me. "And in answer to your question, no, I do not intend to install them there."

"Well . . . where then?"

"That you will learn in due course. You acquitted yourself well on this night. You must be tired. Why not take a rest? That is what I intend."

So saying, he folded his arms over his capacious belly,

leaned back in his corner of the seat, and made ready to doze.

"Am I to be the only one among us all who does not know where we are headed?" I asked in frustration.

"Oh, by no means," said he, "I'm sure our prisoners have no inkling of our destination."

I could but sit in silence, musing upon the events of the night, rehearsing over and over again in my mind that minute (or hardly more) in which all the shots were fired and all the damage done. What I had seen and done in that time repeated dreamlike until at last, lulled by the rocking of the coach, I fell into a dreamless sleep. Whether or not Sir John truly slept during that time I cannot say.

Just as the movement of the coach had put me to sleep, its cessation roused me: the sudden loss of motion brought me up and out of my seat, blinking in the dark, attempting to see where we had stopped.

"Calm yourself, Jeremy," urged Sir John. "We have arrived. Now you'll have the answer to the question that so plagued you."

Indeed I did. The site beyond the window was lit well enough for me to see it exact—and I did truly recognize it, for I had been there only hours before. I was looking at the arched entry into Deal Castle just as the last of the smugglers' wagons, filled with contraband goods, disappeared inside.

A knock came upon the door at the far side of the coach. I slid across the seat and threw it open. There stood Dick Dickens, appearing far more eager and energetic than I felt at that moment.

"Sir John!" said he in an enthusiastic manner which well matched his bright appearance.

"Is it you, Mr. Dickens?" responded Sir John.

"It is, sir, and I see that all went as you wished."

"Not quite all, there were two dead and two wounded among the smugglers, and I would not have wished that.

But in the main, I would say that our operation was a success. But tell me, are you ready for us?"

"Just as I said when last we talked. I can supply storage space for the goods in the wagons. And Deal Castle, like any such, has a place for prisoners."

"A proper dungeon, eh?" asked Sir John. "You needn't keep them in comfort."

"They'll find little of it here."

"Good. I want them good and miserable when I come to question them. But what about the problem of the wagons and the horses? Have you solved that?"

"Yes, I'm sure we have. Once we get the wagons unloaded, I'll have four of my men take them out to a farm outside of town. The owner is someone I trust, and he's agreed to store the wagons as long as necessary and feed the horses with his own as well."

"Can you get them out there before daylight? All this must be done in secret, just as I've said. I'll need about twenty-four hours."

"Oh yes. Believe me, sir, it is also in my interest that all this be kept utterly quiet. If George Eccles should get wind of this . . ."

"We're in complete agreement then," said Sir John, offering his hand. "Look for me back here sometime toward noon."

Mr. Dickens clasped it with his own and gave it a firm shake.

"Till then, sir," said he.

With that, he shut the coach door, and with a word to Mick Crawly, he sent us off to Middle Street.

"Do you trust him?" I asked Sir John, putting it to him bluntly.

"Yes, I do," said he. "He has proven himself many times over. You see, Jeremy, he used this long period of inactivity to put into operation a truly formidable intelligence system. He can tell you whoever in Deal is involved in the smuggling trade—and to what extent. If I were asked—and I may be—who should have George Eccles job, I would say it should be Dick Dickens."

"This in spite of his criminal past?"

"People change, Jeremy. Oliver Perkins changed, as you well know. And I have heard from him that Mr. Dickens's story is even more dramatic than his own."

"Oh?" said I—ever the skeptic at that time of my life. "And how was that?"

"Well, it seems that whilst he was in Newgate, awaiting trial for violation of the excise laws—that is, for smuggling—he managed to write a letter and get it smuggled out and delivered."

"That was bold of him," said I.

"Far bolder than you think, for the letter was written and delivered to the Chancellor of the Exchequer. And boldest of all was its content, for in the letter, Dickens set about criticizing the mode of policing our coasts against smuggling. Not only did he tell him what was wrong, he took it upon himself to tell the Chancellor how it might be put right. The remarkable thing was that what Dickens put forth was all quite practical and helpful. He went so far as to suggest that there were other matters he would communicate, *if given the chance.*"

I laughed aloud at that, so taken was I by the fellow's audacity.

"He was, in effect, asking for a pardon," said I.

"It would seem so, wouldn't it? In any case, he got it—though not immediately. First the Chancellor of the Exchequer wanted to look him over. He had Dickens brought to him, and he found that he liked a number of things about him—his cheek, first of all; though more than that, he liked his direct, plainspoken manner; and lastly, he liked his youth, for when all this took place, Dick Dickens was but a few years older than you are now. So he made an arrangement with the Lord Chief Justice—not Lord Mansfield, but his predecessor—and had him released into his custody. No pardon was necessary, for Dickens had not yet been tried, though the result was the same. He enlisted him in the Customs Service, put many of his suggestions into practice, then promptly forgot about him. Dickens rose in the service, was given positions of trust and command, and finally was made Customs Officer for Deal. George Eccles secured his post through preferment at about the same time, and almost immediately the two fell into conflict. Eccles tied Dickens's hands, just as he did the rest of his officers up and down the coast. And so, unable to operate on his own, Dickens put together a formidable intelligence network. He had made this known to Albert Sarton, and the two were beginning to work together when I made my entrance."

"And so you then continued the collaboration," I offered.

"You might say so, yes." He waited for my response. When none came, he asked, "Are you now convinced of his reliability?"

"I am," said I, "though I confess that it is largely because you approve him. You were ever a better judge of character than I."

"That is because I am older than you," said he, "and have been proven wrong often enough that I've learned by necessity how to judge men."

He said not another word on our journey back to 18 Middle Street. I attempted to draw him out on what might be planned as our next foray against the owling trade. Yet he would not be persuaded. He simply smiled and shook his head, altogether unwilling to commit himself.

It was Molly, the widow Sarton, who wakened me late the following morning. I learned from her that Sir John had been gone for some time and taken Clarissa with him. And where do you suppose they had gone?

"Why, to Deal Castle," said she. "According to him, you would understand."

Oh, I understood—indeed I did. I was to be kept in the dark, just as before. Not even to be present during the interrogation of the prisoners—that did indeed exclude me, did it not?

"He said that he had a task for you that only you or one of the three constables could perform," she continued.

"What sort of task?"

"He dictated a letter to Clarissa and left it for you to deliver."

Once again, it seemed, I was to play the post boy.

"To whom am I to deliver it?"

"To that young lieutenant. What's his name? Tabor, I think it is. He said you're to wear the brace of pistols you wore last night and . . ." She hesitated. "And you're to use them, but only if you have to, so as to protect the letter."

Well, thought I, this errand may be more interesting than I had first assumed. It may even be of some importance in the grand scheme of things.

"I shall certainly get it out to him. You've got the letter, I assume?"

"Right here in my apron pocket."

"Any specific instructions—that is, any others besides the brace of pistols?"

"Oh yes. First of all, you're to take Mr. Crawly's hackney up there to Sir Simon's and no other. If he's not available, then wait till he is."

"All right. That's understood."

"Then, second, you're to wait while the lieutenant reads it through. Tell him to take special note of all the particulars, and then to burn the letter. And if he doesn't do it, you're to take it from him and burn it yourself."

I'm sure my eyes widened a bit at that. I know that my heart pounded an extra beat or two. In my memory, Sir John had never taken such extreme precautions.

The conversation I have just reported took place in the kitchen as I ate a grand breakfast and she did sip at her tea. Molly seemed to relax visibly after she had delivered Sir John's instructions to me. I, by contrast, had been put into an uneasy state of mind, imagining ills that might befall me on my way to the Grenville estate. Perhaps to divert me from such thoughts, she introduced a new topic of conversation, one which she supposed might cheer me.

"I hear you're reading the law with Sir John," said she to me.

"That's so," said I. "I mean to be a barrister."

"You'll make a good one, I'm sure. But you'll make an even better one with a proper law library. I'd like you to go through Bertie's books and choose whatsoever you will and take as your own."

She had quite overwhelmed me with her offer. "Why," said I, "I know not what to say."

"'Thank you' will do quite nicely," said she with a wink. "Shipping will be a bit, but Sir John said that he would cover the cost for those you pick and for Clarissa's, too."

"Clarissa?" How did she figure into this?

"Certainly," said she, rather defensively. "She had the same sort of choice I'm giving you. Surely you think that's fair, don't you?"

"Oh, yes—yes, of course."

"She had not so many to choose from, naturally, for Bertie wasn't much for romances. He did like his poetry, though, used to read me some when we . . ."

There she stopped, quite overcome by the tears that of a sudden welled in her eyes and the trembling in her throat.

"Oh, Jeremy," she wailed, "what shall I do with all this furniture? What shall I do with my *life*?"

I happened to have a clean kerchief in my coat— Clarissa's doing—so I offered it to her that she might regain her composure. And gradually, blowing her nose, clearing her throat, she managed to do just that. When, once more, she could converse, I asked her quite innocently if she could not keep the furniture and live in the house. In response, I saw an expression of absolute disgust upon her face.

"In this town of Deal?" said she, wrinkling her nose. "I would not remain here where Bertie and I were shunned and treated so shabby. You saw a bit of it in the church from the vicar."

"I thought he behaved shamefully."

"There was worse," said she, though she did not care to elaborate. "Besides, even if I chose to stay here, I could not."

"Why so?"

"The house belonged not to us but to the town. Mr. Kemp, the old magistrate—him who was murdered before Bertie—left it to the town of Deal that it might provide shelter to all who succeeded him in the office. I've already received a notice to vacate."

I felt a great sadness and sympathy for her, though I could think of no more to say. From what I had heard, Molly Sarton was now in a state in which a great many widows found themselves. Yet she wanted no pity. She reached across the table and gave my hand a squeeze.

"I must beg your forgiveness," said she in all seriousness.

"Whatever for?"

"For losing control as I did." She sighed deeply. "Oh, don't you worry about me, Jeremy. I've been in tight straits before, and I've always come out of them well enough, for if there's one thing I can do, it's cook. By God, I believe I am the best cook in all of England!"

And with that, she burst out with a triumphant laugh. Her sudden change of heart I found quite contagious: I, too, believed that she would triumph over her circumstances, that she was indeed the finest cook in England. I began laughing, too.

"You'll show them all," said I. "I know you will."

• • • •

Yet afterward, there was much to brood upon. Any reasonable view of her situation would have been considerably darker than what we two, in that final moment at the kitchen table, would have allowed. I realized that once I was out of the house and into the street, the letter to Lieutenant Tabor in my pocket and the pistols to keep it safe there belted round my waist.

I had no difficulty finding Mick Crawly, nor in persuading him to take me up to the Grenville estate. Nevertheless, so troubled was I by what I had heard from Molly Sarton that even though I rode beside Mr. Crawly and listened to him talk excitedly of the events of the night before, I had little to say in response. I found myself troubled, too, by the easy way he talked of roadblocks, ambushes, and the like, for after all, Sir John had been insistent to Mr. Dickens on the need for secrecy. I decided to confront him with my misgivings.

"Mr. Crawly," said I, "surely Sir John impressed upon you the need for absolute secrecy in regard to all that happened last night."

"Oh, he did, he did."

"Earlier, Mr. Dickens gave his assurances that we could trust you not to betray our operations. But betrayal can certainly be unintentional—so I must ask you, sir, have you told anyone of what you saw and heard last night?"

The expression upon his face expressed something akin to horror. And it was real enough and not mere play-acting—of that I was sure.

"I gave my word, young sir, and I would never, never break that. It's just that . . ." He hesitated.

"Yes, what is it?" I prompted him. I would hear the worst.

"It's just that, well, last night—that was proper excitement, that was. Why, it was just about the most exciting time I ever had. I was so worked up I couldn't hardly go to sleep at all. I've been scarce thinkin' of anything else since then, and here I'd sworn I wouldn't say a thing about it. I was grateful when I seen you come along because I had somebody I could talk to about it. I was fair burstin' to tell. Now I have. I'll be all right now, I swear."

"Just so long as you're sure."

"Oh, I am."

We left it at that. Nevertheless, after traveling over a quarter of a mile in silence, Mr. Crawly resumed his excited discussion by asking me how many I had actually killed the night before. He seemed disappointed when I told him.

Lieutenant Tabor, however, took such matters in his stride. I found him without difficulty. Indeed, one could hardly miss the encampment of the King's Carabineers, so near was it to the road leading past the distant manor house. His was the only tent in which one could actually stand to full height. By the time I reached him, he was dressed but unshaven; his servant was preparing to attend to it, stropping a razor, heating the water by the fire. The lieutenant read through the letter quickly and, it seemed to me, rather casually. Then, without a word, he tossed it into the open fire where the pot of water seethed. His indifferent attitude worried me a bit.

"I was to tell you to take note of the particulars which Sir John set forth in the letter, and then tell you to burn it," said I to him. "Since you've already done the latter, I trust I may tell him you've also attended to the former."

"You may tell him what you like," said he. "I am certainly confident that I have mastered the 'particulars,' as you call them—time, place, *et cetera*—or I should not have burned the letter. Will there be anything else? Do you wish to insult my intelligence further?"

I held my tongue. There would be no good purpose in trading rudeness for rudeness, so I simply bowed to him most politely, wished him a good day, and departed.

For a bit, as I returned with Mr. Crawly to town, I mused upon the lieutenant's attitude toward me. Why, he was quite as impolite as Lord Mansfield's butler. Yet hadn't he the day before been ever so much more obliging and mannerly? Ah yes, but the day before, I had but watched him and listened to his exchanges with Sir John and Mr. Eccles; he had had naught to say to me. He would seem then to be one—one of the many—who bowed and scraped to those he thought (or feared) might be his betters, and treated the rest with arrogant hostility. Mr. Patley had not a high opinion of the man. I now understood better the why of that.

I mentioned none of this to Sir John when I came back. There was no need, of course, but more important, he said that he had a task for me that was every bit as important as the one from which I had just returned. I was eager to hear of it.

"Do you wish me to wear pistols for this one, as well?" I asked him.

"What? Oh, no, certainly not necessary. Indeed, if you were to do so, it might create the wrong impression altogether."

"Perhaps I should ask just what sort of task you have in mind for me."

"Simple enough," said Sir John. "I wish you to go down to that sandy beach where you and Mr. Perkins and the two Deal constables prevented the landing by that crew of smugglers—I know not the name of it."

"Goodwin Sands—or so I understand."

"Very well, Goodwin Sands then. Where was I? Ah yes, I wish you to go down to that beach and look for Mr. Bilbo."

This was indeed good news. "Is he coming for a visit?"

"No, no, not the sort you mean. He'll not be coming ashore at all, not even anchoring out there offshore."

This was most puzzling. "How then shall I see him? How can I know him?"

"Why, by the flag that he flies. You've noticed, I'm sure, Jeremy, that ships that ply the Channel hereabouts fly all manner of flags from their rigging and their masts?"

"Well, yes, I have, but I thought them more or less for decoration."

"Nothing of the kind. The Union Jack, which you've no doubt seen, is flown for purposes of identification. It declares that this is a *British* ship. The orange ensign identifies the ship as Dutch, and the *fleur de lys* flag declares the ship as French. Ah, you say, but what about the rest of them—those small flags that flutter all round the rigging? You've seen those, too, haven't you?"

"I have, yes, and wondered at them," said I.

"Well," said Sir John, "they're there as signals—to other ships or to those on the shore."

"What do the signals say?"

"Whatever they might like them to say," said he quite expansively. "It would all be worked out in advance between those in the ship and those on the shore."

"Now I begin to understand, sir. You and Mr. Bilbo have worked out a code between you, have you not? But how did you know when Mr. Bilbo would be here?"

"That was according to his estimate," said Sir John. "I could in no wise dictate to him the time of his arrival. He did say, however, that if all were ready he would sail by Deal morning and afternoon. There's little of the morning left, but he's a man of his word, and we must look for him during the rest of the day. I cannot see him, and so you must be my eyes in this. Do you recall the general look of his ship?"

"I do, yes," said I. "It's called a sloop, is it not? I've seen others like it."

"Very good. Now, what you must do, Jeremy, is to go out there to the beach and keep an eye open for Mr. Bilbo's sloop. Now, as you've said, you've seen others like it. That is both good and bad, for while it should make it easier for you to recognize his as a sloop, it may make it possible for you to confuse his sloop with another. And so keep in mind that Mr. Bilbo's ship is, as I understand, varnished in a lighter shade than most. Had you noticed that?"

"Now that you mention it, sir, I suppose I had. I remember it as a sort of golden brown."

"That is no doubt correct," said he, "but another point to aid identification—he will be flying the Union Jack. And a third point, which is the most important, he will be flying green and white flags from his rigging. Have you got all that?"

"Yes, Sir John—lighter shade, Union Jack, green and white flags."

"Right you are." He gave a crisp nod of approval.

"But what was this about creating the wrong impression?"

"Ah yes, that," said he. "Well, what would you think if you were to walk the strand and you saw a young man, such as yourself, staring out at the sea quite intently. And then you returned some hours later, and the young man was still there on the beach in the same place, still staring just as intent out to sea?"

"What would I think? Why, I would think that rather odd, I suppose."

"I've no doubt of it. And that is the wrong sort of impression. I wish you to be virtually invisible there on the beach, just a part of the larger picture."

"And how do you hope to accomplish that?"

"Well, Jeremy, I know not how it is today, but when I was a lad about your age, it was a common enough sight when down on the seashore to see a young man in the company of a young lady. Whether in conversation or not, either seated in the sand or strolling the waterline—it mattered little what they did, so long as they did it together. Is that not how it is still today?"

"I suppose it is." With each word I hesitated a bit. I was

suspicious of the direction in which he seemed to be taking me.

"That being the case," said Sir John, "I have asked Clarissa to keep you company whilst you search the horizon for Black Jack Bilbo's sloop."

I raised no objection. It would have availed me little to complain. Besides, if this were truly to take an entire afternoon of waiting and looking, I should be glad for someone to pass the time with.

Thus it was that we were there together on Goodwin Sands for a number of hours that day. As Sir John had supposed, we sat for a time, then walked, sat again, then walked again. It was a perfect day for such. The sun shone down bright upon us. It was—in my memory, at least—the brightest and sunniest day we had known since our arrival in Deal. I recalled that when Clarissa and I first visited this place, it presented to us what seemed then to be a somewhat sinister aspect; I carried with me the image of that shipwreck beneath a brooding, gray sky. So was it then; yet on this day, Goodwin Sands seemed a different place altogether: the sky was blue and without a cloud (truly so: I looked and looked and saw not a one); the reflecting sea shone with the same deep blue, except in those places where it caught the sun and glinted silver. It was a day on which to enjoy the generous gifts of nature. And we were indeed not the only couple out on the beach on that afternoon.

Not forgetting why we had come, we paid much closer attention than the rest to the ships and boats out there on the Channel. Most of them were far too small to have taken our attention for more than a moment—fishing boats, most of them, and the largest of them single-masted. A Royal Navy frigate did glide by on its way to Portsmouth, impressive in its graceful bearing. Then finally there came a host of small cargo ships which passed our vantage, homely in appear-

ance and ungainly in passage. Some were large as sloops
but had not their style or shape. Clarissa remarked that she
had never truly been aware just what a crowd of ships was
out there between England and France. I replied that they
were thick as coaches in the Strand on a Monday morn—
and she agreed.

We talked of a great many things during those hours
upon the beach. I remember well that she had heard that I
had been something of a hero in last night's battle at the
crossroads. What pleased me most was the realization that
she could only have heard such from Sir John. "Hero"
would not have been his word, but hers. Even so, to think
that he had been sufficiently impressed to remark upon it to
Clarissa elevated my spirits to a point higher than they had
been since first we came to Deal. Still and again, it was a
bit embarrassing to be told this by her—yes, but at the
same time oddly pleasurable, too.

This led to a discussion of her visit with Sir John to Deal
Castle, which provided her first exposure to his quotidian
labors, save for an occasional visit to his court. She had
seen him in action, so to speak.

"He is terribly impressive when asking questions, don't
you think?" said she.

"I have heard it said that he is the most able interrogator
in all of Britain," I replied. "He seems to sniff an untruth
and hear the lie in the liar's voice. All he lacks—"

"Is the power of sight," said she, interrupting, as she
quite frequently did.

"True enough, but more often than not he seems to see
better with his blind eyes than the rest of us can with our
own, no matter how perfectly they may work. He takes
special pleasure in explaining to all who may ask that if a
man lacks one of his senses, then he must compensate by
strengthening the other four. There. I have heard him say it
so many times that I am sure that I have quoted him exact."

She thought about this for some time. This was during

one of our walking bits, and together we covered quite a stretch there along the water before she chose to speak again.

"I can certainly understand, Jeremy, how you happened to choose the law for your career. I believe that if I were a man, I should be a lawyer, too. Perhaps someday there will be a place for women in the law, too, yet I shall not see it in my day, I'm sure."

While I did not scoff at this remark of hers, I thought it too fanciful to be taken seriously. That, of course, was just the trouble in considering women in such responsible fields as the law. They are creatures of fancy (and none more so than Clarissa), and the law, the discovery and punishment of crime, matters of guilt and innocence—these are areas in which cold logic must rule. Yet of course I said nothing.

"Nevertheless," she continued, "it would do me well to learn a bit of Sir John's work, and the nature of legal procedures, et cetera, so that I might use a bit of this information in some future romance of mine. I can think of nothing better than one which would combine romance with the drama of murder. Perhaps I might write a tale of murder in which the reader must seek to guess the identity of the murderer before him whose role it is to do so in the narrative. How does that seem to you, Jeremy? To my knowledge, it has never been done before."

"How does it seem to me?" It was a clever idea; I gave the question serious consideration. At last I said to her: "I do not think it would please readers."

"You don't? But why?"

"Let us consider the common temper of the readers of romances. Why do they read them?"

"Why, for entertainment, for amusement."

"Exactly, but you would admit, I'm sure, that it is entertainment of an idle sort that they seek. They would not wish to do the sort of mental work that you propose. They expect the author of the romance to do that for them. And so, what am I to say? I do not believe that your idea, clever though it may be, would please readers, for readers are too lazy."

"Hmmm," said she (had she appropriated that from Sir John already?), "perhaps you're right."

We continued to talk, though at some point once more we sought the comfort of the soft, dry sand. I asked a few questions about what, if anything, Sir John might have learned from his interrogations at Deal Castle. From the little she had to tell me, I took it that he had learned little from the prisoners. I felt reassured that I had missed nothing of real importance. He who was captain of the wagon caravan provided Sir John with a list of the London shopkeepers, most of them in Westminster, to whom the contraband goods were to be delivered, thus managing to assure himself of a lighter sentence. Beyond that, there was little. I was, however, relieved to learn that the man whom I had seriously wounded was patched up by Mr. Parker, the surgeon, and it appeared that he would recover as swiftly as Mr. Trotter, the surviving member of Mr. Sarton's tiny constabulary.

Yet to speak of Mr. Sarton was to be reminded of that terrible night of killing in which I saw our friend Molly wailing and keening over the body of her dead husband. And so I then told Clarissa what I had that morning heard from her. Yet I was in no wise surprised to learn that my companion there on the beach had heard all I had and more from Molly Sarton. She knew not only that Molly was unwilling to stay in Deal, but also that she was *so* unwilling that she had even turned down an offer from Mrs. Keen to come on as cook at the tearoom that they might make a full eating house of it. Clarissa knew not only that the house was not Molly's own, but also that the notice to vacate which had been sent her demanded that she leave in five days' time. And she knew, no doubt, a good deal more things about dear Molly's plight. After all, why should she not? The two had shared a bed for nearly a week. Between us, indeed, Clarissa and I knew all about Molly's plight, except how to better it.

"We must do something," said Clarissa most earnestly.

"But what?" said I.

"Perhaps we should tell Sir John. He may think of something."

I considered the matter. There was little or nothing that we two could do to help. But there were avenues and opportunities open to him of which we could not even conceive. At the very least, since he was acting magistrate, he could make it possible for Molly Sarton to remain for as long as he were here. Or perhaps he might know some aristocrat or noble in London who badly needed a cook. He was, after all, a very influential man.

"I think you're right," said I. "Sir John should know, and I think you're the one to tell him."

"I'll do it," said she in a most determined manner, "just as soon as I can find the right moment."

So saying, she set her jaw and turned her eyes out to sea. Clarissa had a strong profile, and among women, strong features are thought to be unattractive and undesirable. Yet I recall reflecting at that moment that in a way peculiar to her alone, she was really quite pretty. Then, of a sudden, she became quite animated. She turned to me and at the same time raised her arm and pointed out into the Channel.

"Do look, Jeremy! Is that not the ship we were sent out to look for? Out there! See? Why, it's positively festooned with green flags."

I looked where she pointed and saw there could be no doubt of it: it was a sloop of a sort of golden brown hue which flew the Union Jack. What could be more certain? She was Black Jack Bilbo's *Indian Princess*. From where we sat, I could even make out figures moving about the ship. One in particular caught my eye: he stood upon the foredeck and jumped up and down, waving both arms for all he was worth. I believed—no, I was certain!—that the figure on the foredeck was my old chum, Jimmie Bunkins.

Then did I stand and wave back. Indeed, I kept right on waving until the sloop was out of sight.

"Come along," said I to Clarissa, "we must tell Sir John."

They would have saved themselves some trouble, thought I, and might even have managed to save themselves altogether, if only they had posted a lookout. Yet so sure were they of the easy success of their enterprise that the smugglers had come in number to Goodwin Sands just a bit before midnight (*our* lookout told us as much) and left no one to watch behind them. They had gone direct to the beach where one of them fired a flink pistol up into the night sky. We watched the progress of its rocket up and up many, many feet above the beach, until at last it reached its apex and exploded, sending a shower of sparks down on sand and water.

That was a signal to the ship that waited out there, not much more than half a mile into the Channel. And in response, from that darkness beyond, an answering rocket went up into the sky and sent its own fiery explosion out into the night sky. Everything was in place, and all was ready. If the rockets were thus signals from shore to ship and ship to shore, they were also signals to us that we might move up from where we had hidden ourselves into the positions that had been chosen in advance. All that would have stopped us would have been word that a lookout had been left—and that would merely have delayed us, for we were ready and eager to fight that night and would in no wise have been held back by one of their band. We were buoyed by our success of the night before.

On this occasion, Sir John's plan demanded a more active role of the King's Carabineers. There would be more for them than pursuing the main body and rounding up the stragglers. Half of them, in fact, were there up above the beach with us, their carabins pointed down alongside our muskets at the smugglers below. The remainder of the mounted troopers, under the command of Lieutenant Tabor, were in the distant dark at the far end of the beach, waiting to ride down upon the owlers. So you see, all was in readiness on our side, as well.

If anything, the moon was even brighter than it had been the night before. Each person, each object, down on the beach—wagons, horses, and men—was clearly outlined before us in the strong moonlight. Mr. Perkins came walking so low on hands and knees that he seemed to be crawling along. He dropped down beside Sir John and gave me a wink as he did so.

"The dragoons is getting uneasy, sir," said he. "They want to know when to fire and when not to fire."

"Well," said Sir John, "there'll certainly be no shooting till boats from the ship out there are on the beach and being unloaded."

"Right you are."

"And I must make my speech, as well. They're not to interrupt that."

"I understand."

"And come to think of it, Mr. Perkins, I'll call out the command to fire good and loud, so none can mistake. Let them hold their fire till then."

"Yes sir." Yet Mr. Perkins delayed leaving. "I wish you could see that moon up there tonight, Sir John—so big and round, so bright. It's what we used to call, in the old days, a smuggler's moon."

"Well," said Sir John, "let us hope that after tonight they will call it a 'magistrate's moon.'"

Then, chuckling softly, Mr. Perkins did leave us, moving swiftly as he had come. Sir John turned in my direction.

"What do you suppose, Jeremy? Shall we triumph this night?"

"We would not be here if we were not sure of it, sir," said I.

"True, but our lads are outnumbered."

"So were we last night, yet we surprised them and took them proper."

"I like your spirit, lad."

Sir John's plan, which he had earlier revealed to all, was simple as could be. As soon as the owlers were down on the beach, we would take positions along the high ground above, behind a natural rampart of sand. Once the boats from the smugglers' ship, a cutter, had landed and were in process of discharging their cargo, the smugglers would make easy targets for us above. It is true that we were out-numbered, though not by so very many. It was true, too, that in any absolute sense the Carabineers were untried in battle, for according to Mr. Patley their duties in Jamaica had been largely ceremonial, but they had been well drilled and presumably knew how to handle their weapons.

Though I had half expected to load for Mr. Patley, as I had the night before atop the hackney coach, I was not at all surprised when Sir John requested that I remain with him. I knew that he felt I should be protected from possible harm both because of my age and my unofficial status; he may have praised my performance to Clarissa, yet he felt in general that I was too young to be involved in shooting cir-cumstances; he used me only reluctantly.

So here we sat, Sir John and I, behind this low wall of sand, simply awaiting the arrival of a boat or boats from the ship. Though it was out well beyond the sandbar, a good half a mile away from the waterline, I could nevertheless make out its general outline in the bright moonlight. And I could certainly see a boat heading for the beach down that stream which cut through the sands. Yes, and there was an-other boat behind it, as well.

"There are two boats coming, sir," said I.

"Well, we shall wait till both are ashore and unloading has begun."

"Yes sir."

"But keep me notified."

That I promised to do and kept a careful eye upon the boat which led the way to shore. It was larger than that which had landed on our first meeting with the smugglers. This one, rowed by four men, would carry a considerable cargo of goods. I saw, too, that the one behind it was of the same size and design. It would not take many trips back to the mother-ship to empty her hold completely.

I looked left and right and saw—again in that bright moonlight—that all within sight were ready and a bit tense with waiting. I noticed something else: all of the constables were to my right, placed each to the next at a distance of thirty feet or a little less. To my left were six of the Carabineers, placed at the same rough distance, each to the next. Mr. Benjamin Bailey, captain of the Bow Street Runners, had assigned us our separate positions. He, of all people, must know what he was about, I told myself. Still, would it not have been better if the constables—and Sir John and I—had been mixed in among the untried Carabineers? All except myself were steady, confident men who might well stiffen the nerves of those off to my left, should resistance from below become unexpectedly fierce. Ah well, 'twas not up to me to decide such matters.

"The first boat has landed, Sir John."

"They've pulled it up on the beach, have they?"

"Yes sir—and now the second boat is in. They're pulling it alongside the first."

"They're unloading them?"

"Just begun."

"Well then," said he, "it is no doubt time to notify them of our presence."

He raised himself up on his knees (for he would not dare to stand and offer those below so fine a target) and cleared his throat. Then did he present his speech of the night before, repeating it near word for word. It was, of course, an appeal to surrender, yet it ended with a threat: "If you resist or try to flee, you will be shot dead."

There was wild laughter below. Yet they were not so disorganized as the drunken caravan guards of the night before. Immediately they sought the protection of the wagons. There must have been near twenty—nay, more—who scattered behind them in less than a minute. A man on horseback, whom I had taken previously to be the leader, rode from one to the next, shouting encouragement to his men. He dismounted behind the third wagon and sent his horse galloping, riderless, out toward the darkness at the north end of the beach (where, unbeknownst to them, Lieutenant Tabor and six of his troopers waited to ride down upon them). All that took place more or less simultaneous, but what soon became evident from all this hurly-burly and running about was that the owlers were determined to make a fight of it.

As best I could, I described this confused scene to Sir John as he nodded eagerly, taking it all in. He had but one question.

"Do you recognize the man on the horse?"

"No sir, I don't," said I. "His hat's pulled down, and his cape collar's up. I can see naught of his face. And even if I could, he's pretty far away."

"Remember then how he was dressed," said he. "Keep an eye on him as things progress."

"Yes sir."

As he had the night before, Sir John gave to them the first shot—or shots, really, for they came in ragged succession—*pop-pop-pop*—so that it took near half a minute for the owlers to waste their bullets and wonder if they had had any effect. What was most plain from the shots which were fired was that they had not an inkling of where we were hid. Most of the shots—which were from pistols of no great size—had hit the sand below us along the hill which led down to the beach. Still did Sir John withhold the order to fire. Soon I saw why. A minute passed, then more. Three or four heads popped up above the wagons and two exposed their whole bodies, stepping out from behind the tailgate of one of the wagons. One walked boldly from one wagon to view the hill above. There was uneasy laughter to be heard. Curiosity had made them incautious.

"Are they coming out yet?" Sir John asked in a whisper.

"They're starting to do so."

"Let us wait just a little longer."

A full minute passed. I know that to be accurate, for I counted off each one of those sixty seconds. And during that time, more heads came up, and a growl of talk was heard amongst the owlers.

"Would you say now, Jeremy?"

"Yes sir. Now."

"Fire!"

The volley from the nine muskets felled three, which I could plainly see. Yet I'm sure there were more—heads and shoulders, whole trunks, presented as targets which simply could not be missed. As many as a third of their number may have been hit by those first shots—and I told Sir John of it. Yet the survivors of that volley now knew our location, and balls from their pistols began digging holes in our barricade, spraying sand this way and that. Nevertheless, the effective range of a pistol is not very great, nor is it very accurate, and so, what they offered us was more in the nature of an annoyance than a danger.

The constables and the Carabineers then fired at will as targets presented themselves, but now, of course, targets presented themselves far more reluctantly than before. Heads were kept low; none ventured from behind the cover of the wagons. Would it continue so till morning? No. An indication that things were about to change came when, surprising us all, the flink pistol fired again and another rocket was launched into the sky. When it exploded, it sent an even grander shower of fiery sparks out into the night. This was obviously a signal, yet a signal for what? After informing Sir John of this odd development, I waited for an answering rocket from the ship—but none came. What did it portend? Little good for us.

A goodly space of time passed before the rocket achieved the desired result. Indeed, I had quite forgotten it and was looking up the beach, wondering if Lieutenant Tabor and his men would ever join the fray—and if it would make any difference if they did. This I was pondering when, of a sudden, I heard a great boom, a whishing through the air, and a powerful thud not too far behind us. Good God, the smugglers' cannon! I had quite forgot the cannonball that had been thrown our way but a week ago as we marched our prisoners up the hill.

Did I write "the smugglers' cannon" but a few lines past? It should have been writ "the smugglers' three cannon," for if there be such a thing as a volley of cannon, we were then offered one from the ship. I was watching it closely (as close as the darkness permitted) when the side of it suddenly seemed to burst into flame. What I had seen, reader, were three good-sized cannon erupting simultaneous in powder and shot. Then came the great roar they made together, and the separate thuds—one which hit below and two directly on either side of our place behind the sand wall. If the pistol shots did little more than spray us with sand, the cannonballs fair drowned us in it. Sir John and I had it in our faces—our nostrils and mouths—so that we came up coughing and spitting out the gritty stuff. But Sir John quite amazed me, for it seemed that between coughs and spits, he was laughing! Not great guffaws, but mirthless chuckles of a sort that somehow said he was anticipating something quite jolly. It would have to be something very jolly indeed to make up for this.

A glance off to my left assured me that the King's Carabineers were certainly not amused. The trooper nearest us seemed to have taken in quite as much sand as Sir John and I—and swallowed deeper; the poor fellow was retching to rid himself of the stuff. But the one beyond him worried me more. I saw fear writ upon his face plain as if indelibly in ink. The next barrage, which fell farther to the left though no nearer, put him into such a state that he threw down his weapon, turned, and ran. To what destination I cannot be certain, nor could he; his only thought, I'm sure, was to be away.

Meanwhile, however, the shooting continued. The constables, as well as two or three of the Carabineers, kept up a steady fire down upon the owlers. Yet the latter, assuming we would be driven away soon by the cannonballs raining down upon us, did not even bother to return fire with their pistols. Thus we had achieved a sort of lopsided draw. It would only turn in our favor if Lieutenant Tabor committed himself and his six mounted troopers to the fight. Why did he hold back?

There was but one other possibility, and that one seemed now so dim and distant, a mere phantasy, so that I—

The sound of booming cannon came from a distance, though not a great one, as great fountains of water erupted all round the smugglers' cutter. That possibility for which I'd hoped had suddenly become a probability! Another barrage from the mystery ship, and it hove into view flashing flame. My wish had been granted, my hope fulfilled: Black Jack Bilbo had made a most dramatic entrance.

"Sir John," said I, "I believe it's Mr. Bilbo come to save us."

"You believe so, do you? Well, it had better be him and not some other pirate."

There was a flurry of disordered activity aboard the smugglers' ship.

Seamen raced about the deck, attempting to weigh anchor while at the same time others were attempting to get off one last shot from their cannon at us up on the hill. Rushed as they were, they aimed false and fired from the trough of a wave, utterly destroying one of the wagons on the beach and wounding, perhaps killing, a number of those who had sought cover behind it.

But now at least the ship was free, anchor aweigh, able to attempt an escape from a larger, potentially faster ship, one that had them outgunned (I later learned) thirteen cannon to seven. It wouldn't be easy, though it might be possible. The captain of the smugglers' ship tried a daring maneuver, tacking into a light wind and proceeding parallel to the sandbar. In such a way, he might just manage an escape.

But Mr. Bilbo was not to be so easily outdone. He, too, threw the *Indian Princess* into the wind, duplicating the same maneuver the smaller ship had performed with such swift grace. At the same time, his gun crews made ready to fire once again. When the two were parallel, side by side at a distance of no more than a hundred and fifty feet, Mr. Bilbo gave the order to fire and, well aimed, the cannonballs burst through the rigging, bringing sails down and snapping the main mast. The smugglers' ship was doomed.

An audible groan was heard from the owlers. They had left the shelter of the wagons and lined the beach in order to watch the action in the Channel waters. What were they to do? Must they surrender?

Mr. Bilbo's *Indian Princess* was now alongside its half-destroyed victim, which floated dead in the water. Grappling hooks were thrown. Men leapt and swung across to the smaller ship. The rattle of small-arms fire swept across the water to us. It seemed now that all would be over in a few minutes' time.

All this I had described to Sir John as it was happening. And at this point I had a surprise for him.

"You may not credit this, Sir John," said I to him, "but

Lieutenant Tabor is now riding down upon the owlers to demand their surrender."

"At last, eh?"

"Indeed, he—" I broke off sudden, for I had seen something that disturbed me. "Sir, the man you told me to watch—the one who was on horseback—he seems to be getting away."

And indeed he did! He had moved stealthily through the clustered owlers, seeking the darkness at the south end of the beach. He blended in well with the rest. He might well be gone before his absence was noted.

"Then after him, Jeremy," said Sir John. "Shoot him in the leg, if necessary, but you must not let him escape!"

That was all that I needed to hear. I was up and over our sand wall and running down the hill of sand so swiftly that it seemed for a moment or two that I must tumble heels over head to the bottom of it. I went fast as I could then, close behind him but aiming at a point ahead where our paths would intersect. He was in no wise capable of besting me in such a footrace. He must have known that, for when I was close, he suddenly stopped, threw back his cape, and drew a pistol. My momentum carried me all too near: He could hardly miss at such a space. What was I to do?

I ducked, scooped up a handful of sand, and threw it in his face just an instant before he fired. Yet in that instant, his hands—including the one which held the pistol—had gone up involuntarily to protect his eyes. The pistol shot sailed above my head.

Before he could recover and perhaps draw another pistol, I had wrestled him down to the sand and was fighting to keep him down. He, on the other hand, was trying with all his might to bring up the empty pistol and knock me unconscious with it. He was no match for me. I pinned his left arm with my right knee, then I used both hands to take the gun from him (easily done: the wrist is the weakest part of the arm). It was mine now to do with what I wished, and what I wished most was for this fellow to stop thrashing beneath me like some wild brute. I beat upon his head with the butt of it until he lost consciousness. At last I could know who he was.

I jerked off his hat, unbuttoned his cape collar, and pulled it down. Who then was revealed? Why none but Sir Simon Grenville, Baronet.

and of those who displayed the outward signs of wealth. It is a fault which I have since overcome (or pray God I have).

It was Sir John, of course, who explained it all to me, tying together the bits we had learned and seen along the way so that they told a continuous story. This took place after Sir John, as acting magistrate, had devoted a whole day to a single session of the magistrate's court, which was held for convenience in Deal Castle. All who had been placed under arrest during those two successive nights (with the exception of those subjects of France who were held whilst their status was negotiated) were bound over for trial in London. This was a considerable number, and hearing each man's statement, managing the paperwork, et cetera, took a considerable amount of time. I could not remember Sir John ever working as hard or as long as he did that day. Yet the dinner prepared for him by Molly Sarton did rouse him from his torpor, and rather than retire immediately thereafter, he chose to sit for a bit in the little room off the hall which Mr. Sarton had called his study. It was there that I approached him. And it was there that I heard his account of events which led up to the battle on Goodwin Sands and began well before our arrival in Deal.

"It all goes back," said he to me, "to his second marriage. As I understand from Molly Sarton, the death of the first Lady Grenville came of pneumonia following the coldest and the wettest winter they've known here in Kent in many a year. There was one child, a boy named Robert, who boards year-round at the Cathedral school in Canterbury. Somehow, the first Lady Grenville had exercised some restraint over her husband whilst she was alive. Now that she was gone, he was free to pursue a course he had considered, even planned, for years. Not content with the rents he gathered each year from his thousand acres, he wished to take part in the most lucrative trade of all in this region, which is, of course, smuggling. He intended to en-

ter at a high level and organize all under his direction. He
would turn a simple trade into an industry.

"How would he go about this? First of all, by marriage.
He arranged a match with the daughter of one of France's
oldest families—in the smuggling trade. Marie-Hélène's
family, the Casaleses, had contacts among wine-growers,
weavers, lace-makers, tobacco-traders, all of those suppliers of goods which the aristocracy, and the merely prosper-
ous, felt they could not live without. The Casaleses also
owned vessels with which they might move their goods
across the Channel. It seemed quite like a perfect arrangement—and it might have been, had he not wished to take
the matter even further.

"Was there any safe way to engage in the smuggling
trade? To be safe—that is, from detection and prosecution?
Why yes, if he were the magistrate of Deal, then he would
certainly be safe. The only difficulty there was that Deal had
a magistrate, old Mr. Kemp, and he could not be persuaded
to step down. And so, Sir Simon had him murdered. You
know how it was done, Jeremy: Sir Simon appeared at the
magistrate's window in the middle of the night, persuaded
him to open the door that they might talk, and had him shot
down before his very eyes. However, just as he was preparing himself for the job, the Lord Chief Justice, a friend of his
father's to whom he owed more than one favor, asked Sir Simon if he would use his influence to seat young Albert Sarton as magistrate in Deal. He did not feel that he could deny
Lord Mansfield; and after all, he could no doubt use one so
young as Sarton to achieve his own ends—or so he thought.
We know a good deal of this from Mr. Eccles, of course,
whose friendship he had cultivated; the rest is reasonable
speculation.

"There was one more obstacle to his domination of the
smuggling trade, and that was the small gangs in and about
this part of the Kent shore. If he could not persuade them to
join him and accept his direction, then he would have to

eliminate them. This process began with the hiring of one gang, which he housed right there upon his estate, and with the apprehension of another, the single occasion whereon he was able to 'use' Mr. Sarton. He made some successful runs from France—or rather his wife had done so, for it was she who oversaw the delivery of the goods to England—and a proper sailor she is, or so I've been told. In any case, there were smuggled goods of all sorts stored in a chalk mine on the Grenville estate. One night, one of the roughest of the gangs came in stealth to the estate, murdered the guard who had been posted at the mine, and escaped with a wagonload of goods to dispose of in London. They should have stayed in London, for when they returned, he had them killed.

"That was on that single night when so much blood was spilled. In addition to the three whom you found, there was Mr. Sarton, whom we can now be certain was murdered in the same way his predecessor had been, and the constable who was guarding the captives taken down there on the beach. The three on the beach were killed as an example to all the rest of the smugglers in the region of Deal; thereafter he would have had no difficulty enlisting the remainder. Mr. Sarton was murdered because he had proven himself altogether too independent and had had the temerity to order an operation which intercepted a specially ordered shipment of perfume; Sir Simon took it as an insult, too, that Lady Grenville had, in the course of the operation, herself been shot at. You do recall, don't you, Jeremy, that Mr. Perkins said he believed that one of the two passengers in the boat which escaped was wearing skirts? He was quite right. She was—though I understand that she does not always do so. And ah yes, the poor fellow, who was killed at the inn guarding the prisoners, and his mate, who was badly wounded—just another demonstration by Sir Simon of his power: his men were rescued and their captors shot down. This was meant as a lesson to all. And all the rest of the story I'm sure you know as well as I—indeed, perhaps better."

"Better? Oh, I doubt that, sir," said I.

"But you took an active part in those events, played your role well, and there is nothing like the participant's knowledge," said he rather plaintively. "But perhaps you have some questions . . ."

"Oh, I have many."

"Well," said he with a sigh, "I'm not sure that I'll be able to answer many. Why not ask me two or three that plague you most?"

"All right," said I. "When did you first suspect Sir Simon?"

"Almost from the very first. He could not satisfactorily account for his sudden change—nay, reversal—of opinion with regard to Mr. Sarton. He was completely for him, then of a sudden, he was completely against him."

"Was Mr. Eccles his collaborator, or simply his dupe?"

"From all I can ascertain—and believe me, I have tried—Eccles was simply his dupe."

"I noted," said I, "that Sir Simon was bound over to be tried for the murder of Albert Sarton, with a lesser charge of smuggling. Can murder be proven?"

"Oh, it can be proven. I have a witness." I would then have pressed him for the answers to more such questions, but with a wave of his hand he silenced me. "Let that be all," said he. "The answers to the rest you may have tomorrow night."

"What then?"

"Molly has asked us to what she, in her way, calls a victory feast. Let it be called whatever she wishes. It will be a proper celebration, and the celebrants will be those, like you, who took an active part in the doings of the last couple of nights."

•　•　•

It was indeed so. With the exception of Lieutenant Tabor and his men, all who had played some part were present. And why were they not? I put the question later to Sir John, and he explained that he felt the lieutenant had not taken a sufficiently active role on either night to merit an invitation; and those of the Carabineers who had contributed could not be invited whilst their officer was excluded.

It was a proper English feast, prepared by Molly Sarton and served up by Clarissa. Which is to say, there were potatoes and carrots for all who wanted them, but the centerpiece of the meal was a joint of beef roasted quite perfect and offered with pudding and dripping. A modest menu, to be sure, but what it lacked in courses, it made up for in quantity. There was God's own plenty there for all to eat, and enough good claret so that all might leave the table tipsy if they so chose.

Though in the beginning a fair quiet reigned at the table, as we filled our stomachs and drank our fair share of wine, tongues loosened and talk began to flow round the table.

Sir John, who sat at the head as Molly had insisted, rose and toasted our hostess and cook. Then did he raise his glass to one after another at the table, speaking of each and describing his contribution to the outcome of our signal victories.

He raised his glass, first of all, to him who sat across from Clarissa and me: "To Will Fowler," said Sir John, "who, for no reasons of personal gain, but rather to maintain the good name of the Grenville family, kept Mr. Dickens apprised of the illegal activities of Sir Simon. Specifically did he tell us of the movement of the smugglers' caravan to London and of the landing on the next night at Goodwin Sands."

All drank to Mr. Fowler as I picked up a bottle of claret and raced round the table, filling glasses.

"To Mr. Richard Dickens who, having found his way to the right side of the law, discovered a way to remain active in his chosen profession, even though kept in a state of involuntary retirement by one we need not name here. To wit, he formed a model intelligence network and used it to aid Mr. Sarton—God rest his soul—and me. 'Twas he who passed on the information regarding the caravan and the landing and assisted me in the planning of the two operations which resulted."

The table drank to Mr. Dickens. One or two signaled to me that their glasses were empty. I filled them.

"To Mick Crawly, hackney coach driver extraordinary, who took our little force up the hill to the crossroads where the first battle was fought. He did this at some risk to himself and to his fine team of horses. And he generously permitted us to make use of his coach to block the road to London. It might have suffered considerable damage, yet miraculously it did not."

I wondered that I myself might well be tipsy once all the toasts had been drunk; there were ten besides Sir John at the table, after all.

"To Oliver Perkins, Benjamin Bailey, and Will Patley, three trusty members of my London constabulary, the Bow Street Runners. They came here to Deal without condition and proved invaluable each time they were called upon. I owe so much to them and their fellows, I know that I shall not begin to be able to repay the debt, except with my deepest thanks."

Here Sir John paused as we drank. His forehead then wrinkled in a frown.

"John Bilbo," he called out. "Are you here, Mr. Bilbo?"

"I am, sir. I'm here at the other end of the table, a bit below the salt."

"Where you belong! I had not heard you say a word for a bit, Mr. Bilbo, and I wondered perhaps you'd slipped out without my knowing of it."

"Little chance of that, Sir John, so long as there's a bit of that roast beef left." Mr. Bilbo then laughed heartily at his own joke.

"Then let us, one and all, drink to him, ladies and gentlemen, for without him, his sloop, his cannon, and his seamanship, most of us would not be here at all. We had heard rumors of Black Jack Bilbo, of his shady past. Stories were told that he was a pirate, and others that he was a privateer, yet on one point they did all seem to agree—that he was a fine commander and a great seaman. Well, that was demonstrated in the waters just off Goodwin Sands two nights back. He is a grand fellow and a great one on whom I knew we all could depend. He is a friend and will ever be—I give you, Mr. John Bilbo."

"Hear, hear," was heard from Mr. Perkins, and a scattering of applause came from his fellows. They held up empty glasses. I grabbed a bottle from the sideboard and rushed to provide remedy.

"And now," said Sir John, "we come to Jeremy Proctor."

He caught me offguard. I had not by then recovered my place at the table. I could not do so at that moment, and so I simply stood rooted by the sideboard with what I'm sure must have been a look of surprise upon my face. I knew not what to expect.

"Oftentimes," he continued, "Jeremy is denied his due. This, I believe, is because I have come to think of him as a son. If he were my son, I should think of him as satisfactory in every way, yet I would still deny him his due. This is unfair of me, I know, yet it is how I myself was brought up. My father was a military man, and he was always sure that whatever was good could be made better. I entered the Royal Navy as a midshipman and found that the same rule applied. And so I, the prisoner of my past, have tended to treat Jeremy as I was treated. And in this instance—I might say, in these two instances—he deserves better than that. In the battle at the crossroads, at considerable risk to himself, he protected our sharpshooter, Mr. Patley—"

"Saved my life, he did!" Mr. Patley called out, interrupting.

"So I understand," Sir John agreed. "And the next night on Goodwin Sands, when Mr. Bilbo's successful attack upon the smuggling vessel had ended the resistance of those on shore, their leader, Sir Simon, thought to escape, undetected and unidentified. It was Jeremy detected his escape and identified him to me as the leader. I sent him to capture him, not realizing that I could have been sending him to his death. Yet he acquitted himself just as well in that instance as he had earlier, catching Sir Simon and, braving a shot aimed point-blank at him, overcoming the smuggler chief. So let us drink also to Jeremy Proctor, who did wonderfully well, though I suppose he could have done better—yet I can't, for the life of me, think how."

Having spoken thusly, he extended his glass in the ceremonial gesture toward me, then brought it back and sipped from it whilst those at table mimicked the gesture. For my part, I burned with embarrassment; my eyes filled with tears. Will Patley led a round of applause. Somehow I found my way back to my chair and sat, quite overcome, yet forcing a smile.

"Now then," said Sir John, "have I slighted any? Is there one, or even two, here this evening whose part in this has not been recognized?"

There were calls from Mr. Crawly and Mr. Fowler, repeating Clarissa's name.

Then did Molly Sarton make her voice heard above the rest: "Just like a man to fail to give a female rightful credit. Yes indeed, Clarissa!—the girl who served you your dinner. Does that count for so little?"

"Not at all, not at all!" cried Sir John. "Let it be known to one and all that I am second to none in my appreciation of that young lady and well she knows that, or so she should. Let me make amends by offering this toast:

"Gentlemen, I give you Mistress Clarissa Roundtree. Let

it be known that she is much in her own right—secretary to Lady Fielding, poet, a writer of romances yet to be written, and incarnate proof that women are, in ways yet uncounted, equal, if not superior, to men. Her contribution to the victories we celebrate here may not be material, nonetheless it was real enough and can be measured. Her insatiable curiosity set her wandering about Sir Simon's estate, making discoveries of perfume, wine, and a corpse that kept alive my suspicions of him. Thus, her misadventures provided the impulse which drove forward my investigation. Also consider her influence upon Jeremy . . ."

At that there were a few chuckles heard from that corner of the table where sat the three London constables. Sir John ignored them.

"Could he have accomplished the feats which I have described, without her womanly inspiration?"

There was laughter all round the table at that. It rose in volume and pitch as Sir John bellowed forth:

"Surely not!" He raised his glass to Clarissa and drank, as did the rest.

Then, reader, as if I were not sufficiently chagrined by all this merrymaking at my expense, Clarissa, who sat next to me, leaned over and planted a hearty buss upon my cheek. Then did the table go quite mad with foolish laughter. Alas, even I, in spite of myself, did join in; it would have taken a more sober-sided individual than I to have resisted.

In all, though we were at table well over an hour more, Sir John's toasts to one and all there at dinner provided the climax to a jolly evening. We were perhaps a bit rowdy, yet harmlessly so. And there was to the occasion also something a bit melancholy, for I believe that all who were there realized that in spite of the abundant good feeling, this would almost certainly be the only time we would all sit together at the same table. For those of us who knew the late magistrate—and for Molly most of all—there was the added disappointment that Albert Sarton was not present to celebrate the fruition of his work in Deal.

With those melancholy circumstances no doubt in mind, Clarissa began a conversation with Mr. Fowler which had a most surprising result. He sat, as I believe I have already mentioned, across the table from us. And the hum of talk around us was such that she was obliged to speak up a bit in order to be heard. Yet all the rest were so absorbed in their own conversations that none but I paid them much attention. I know not if I can quote them exact, yet I shall try, knowing full well that any mistakes I make will certainly be corrected.

I recall that she waited till Mr. Fowler had concluded with Mr. Dickens on his right when Clarissa called out to him and gained his attention.

"Mr. Fowler," said she, "I wonder if you would clear up a few things for me."

"I'd be happy to try, Miss Clarissa," said he.

"That last walk I took round the estate . . ."

"Ah, I was thinkin' you might get to that sometime this evening. What is it you want to know?"

"Well, a number of things, really. For instance, I believe I fainted whilst out alone in the night, though I'm sure I was grabbed from behind."

"You was grabbed from behind, true enough, by a guard put out to keep all away from the chalk mine."

"And did I faint, or was I somehow sent into an unconscious state?"

"Both, I fear. You fainted, p'rhaps from the shock of bein' grabbed so rough. But then they, not knowing what to do with you since they was aware you was with Sir John, put a sponge to you which put you to sleep till I was sent for and came."

"What was in the sponge that kept me asleep so long?"

"It was a potion, so to speak, of all the worst, such as squeezed mandrake root, opium—if you know what that is—and the whole of it soaked in wine. It kept you sleeping for the better part of an hour whilst I was sought out and summoned. They'd no idea of the plan of the house and must have wakened half the household staff before finding me."

Clarissa giggled, something she didn't often do. "It must have taken you half that time to get out of that silly ghost costume and get the paint from your face."

He looked at her oddly. "Pardon? I remembers you had something to say about the ghost, but I put it all to that potion you'd been given."

"Nothing of the kind," said she. "I assure you that I saw you dressed up as the ghost in that silly last-century costume. I know it was you."

"Miss Clarissa," said he. "I assure you it were not."

"But he looked like you," she protested. "Quite like you."

"Be that as it might . . ." But then did he hesitate. "P'rhaps I should confess to you something of my family's history. You see, Sir Simon and I share the same great-grandfather. I carry the family face better than he does. You remarked upon it once yourself."

"A bar sinister!" She fairly shouted it. Heads turned, and Mr. Fowler looked away as if to deny his part in this conversation. Clarissa, on her side, clapped her hand over her mouth and rolled her eyes in shame. To me she muttered, "When will I ever learn?"

There was little more to say to Mr. Fowler. (I'm sure he thought she had said quite enough already.) And so, for a lengthy period of time she remained unusually quiet. Then, of a sudden, as if the thought had just struck her, she turned to me with an expression I might call stunned. Then did she say to me in a whisper: "Good God, Jeremy, do you realize what this means? I've seen a ghost."

A good deal of the talk round the table that evening had far greater import. As an instance of this, Mr. Bilbo fell into discussion with Mr. Dickens and learned from the latter than an awkward situation had developed with the prisoners held in Deal Castle. They had to be moved to London at once, or his chief, Mr. Eccles, would discover their presence, listen to his old friend, Sir Simon Grenville, and set them all free. He was capable of such treachery. The difficulty was this: They had not transportation sufficient in Deal to move so many. Mr. Bilbo asked how many there were and was told that there were over forty, if they were to include the Frenchmen from the ship. "Why not include them?" Mr. Bilbo was heard to say. "I can take them all. We'll lock them in the hold, and they'll make good ballast." His offer was then passed on to Sir John; he liked it so well that he asked if he and all the rest of the London-bound party might also come along. Nothing could have pleased the old privateer more.

"I should make it clear," said Sir John, "that this will include our hostess, as well."

He spoke loudly so that all at table might hear, and in response, Molly Sarton gave a broad smile, which seemed to include both Clarissa and me.

"Then you told him of her situation?" said I to Clarissa.

"At the first opportunity," said she.

Speaking in the same loud voice, Sir John announced that Molly would, for a time, be serving as our new cook there at Number 4 Bow Street. "She deserves better and will get it soon at one of the great houses, but this will give her a chance to find her way in London, and also in the meantime, to pass on her kitchen secrets to Clarissa."

TWELVE

*In which the judge
quails, and I
am embarrassed*

And so it seemed that all had been arranged. Two days later we left Deal. All but one of the prisoners were locked away in the hold; those who were not in irons were bound with rope and would, Mr. Bilbo assured us, cause no problems. The extra day gave Sir John a chance to dictate a letter to the Lord Chief Justice and explain the outcome of the events he had described in his earlier letter; he also requested that transportation be provided from the dry-dock to Newgate Gaol. The dry-dock in Wapping was specified because Mr. Bilbo announced that he would be claiming *La Belle Voyageuse* and towing it up the Thames to Wapping for repairs and sale. Clearly, he had no intention of losing the opportunity to benefit monetarily from his trip to Deal.

The extra day taken by them before their departure also gave Molly Sarton time to put her affairs in order. She took along with her little more than the clothes on her back—

and a frock or two in her portmanteau. Most of the furniture in the house in Middle Street had belonged to its former owner, Mr. Kemp. But there were keepsakes and a few pieces of her own which Molly stored in the cellar of Mrs. Keen's tearoom. Though the two veterans of service in the Grenville household had a tearful parting, Molly was adamant that she had no desire to remain in Deal. In a way, I thought she was wrong in that, for even though the circumstances in which I had come to know the town were far from ideal, there was much about it I had come to like. Yet of course I had not endured there what she had.

There was, as earlier indicated, one smuggler who had managed to avoid imprisonment with the rest in the hold of the *Indian Princess*, and that one alone was Marie-Hélène, the Lady Grenville. This was partly out of respect to her sex, of course, though for the most part, I think, it was because Black Jack Bilbo had taken a liking to her. He had provided her with a cabin (his own) and given her the freedom of the ship—with the exception of the hold, of course. She was not to talk to the prisoners through the grate or air holes, nor in any way attempt to communicate with them by letter, or by note, or by sign. These prohibitions seemed to bother her not in the least. She wandered about the vessel, speaking with whomever she would in accented English which set some laughing and charmed the rest. Clearly, Mr. Bilbo was one of those charmed. He managed to spend a good deal of time with her, in spite of the demands upon his attention as captain of the ship. And Clarissa pointed out that he always seemed to come away from such encounters with a smile upon his face.

My chum, Jimmie Bunkins, acknowledged, with a sigh, the accuracy of her observation.

"An't it so," said Bunkins with a troubled look. "Seems these Frenchy blowens got a certain way with the cove. Been so as long as I knew him."

"He's certainly interested," said I, meaning to imply with that a good deal more than mere interest.

"I fear that if he were any more interested, we would never reach London," Clarissa commented dryly.

"Least this one's got a proper cut to her jib and a pair of bollocks would do any man proud." At that point he halted and looked uneasily at Clarissa. "Beg yer pardon," said he to her.

She simply chuckled.

"Look at her now," said Bunkins, nodding across the deck at Lady Grenville. "Looks right rum in that dress, don't she?"

"Mmmm, she should," said Clarissa. "Must've cost a pretty penny in Paris."

"Well," said he, "first time I seen her she wasn't wearin' no dress. She was wearin' kickseys, same as any man. She had a cutlass in her hand, wavin' it about, tryin' to get her crew to fight the *Anglais*—that's us—but they was all for givin' up, hands up in the air, an' that. But all this time she's yellin' at them, cursing them in French, like. And then she sees the cove jump on board, an' he's a-wavin' his cutlass about, an' without anybody tellin' her, she knew he's the captain, so she runs at him with her cutlass and would've kilt him right there had she the chance. The cove knew right enough she was a woman and didn't want to fight her, but by God he must, or she would've sliced him dead. So they go at it, the two of them—hack-hack, klink-klink—but he's just blockin' her thrusts. And the queer thing was, all those aboard—all the Frenchies and all of us—just stopped everything to watch. It was the damndest, funniest thing you ever saw."

And there he stopped, as if he had brought the story to a proper end. This infuriated Clarissa, who had been hanging upon Bunkins's each word.

"Well, what happened?" said she through clenched teeth.

"Oh," said he, "well, sure enough, with all that hacking away at him, she did finally give him a nick on the arm, and the cove didn't like that much, so he went after her for the first time, did a little trick I've seen him do before, and sent her cutlass flying, just like that." And so saying, he snapped his fingers.

"Just like that?" Clarissa echoed, sounding terribly disappointed. Then, cheering up a bit: "But she did at least draw blood, did she not?"

Bunkins gave her an odd look. "Whose side are you on, anyways?"

"Well . . . Mr. Bilbo's, of course, but I'm always happy when a woman distinguishes herself. So she was the captain, was she?"

"Oh, no doubt about that. It was her at the helm when they pulled anchor and turned into the wind. She thought that up. It surprised us, it did."

"Bravo, Marie-Hélène!" said Clarissa, and to me: "I should like to meet her."

That certainly was not difficult. The *Indian Princess* was not a large vessel, and she wandered about the deck as restlessly as we two did. We soon began nodding at her as we passed, and she at us. She had lively eyes and seemed not the least fearful of her future; nor, for one who would in all probability soon be a widow, did she seem greatly distressed. I believe that I was as eager to meet her as was Clarissa.

We had our opportunity in the morning when, having waited all night in the London roads that we might proceed up the Thames, the wind suddenly shifted and Mr. Bilbo left Marie-Hélène at the railing and went off to see the sails set and the anchor hauled. He left laughing, and she, staring after him, stood shaking her head, as if in surprise or bewilderment. We happened to be close by just as the ship began to move, with the smugglers' cutter in tow; she waved us over to her. Then without preamble or introduction, she began to speak to us quite like we were all three the best of friends.

"Do you know well thees man, Bilbo?" she asked.

"Oh yes," said Clarissa with great assurance, though in truth I had known Black Jack far better and far longer.

"Tell me then, is he famous in England?"

"Famous?" said I, echoing her word, not quite understanding.

"Do I say right? Fa-mous?"

"Oh yes, it's just that I'd never thought of him quite so."

"Tell me about him," said she. "I want to know all about him."

"What is it you want to know?"

"Everything. He tell me little stories, funny stories, but not who he is, what he does. I think he must be famous in England. Such a man should be famous."

"Famous in London, perhaps," said I, "but not in all of England."

And so at her invitation we stood with Marie-Hélène at the taffrail and told her all that we knew of John Bilbo, and of his gambling den, which was established from the proceeds of his long career as a privateer, *et cetera.* She found it difficult to make the distinction between privateer and pirate (as many do), and I settled it to my satisfaction by explaining that a privateer was a sort of legal pirate. Hearing that, she laughed sweetly and said, "Oh la! You English!"

For her part, she told us all about herself, as well, and the more she told, the better Clarissa and I understood her evident indifference to her husband's fate. She was offered to him by her father simply to seal the agreement made between them: the Casales family as suppliers and Sir Simon as the English buyer.

"You were a mere pawn!" cried Clarissa in shocked sympathy.

"*Exactement!* You play *échecs?*"

"Chess? Why, yes I do." Then, leaning forward and speaking confidentially: "Did he treat you badly?"

"He did not treat me at all. He was so busy with his assassinations and the hunting of the poor fox that he has no time to be my husband. He is a stranger to me, a stranger who is my father's partner. The only pleasure I have from this is that I am the *capitaine* of the little ship that goes back and forth to Deal. I learn all about this from my brothers and my uncle."

On and on they talked. I was as much intrigued and entertained by Marie-Hélène as was Clarissa. Nevertheless, I could not but wonder what would become of her when we reached London. As I listened, my eyes wandered across the deck, and I saw Mr. Bilbo deep in serious conversation with Sir John. Could it be regarding the fate of Marie-Hélène? As I considered this, I saw that further preparations were being made for our return to London. The swivel gun on the foredeck was lifted from its mount and taken away to be stored. One by one, the six guns either side the gun deck were pulled back from their gun ports, secured, and hid beneath the canvas. The prisoners were brought up two at a time from the hold by Mr. Bailey and Mr. Patley. (Mr. Perkins had remained behind in Deal, so as to help Constable Trotter, now recovered, to police the streets of the town.)

As Clarissa prattled on to her, I happened to catch Marie-Hélène's eyes as she looked down at the assembly of prisoners. For the first time since we had begun talking, she seemed unsure of herself, perhaps even afrighted. And it helped little when Mr. Bilbo appeared upon the poop deck and asked Marie-Hélène to accompany him. For the first time in her presence he did not smile. Once they had gone, Clarissa and I looked fearfully at each other, half-expecting her to appear on the main deck with the other prisoners. I saw Sir Simon look round him, no doubt for her, yet she was nowhere about. We saw no more of her then.

As we passed Tower Wharf, a Royal Navy longboat joined us, escorting us to a place opposite the Wapping dry-dock. There, we dropped anchor and it pulled alongside; a ladder was tossed down to it. The transfer of the prisoners to the shore began. And once begun, all was accomplished in a few short trips. That done, the rest of us descended the rope ladder—not easy for Molly and Clarissa—and were taken to the little wharf to the side of the dry-dock. By the time we arrived, the prisoners were gone, conveyed to Newgate in two large, barred wagons, specially made to transport large numbers of prisoners.

I watched the watermen make preparations to tow *La Belle Voyageuse* into dry-dock, but only for a moment or two, for Sir John called me over to him and instructed me to go out upon Wapping Dock and see if it were possible to find a hackney coach to carry the six of us back to Number 4 Bow Street. I had not far to look, for there, pulled over to the side of Wapping Dock, was a coach-and-four that had by then become quite familiar to me—that of William Murray, the Earl of Mansfield, the Lord Chief Justice. It seemed that he desired to see Sir John at the latter's earliest possible convenience. He had sent his coach to ensure his compliance. There seemed in that an implicit threat.

"But how can you be so sure that Sir Simon killed this fellow—what was his name?—Sarton, yes, Sarton. How do you *know* that?"

"I didn't *say* he pulled the trigger. I said he *ordered* Mr. Sarton killed."

"There! You see? He wasn't actually the direct cause of his death, was he? Perhaps there was some misunderstanding between Sir Simon and the fellow who actually did the deed. Perhaps he said, 'Oh, I wish that man were dead,' meaning it in a figurative way—not literally *dead*, you understand. And taking that as an order, the killer went out and shot the man dead. It could have happened just so—now, couldn't it?"

"Hardly. Sir Simon was present at the scene. He was literally but a few feet away when the magistrate was shot down. He could have stopped it with a word."

"But how do you *know* that?"

"I *know* that because I have a *witness*."

Lord Mansfield had begun roaring the moment Sir John appeared before him. He was louder and more unbridled in his anger than I had ever seen him before—or for that matter, since. For his part, Sir John responded with remarkable restraint, knowing that if he were to speak as he was spoken to, then the interview would have collapsed into an intemperate duel of shouting and stomping.

Though I had no suspicion of what awaited us when we boarded Lord Mansfield's coach, I am nearly certain that Sir John did. That must have been why he insisted that the driver take us first to Bow Street that Clarissa and Molly might go to our living quarters there, and constables Bailey and Patley might continue from there to their rooms.

Yet even Sir John must have been taken aback at the vehemence and lack of reason exhibited in the arguments put forth by the Lord Chief Justice. Had the latter heard such in Old Bailey, he would have dismissed them in an instant. Lord Mansfield must, in any case, have reconsidered his position to some extent, for he paused and remained silent for a bit, and when he began again, he spoke in a more controlled manner.

"Who is this witness of yours?" he asked. "Is he the man who did pull the trigger?"

"By no means," said Sir John. "That man was killed when he offered fire during our first battle with the smugglers there on the road to London."

"Who then? Who was it? What part had he in this alleged assassination?"

"Ah! Alleged, is it? Well, his name is Edward Potter, and

he was as near to an innocent observer as one could have been. He simply held Sir Simon's horse as he tapped upon the window to Mr. Sarton's study and asked to be admitted that he might talk with him on a confidential matter. When the magistrate opened the door, rather than Sir Simon's confidence, he was given a bullet in the head."

"Is that how it was done? Is that what your man Potter told you?"

"That is as I earlier reasoned it," said Sir John, "and that is also what Potter told me."

"You led him so?"

"Nothing of the kind. His testimony merely confirmed what I had supposed. I did not prompt him. I would not."

"And what did you promise him for this testimony so freely given?"

"I promised him nothing. That is not my way. I hope that by now you know that of me. The most I have ever done is to tell a prospective witness that I would recommend leniency of some kind—transportation in capital crimes and a reduced sentence in the rest."

Sir John hesitated; he faltered a bit for the first time. "In this case," he continued, "I . . . I did tell him that I would recommend a reduced sentence."

"And did you say that your recommendations are always followed?"

"I did say that they have been, yes."

"Well, you may tell him for me that in his case your recommendation will *not* be honored. Let us see then just how readily he comes forward to testify against his former master. I am not bound by your recommendations, as I'm sure you know."

Sir John Fielding was silent for a long—oh, an interminably long—moment. But when he spoke again, his voice was strong and certain.

"You will have my letter of resignation on your desk in the morning."

Lord Mansfield was evidently shocked. This was not the outcome he had foreseen. "If I do receive such a letter from you, I shall tear it up immediately," he declared. "Let me put it plain: I shall *not* accept your resignation under any circumstances."

"Then you must put Sir Simon Grenville to trial and allow my witness to testify against him if he so chooses. My recommendation for leniency will stand. I shall let Potter know that it may not be honored. You cannot, in other words, have both Sir Simon and me. You must choose between us."

"Must you vex me so, sir?" Lord Mansfield fair wailed forth his response.

"Yes, I must," said Sir John forthrightly, "for if our positions were reversed, you would do the same."

"Oooooh." It was a strange sound, something between a moan and a growl. And when Lord Mansfield spoke, it was as if it were a great strain to speak above a whisper: "If you but knew how close I was to his late father at Oxford—and after. Oh, for many years afterward. Why, I held Sir Simon as a baby. How can he be tried now for murder?" He stood, panting, clearing his throat repeatedly, then struggled to speak: "Now go, please. I do not wish to be seen weeping."

Sir John nodded at me and groped for my arm. When he had found it, I led him out of the room, down the hall, and to the door. There the butler appeared and, saying nothing, swung open the door. Once outside, we set off in the direction of Southampton Street, where we might find a hackney waiting. And it was then yet a bit till Sir John spoke.

"I do not envy Lord Mansfield," said he then. "By God, I do not."

I shall not dwell long upon the remaining events of that day. They included a visit to Newgate, then only the second time I had been inside that foul and frightening place; it had not improved since the first; and today it is worse still.

There, after some difficulty in establishing his whereabouts in that overcrowded rat's nest, Sir John held an interview with Edward Potter through the bars of the great holding cell wherein all from Deal, except Sir Simon, had been jailed. There is no privacy in Newgate, no place set aside for conversations between those awaiting trial and representatives of the law; and so, with Potter's fellow prisoners crowding about, openly attempting to listen in, it was necessary for Sir John to speak in hints and generalities.

Potter, an unpleasant-looking little fellow no older than I, was a stable boy from Sir Simon's household staff. I had seen him about during those few days that we had stayed at the manor house but had formed no high opinion of his character or his intelligence. He had, Sir John later told me, come forward with what he described as "something you want to know," but had made it clear that it would only be made available if he were promised, *quid pro quo,* something in return. The deal was made in private. Thus, Sir John's appearance was greeted by him with some alarm: he could only be bringing Potter bad news. When at last he came forward to the bars, he looked at the two of us with great suspicion in his eyes.

"What you doin' here?" he whispered to Sir John. "What you want from me?"

"Only your attention. You recall the recommendation I made in your behalf?"

"'Course I do. We made a deal."

"Well, I've come to tell you that my recommendation may be rejected. It's unfortunate, but you deserve to know."

"That an't fair," said Potter, forgetting to whisper, "not by half, it an't. You said they always do what you tell them to."

Sir John sighed. "I said they've always accepted my recommendation in the past. That is true. This is the first time in seventeen years there has been some doubt. But if you choose to, you may still . . ." He left the sentence unfinished.

"Forget that! They'll get naught from me. The deal is off. I'll take what everyone else gets."

Having said that, he turned and pushed his way through the little crowd that had gathered round him. Two or three turned, frowning suspiciously, and watched him go.

"Let us be out of here, Jeremy," said Sir John, and fast as we could go with only one pair of eyes between us, we left Newgate behind.

Returning to Number 4 Bow Street, Sir John gave a perfunctory greeting to Mr. Fuller and Mr. Baker, for it was that time when day turns into night, and the Bow Street Runners report one by one to go off upon their separate assignments. It was also that time, or near it, when supper was served in the kitchen above.

We ascended the stairs and stepped into the kitchen. I believe that Sir John and I were both surprised to find Lady Fielding had returned, and even more surprised to find all three women (Lady Kate, Clarissa, and Molly) in the kitchen together—and not a word being said. I know not your experience, reader, but in mine, three women in a room together over a period of time nearly always find something to talk about. Yet into the kitchen we came, and there we did see Lady Kate in the middle of the room, her arms folded before her, a frown upon her forehead, and her lips pursed; Molly was bent over the stove, pulling from it five sizzling mutton chops; and Clarissa between them, looking unhappily from one to the other.

Lady Fielding was the first to rouse. "Jack! You're back!"

"Indeed I am," said he. "And I trust your mother is well, safely through her spell?"

"Oh yes," said she. Then, *sotto voce* into his ear: "Who *is* this woman?"

Then he, just as quiet: "She is our new cook."

"But—"

He interrupted: "Come upstairs, and we shall discuss the matter between us."

And so they went, he leading the way and she following. The door to their bedroom closed behind them. The three of us then breathed a simultaneous sigh of relief.

"I was afraid something like this would happen," said Molly.

"Well, I tried to explain all to her," said Clarissa.

"I know, I know," said Molly. "That was when I went off to Covent Garden to buy for dinner. I skipped right out, thinking it best if you and the lady had a bit of time together so that you might make things clear."

"Oh, don't worry," said I, waving my hand dismissively (in a gesture I had copied from Sir John), "all will be made right. You'll see."

"Well, what would you think," said Molly, "if you found a strange woman in your kitchen?"

"From what she said, it wasn't so much that," said Clarissa, "as not being consulted, not having any say in the matter."

"I can understand that," said I.

"So can I," said Clarissa.

"Oh dear," said Molly.

Voices were raised behind the door to their room above. Clarissa set the table rather hurriedly, and Molly put out the food. I waited—but not for long. It seemed but a moment or two until they returned. Happily, Lady Fielding went straight to Molly and offered her hand.

"Please forgive me for my failure to welcome you," said she. "It was simply surprise which made me forget momentarily to tell you that we are very happy to have you in our household." With that, she looked round and smiled modestly. "Well then, shall we eat?"

We four took our usual places at the kitchen table, leaving Annie's old chair to Molly Sarton, who seemed to be waiting for the rest of us to begin. Lady Fielding cut into the mutton chop and took a bite. Her face brightened immediately.

"This is really quite wonderful," said she. "How did you manage?"

With that, Clarissa and I exchanged relieved glances. A crisis, it seemed, had been averted—or at least delayed.

Quite early the next morning, when I was the only one up and about, Mr. Baker came up the stairs and informed me that a message had come from Newgate for Sir John. He asked me to summon him. Answering my knock, Sir John appeared in his nightshirt, and not bothering to dress further, went down directly to Mr. Baker and received the news that Edward Potter had been murdered during the night, his throat cut, his body cold and rigid when it was discovered during the early morning. All those in the big holding cell naturally proclaimed their innocence and insisted they had neither seen nor heard anything of a suspicious nature during the night. Having listened carefully to Mr. Baker, Sir John thanked him and sent him on his way. Then did he turn to me with a most woeful look upon his face.

"You know what this means, Jeremy, do you not?"

"That there will be no murder trial—is that not so?"

"Exactly so." He sighed. "Potter might have been put upon the witness stand and badgered into telling what he had seen in spite of his intentions to keep silent. But now, with no witness at all . . ."

"There would be no point in bringing Sir Simon to trial for murder."

"My certainty of his guilt counts for nothing. Well, I shall have a letter for you to take down as soon as I am dressed."

"A letter to whom?" I asked.

"To the Lord Chief Justice."

"Surely not your letter of resignation?" I was for a moment truly alarmed.

"No, that would serve no good purpose. I shall simply inform him of this event and make a few comments upon it."

Yet the letter, as dictated by him and taken down by me, was a good deal more than what he described. I should like to have had a copy of that letter so that I might present it here verbatim, for it was a good example of how Sir John's mind worked. He began by informing Lord Mansfield of Potter's death and assuring him that there could be no doubt that he had been murdered, since his throat had been cut. Why had he been murdered? The most likely reason, Sir John suggested, was that Sir Simon had ordered it, sent word down from his private cell that Potter, poor specimen that he was, nevertheless constituted a danger to him as a witness to the crime he most certainly had committed. If Lord Mansfield believed that because Sir Simon and the smuggler crew were in separate cells, some distance apart, such communication would be impossible, then he had no practical notion of just how corrupt was the guard force there in Newgate Gaol. A proper bribe would bring a prisoner anything he desired. Notes delivered within the prison were the least of it; a guard might well oblige with murder, if murder were required and if the sum paid were sufficient.

Of course, said Sir John in the letter to the Lord Chief Justice, there could be no question now of trying Sir Simon on the charge of murder. Without a witness to the act, all that could be held against him were Sir John's suspicions and his theory of the crime. But (I recall these concluding lines so well that I believe I may put them within quotation marks): "I would remind the Lord Chief Justice that in addition to the charge of homicide, Sir Simon Grenville was also bound over for trial on the lesser charge of smuggling. He will not, I hope, be forgiven this simply because his father was lucky enough to be your friend."

Though put more eloquently than I have done here, this was what I remember of the letter to Lord Mansfield—direct, forceful, and challenging. By the time he had read to the end of it, the Lord Chief Justice may well have wished that he had instead received that letter of resignation with which Sir John had threatened him.

The letter was delivered by me into the hands of Lord Mansfield's butler. With that, he seemed actually to be disappointed that we were not to have our usual disagreement over whether or not I was to be admitted into the great man's presence that he might scrawl an answer in the margin of the letter.

"No need for that," said I to him, "though it might be best if he were to be given the letter before he leaves for the day."

Having said that, I danced down the stairs and set off along Bloomsbury Square to continue on my way. I had a number of other errands to run. Though they were of no real consequence, they took up the rest of the morning. As a result, I did not return to Number 4 Bow Street until after the noon hour. At such time, of course, on nearly any day of the week, Sir John Fielding holds his magistrate's court. For more than a week, however, he had been absent. This day's session was the first he had held in quite some time, and when word went out that he was back, a great crowd turned out to greet him. It was composed of friends and relations of the prisoners and disputants before the court, as well as those who came from the district round Covent Garden. Now, those who live and work thereabouts are not all of them greengrocers. For a district of modest size, it has more than its fair share of pickpockets, sneak thieves, burglars, prostitutes, procurers, drunks, et cetera, and so a good many of these turn out at noon each day to attend Sir John's session of his magistrate's court. Add a few of the aged and infirm, those too poor to afford any other form of entertainment, and you have a sense of the sort of people who might be in attendance on any given day of the week.

There were so many present on that day that when I entered, it seemed I might not find a place to seat myself. But far to the front I saw space enough for me upon a bench just opposite the prisoners' section. There was nothing more that I could see, and so I blustered down to it, claimed it, and sat myself down.

I looked over at the three prisoners. I meant only to glance, but one of them held my eye. He was an ordinary-appearing fellow, a little stronger than most from the look of his chest and shoulders, but not the sort that one would otherwise notice. I had seen him before, had I not? Ah well, probably in or about Covent Garden. I saw so many in my daily rounds. Then he looked my way and obviously recognized me. His eyes brightened, and he smiled at me. It was clear that he was glad to find me present. Yes, I *had* seen him before—and more than that, we had conversed. I was in some sense acquainted with the man.

Sir John had been conferring in whispers with Mr. Marsden, his clerk. But then he turned toward the court and bellowed out: "Call the next case, if you will, Mr. Marsden."

"Henry Curtin, come forth!"

The man who looked so familiar—he who had smiled at me—then rose and took a place before the magistrate. He glanced back at me, as if looking for assurance. Why should he seek such from me?

Yet of a sudden I knew the answer to that. Henry Curtin was the coachman in whose care I had entrusted Lady Katherine Fielding. I had tipped him a shilling—a goodly amount—but thinking that somehow insufficient, I had gone on to ask his name and to hint broadly to him that I would pass it on to Sir John, and if ever Mr. Curtin came before the magistrate of the Bow Street Court, then he would receive special consideration. A sense of horror swept over me. I had been trapped by my foolish desire to seem important. It was necessary for me to fight to keep my place on the bench, for I felt a nearly overwhelming desire to bolt from the courtroom.

"What is the charge against this man, Mr. Marsden?"

"Public drunkenness."

"What have you to say for yourself, sir?" asked Sir John.

"Well . . ." The prisoner cleared his throat. "My name is Henry Curtin . . ." There he paused.

"I understand who you are. Get on with your story, man."

"Uh, yes, yes sir. Well, *Henry Curtin* is my name, and I work as a coachman on the run to York and back, and I come by a bit of money just yesterday."

"Let me stop you there and ask you how you came by this 'bit of money'?"

"It was won on a wager, sir."

"What sort of wager?"

"'Twas a contest of fisticuffing. 'Twas held in a field just north of Clerkenwell. I bet on the black fella and Charlie Tobin bet on the white one."

"Hmmm," Sir John mused, "and I assume the black pugilist was the winner?"

"Weren't he though!"

"Very well, you came away from the contest five shillings richer."

"That's right, and I then and there decided I would take that money and drink my way home on it."

"Drink your way home? What a novel idea."

"Yes sir. Thank you, sir."

"I did not say it was a good idea. I simply said it was a novel one. Now get on with it."

"Yes sir. What I was going to do was drink a drink of something—gin or rum or brandy—every place I took a notion from Clerkenwell to home."

"And where is home?"

"Just round the corner in Tavistock Street. I made it as far as Drury Lane, then I fear I ran out."

"Ran out of money?"

"No, ran out of sense, just completely lost out, like I'd been hit hard by the black fella."

Sir John turned to Mr. Marsden and asked if there were any comments by the constable who made the arrest. "Who was that, by the bye?"

"It was Constable Langford," said Mr. Marsden. "He said he found this man, Curtin, asleep in the gutter."

"Did Mr. Curtin resist arrest? Give him any trouble at all?"

"No sir, not according to the arrest report. Just keeping him upright was the hardest part."

"All right, thank you, Mr. Marsden." Sir John turned back to the prisoner and addressed him directly: "Henry Curtin, I know who you are. I am aware that you expect special treatment in my court and—"

"Oh, no sir," Curtin said, interrupting, "I wouldn't dare to—"

"Don't interrupt! I do the interrupting hereabouts. Now, as I understand it, what was said to you was something less than a promise of leniency, yet it was enough to allow you to suppose you would receive easy treatment from me. I am not bound by what was said. In fact, I should like to burden you with the severest penalty that the law allows just to teach the individual involved to make no more promises in my name."

At that, Curtin threw at me a look expressing great misery.

"But it would not be fair to you to make you suffer in order to teach another a lesson." Sir John paused at that point, then asked, "Tell me, Mr. Curtin, have you money enough to pay a fine?"

"No sir," said he. "All I got is a little at home to eat on

till next I get paid. The five shillings was drunk up or stolen from me whilst I lay in the gutter."

"Well, I wouldn't see you starve whilst waiting to be paid, nor would I wish to see you lose your job as coachman because you were serving a term in jail. But let us fix a fine of five shillings, for that is the sum you foolishly threw away on drink. Let it be payable to the Bow Street Court when next you are paid. You may work out the date, et cetera, with Mr. Marsden here. But I warn you, you must pay the fine, or we shall come after you, and next time I shall not be so accommodating. Are we done, then, Mr. Marsden?"

"We are, sir."

"Then the Bow Street Court is adjourned until noon tomorrow." Sir John beat upon the table with his gavel, then laid it aside and made a hasty exit through the door behind him, which led directly to his chambers.

Because Mr. Curtin had been charged to settle matters with Mr. Marsden, I was able to evade him. I managed to slip out through the door which led back to the strong room and, by a longer route, to Sir John's chambers; it was to him I went, as one to receive just punishment.

"Is that you, Jeremy?"

He had barely settled in his chair and taken up the bottle of beer from the desk when I entered.

"It is sir," said I, properly humble.

"I take it you were present during Mr. Curtin's appearance?"

"Yes, I was."

"Well, shut the door and seat yourself. Let us talk about this."

I did as he said, and once I was settled, he resumed.

"Jeremy, we who have to do with the law must keep a firm hand upon ourselves. Now, we discussed your slip with Henry Curtin. You know you did wrong, so there is no need to repeat what was said. I'm confident you will not repeat that error. But I have had reason during the last day or two to question myself. As a personal favor to me, John Bilbo sailed in with his crew and saved us there on Goodwin Sands. We could not have won the day without him, his sloop, and his cannon. Then yesterday, he asked, as a personal favor to him, if I might put Lady Grenville in his charge that she might not be forced to languish in Newgate Gaol awaiting her trial—or her rescue by the French ambassador. I allowed it. I pray God that I am not given reason to regret granting that favor.

"And you saw the Lord Chief Justice himself bend law and legal practice for personal reasons. He denied my recommendation for leniency to that fellow Potter simply because Sir Simon's father had been his friend. The judge who had condemned hundreds to death could not bear thus to condemn a murderer whom he had held as a baby.

"We all have our weaknesses, and perhaps it is just that we should. Justice may be blind, but you may believe me, blindness is an affliction and only rarely an advantage. If you—"

A knock sounded upon the door.

"That will be Mr. Marsden. Go now, Jeremy. We may talk about this again sometime—and then again, we may not."

As an addendum to this, let me say that Lord Mansfield regained at least some of his resolve, for Sir Simon was tried along with the rest of his crew on a charge of smuggling, and no preferment was given him. He was sentenced to three years to be served in Newgate Gaol along with the rest. The French seamen were allowed to return to France through the diligent efforts of the French ambassador.

And Marie-Hélène, Lady Grenville? What of her?

Another time, perhaps.